Biddy's heart soared. Imagine her being put in front of someone like *Kate Thornley*! And Tara telling her she needed her.

'I feel I could just about cope if you came – you understand the way things are back in Ireland.'

'I'll be there, Tara,' Biddy said, her voice suddenly sounding confident and strong. Strong enough to face anything that might come her way back in Ireland. Strong enough to face all the gossips and the backbiters and the people who never knew the truth of the terrible things that had happened to her. Strong enough to be Tara Flynn's oldest and truest friend. 'You an' me will be together back in Ballygrace . . . I'll be with you every step of the way.'

A few minutes later, Biddy hung the phone up and laid her head in her hands. When she had composed herself again, she walked straight from the hall into the sitting room and opened the cupboard that housed the sherry bottle which she now so desperately needed.

Geraldine O'Neill lives in County Offaly, Ireland, where she teaches in the local National School. Her previous novel, *Tara Flynn*, is also published in Orion paperback.

TARA'S
FORTUNE

Geraldine O'Neill

ORION

An Orion paperback

First published in Great Britain in 2004
by Orion
This paperback edition published in 2005
by Orion Books Ltd,
Orion House, 5 Upper St Martin's Lane,
London WC2H 9EA

First published in Ireland by Poolbeg Press Ltd

Typeset by Deltatype Ltd, Birkenhead, Merseyside

Printed and bound in Great Britain by
Clays Ltd, St Ives plc

www.orionbooks.co.uk

Acknowledgements

I would like to give a big thanks to all the staff at Orion, particularly Kate Mills for her editorial advice given in such a friendly, encouraging manner, and Susan Lamb for her support.

Thanks to my fantastic literary agent, Sugra Zaman, of Watson, Little Ltd., London, for always being there for me, through the ups and downs of the literary world.

Sincere thanks to my friend, author Lyn Andrews, for her generous advice and unstinting encouragement.

I would like to express my sincere gratitude to the Offaly Arts Office for awarding me the Artist's Residency at the Tyrone Guthrie Centre in Autumn 2003, which helped enormously with the writing of *Tara's Fortune*.

Thanks to my mother-in-law, Mary Hynes, and her lovely friend, Elsie Thompson, for all the information about the Stockport mills, and our pleasant nights discussing it.

Grateful thanks to Martin and Mary O'Donoghue from Daingean National School for providing me with an original poem as *Gaeilge* by Donuchadh ð Donnchadha, Martin's late father.

Thanks again to my parents, Teddy and Be-Be O'Neill, for their love and constant encouragement; my sisters and their husbands; and my brother and his wife. Also, Mike's brothers, Kevin and John, and his sister Helen for all their support.

Grateful thanks to my Stockport friends – a special mention to John and Helen Fahy, Geoff Neeble, Ann and Phil Read, the Lowrys, the Ashtons (and friends!), the Singletons and Elaine – and of course Alison and Michael Murphy.

Thanks to Eileen Burns for her great support of my writing, and for all the hard work involved in making the two literary lunches at Adlington Hall so successful for Francis House in Stockport.

A final thanks to my loving husband, Mike Brosnahan, for his endless support and patience with my often erratic ways.

This book is dedicated with all my love
to my two children, Christopher and Clare Brosnahan,
who are more precious to me than they will ever know

Part One

Life is a series of natural
and spontaneous changes.
Don't resist them – that only creates sorrow.
Let reality be reality.
Let things flow naturally forward
In whatever way they will.

LAO-TSE

Stockport, England
1963

Even in jeans and a casual blue-checked shirt, Tara Fitzgerald cut a slim, elegant figure as she stood, long Titian curls lifting in the summer breeze, in the middle of what had once been a beautiful, rambling Edwardian garden.

She stepped back a couple of yards to a safer distance, watching as the crumbling old chimney stack divided into individual red, orange and sand-coloured bricks before tumbling down the slate roof and crashing on to the ground.

Yesterday she had watched as numerous disintegrating window frames had been given the same treatment, and she'd watched the day before, too, when all the outer doors with their cracked, stained-glass windows had been unceremoniously ripped off. She continued to watch each day as the old building was stripped back to the bare bones and then scrutinised and studied by the builders and tradesmen she had hired. Eventually, they would reach a point when it would be decided that they had removed all traces of decay and dilapidation – all traces of the neglect that the building had endured. Then the rebuilding and renovation process would start and it would be restored to its former Edwardian glory.

When the swirling grey dust from the chimney stacks had settled, Tara moved across the garden to investigate the two overflowing skips. Piles of torn and faded velvet curtains lay heaped on top of broken chairs and mirrors – part of the clearing and cleansing process.

As she stroked the crushed velvet material, she felt a tinge of sadness, witnessing the last, faded remnants of the old being cast aside to make way for the new. Like the elegant building, she, too, had been brutally forced into shedding the old and comfortingly familiar: the building and Tara Fitzgerald were both heading into a new and unknown future.

Chapter One

Tara Fitzgerald stood at the tall bay window in the drawing room of Ballygrace House, holding several blue sheets of Basildon Bond notepaper in her hand and an envelope that bore a Stockport postmark. She was dressed for going into town in a short-sleeved sweater with an amber necklace and earrings and a russet-coloured knee-length flared skirt – but the arrival of the post had halted her departure.

Her eyes gazed into the cloudy distance – over the house's garden to the fields beyond – far beyond the slightly bowed figure who pushed the lawnmower back and forth over the already tidy grass.

She stood motionless for a good five minutes, then moved purposefully out into the hall and down to open the front door of Ballygrace House. 'I've had a letter from Biddy,' she called out to her father, waving the sheaves of paper she had just received from her oldest and dearest friend. 'There's some news about Fred in it.'

Shay brought the lawnmower to an abrupt halt. He pushed his working cap back on his greying curls, and wiped a brown forearm across his brow. Then he stood looking at Tara, waiting to hear what she had to say.

She came down the high steps at the entrance smartly, but taking care with her high-heeled brown shoes that toned perfectly with her skirt.

Shay folded his arms over his chest. 'Poor oul' Fred,'

he said, shaking his head. 'Is there any change for the better at all?'

'A slight one,' Tara replied, coming across the lawn to her father. 'Biddy says they have him sitting up now . . . and that he's able to eat soft foods rather than just liquids.' The description of the sad state of Biddy's poor husband suddenly struck her silent – and she held out the letter to her father.

'Go on, work away.' Shay prompted her with a wave of his hand. 'You read it out, you'll make a better fist of Biddy's handwriting than I will, for I've left the oul' glasses back at home.'

She scanned the first page, which was full of thanks for Tara having visited them the week before last, and saying how much Biddy and the children had enjoyed having her over. She then moved on to the second page that concentrated on the details of Fred's slow but steady recovery.

They have Fred sitting up in the bed now [Tara read out to her father], and they're feeding him soup and custard and semolina and that kind of thing. They've taken down most of the tubes, so that's a relief. The doctors have told me that he has a long road to recovery, and not to hope for too much as he may never be the same man again. But I have to say, Tara, that I am hoping for a lot more. I don't care how long it takes, he'll always be the same big Fred to me.

Tara and Shay looked at each other and shook their heads sadly. Poor, poor Fred. It was now nearly two months since his accident in the wrestling ring. It seemed that a simple enough wrestling bout had gone tragically wrong when Fred had fallen out of the ring and had suffered serious head injuries.

The fight had been with an old adversary, with whom Fred often met up in the ring. They were more or less evenly matched, even though Arizona Jack was nearly a head taller than Fred. They knew each other's moves well enough, and whoever was beaten in one match was often the winner in the return fight.

According to Biddy, Fred had left home as usual on the Friday night for the match in Bellevue in Manchester. Apart from repeating to his wife that he was going to give up on the wrestling shortly – because he hated being away from home at the weekends – he was in grand form. 'And now', Tara continued reading, 'it seems that the wrestling has given up on Fred. If he manages to walk and talk normally ever again, it's as much as the doctors could hope for.' Biddy said she hoped that Tara would visit them again soon, and that her houses were being well looked after by the tenants, and that before Fred's accident he had paid regular visits to check up on things. Biddy herself had visited the two houses at the weekend, and all was well. She didn't want anything to go wrong there; she knew all the hours of working in hotels and teaching music that Tara had put in to pay the mortgages. *We all miss you here in Stockport*, Biddy concluded, *and, God-willing, Fred will be up and about on his feet when you pay your next visit.*

Shay rubbed his cap over his face, catching the start of a tear in the corner of his eye. 'Wouldn't it make ye wonder', he said in a low voice, 'how the biggest-hearted ones are the ones that get the worst of luck?' He paused. 'And d'you know something, Tara? I'm beginnin' to wonder about that house in Maple Terrace . . . they've had nothin' but bad luck in it.' He shook his head. 'And I'm not a superstitious man as a rule, but it would make ye wonder.'

Tara patted her father's shoulder, knowing that he was referring to Ruby Sweeney, Biddy's old landlady, and Shay's close friend. *Too close* friend, for the married man that Shay was when he was living and working over in Stockport several years ago.

But that was all water under the bridge now, and poor old Ruby was dead and gone. Shay's life in Tullamore with his second wife, Tessie, was more or less back to normal.

'We'll go in and have a cup of tea,' Tara told her father, glancing up at the cloudy sky. 'I think Angela has some bread and scones just out of the oven.' Tessie and Shay's youngest daughter, who had a considerable talent for cooking and baking, now worked alongside Ella in keeping the domestic side of Ballygrace House ticking over. Tara was actually delighted to have her half-sister in the house, as she brought a breath of fresh air with her lively chat and enthusiasm about everything. Gabriel liked Angela, too, and often stood chatting with her and Tara in the kitchen whilst drinking a cup of coffee – something that would have been unheard of back in his parents' day when everything was so formal.

Shay wiped the cap across his face again, and put it back on his head. 'I was all but finished here, anyway,' he said in a choked voice, 'tryin' to beat the feckin' oul' rain. We've had nothin' but rain this whole summer long, and now we're headin' into the winter it'll only get worse. The weather in this country isn't worth a feckin' damn!'

Tara pursed her lips tightly, knowing that her father was only using the weather as an excuse to give vent to his frustration about Fred's condition.

They walked across the lawn together towards the front of Ballygrace House, then when they reached the front steps of the house they parted wordlessly, Shay to walk round to the kitchen entrance at the back of the house, and Tara to walk up the front steps.

Tara made her way in first, her heels tapping down the long hallway to the kitchen. Shay was still outside, kicking the grass and earth from his work-boots until he felt he was in a fit state to step into the house. It didn't matter how many times Tara told him to come in through the front door, he never would. The ghosts of too many Fitzgeralds and their like, who had owned Ballygrace House, hung too freshly in the air for Shay. He was far more comfortable entering and leaving through the kitchen, where he could mix with the people he felt on a level with. And at times that was his daughter, Tara Fitzgerald. And at other times, it was not.

Chapter Two

Tara slowly climbed the staircase, her hand trailing thoughtfully along the polished wooden banister. Hopefully things would soon get back to the way they were. Back to the more relaxed, carefree days that she and Gabriel had taken for granted up until recently. The days when they had nothing to worry about apart from which film they might go to see, or which play they might drive up to Dublin for at the weekend. Or the planning of trips away which they enjoyed so much. Visits to their friends in Stockport and to Gabriel's family in London – and their trips further afield to places like Italy and France.

Maybe when things settled down, she and Gabriel could think of having a nice relaxing break away on their own again – hopefully before the summer ended. By then Fred might be back to his old self and they wouldn't be on tenterhooks all the time, worrying about how he was, and Tara wouldn't feel so concerned about Biddy being so far away and having to manage the boarding-house on her own.

But the important thing was that Fred Roberts was definitely showing signs of recovery and he would continue to improve. Looking at things positively, Gabriel had recovered well from the bad bout of pneumonia he had suffered last year – and had little or no effects to show for it now. Of course, he still had to watch that he didn't overdo things, but he had definitely come out the other side of a tough time.

Maybe, she thought, she would try to persuade Gabriel to spend a month over in Stockport with her. Or, if Gabriel didn't fancy the whole month in the Northwest where people were basically Tara's friends, then maybe he could spend a couple of weeks down in London with his mother and younger brother. Elisha still needed constant reassurance that her eldest son's health was back to normal, and a visit from him was always guaranteed to lift her into a more optimistic frame of mind. Also, his younger brother, William, completely hero-worshipped Gabriel and would be thrilled to have him to himself for a few weeks.

Yes, Tara decided, a month over in England would give them both ample time to spend with friends and family, and to feel satisfied that their presence was making a difference. They could even take young Angela over to Stockport with them, she thought suddenly. It would give the girl a bit of a change from the domestic work in Ballygrace House, and it would be a great help to Biddy with young Michael and little Helen. There was already an older woman who helped with the cooking for the boarders and the general running of the house, but Angela would be another pair of hands and would be company for Biddy in the house at night.

There would be no problem with accommodation, for Tara still kept her bedroom intact at her own house in Cale Green, just outside Stockport town. She still had all her personal effects in the drawing room, including the beloved baby grand piano that her old love, Frank Kennedy, had bought her some years back. She kept a wardrobe with several outfits, with matching hats, shoes and handbags, and the housekeeper made sure the bed was aired regularly. This meant that Tara could set off at a moment's notice for England, anytime she felt like a break from Ballygrace. Of course she knew she was very lucky having the best of both worlds. The

11

lovely quiet, country surroundings of Ballygrace House, and then the hustle and bustle of town life over in England.

Apart from seeing Biddy and her other friends, visiting Stockport and Manchester meant a bigger choice of shops and theatres and general places to visit. When he relaxed into the visit, Gabriel usually enjoyed himself too. Of course, Tara knew that he would never feel as entirely comfortable with Biddy and Fred as she did, but it was still a break away from the businesses back in Ireland, and the other business interests he still kept an eye on in London.

Tara always felt happier when Gabriel came with her, because there was so much to do and see, and she preferred to share the experiences with him, rather than describing them all to him later. Apart from enjoying things more when she was in his company, she felt safer if he was with her when she went to the theatre or to a restaurant.

Only twice in the last three years had she come face to face with her old flame, Frank Kennedy. But that was twice too often. On the first occasion – when she had been at the Opera House with Gabriel – he had been perfectly polite and pleasant, and had even congratulated them on their marriage. But the next time she had been in a restaurant with a friend, and Frank had behaved very differently.

Tara shuddered at the memory. She and Kate Thornley, her friend from the estate agent's in Bramhall, had been sitting at a dimly lit corner table, relaxing over coffees after their meal, when he had spotted them. He left the group of businessmen he was with to come over and join them, once again congratulating her on her marriage. Within minutes a bottle of expensive champagne and three glasses had appeared on the table.

'No, really, we're just going,' Tara had protested, her face flushing at the awkwardness of it all. But the cork was off the champagne bottle and Kate was holding out her glass – laughing as Frank poured the bubbly liquid into it. The chat had been light and easy until Kate had gone off to the ladies', and Frank had leaned across the table and taken Tara's hand tightly in his. 'I'll never forgive myself', he said quickly, 'for getting everything so wrong. For not trusting you to understand . . .'

Tara pulled her hand away. 'Frank,' she said in an ice-cold voice, 'I'm a married woman, and you shouldn't be speaking to me like this.'

'It should have been you and me,' he told her. 'My divorce has come through . . . and we could have been married.'

'*Never*,' Tara hissed, her green eyes brittle with anger. 'I wouldn't have married you if you were the last man on earth!' She halted for a moment, finding the words that would end this nonsense. 'Yes,' she said, nodding, 'I admit I *was* horrified when I discovered that I'd been seeing a married man, and it took me a while to get over it. I won't deny that. No woman likes to feel she's been cheated and lied to. But, in the long run, it didn't matter, because breaking away from you left me free to find real love again with Gabriel.'

His whole body stiffened at her words.

'Make no mistake,' Tara went on. 'It was *always* Gabriel Fitzgerald. From when I was a very young girl, it was always Gabriel I was in love with. You only filled a small gap until we got back together.'

Frank Kennedy's eyes had clouded over when she started, and his face and shoulders had sagged by the time she had finished. He sat there for a few moments in silence. Then he said in a low whisper, 'Is that your final word?'

'It is,' Tara said firmly, 'and if you don't leave the table now, then I will have to walk out and leave Kate on her own.' She pushed her hardly touched champagne glass to the side and lifted a glass of water to her lips instead.

Frank stood up, and without another word he walked back to his table. He had a brief word with one of the other men, then lifted his coat and walked out of the restaurant without a backward glance.

Tara still felt a clammy anxiety when she remembered the scene – but she had been glad of the opportunity to let Frank Kennedy know exactly where he stood.

She went into the master bedroom now. A bedroom that had been newly created for her and Gabriel after their marriage, when they moved into the renovated Ballygrace House. Originally it had been the nursery and Gabriel's old bedroom, which had been knocked together to make a large, airy bedroom. The only bedroom that Tara could contemplate sleeping in, in Ballygrace House. A new, fresh bedroom that held no ghosts for her.

She had not been willing to contemplate sleeping in what had been Gabriel's parents' bedroom, nor in his sister Madeleine's bedroom. This had left only the smaller guest bedroom, the nursery and Gabriel's bedroom, which overlooked the main flower garden. Using the excuse that she wanted that particular view, Tara said that she would only be happy living in Ballygrace House if there were some changes made to allow her to have exactly the bedroom she wanted. Gabriel was surprised at how adamant his fiancée was over the situation, but was happy to agree to any changes she wanted.

If Tara Fitzgerald was happy, then Gabriel Fitzgerald was happy.

Later, when she came out of the bedroom, Tara halted, a thoughtful look on her face. Ballygrace House was exactly the way she and Gabriel wanted now – apart from one thing. The house needed more life in it.

It needed a *baby*. They had everything else they needed in their lives. They had a happy, contented marriage, a beautiful home and more than sufficient money. The more she thought about it, the more determined and excited she felt about it. The time was right *now* for them to start a family.

When Tara thought back to her own simple upbringing with her Granda and uncle in the little cottage in the Ballygrace village, it was almost inconceivable that she should have travelled so far in her life. She had got there by her own hard work and determination, and ultimately by her marriage into the Fitzgerald family.

Tara Flynn had travelled just over a mile from her cottage to the imposing Ballygrace House, but socially she had travelled a great deal further.

She walked down the staircase, a smile lighting up her emerald-green eyes and her beautiful face. She suddenly had a good feeling about things. In spite of all the recent difficulties, things were definitely improving. Summer was a good time of year – a time that often brought changes for the better.

When the moment was right, she would mention to Gabriel again about turning one of the bedrooms into a new, modern nursery. Perhaps this time next year there might be new light and life in Ballygrace House.

Chapter Three

STOCKPORT

Biddy sat at the large round table in the kitchen, her elbows leaning on the flowery oilcloth cover – the table that normally seated a good half a dozen or more hefty builders, who all possessed equally hefty appetites. But at this time of the morning Biddy, dressed in blue-checked nylon working overall and old grey working slacks, had the table to herself. Both she and Elsie – her middle-aged daily help – had cleared up after the lads' breakfasts and given the kitchen and the whole of the downstairs a really good going-over. A typical Monday going-over, which was always the most thorough cleaning day of the week. This was deemed necessary after a weekend of builders cluttering up the rooms. The heavy routine involved changing beds, hoovering carpets, beating rugs, washing and polishing floors, bleaching and cleaning sinks and lavatories.

It was hard work, but Biddy felt an awful lot better than when she had started at half past eight that morning. Seeing everything clean and tidy and back in its proper place gave her a feeling of satisfaction – as though she had regained some kind of control in her life.

The kettle on the gas ring started the low rumble that signalled the piercing whistle was ready to go off shortly. Biddy soundlessly pushed back the chair on the new linoleum floor that Fred had helped to lay only a week before his accident. That was Fred all right – always helping people out. Helping the fellow to lay the linoleum even though the man was being paid to do the job himself. Fred had known that Biddy wanted the floor finished before the lads got home from work, and when it was gone three o'clock and there was no sign of it being finished, he had pitched in with the man.

It was the same with any jobs that needed doing in the house: whether it was domestic or electrical or bathing and dressing the children, Fred had turned his hand to anything within his capability that needed doing. There was no doubt about it. Biddy had made the best decision of her life when she had married Fred Roberts. They were a good team, Biddy and Fred. Everybody said so. They said it themselves, often.

And now this – this cruel, cruel accident that had torn their lives apart and left Fred lying useless in a hospital bed and his wife struggling to cope on her own with the children and the lodgers.

Biddy put two heaped spoonfuls of tea in the pot – enough for several cups. Elsie would be back from the shops with the children shortly and would be ready for a cup. She left the teapot on the edge of the low flame for a few minutes to brew, and then went to one of the high kitchen cupboards where she kept the cakes and biscuits. She stretched high on her tiptoes to reach the cake tin, tutting to herself as she lifted it out. She had told the bird-like, grey-haired Elsie only yesterday to stop her from eating cakes or biscuits every time she had a cup of tea. But that was yesterday – and the diligent Elsie wasn't here now. And all the thoughts in the world about how her skirts and blouses were getting that little bit tighter couldn't fend off the overwhelming need for something sweet and nice and comforting.

Biddy cut herself a large slice of fruitcake and picked a Kit-Kat from the biscuit tin, then she poured herself a cup of tea and sat down at the table to enjoy it all.

17

There would be plenty of time for watching her weight when she had her big, smiling, safe Fred back home – and her own life was back to normal.

The afternoon slid away easily as Biddy and Elsie continued working through their list of chores, occasionally humming along to Frank Ifield or Cliff Richard on the small transistor radio they carried with them from room to room. While Biddy was younger and lighter on her feet, Elsie's nervy energy and constant need to be doing something made them an ideal working team.

Monday had the heaviest workload, but was only the start of the week's domestic routine. Tuesdays were dedicated to the washing and ironing of the bedlinen that had been taken off, and each day following had its allotted jobs. The routine of running the boarding-house had been established back in Ruby Sweeney's early days, and Biddy had carried on with it because she was used to it – and because it worked as well as any other.

'It's gone four o'clock, you know,' Elsie said, gathering up sheets and pillowcases in a sack-like bundle in the square of her floral apron. 'Shall I make a start on the potatoes and vegetables?'

Biddy ran a hand through her dark, bobbed hair. It was the previous year when Tara had suggested that she might suit the hairstyle, as Biddy had been complaining that she found her shoulder-length hair hard to handle. 'You might as well,' she said to Elsie, stretching to smooth down a green padded-nylon bedspread. 'We'll want everythin' organised for them coming in at six on the dot, so that I'm ready to run for visiting at the hospital.' She turned to the Hoover now, and started winding up the flex. 'I'll look in on the kids for a few minutes, then I'll come down and see how the pork is doing, and get the rice pudding into the oven.'

The two children were happily occupied sucking Spangles and watching a television show involving rabbits and a rag-doll, so Biddy left them to it, and went out into the hall to phone the hospital – another afternoon ritual.

'Fred's had a good day so far, thank God,' she told Elsie as she reached for the oven gloves. 'The nurse said the doctors were talking about moving him soon to another hospital in Leeds for physiotherapy.'

'That's a great sign,' Elsie said, smiling broadly. 'When me mam had her stroke, they gave her physiotherapy and it worked wonders on her. They can do miracles these days.' She nodded her head, her well-pinned greying bun sitting stiffly on the back of her head. 'You'll have him home before you know it.'

Biddy prodded a fork into the large piece of pork. It was cooking nicely. Tears suddenly sprung into her eyes. Pork was Fred's favourite meat – especially the crispy crackling on the outside. 'But will he ever be the same again?' she said in a croaky voice to Elsie.

Elsie dropped her potato and peeler into the sink, and rushed over to throw a comforting arm around her employer's shoulder. 'He'll be right as rain,' the older woman told her. 'In't he improving every day? Me mam came round from her stroke to more or less normal – and she was in a far worse state than Fred. Far worse altogether.'

They both knew this was a gross exaggeration, because Elsie's mother had been a frail woman in her late seventies to start with. But saying it made Elsie feel slightly better – and hearing it made Biddy feel slightly comforted.

Biddy had washed and changed into a brown jersey skirt and matching jumper with a cream collar and cuffs, and was just finishing off her make-up when the phone rang. She put a slick of pink lipstick on, checked her hair, then ran downstairs to see who wanted her now.

'A man – Irish accent, I think,' Elsie mouthed in the almost-silent way she had learned from working in the noisy mills in Stockport for a number of years. She handed the receiver to Biddy and then went off to finish giving the children their supper.

Biddy paused for a moment before speaking. 'Hello,' she said in a hesitant tone. Calls from Irish people were few and far between – especially Irish *men*.

'Hello there, Bridget,' said a rich, refined voice. 'I was just thinking of dropping in on Fred at the hospital this evening . . . and I wondered if that would be OK by you?' Biddy's face broke into a wide, relieved smile. In the past, phone calls from Ireland or Irishmen had often been bad news. 'And why wouldn't it?' she said warmly. 'You know that Fred is always delighted to see you, Frank Kennedy – and so am I, for that matter. You always cheer him up.'

'He's had a good day today, Mrs Roberts,' the ward sister said in a cheery, headmistressy kind of voice. All the nurses on Fred's ward knew Biddy by now, and they usually stopped by to have a word at visiting time. 'He's eaten up all his meals today,' she said, checking the chart at the bottom of the bed, 'and he slept all last night.'

Biddy, sitting close up at the top of the bed, squeezed Fred's hand tightly at the good report. He responded by nodding his head and smiling broadly, although his eyes were dull and heavy and looked large in his thinned-down face.

'You ate all your dinner today,' Biddy said, 'that's grand.' She looked at him closely now. 'What did you have for dinner, Fred?'

Fred's brow creased in thought. After a few moments, he whispered, 'Shepherd's . . . pie and peas.'

Biddy's gaze shifted over to the nurse.

'Shepherd's pie and peas,' the nurse confirmed, winking over at Biddy.

'And . . . trifle,' Fred suddenly remembered.

Biddy felt a surge of joy rising up within her. *His memory was coming back! And his speech was clearer than yesterday!* 'Oh, Fred!' she said in a choked voice, gripping his hand tighter. 'You're definitely, definitely getting better.'

They spent the next half an hour or so with Biddy telling Fred any news she had, then she gave him a rundown of her day at the boarding-house – from the minute she had got up until her arrival at the hospital. Then Biddy reached into the bedside cabinet and took out a packet of photographs. She held up one of the photos, asking, 'Who's that?'

Fred studied it with great concentration. 'Me and you,' he said, looking up at Biddy, 'on a night out at the hotel.' It was a snap taken at a Christmas do in the Grosvenor Hotel a couple of years ago.

'Well done,' Biddy said, holding up another.

'Tara,' he said after a few seconds, then, 'christening.'

They finished the photographs, Biddy feeling more optimistic than ever, since Fred had been successful in naming everyone in the photographs tonight, and he had even kissed the photographs of the children. Satisfied, she put them back in the locker, and then she bent down to her large handbag, and took out the *Manchester Evening News*. Biddy moved her chair back, and came to stand close by the bed. She spread the newspaper out in front of Fred, then turned to the sports section at the back. She pointed out articles about his favourite football team, Manchester United, and the results from the wrestling bouts over the weekend, and read out to him any that he showed the slightest reaction to.

Biddy had serious reservations about wrestling now,

after what had happened to Fred in the ring. But there was no point in worrying about that now. It would be a long time before she had to worry about Fred and wrestling again – if ever.

They took a rest after the newspaper, then Biddy helped Fred to drink some Lucozade, and gave him some soft marshmallow sweets. She finished off with a wrapped chocolate caramel, and watched with great satisfaction as Fred unwrapped the wax paper and managed to chew the sweet without any great difficulty.

'Did I tell you about Tara and Gabriel coming over?' Biddy said to her husband now. She knew very well that she had told him last week, but apart from checking his memory again, she felt she needed to keep Fred's concentration focussed on conversations as much as possible.

Fred's brow creased.

'I got a letter from Tara last week,' Biddy reminded him, 'and she said that she would be coming to Stockport for a month, and that Gabriel would spend maybe a week or two here and the rest of the time in London.'

'London?' Fred said, looking surprised.

Biddy nodded her head. 'Gabriel will be going to London,' she repeated patiently, 'and Tara will spend the whole month in Stockport.'

Just then, footsteps sounded at the bedroom door. 'And how's the big fella today?' came a warm, velvety Irish tone.

'Frank!' Fred's eyes lit up and, after a few moments, his hand stretched out towards his visitor.

Frank Kennedy handed a gift-wrapped box to Biddy, and then moved to the far side of the bed. First, he took Fred's outstretched hand, and then he enveloped Fred in a bear hug. A careful, very gentle bear hug. 'And how's me oul' pal today?' Frank asked.

'Champion!' Fred answered, holding a fist up. 'Just champion!'

Frank stood back. 'I didn't need to enquire – sure, you can tell by the look of you that there's a marked improvement.' He turned now to Biddy, nodding his head. 'A marked improvement indeed.'

'How long is it since you saw him?' Biddy asked.

He calculated for a few seconds. 'A week today, I think it was.' He paused. 'It has to be . . . it's nearly always a Monday that I'm out this way on business. On my way back from Buxton.' He went over to the corner of the room and lifted a high-backed chair over to the bed, so that he was sitting opposite Biddy.

Biddy motioned to the fancily wrapped box. 'You shouldn't have brought anything – I told you that last time. Fred's just happy seeing you, he's not looking for anything from you.'

'Well,' Frank said, winking over at Fred, 'by the cut of him, it might be the last present he'll be getting from me. Anyway, it's only a light dressing-gown. The last time I was in here, I thought it was getting a bit hot for the heavier ones.' He touched Fred's foot under the bedclothes. 'Sure, there's nothing wrong with this fella now, he's nearly back to his oul' self. I think he's only codding us all now, enjoying the bit of attention.'

Fred looked across at Biddy, checking – and when he saw his wife's face creasing in laughter, he started to laugh, too. Loudly and heartily, looking for all the world like the old, good-natured Fred.

Frank Kennedy turned a few heads as he returned from the bar in the Plough Inn, carrying a tray of drinks. The heads of both men and women. His fashionable, well-cut suit and expensive shirt and silk tie shouted 'money' at the men, and his dark, good looks and confident air caught the eye of the barmaid and the other women in the pub. If he noticed any reaction, he certainly didn't show it. Frank was well used to causing a bit of a stir wherever he went. The older he got, the more confident and charismatic he became.

Biddy sat at a table in the window, finishing off her second whiskey and dry ginger.

'You're very good,' she said as Frank put the third tumbler in front of her. 'That little drink has done me the power of good.'

'You deserve it,' Frank said, 'all you've been through these last few months.' He pulled a chair out. 'It's been a tough old time for you, make no mistake about it.'

Biddy nodded her head and took a gulp of the whiskey. 'Who would believe it?' she said. 'After all the times he fell out of the ring without a problem – and then suddenly he falls at an awkward angle, and the next thing we know is that he has a really serious head injury.'

Frank lifted his own whiskey glass and looked down into it for a few moments.

'That's life, Bridget,' he said quietly. 'It always catches us out when we least expect it.'

Biddy took another quick gulp of her drink, the golden liquid sliding down her throat and giving her that lovely warm feeling. 'The thing is, Frank,' she said in a low voice, 'I never really appreciated Fred as much as I do now.' Her hand came up to brush her dark hair behind her ear. 'Don't get me wrong . . . I always knew I was lucky that Fred had taken me on . . . given all the problems I'd had back in Ireland and everything.' She lifted her eyes up to Frank, wondering how much he knew of her past.

He inclined his head a little, the merest nod – an understanding nod. The nod of a man who had seen more than a bit of life's difficulties himself.

'We're a good team, me and Fred,' Biddy went on, enjoying having someone listen to her. 'We worked well together. Hand in hand, as they say. Between the boarding-house, and Fred's bar work at the Grosvenor and wrestling at the weekends, we were making a good living. Providing a good home for ourselves and the kids. But at times it seemed that it was all work, with little time for ourselves.'

'You certainly have worked hard,' Frank said. 'You've maintained and improved the house to a high standard – Ruby Sweeney would be amazed to see the changes you've made.'

Biddy nodded, her face clouding over at the mention of her old landlady and motherly friend, whom she still missed very badly. She could do with someone like Ruby being around right now. Somebody to put their arms around her and tell her that everything would be all right. 'I suppose I just thought Fred would always be there . . . and that the time would come when we would have more time for ourselves.'

Frank reached across and covered Biddy's hand with his. 'And you will, Bridget,' he said, squeezing her hand encouragingly. 'You'll get a second chance to do it exactly the way you want it, when Frank comes out of hospital.'

'Do you think so?' Biddy said, looking up at him with large, watery eyes.

'I *know* so,' Frank said.

A relieved smile came over Biddy's face.

'Fred's improving by the day. He'll be back to his old self in no time at all, and then you'll be able to spoil him and spend more time with him.' Frank gave a deep sigh. 'You'll be thinking how lucky you are . . . for not too many people get a second chance to put things right.'

Biddy's smile slowly faded. She looked down into her whiskey glass, and then took a sip from it. 'You're thinking about Tara . . . aren't you?' she said quietly.

There was a silence. 'Ah, sure, I often think about her,' he said in a low whisper.

Biddy took a big gulp of her drink, almost finishing it

in one go. 'There's no point in wishing for something you can't have,' she said quietly. 'I've told you that before, Frank.'

'I'm always hopeful,' Frank said ruefully. 'But you did say that things weren't great between them . . . the last time they were over. You said—'

'I said he didn't seem great *in himself*,' Biddy corrected him sharply. 'I just said that Gabriel seemed quieter than usual. But in actual fact, I shouldn't have said *anything* to you at all. I had no business talking about Tara and Gabriel.' She finished the drink off now, swallowing it down slowly. 'Tara doesn't even know you call out to the house. I don't know what she'd say if she knew. She might never speak to me again.'

'Surely she wouldn't mind me calling out to see how Fred is?' he said in an injured tone. 'Haven't I known Fred since I came over to Stockport? Between the wrestling and the time I was doing business with the Grosvenor, I saw Fred as regularly as I saw anyone else. Surely Tara wouldn't expect me to drop all interest in you and the family at a time like this?'

Biddy shrugged and stared down at her empty glass. 'It's hard, Frank,' she said, 'it's very hard.' She looked up at him now. 'I don't think you'll ever realise just how much you hurt Tara. She's a very proud girl – she always was.'

A little gleam of hope came into Frank's eyes. 'I never really knew the extent of her feelings for me,' he said, his voice strained. 'She was always a deep, mysterious kind of a woman . . . and I was always waiting for the right time to tell her about . . . my situation. I was waiting until I was more certain of her – until I was confident that she could handle it.'

Biddy shook her head. 'You should have trusted her . . . or at least asked *me* what I thought. I would have understood about you bein' married and everythin'. I'm more a woman of the world than Tara, what with everythin' I've gone through myself. I would have advised you. I would have told you if it was the right time.' She tilted her head. 'I am Tara's oldest and best friend, you know. We go back an awful long way. She's told me things she'd never tell anyone else . . .'

Just then a barman came to take the empty glasses and wipe the table.

'The same again,' Biddy said, reaching for her bag, 'and this round's on me, I can't have you payin' for the drinks all night.' She rummaged inside the bag for her purse.

'No – no – I've had enough,' Frank said, holding up his hardly touched drink. 'And anyway, I have the car.'

'One more won't do any harm,' Biddy insisted, pressing some money into the barman's hand.

Frank took a small sip of his drink, his brow in a deep frown. He had said too much tonight. He hadn't meant to get involved in discussing Tara like this – but he couldn't help it. It just seemed to overtake him. Bridget Roberts was the only contact he had with Tara, and he knew he would have to tread carefully or he would put a strain on their friendship. And a friendship it was, because he liked both her and Fred, and he liked visiting their house. He liked the banter with the working lads and the bit of fun with the kids. He liked being part of a family for a few hours, especially since he didn't get to spend much time with his own any more. But if he were truly honest with himself, the thing Frank Kennedy liked the most about Bridget and Fred was the lifeline they gave him to Tara Flynn.

A few hours later, back at Maple Terrace, Biddy sat watching the last flames of the fire flicker into cold, grey ash. She drew her thick blue and grey Fair Isle cardigan around her shoulders, and moved her cramped legs into a more comfortable position. She took another sip from the glass of hot brandy, and closed her eyes to

27

concentrate as it warmed her throat and then spread a warm glow down into her chest.

This was Biddy's favourite part of the day, since Fred's accident. When everyone was in bed – the children and the lodgers. It was the time when she could eventually blot out all the things she didn't want to think about. Things like how she was going to keep going until Fred came out of hospital. How she was going to keep going if Fred *didn't* come out of hospital soon. How she was going to keep going every night without Fred to put his strong arms around her when she got nightmares, and tell her everything was all right. How she was going to keep going at all.

Elsie had been an absolute rock to her since all this had started, and Biddy didn't know how she would have managed without her. In truth, Elsie had kept everything going – the kids, the boarding-house, and Biddy herself. She had turned up at just the right time, and taken over the reins any time of the day or night that Biddy needed to visit Fred. And she was happy to come over and sit up late with Biddy if she needed someone to talk to.

Biddy took another drink of her brandy, and sank further into the warm, comfy sofa. She pondered over the happenings of the day – the little things with the children, the little improvements in Fred, and then her conversation with Frank Kennedy.

When she tried to remember exactly what they had been talking about, Biddy was a little foggy on some of the details of the chat towards the end of the evening. Maybe, she thought, she might have drunk her whiskey down a little too quickly.

She knew they had discussed Tara. Exactly *what* they had discussed about her, Biddy couldn't be sure. But she knew one thing. Frank Kennedy still loved Tara Flynn – whether she was married or not.

Biddy suddenly had a vague, uncomfortable feeling

that she might have said something she shouldn't have. Her brow furrowed deep in thought. She hoped she hadn't given anything confidential away – anything that might give Frank the impression that Tara's marriage wasn't as happy as it should be. Because, in truth, Tara had never said anything to that effect. In fact, Tara said very little when it came to her private life. Not like Biddy, who liked to talk things out with friends, especially older and more experienced friends who she thought could advise her, like Ruby Sweeney and Elsie. Tara had always been the same – closed and private. But Biddy knew the way Tara was. Wasn't she Tara's best and oldest friend?

She took another drink from her hot, sweet glass. Biddy had always known where her friend's feelings lay, because she'd been with Tara from the very early days. She'd been with her when the first spark of romance had ignited between Tara and Gabriel – and it had never gone away. Tara had always had a fascination with Gabriel and Ballygrace House and that whole way of life. And Biddy knew that it was the only life, and Gabriel the only man, that Tara Flynn truly wanted. Frank Kennedy had only filled a gap in Tara's life when she thought she couldn't have Gabriel.

It was strange the way things went, because, if it had been Biddy's choice, she would never have hesitated. She would by far have preferred Frank to Gabriel, because they had more in common. Although Frank was a wealthy, successful businessman, he was from ordinary people down in County Clare – just like Tara and Biddy were from ordinary people.

But it was all water under the bridge now. Frank had lost his one chance with Tara because he made a huge, fatal mistake. But while Tara couldn't forgive him, that didn't mean to say that everyone else felt the same. Who was Biddy to judge? Hadn't she made plenty mistakes herself?

She nodded to herself now, thinking how lucky Tara was that she'd never made any terrible mistakes in her life. And the more she thought about it, the more she realised that Tara Flynn had *always* been lucky in a way. She might not have had a mother, but she had everything else – a doting grandfather, lovely long red hair, lovely tall slim figure, lovely clothes. And she had two wealthy, handsome men who had fallen madly in love with her.

Yes, Biddy thought, Tara was indeed lucky – she'd had what a lot of people would describe as a charmed life. She didn't have to worry about where the money was coming from to pay bills, nor – as in Biddy's own case – worry about having to run a busy boarding-house all on her own. She didn't even have children to worry about. Tara was her oldest and dearest friend – but she had definitely had an easy life compared with her own. Tara and Gabriel hadn't had anything *really* serious happen since they got married. Apart from Gabriel being sick last year – and hadn't he made a fairly quick recovery?

Biddy drained the end of the glass now, and then moved to go upstairs to her cold, lonely bed.

She hoped she hadn't said anything too careless to Frank. But if she had, it was too late to do anything about it. She'd worry about it tomorrow.

If she happened to remember any of the evening at all.

Chapter Four
BALLYGRACE

Tara stood on the top step of Ballygrace House, staring up at the sky and debating whether to take the bicycle or the car. There was a bit of a breeze which lifted wisps of her long curly red hair and puffed out the skirt of the fashionable blue shirt-waister dress that she'd bought on her last visit to London. A particularly dark cloud hovering over the high pine trees made up her mind. She walked back into the house to collect her cardigan, her handbag and the keys of her grey Morris Minor car.

Ten minutes later she pulled up outside her childhood home, the home she had shared with her grandfather, her father and her father's brother, Uncle Mick, from a very young age after her mother had died. Coming back to the old cottage always aroused mixed feelings. She was happy to see Mick and Kitty – the wife he had married late in life – but she never entered the house without a pang of regret about her granda.

Her Uncle Mick came round the side of the house, the sleeves of his checked working shirt rolled up and a rake in his hand. 'Hello, my girleen, how are you?' he greeted her with a wave of the rake, his face a ruddy red from the vigorous work and his customary shyness which manifested itself even with someone as close to himself as Tara. He walked backwards a few steps. 'You have a visitor!' he called in through the kitchen window to his wife.

Tara waved back and bent into the car to retrieve a bag with two cakes that Tessie had sent in with Angela that morning. Tara knew they would never eat them before going to England and that they would end up being wasted.

'Tessie made them,' Tara told her aunt, pulling a chair out from the well-scrubbed pine kitchen table and sitting down. 'Although Angela has surely inherited her mother's baking skills. You can hardly tell the difference between their apple tarts.'

'Oh, she's a grand little worker,' Kitty said, putting the kettle back on the hob. Although the older woman was dressed in her plain working overall for the grimy job of cleaning the turf-fuelled cooker, her tinted hair was set in perfect waves and she had the lightest dusting of powder to tone down her rosy cheeks. Kitty Dunne might have married her second husband late in life, but she reckoned that was no reason to let her looks go. 'All the family are a credit to Tessie, considering the houseful she always had.' She came back to the table and started to slice up a freshly baked soda-bread cake.

'And considering she didn't get much help from my father when they were young,' Tara pointed out, a disapproving look on her face. 'Although Tessie says he's improved over the years. He's grand with the heavier jobs around the house now, and I have to say he puts in a good bit of time on the gardens out at Ballygrace House.'

Kitty lifted some shamrock-patterned cups and plates down from the old pine dresser, and then stood across from Tara, her hand resting on the back of one of the chairs. She gave a quick glance out of the window, checking that Mick was still occupied in the garden. He had been up early that morning, repairing and tidying around the area at the back of the garden where they kept the chickens. 'Well?' she ventured, looking anxiously at her niece. 'Any news?'

Tara glanced up, held her aunt's gaze for a few seconds, then shook her head.

'Nothing again . . .' Her voice trailed off, and she fiddled with the gold cross on her neck, running it back and forth on the chain. 'It came this morning.'

'Oh, Tara,' Kitty said, coming over to put her arms around her. 'I was sure it was definite this time . . . I was really sure. You're nearly a week late.'

Tara buried her face in her aunt's shoulder. 'It's never going to happen, Kitty,' she whispered. 'Every month it's late, and every month I think *this is it* . . . but it never is.'

'It will happen . . . it *will*,' Kitty said, hugging her. 'With *me* it was different. Don't go thinking it's the same problem I had. My periods were too often and too heavy. I always knew I was going to have problems from when I was young. Your situation sounds completely different. And these days they can do more. There are tests and that kind of thing.'

'But it's not that straightforward,' Tara said in a low, tearful voice. 'There's not really much chance of it happening. You see, I'm not sure if we're doing . . . if things are happening at the right time.' Her red curly head drooped even lower. 'Gabriel doesn't seem to have the same energy . . .'

Kitty bit her lip, unsure which way to go. She gave Tara another reassuring pat, then moved back towards the steaming kettle. She moved it to the edge of the range and then poured the boiling water into the teapot and left it to brew for a few minutes.

'Not that I mind, really,' Tara went on. 'I understand . . .' She halted for a moment, wary of embarrassing her aunt. 'I know there's more to marriage than . . . than the physical side of things – but if things aren't happening at the right time between us, then it's going to be very difficult for me to conceive a child.'

Kitty's eyes darted in the direction of the garden

again. She'd warned Mick to stay outside until she called him, and she certainly didn't want him barging in at such a sensitive time. She knew that there would be a few female things that Tara would want to discuss with her – but she hadn't realised the extent of the situation. 'I'm sure things will be fine, Tara,' Kitty said, pouring out the tea. 'Ye're both still very young, and ye have all your lives ahead of ye.'

'I'm sure if we had a child,' Tara said, fiddling with the cross again, 'that *everything* would be grand. Ballygrace House would be like a real family house again, and there would be more of a purpose to everything.'

'It's early days, Tara,' her aunt said soothingly, handing her a china cup and saucer. 'Just give yourself time. It'll all work out in its own way.'

She rapped on the window now, and beckoned her husband in.

Tara walked down the cottage path with her aunt and uncle, feeling much better after the chat with Kitty. She was lucky to have Mick's wife to talk to because she couldn't think of any other person she could talk to about such personal, confidential things. She had almost considered confiding in Biddy at one point, but then the awful accident with Fred had taken over everything else. Looking back, it was really just as well she hadn't said anything. Biddy really had enough on her plate without having to listen to Tara's much smaller problems.

She turned the engine of the car over, and just as she was about to pull off, Mick suddenly knocked on the driver's window. Tara wound down the window.

'Joe,' her uncle said. 'Any further word from him?'

'I forgot to mention,' Tara said apologetically, 'he's coming up next weekend. I'm picking him up at Portlaoise Station on Friday evening, and leaving him back on Sunday afternoon.'

'How's he doing?' Mick asked. 'Has he settled in, down below in Cork?'

'I think so,' Tara said, a small frown coming over her face. 'We'll hear all at the weekend, no doubt.'

'I'd say it's a big change to him now,' Mick said, rubbing his ear thoughtfully. 'A big change from Dublin.'

'I'll call out again before the weekend,' Tara told him, starting up the engine.

Thank God that Joe and the priesthood was one area that seemed to be going well, Tara thought as she drove along the pot-holed road to Ballygrace House. There was a time when she had worried about his vocation. But, thank God, he had got over any doubts, and had gone straight ahead to his ordination without a hitch. Although he was young and relatively new in his vocation, there was no doubt about it – Joe Flynn was a very good, very dedicated priest. A priest who put his own needs long after everyone else's. Tara smiled to herself now, the thoughts of her good-natured brother having lifted her spirits.

Yes, Father Joe Flynn was one part of her life that she need have no worries about.

Chapter Five

STOCKPORT

Biddy looked with some satisfaction at the pile of newly done ironing on the kitchen table – and then she looked up at the clock. It was nearly a quarter past eleven. *Where on earth had the day gone?* she wondered to herself. Yet another busy day of cooking and cleaning and making sure the children and the lodgers had everything they needed.

She turned the transistor radio off and then lifted a little cream liberty bodice of Helen's to her cheek, noticing that it was still warm from the iron. Thank God and his Blessed Mother that they were two very good children, who gave her little cause for concern. And thank God they had handled the situation with Fred very well. They missed him, of course, but they accepted Biddy's explanations about how he needed to stay a little bit longer in hospital until he was completely well.

Biddy found it much harder to accept than did Michael and Helen. It was overwhelming at times being responsible for absolutely *everything*. She didn't mind all her usual household chores – in fact she quite enjoyed them – but Fred would never have allowed her to do the heavy jobs, like lifting in the coal or chopping the firewood. First thing in the morning he always emptied the ashes and cleaned the grate and did any other dirty jobs that were necessary before leaving the house. Now Biddy had to do most of these jobs herself. Elsie was already doing over and above her usual chores, helping with the evening meals and minding the children when Biddy went to visit Fred.

Thank God for Elsie – she had been a lifesaver, filling a whole lot of gaps at this terrible time.

She unplugged the iron, folded the ironing board, and put it back in the cupboard under the stairs. Then she went into the family sitting room and set about shaking cushions and straightening the arm-covers on the sofa and chairs and, as she did so, her thoughts came back to Elsie's son, Eric.

He had dropped in early that afternoon, offering to do any of the heavy jobs that Biddy was having difficulty with. Things such as cutting the grass in the back garden, and finishing off the new fence at the front which Fred had started the day before his accident. Up until now, the boarders had lent a hand, but Biddy couldn't always wait until they came in, and it wasn't fair to expect them to do big jobs in the house after a day out at work.

It would certainly be handy to have a strong young lad about the place, and she knew that Elsie would be delighted if Biddy took him on for a couple of hours every day. It would keep him busy and give him a few pounds in his pocket. In fact, it was odds on that Elsie had suggested to Eric that he ask Biddy for a job – because it was unlikely that anyone else would give him one. He wasn't finding it easy to get work since coming back to live with his mother. Not since his year-long stint in the remand home. And then there was his appearance: his Teddy-boy quiffed hair and his tight drainpipe trousers did not endear him to would-be employers. But as Elsie constantly said, he wasn't a *bad* lad – only easily led.

Getting caught up with a bad crowd was a simple enough thing to happen to any young fellow. There were plenty that got up to stupid things after a few drinks. As Eric had said, how was he to know that there was anyone in the old caravan on the building site when he and his mates set fire to it? How were they to know that there was a nightwatchman fast asleep in it when he should have been out working and minding the place?

Apart from that one tragic mistake, Elsie told Biddy, he'd only been involved in the usual teenage stuff of nicking from shops or taking items from washing-lines for a bit of a laugh. All the stuff that most lads got up to at one time or another in their life. All devilment and no real harm.

Biddy moved and put the fireguard back in its place. Then she went around the room tightly closing the curtains and unplugging the television and standard lamp. She closed the sitting-room door and then went out and checked the plugs in the kitchen and that the back door was properly locked.

She halted for a few seconds in front of the kitchen cupboard with the whiskey. 'No,' she said aloud to herself, 'that's not the answer to things.'

Then she came out of the kitchen and along the hallway to check the front door. All Fred's little nightly rituals. Now they were *her* nightly rituals and Biddy had to stick to them, because they were part of the routine of their family life together. All the little things she had never had as an orphan growing up in Ireland. All the little things she might lose if Fred didn't get back to his old self. She clapped a hand over her mouth to stifle the sob that suddenly caught in her throat and forced herself upstairs and into bed without the fortification of another whiskey nightcap. Tomorrow was another day and, depending on how things went at the hospital, she would decide on whether or not the errant Eric might be suitable to lift some of the burden from her shoulders. Whether or not he might be suitable to step into Fred Roberts's shoes.

At around three o'clock in the morning, Biddy decided that she'd had enough of staring up into the black ceiling and periodically switching on Ruby's china bedside lamp to check the time.

She padded about barefoot until she found her slippers, then took her pink nylon quilted dressing gown from the hook on the door and tiptoed quietly downstairs and into the kitchen. She filled the kettle and lit the gas under it, then went into the sitting room. Seeing that the fire was well and truly dead, she got the small electric fire from behind the sofa. She plugged it in to the wall socket and dragged it over to the armchair near the door.

She went out into the hall and, lifting the phone from the little table, stretched the cable back across the floor and into the sitting room. The phone came just as far as Fred's armchair, which Biddy knew it would. When she had everything in position, she went back into the kitchen to make herself a cup of tea.

A short while later, after a few sips of the hot tea and with the electric fire warming her legs, she lifted the phone receiver and dialled the number she knew off by heart. The usual thoughts of a large bill after phoning London or the fact that it was the early hours of the morning didn't enter her head. Biddy needed to talk to someone who understood her situation – whatever the cost.

The phone rang several times, and, just as she was about to give up, a half-asleep, grunting male voice answered.

'It's me,' Biddy said in a low voice. 'You said you didn't mind how late I phoned . . .'

There was a pause. 'Is it Fred?' the man said in a cockney accent. 'Has he taken bad?'

'No . . . no,' Biddy replied, 'he's still the same. In fact, he's coming on quite well now.'

'So what's the big panic?'

'None, really,' she said. 'It's just you said to phone if I was ever lonely on me own . . . or had any worries I needed to talk out with someone. D'you remember? Last time you visited Fred in hospital.'

' 'Course I remember, darlin',' the man said, sounding more awake now. 'What's on your mind?'

Biddy tucked her legs up under her, making herself more comfortable in Fred's armchair. 'It's just that I'm findin' things a bit hard here . . . managin' everything on me own, like.' She took a sip of her tea. 'I've had the offer of a young lad comin' in to help. I know his mother and she's nice, but I'm not so sure about him.'

'Is he a decent enough lad?' he asked.

'Well . . . the thing is, he's done time inside . . . not prison exactly, some kind of detention centre for younger fellows.'

'That don't sound too good, girl,' the London voice said now. 'You don't want to go adding to your problems havin' some kind of wide boy there.'

Biddy gave a little sigh of relief. This was exactly what she wanted – what she needed. A man to listen to her and advise her. A man to look after her. Just the way Fred did.

'Well,' Biddy said, 'I think he's learned his lesson. His mother says it was all a mistake, really; he'd got in with a bad crowd and everythin'. That deep down he's got a good heart.'

'Mothers have been known to say that kind of thing. Some find it hard to find any wrong in their kids, no matter how bad they are.' There was a pause. 'Listen, Biddy, as it happens, I'm coming up to Manchester this weekend checking out a job. Maybe I could come across to Stockport on Saturday and visit old Fred, then I could take a look at this youngster – suss him out, like.'

Biddy's heart leaped. 'Oh, that would be grand! Maybe we could go out for a few drinks as well . . . after we've been to the hospital. I don't get out much these days with the kids and the lodgers and everythin'.'

'Sounds good to me – we might even catch a bite of dinner somewhere,' he said. 'A treat – make a change from you cookin' for me.'

Biddy closed her eyes in delight. 'Lovely,' she breathed. 'I'll really look forward to seein' you . . . and to sortin' all this business out with Elsie's lad.'

'That's it sorted, then, darlin',' he said now. 'Didn't I say you could always rely on old Lloyd?'

'You did, you did,' Biddy said. 'You've always been a true friend, Lloyd – through thick and thin.' She moved her cramped legs from under her a little. 'D'you remember the good times we had here with Ruby and the lads? The great nights at the dancehalls in Manchester?'

'How could I forget them?' Lloyd said. 'Any news of Tara?'

'Oh, Tara's grand,' Biddy chattered on, 'livin' back in Ireland in a fine big house with her nice, fancy husband.' Then, feeling guilty, she added, 'Gabriel's a bit uppity, but it's the way he was brought up. Of course I've known him since we were children, and his sister Madeleine as well. He's nice enough in his own way and he makes Tara happy, and isn't that what counts in life?'

'It certainly is,' Lloyd said. 'Being happy is all that counts in life.' There was a pause. 'I think I'd better get back for some kip now, or I won't make it up in the morning for work.'

'Tara's hopin' to come over in the next few weeks,' Biddy added. 'She's been back and forward to see Fred regularly—'

Lloyd cut in. 'I'll look forward to hearing all your news at the weekend, darlin' – I don't want to cost you a fortune talkin' about it all now. You take good care of yourself.'

'I've enjoyed our chat . . . thanks for cheering me up, Lloyd,' Biddy said quickly. 'You're one friend that never forgets me.'

And then, feeling much better now, Biddy put the phone back in the hall and went into the kitchen to make herself another little hot toddy to take back to bed. Just a very small one. Just enough to keep her warm in bed while she mulled over the chat she'd had with Lloyd, and decided what she'd wear when they went to the nice restaurant on Saturday night.

Chapter Six

BALLYGRACE

Tara parked the car in Harbour Street in Tullamore, just beside the church. It was a lovely sunny day today, and she was wearing a peach-coloured, boat-neck dress, with a white belt and matching white cuffs on the three-quarter-length sleeves. She had picked up the *Vogue* pattern for the dress in a shop in Manchester, and had an excellent Tullamore seamstress, Mrs Lynch, make it up for her.

She leaned into the back seat of the car and lifted her white handbag and black lace mantilla. Then she quickly strode the short distance across the yard and into the church. She hadn't much time, as she had a number of things to do in Tullamore today, but it wouldn't take long to light a few candles and say her prayers.

She paused in the doorway of the church for a few moments to cover her flowing red hair with the mantilla, then she pushed the heavy door open and went inside.

The church was cool and dim as always, in spite of the sunny weather outside, and it was completely empty. It was ten o'clock, and the worshippers at the early Mass were long gone. She walked up the centre aisle, genuflected, then went over to the side altar with the statue of the Virgin Mary and the candle stand. She picked up two candles and quickly lit them.

43

She knelt down on the prayer bench, joined her hands, and closed her eyes. Her first prayer was for Fred's continued recovery, and the next one was for the conception of a baby.

In just over an hour, she had been to the bank to organise English money for next week, had looked into the auctioneer's office to pick up some business papers for Gabriel, and had gone into Oliver Gayle's gents' outfitters to buy him two new shirts and some other bits and pieces such as hankies and lightweight summer socks which she thought he might need. On her way back to the car she had stopped off at the florist's to pick up her weekly order, and shortly afterwards was driving back out to Ballygrace to organise things for Joe's arrival that afternoon.

The phone was ringing as she stepped in the door, and Tara – arms full of shopping parcels and flowers – was almost knocked down as Angela came flying out of the drawing room to answer it.

'God almighty!' Tara gasped, flattening herself against the wall.

'Oh, Janey! I'm sorry, Tara.' The girl's hands flew to her mouth. 'It's just that the phone has rung three times already and every time I go to get it, it rings off.'

'It's OK,' Tara said, straightening up and smiling ruefully. 'I'm grand . . . go and answer it before it stops again.' As Angela hurried off down to the bottom of the hallway, Tara put the flowers and parcels on the table inside the door and hung her coat and handbag on the hallstand.

'It's Gabriel,' the girl said, holding out the receiver to her.

Tara's face lit up. 'Thanks,' she said. 'Would you put the flowers in the sink for me, until I get a minute to sort them out?'

Angela went to the table and lifted the bundles of

flowers up to her nose. 'They smell gorgeous!' she mouthed to Tara, before heading back into the kitchen.

'Tara?' Gabriel's voice sounded over the line. 'I was just thinking about you, so I decided to give you a ring. How did you get on in town, darling?'

'Grand, I got everything we needed,' she told him. 'I picked up the papers you asked for from the office, and I sorted out the sterling money.'

'Good girl!' he said. 'I only wish Jim Tierney was quite so dependable. He rang in sick again today, and I've spent the last two hours trying to sort out all the things he's half done, and I still can't make much sense of it.'

Tara bit her lip. 'Can no one else sort it out?' she asked in a low voice. 'What about the new fellow who started in the office after Christmas?'

Gabriel sighed. 'Jim has either forgotten or ignored what I said, and hasn't let young Connors near any of the accounts or files. He's kept him to the outdoor work, the viewing and selling.' He paused for a moment. 'But this isn't fair on you, boring you with all my business problems.'

'Don't be silly,' Tara told him, 'you know I'm always interested in your work. I only wish I could drive over to you this afternoon and help you out with some of it.'

'Not at all,' he said, 'but you're a darling for even thinking of it. *And* you'd make a better office manager any day than Tierney.' His voice dropped. 'I'm sure he's hitting the bottle again . . . his wife sounded very fraught on the phone.'

A vehicle engine sounded in the driveway, and a few moments later the kitchen doorbell went. 'Are you sure I can't do anything?' Tara said, moving to a safer space as she heard Angela's heels clattering down the hallway to answer the door.

'I'm certain,' Gabriel reassured her. 'Listen, I'll get back to this pile of papers, and I'll ring you before I leave the office this evening. I could be late, so don't hold dinner up for me.'

'I'll leave it as long as possible,' Tara told him. 'Joe's easygoing, and he won't mind what time we eat.' She stretched the phone wire until she could see from the hallway through into the kitchen. It was the local butcher's assistant bringing in the weekend delivery, and he would be waiting to be paid. Also, he had an eye for the girls, and Tara had not been impressed with a comment she'd heard him make to Angela the last time he was at the house. She had been even less impressed when she'd heard her half-sister's appreciative laughter.

'I'd better go,' she said into the phone now. 'I have someone at the kitchen door.'

'See you later,' Gabriel said, 'and I love you dearly.'

'And I', Tara said, 'would be lost without you, Gabriel Fitzgerald.'

As he stepped off the train with case in one hand and book in the other, Tara suddenly noticed for the first time just how good-looking her brother really was. She had always known he was attractive enough, although the frown he often wore lent him a serious air that kept people at a distance. But the frown was gone today. The dark, priestly colours with the white collar really suited him, and as he strode towards her, Tara noticed all the women's heads turn in his direction. As usual, when they caught sight of the collar, the hands went up covering heated whispers to their companions, amazed that this young, handsome man was a member of the clergy.

'Tara!' he said, coming towards her with the bright-eyed smile that made him look like their father, in Shay's younger days. 'It was good of you to come all the way over to Portlaoise for me. That old car I have down in Cork hardly takes me around the parish.'

'Amn't I only too delighted to come for you?' Tara

46

smiled broadly, giving him a hug, much to the entertainment of the other people coming off the train who couldn't have known that the vivacious redhead was his sister.

The two of them walked through the small stone-built station and out to where the car was parked. 'Any news about Molly?' Joe asked, throwing his slightly battered brown leather holdall into the back seat.

'Still the same,' Tara said, starting up the engine. 'Still very muddled and calling everyone by the wrong names. The poor soul's latest obsession is going on about my granda as though he were still alive, and him gone these past ten years.' She started up the car engine. 'She was giving out hell about my granda never coming to see her, and him and Mick with the ass and cart and they couldn't think to take a drive out some Sunday afternoon to visit her.'

They pulled away from the station and on to the empty road.

'How is she coping with the domestic side of things?' Joe asked, his voice sounding flatter. 'Is she able to cook and keep the house clean – that sort of thing?'

'Not too grand at all,' Tara admitted. 'She's liable to leave the kettle and pots on till they boil dry, and you would worry that she wouldn't cook things properly and end up with food poisoning.' She stopped at a road end and then turned the car towards Geishill. 'You know I organised Tessie to help her out since you were last here?'

'I do,' confirmed Joe, 'and I'm more than grateful to you for organising it, and for paying for the help.'

'I just add a little bit extra to her pension,' Tara said. 'And weren't Molly and Maggie good enough to us when we were young?'

'They were,' Joe sighed. 'And I've more to thank them for than anyone.' He paused. 'Thank God we have somebody as reliable as Tessie in the family to do the

47

necessary, because it's not easy to deal with old people when they turn out the way poor Molly has.'

'Tessie goes in every morning to help Molly get dressed, and to see she has a good breakfast, then she leaves everything clean and tidy for her and takes her to ten o'clock Mass.' There was a little silence. 'Sure, if Tessie didn't check, she could go up the town in her slippers or end up putting her clothes on over her long nightdress. She's done that on several occasions recently.'

'To think poor Auntie Molly would end up like this!' Joe's face clouded over. 'I wonder if a new doctor would do any good . . . maybe there's some treatment they haven't tried.'

'I doubt it,' Tara said gently. 'When I spoke to Doctor Morrell, he said that it's just the way some people go with old age and that nothing can be done. He said that it's parts of the brain wearing out, like parts of an engine – except they can't be replaced.'

Joe shook his head. 'God almighty!' he whispered. 'What's going to become of her?'

Gabriel joined Tara and Joe for a meal that evening in the dining room. While the two men chatted animatedly over a glass of wine about the differences between life in Dublin and Cork, Tara sat quietly, delighted with how well her brother and her husband got on together – in fact, over the years they had actually come to be very good friends. Considering the differences in their backgrounds when growing up as children, who could ever have thought that one day Tara and Joe Flynn would sit comfortably, chatting and laughing with the blond, handsome Gabriel Fitzgerald in Ballygrace House?

It was all the more surprising when one considered how little contact she and her brother had as children, what with her being brought up with her granda and

Uncle Mick, and Joe being looked after and doted on by the two maiden grand-aunts.

Even more incredible would have been the thought that one day she herself would be the mistress of Ballygrace House. When she thought back to her teenage years, when she was coming and going to the house as the only friend of Madeleine Fitzgerald – Gabriel's younger sister – she felt a darkness descend upon her. Poor Madeleine had developed a mental illness, and had then been killed along with her father in a tragic car accident.

A claustrophobic hot flush came over her face and neck, and Tara reached out for her wineglass and swallowed a mouthful of the fruity red liquid. Then she stood up, excused herself to the two men, and went out into the hallway in the direction of the kitchen.

Angela turned from the soapy dishes in the sink, her thick, straight blond hair tied back in a sensible ponytail. 'Did you hear anything from Biddy yet?' she asked, her blue eyes sparkling with excitement.

Tara smoothed a hand over her curly hair. 'It looks like next weekend is the most suitable to travel over,' she told her young half-sister. 'Does that still suit you?'

'Grand,' Angela said, beaming. 'Oh, I'll be all organised long before then. I've already started packing my case. I can't wait!'

Tara's face softened, pleased at the girl's excitement. 'You'll love it in Stockport,' she told her. 'The shops and the markets, and the parks and everything. I know Biddy and I did when we first went over.'

'How old were ye, when the two of ye went?'

Tara thought for a moment. 'I shouldn't think we were much older than eighteen, the pair of us.'

'Well, I turned twenty last month,' Angela reminded her, 'so I suppose it's about time I saw a bit more of the world.'

Tara nodded, smiling now. For some reason she

always imagined Angela to be younger than her years – she still seemed like a giddy teenager in many ways compared to how she and Biddy had been. How they had had to be. 'I suppose it is time to spread your wings a bit,' she agreed, turning towards the door now. 'Gabriel has some work to finish off before we go, and I've a few things to sort out here and in Tullamore with Auntie Molly.'

Angela's brow suddenly creased. 'You know, Tara, I think Auntie Molly's gone fierce queer in the head. She's always repeating herself, telling you the one thing over and over again. And she gets cross at the slightest little thing.'

'Don't I know,' Tara sighed.

She was givin' out to Mammy last week,' Angela said in a low voice. 'She made a swipe at her, an' poor Mammy only tryin' to put a few rollers in her hair.' She looked at her older half-sister as though waiting for a solution to the problem.

Tara bit her lip and turned towards the hall. She said nothing.

What was there to say?

Chapter Seven

STOCKPORT

Lodgers weren't the same these days, Biddy thought as she cleared up the messy breakfast table. They weren't the same as the ones back in Ruby Sweeney's days. The young lads she had at the moment couldn't lift a paintbrush or a spade to save themselves – or to save an overworked landlady like herself.

The lot she had in at the minute were too young for one thing, and they talked a load of rubbish about how great things were back home in Ireland. If things in Ireland were that great, why didn't they go back there? Why did they stay in a nice town like Stockport – and in reasonably well-paid jobs – if they were going to moan about it all the time? She shook her head as she carried a pile of greasy breakfast plates over to the double sink.

She lifted the bottle of Quix washing-up liquid from the side and gave a few quick squirts into the sink before running the hot water in on top of it. *She* had no complaints about Stockport or England in general, she thought, as she swished the water around to make it more bubbly. Stockport had been good to her on the whole. Very good indeed.

Here, Biddy was a respected landlady with a nice husband and two lovely kids. Thanks to Ruby Sweeney who had left her the boarding-house in Shaw Heath, she was now a woman of independence. Back in Ireland, she'd be forever known as poor Biddy Hart, the little orphan that Lizzie Lawless had taken in. The same Biddy Hart who would have gone with any lad that gave her a good look or a kind word. The Biddy Hart that had left Ballygrace under suspicious circumstances and never once returned.

She looked up at the clock – it was going on for nine o'clock. It was unusual for Elsie to be this late; she'd missed helping with cooking the breakfast and now it looked as though she mightn't make it in for the clearing up. Still, it wasn't too bad for a Saturday morning, considering most of the lads had gone out to work this morning. There were only two of them who weren't working today, and they probably wouldn't emerge until eleven or twelve. The lodgers were harder work when they were in the house causing mess, leaving newspapers and cups everywhere. It was easier when they were all working to get the breakfast over and done with nice and early, and then to have the rest of the day for doing whatever housework was needed. The two children weren't up yet either, which was a blessing, as they demanded far more of her attention at the weekend than they did on schooldays.

Hearing one of her favourite tunes, Biddy stretched up to the shelf where she kept the transistor radio and turned the volume up. Petula Clark's clear voice singing 'Sailor' suddenly filled the kitchen, and immediately lifted Biddy's spirits. She turned back to fill the sink with hot bubbly water to tackle the dishes, singing along with the catchy song.

A short while later the back door opened, and a harassed-looking Elsie came bustling in. 'I'm sorry I didn't make it in for the breakfast, Biddy, but I slept in on account of our Anne keepin' me up all hours again last night.' Elsie's daughter and her husband and toddler son were living with her while they waited for their names to come up for a corporation house.

'Don't be worryin', you're grand,' Biddy told her in a

soothing voice, stretching to the shelf to turn down the radio. Elsie was always saying how she couldn't stand loud music. 'Get yourself a cup of tea and calm down. If it's too stewed we can make a fresh pot.' She filled the kettle with more water and put it back on to the cooker, lighting the gas ring under it. 'Was it trouble with the husband again?'

Elsie took her old duster coat off and hung it behind the door, then she untied her souvenir Blackpool headscarf, emblazoned with pictures of the pier and the beach. She folded the scarf carefully, and tucked it in her coat pocket, then lifted her flowery cross-over apron from behind the door. She patted her greying bun to make sure that all the hairpins securing it were still in place. 'Oh, they were rowin' for hours – a big to-do about nothing. It started over him readin' the newspaper when Anne was trying to tell him all about somethin' she'd bought down the market for the young lad. At times I think it's six of one and half a dozen of the other,' she sighed, putting her head through the gap in her flowery pinny. 'They'd both been at the drink again, and our Anne is no good with drink – she'd fight with her shadow when she's had a few too many.'

'It's not fair on you,' Biddy said, pouring two cups of tea. 'You have your own problems and work to be thinking of.'

'And then there's our Eric,' Elsie said, expertly tying the apron-strings behind her back. 'It's not fair on him. How's he ever going to get into a routine for getting' up for work, if they keep him awake half the night with their bleedin' rowin'? He ends up goin' up to his room and puttin' Elvis Presley on the record player full bung to drown out the racket. I don't know whether I'm comin' or goin' between the lot of them, I don't. I've got Elvis Presley goin' round and round in me head half the flamin' night.'

Biddy cleared a space on the cluttered table, and set

down the cups and the fancy biscuit tin, then she looked at the cooker. 'Did you get any breakfast, Elsie? There's a few rashers an' some sausages left in the pan. D'you want me to warm them up for you with an egg an' a bit of fried soda bread?' When there was no answer, she turned to look at the older woman. Elsie was holding the front of her apron up to her face like a hanky.

'Oh, what's wrong, love?' Biddy said, coming over to put an arm around her.

'Nowt,' Elsie said, snivelling into the flowery material. 'It's just that you're the only friggin' one that gives me a nice word. You're the only one that would think to ask if I'd had a bite to eat before comin' out. That lot back at the house wouldn't care if I went the whole day without eatin'. They wouldn't even notice if I didn't eat for a whole week . . . as long as I'm there to cook and clean for them and mind the little lad.' Her words trailed off into a long sob.

'Come and sit down and drink your tea,' Biddy said, guiding her over to the table. 'It won't take me two minutes to have a bit of breakfast ready for you, and you'll feel much better.'

Half an hour later, with Elsie fortified and comforted by her hearty breakfast, the two women set about clearing up the kitchen.

'Did you give any more thought to our Eric givin' you a hand?' Elsie asked, as she attacked the top of the grease-splashed cooker with a foaming Brillo pad. 'I hate the thought of you havin' to lug all that coal by yerself. An' I was just thinkin' that he could have that fence all fixed up for Fred comin' out of the hospital . . . he could be doin' it while the weather's fine.' A smile suddenly lightened her worried face. 'He's good at the woodwork – he got a C for it in his school exam.' She gave a wry smile. 'It were the only bloody exam he passed – mind you, he never went in for half of them anyway. He hated school, our Eric.'

'I was thinkin',' Biddy said, as she rubbed a stripy tea-towel over one of the breakfast plates, 'that if he called round for a little chat about five o'clock this evenin', I have a friend comin' to the house . . .' Biddy halted for a minute, wishing Elsie hadn't brought the subject up again so quickly.

'A friend?' Elsie's eyebrows shot up inquisitively. She halted her scrubbing for the moment.

'A friend of mine . . . and Fred's,' Biddy clarified. 'Lloyd his name is – an old lodger of Ruby's. He's a grand lad. Anyway, Lloyd is goin' to have a look at what needs doin', and he'll be able to tell me if a young lad is fit to do all the jobs.'

'*Lloyd?*' Elsie said, her eyes narrowing. 'I don't think I've heard you mention him before . . . what kind of name is it? It don't sound Irish to me.'

Biddy suddenly flushed. 'Oh, he's not one of the Irish lads . . . he's from London.' She picked up another plate to dry. 'Actually, he's a coloured lad . . . kind of half-caste, I think. Half West Indian or African or something like that.'

'A *darkie*?' Elsie said, obviously shocked.

'I've never heard anybody call him that,' Biddy said, 'they wouldn't dare. He's a fit lad and a good worker. All the other lads thought the world of him, and so did Ruby.'

Elsie paused, pondering the situation. 'I didn't mean any offence or nowt like that . . . it's just that black lads aren't liked by everyone. You don't see many of them around Stockport. And did you say he was one of Ruby's old lodgers?'

'I did,' Biddy said, lifting the pile of dried plates over to the ribbed-glass dish cupboard. 'And one of Ruby's best lodgers, a great worker around the house for her and everythin' like that. He was great at the paintin' and decoratin' – did the hall outside all by himself in a matter of days.' She rubbed at a mark on the outside of the cupboard door. 'I could do with a few lads like Lloyd around the place now.'

Elsie pursed her lips. 'An' you don't mind the black lads yersel'?' she said. 'You wouldn't mind havin' one for a lodger, like?'

Biddy shook her head. 'Not at all – not as long as they're decent like Lloyd. He's no different to any other lad – only the colour of his skin.' She wished Elsie would drop the subject now. She went to put the plates in the cupboard, then noticed that the side plates and breakfast plates were all mixed up together, making the pile unsteady.

'God!' she muttered. 'This delft is in a fierce muddle.' She put the plates down on the table, and started to sort out the piles in the cupboard.

Elsie dropped her Brillo pad on the top of the cooker. 'Here,' she said, coming over to the cupboard, 'let me give yer a hand with that – an' if ye've any sense, you'll get our Eric in to help you with all the heavier stuff.'

Biddy lay back in her nice warm bath and waved her hands around in the water to disperse the rose-scented pink bath cubes that had settled in two soggy lumps at the bottom of the bath. They were part of a set that one of the girls from the Grosvenor Hotel had given her last Christmas. Normally, Biddy was too busy to be bothered with putting them into her weekly bath, but this afternoon she felt she deserved a little bit of pampering. She had left the box with the hand-cream, body lotion and talc on her bedroom dressing-table, intending to use them all when she came out.

Elsie had taken Michael and Helen off to the market in Stockport for some new socks and underwear, and some colouring books and crayons and a jigsaw puzzle to keep them occupied later that evening. Elsie said she would probably take them into one of the cafés in the town for chips and sausages and a drink, so Biddy needn't worry about cooking for them.

The shepherd's pie and the tinned carrots and peas were already sorted out for the boarders' dinners and just needed heating up, along with the apple tart and a couple of tins of evaporated milk to pour over it for pudding.

The house was all clean and tidy – everything done and dusted by three o'clock – and Biddy was now taking the chance of a quiet hour to herself while the kids were out of the house, and before the first of the lodgers arrived back from work or a football match. Her bath over, Biddy padded barefoot along the hallway to her bedroom, wrapped in a bath towel and with another smaller towel around her shampooed hair. Once in the bedroom, she rubbed herself vigorously with the towel, and when she felt dry enough she dropped it on the end of the bed and walked about the room naked.

This was something she didn't get the chance to do very often, and usually only when Fred was in the room with her. The sight of his wife's relatively slim, attractive body always got to him, and then they usually ended up in bed. But this afternoon poor Fred was not there, and it would be another few hours before Biddy saw him in hospital, so she just enjoyed the freedom of moving around naked in the privacy and warmth of the room. She covered herself in the sweet, rose-scented body lotion, and while it soaked into her skin, she plugged in the hairdryer.

She looked at herself in the dressing-table mirror, grateful that her hair was easier to style these days. She'd kept the shortish, wavy bob that Tara had suggested, although she wasn't too sure about the colour, as it was beginning to look a bit mousy and drab. She ran her fingers through her hair, wondering what she'd look like as a blonde. The sort of ash-blonde that Ruby used to have. She lifted the gilt-framed photo of herself and Ruby which she kept on her bedside cabinet, and stared at her old landlady. *Don't forget,* Ruby used to tell her, *gentlemen always prefer blondes!* And then Ruby would add, laughing, *And so do the others who are not gentlemen – and they're a lot more bleedin' fun!*

Biddy nodded to herself in the mirror, holding up two strands of hair one on either side of her head. Maybe she might go blonde after all. Just for a change. She could always dye it back to brown if she didn't like it. She might just pay a visit to Ruby's old hairdresser down in Underbank in Stockport next week, and get her opinion about going blonde. She would also ask Fred when she was in visiting him this evening – it would be something fresh to talk about. And then there was Lloyd. She could ask his opinion, too, she mused. He had a good eye with fashion, had Lloyd – plus he would know what all the latest hair fashions in London were.

Biddy stood up and with narrowed eyes appraised her naked figure in the mirror. *Not bad*, she thought, *not bad for someone of nearly thirty, with two kids*. Of course she'd put on a couple of pounds here and there with all the extra biscuits and sweets lately – but she still wasn't fat or anything like it. She still looked good enough for her age. And she looked after herself well. She'd taken on board a lot of the advice that Ruby used to give her, and when she had time she varnished her nails and put cream on her face. Fred didn't mind what she spent on herself, he said he liked to see her looking good and he said she deserved it.

As she went over to her chest of drawers for her bra and knickers, Biddy suddenly wondered what Lloyd would think if he saw her naked – or maybe in one of the little lacy underwear sets she bought from Stockport market. And as quickly as the terrible thought came into her mind, it was replaced by a picture of her poor, sick Fred lying in a hospital bed.

Hot tears of guilt sprang into Biddy's eyes, and she quickly grabbed the towel from the bed to cover herself up. What a terrible, terrible thing to be thinking at this time. Next week she would go down to the priest in Our Lady's in Shaw Heath and make her confession. She would have to. A married woman with two children thinking such terrible things about another man. And a *coloured* man at that.

Biddy shivered now, suddenly cold, and goosepimples came out all over her body. She opened her underwear drawer and picked out a plain white underset of bra and knickers. The plainest ones she could find. Fred liked her in the lacy or flowery little things – but Fred wasn't in a position to appreciate those things now.

She would wear sensible underwear and a sensible outfit to visit Fred, and that's what she would be wearing when she went out for the meal tonight with Lloyd.

Chapter Eight

TULLAMORE

'Do you think she'll be all right?' Tessie Flynn said in a low voice, nodding towards the bedroom where Angela was finishing off the last of her packing. She'd been at it on and off all day, putting this in and taking that out, and calling for her mother's opinion every so often. Mary and Assumpta had both come home at lunchtime to wish their sister well on her trip, and had brought her gifts of toiletries to take with her, which meant that the already packed case had needed reorganising to accommodate the last-minute additions.

'Oh, she'll be the finest,' Shay said from behind the local newspaper, in a voice that harboured no doubts whatsoever.

'I'm not so sure,' Tessie said, pursing her lips. 'Angela isn't as easy as the rest of the girls . . . she can be fierce awkward when she gets a mood on her. I hope her and Tara don't clash too much.' Tessie had found Angela so difficult that afternoon that she'd slipped out to a neighbour who did a bit of hairdressing, and had spent a relaxing hour having her brown hair trimmed and set. When she returned home, she decided to change into one of her decent Sunday frocks in honour of Angela's departure.

'Well,' said Shay, putting his newspaper down, 'if they clash, they clash. Between them be it.' He rose to his feet now and went across to sit beside his wife on the small wood-framed settee. 'You worry too much about everythin',' he told her, putting his arm around her and pulling her close to him.

'I can't help it,' Tessie whispered, leaning her head on his shoulder. 'She's the first one of ours to go over the water.'

'Well, you only have to look at Tara to see how well she did over in Stockport,' Shay reminded her. 'And anyway, Tara will keep a close eye on Angela – she's the very woman that won't take any nonsense from her.'

'True,' Tessie mused, 'that's true.'

'You smell nice . . . is that perfume you're wearing?' Shay suddenly said, sniffing at his wife's neck. His hand moved up now to cup one of her generous breasts.

'Just a touch,' Tessie said, delighted that he'd noticed. Then, when his hand came to her chin to lift her face to his, she closed her eyes in anticipation of the kiss she knew would follow.

'For God's sake!' Angela's voice came from the doorway. 'You can't even come into your own living room without finding ye two all over each other.'

Tessie moved away quickly, almost pushing Shay off the settee. 'Mind your tongue, young lady!' she snapped, mortified at being caught out in such an intimate situation.

'We'll have less of that kind of talk from you,' Shay said, getting to his feet.

'No wonder!' Angela huffed, going over to look out of the window. 'Imagine if Tara and Gabriel had come in to find ye canoodlin' on the couch!'

'I'm sure they wouldn't mind a bit,' Shay said, laughing now. 'I'm sure they often do a bit of canoodlin' themselves. Isn't it only natural with married couples?'

Angela threw her father a derisory look over her shoulder. 'Gabriel and Tara are an awful lot younger than an oul' pair like you two.' She turned back to the window, muttering to herself, then lifted the curtain to get a good look along the street. 'Mary Slattery said she might call in to see me before I leave . . .'

'Oh, I meant to tell you,' Tessie said quickly, 'I met her up the town this morning, and she said to tell you she had an appointment at the doctor's—'

'Well, thanks for lettin' me know,' Angela sighed, dropping the curtain back in place.

'Have you nearly finished your packing?' Tessie asked.

'Yes,' Angela said, wishing they would stop checking every single thing she did. She couldn't wait to get away to Stockport where she could do things any way she wanted, without having to answer to anyone.

Shay went to take up a position by the window now. 'Make sure ye don't keep Tara and Gabriel waiting,' he warned his youngest daughter. 'Be ready to go the minute the car pulls up, for they said they didn't want to be cuttin' it neat for the boat.'

'I'm ready,' Angela said, her eyebrows shooting up in indignation. She turned towards her bedroom now, her mother following close behind.

'Are you sure you have everything you need?' Tessie checked anxiously, then started going through the neatly packed case again. She lowered her voice. 'Have you a few spare sanitary towels in your toilet bag, like I told you? You never know . . . it could come a few days early with the travellin' and everythin' and you don't want to be running around looking for chemists the minute you arrive in England.'

Angela gave a loud, exaggerated sigh – they had been going on to her all afternoon about the most stupid of things. '*Mammy!*' she said. 'I'm not a child. I know what to take – and anyway, didn't Tara give me a list as well?' She banged the lid of the case down now, and started to zip it up. 'You'd think I was some class of an eedjit the way you're all goin' on . . . as if I hadn't a brain in me head.'

'Here!' Shay said in an authoritative tone. 'Mind that case! That's not yours to be treatin' so roughly. That's no ordinary case – that was a Christmas present I got from me eldest son.'

Thank God he didn't mention the fact that his eldest son happened to be a priest, as he so often did, Angela thought. If he wasn't braggin' on about Tara and Gabriel and Ballygrace bloomin' House, then he was going on about Joe bein' a priest.

Shay ignored the huffy looks Angela was giving him. He was well used to the tantrums of young ones – particularly the girls. Women could be fierce hot-headed and touchy at times, and he was the man that knew all about it – God help him. 'Have you your wallet separate, like I told ye? Ye couldn't be up to some of them lads on the boat, they'd steal the eye out of yer head if ye weren't looking.'

'How many times have I told you?' the girl said, tutting. 'The wallet is safe in my handbag. God! Youse are both beginning to sound like Auntie Molly – repeatin' the same oul' things over and over.'

'God forgive you!' Tessie Flynn scolded. 'Isn't that a lovely thing to be saying? Talkin' about your father's poor old auntie like that.'

'An' it's to be hoped', Shay added, 'that *you* never find yourself in that predicament one day, m'lady. D'you think poor oul' Auntie Molly imagined it would happen to her?' He folded his arms and craned his neck to look out of the window for the car once again. 'She was a *lady*, ye know – a pure lady. An' my poor father an' Auntie Maggie would turn in their graves if they knew the way her poor oul' brain has gone.'

Angela lifted her handbag and checked through her documents and money again, and the new striped make-up bag she had bought from Quirke's Medical Hall in Tullamore only yesterday.

'Here it comes!' Shay suddenly said, making a dive for the case as Tessie ran all flustered to answer the door.

A surge of excitement ran through Angela. She'd been awake a lot of the night, waiting for this very moment. Her big adventure – and maybe even a new life – started *now*, because the few hours' drive up to Dublin in Gabriel's car was excitement enough in itself, never mind the thought of the trip to England in a big, fancy boat, for they were going *First Class* on this trip.

Tara got out of the passenger side of the big shiny black car to have a word with her stepmother, while Gabriel wound down the window to have a word with Shay and to give him the keys of Ballygrace House. Both men were suitably dressed for the warm evening in short-sleeved shirts – although there was no denying the difference in cut and material in the cream linen shirt that Gabriel was wearing.

'You've had your hair done,' Tara told Tessie, 'it looks lovely – and your dress does, too.'

Tessie smiled delightedly at the comment, touching a hand to her curled hair. 'You have to make a bit more of an effort when you get to my age.'

'Go away,' Tara laughed, 'you never look a bit different to me.'

'And what about my new slacks?' Angela asked, tossing her long blond hair over her shoulders. 'I took your advice and wore my trousers for travelling on the boat.'

'We're both in the same fashion, then,' Tara said smiling, for she was wearing a pair of light-green tapered slacks and a cream sweater and cream loafers.

'Here, Daddy.' Angela handed her father her beige

raincoat, and then stepped back, posing hand on hip, to let Tara get a look at her outfit.

'Fantastic!' Tara said, admiring the blue slacks and the short-sleeved pale blue jumper that showed the young girl's slim, petite figure to perfection. 'The colour suits your hair perfectly and the string of pearls really sets the outfit off.'

Angela smiled warmly at her mother. 'That was my last birthday present from Mammy and Daddy.'

'That's a fine big boot ye have there,' Shay commented, as he placed Angela's case and coat in it. 'Ye're a lucky girl,' he told Angela, 'travellin' over in a grand vehicle like this.' She was indeed lucky, for Shay had had very few comfortable journeys back and forth to England in his time. Most of his journeys were spent cramped up in the front seat of a van, with a battered old hold-all on his knee, or in the old rickety coach that hit every pothole between Tullamore and Dublin as it wound its way through the winding country roads.

'I'll write to you when I get time,' Angela declared, then suddenly moved to throw her arms around her surpised and delighted mother and then followed suit with her father, before depositing herself in the back seat of the car.

'See and make sure you behave yerself,' Shay said, holding his thumb up to her now.

'I think we've covered everything that needs doing,' Gabriel said, handing the bunch of keys over to his father-in-law. 'The biggest job is keeping the grass down at this time of the year.'

'Sound as a pound, Sir,' Shay said, beaming with delight. 'Sound as a pound. I'll be keepin' a close eye on everythin' for youse while you're on your travels.'

'An' I'll keep the house good and aired for ye,' Tessie assured Tara. 'An' if you let me know when ye are due back, I'll have bread baked an' all your orders in from the shops.'

Tara smiled and nodded. 'You're both very good,' she said. 'We'll have no worries about the house at all.' She paused for a moment, then added quietly, 'And I hope you don't have too many worries with Auntie Molly.'

Tessie and Shay stood waving until the big black car had disappeared out of sight.

'Ah, well,' Tessie said, a catch in her voice. 'That's her gone now. The house is going to feel fierce empty without her.'

Shay put his arm around his wife and guided her back into the house. 'It's going to be fierce *peaceful* without her,' he said laughing. 'And don't deny it, Tessie – for she's been like a bag of feckin' cats these last few weeks!'

Chapter Nine

STOCKPORT

Biddy got a shock as she and Lloyd walked into the ward to see Fred's bed empty. The pillow-cases and the bed-linen were fresh and looked as though they hadn't been touched since being made up in the morning. Her heart was pounding as she rushed up the corridor to the nursing staff office, leaving Lloyd with the bottle of Lucozade and the bag of Fred's favourite biscuits and sweets.

A few minutes later she came out all smiles, after having been reassured by a cheery young Irish nurse from Cork that Fred was just grand. In fact the physiotherapist had just commented yesterday afternoon that he was literally making great strides in all directions.

He had been bathed and changed that morning into fresh pyjamas and the new wine-coloured dressing gown that Frank Kennedy had brought him, and had spent most of the afternoon in the day room watching sport on television and chatting with the other patients. He'd had his evening meal at the big table in the middle of the ward, and had just been wheeled back down to the day room half an hour ago.

'I don't believe it,' Biddy said as they walked down to the bottom of the busy ward, bustling with visitors and nurses, 'I thought he was stuck in that bed for ever.'

'Not old Fred,' Lloyd said cheerfully. 'They'll have to

shoot him before they can put him down. Fightin' is in his blood – he's a wrestler to the last.'

'An' it nearly *was* his last,' Biddy told him wryly. 'That damned wrestling nearly killed him. Thanks be to God he'll never go near a wrestling ring again.'

Fred was sitting in the corner, chatting with a young lad who didn't look more than a teenager. When Biddy called out his name, he turned his whole body slowly to look round at her – and when he recognised her, a huge smile spread across his face.

'This is my girl!' he told the young lad proudly as Biddy came towards him with outstretched arms. 'This is my lovely wife, dressed up all nice to come and see me.' Biddy felt herself blush, feeling guilty that her pink twin-set and fairly tight pencil skirt had been more influenced by the meal out with Lloyd later, than her hospital visit, for she had changed her mind at the last minute about a too-sensible outfit.

It turned out to be a good thing that Fred was in the day room, because Biddy and Lloyd got decent arm-chairs, and they could all talk loudly and laugh as much as they liked without disturbing the other patients and their visitors.

'Big change in you since I last saw you, mate!' Lloyd told Fred. 'Next time I come, you'll be out of that wheelchair and runnin' around all over the place.'

'That's the last hurdle now,' Biddy said, reaching over and squeezing her husband's hand. 'Isn't that right, love?'

Fred nodded his head. 'Last hurdle.' he repeated, 'definitely the last hurdle.'

Biddy gave him one of his favourite Eccles cakes and then left him chatting with Lloyd about the wrestling bouts on television that afternoon, while she went off into the ward in search of a tumbler for his Lucozade.

'I was thinkin' of gettin' my hair done all blond,' she told Fred later, as she poured him his drink. 'Like

Ruby's used to be. D'you think that blond hair would look well on me? Lloyd said he thinks I'd look nice blonde.'

Fred stared at her for a few seconds as though considering her question very carefully.

'Your hair's very nice,' he eventually said. 'Your hair always looks very nice.'

Biddy looked at Lloyd and bit her lip. She decided to let the subject of her hair drop.

Biddy dabbed her eyes, then blew her nose on a tissue and went back to looking at the menu. It was a new steakhouse restaurant that Lloyd had picked, and in a nice part of Didsbury – a not-too-far taxi-ride from the hospital.

'Get that drink down you, girl,' Lloyd told her gently, 'and you'll soon be in crackin' form again.'

Biddy nodded and took a gulp of the brandy and Babycham. 'His brain's still not fully right,' she whispered, 'is it, Lloyd?'

Lloyd shifted his shoulders in a half-shrug. 'It's hard to say, sweetheart . . . it's just gonna take time.' He reached a hand to her across the restaurant table, studiously avoiding the lit candle and the small vase of pink plastic roses. 'You've just got to be patient. He's improved no end since the accident and, as the nurse said, he's improving every day.'

'But it's his *brain*,' Biddy emphasised, 'it's his brain I'm fierce worried about. There's times when I'm not sure he understands everything.'

'Well,' Lloyd considered, running his hand through his short, thick curly hair, 'don't forget it's his brain that makes his body work – and his body and brain have had to learn everything all over again. It's all very complicated . . .' Then, to his immense relief, a stout, elderly waitress came slowly, puffing, towards the table for their order, and Biddy turned her attention to whether she wanted her steak well done or *very* well done.

'Let me buy a round,' Biddy said in a loud voice, pushing the pound note across the table. 'It's only fair – you said I could buy them – the next time.'

'OK, darlin',' Lloyd said quickly, getting up from the table. 'If it makes you feel happy, old Lloyd's not gonna argue.' He headed off towards the bar.

Biddy nodded and lifted her glass of rum and port. 'It's my round,' she said to herself, 'an' it's only fair to pay me way . . . only fair.' She took a drink from the almost empty glass, and then very carefully negotiated a place to put it back down on the table. She lifted her head up to look around the restaurant: it was almost empty, and the waitress had disappeared into the kitchen a while ago, leaving Lloyd to make his way to the bar downstairs.

Biddy blinked a couple of times to focus her vision, because at times she was seeing two of everything. It must have been the rum and port mixed with the brandy and Babycham, she vaguely thought. Maybe she would have been better sticking to one or the other . . . maybe she would have been better not mixing them.

'Here, I'll do that,' Lloyd said, attempting to take the front-door key from Biddy.

'Ye're all right,' Biddy slurred, making a third stabbing attempt at getting the small Chubb key into what she saw as the ever-moving, ever-decreasing keyhole. Lloyd leaned over and covered Biddy's smaller hand with his, then guided it firmly towards the keyhole.

Suddenly, a feeling that Biddy had not felt in a while rushed from her covered hand right through her body. The lovely feeling of having a man standing close to her. The lovely feeling of a man's hand touching hers.

Instinctively – just as Lloyd turned the key in the lock – Biddy turned her body around towards his, and the sudden movement sent her flying backwards into the hallway. Lloyd made a move to catch her arm, but the half-dozen or so pints of beer he had consumed did not allow him to move swiftly enough to save her.

'Jesus, Mary and Joseph!' Biddy uttered, as she landed in an ungainly heap on the hall floor.

'Up you get, girl!' Lloyd said, coming forward to help her up. 'Up you get . . .'

But Biddy was not making any moves to get up, and instead, taking Lloyd's outstretched hand in both of hers, she pulled him down on top of her, giggling as she did so.

'What you doin'?' Lloyd protested in a loudish whisper. 'We'll have the whole bleedin' house up in a minute.' But his protests were abruptly cut off, as Biddy's lips came up to meet his, and suddenly they were kissing passionately. In moments they had rolled over, and Lloyd was on top, and the hardness Biddy could feel pressing down on her stomach told her exactly where it was going to lead. Then, just as Biddy was attempting to pull Lloyd's jacket off, the click of a landing light going on upstairs brought their passion to an abrupt halt.

'That you, Biddy?' Elsie's voice sounded in a loud whisper from upstairs. 'Is that you come home?'

Both Biddy and Lloyd scrambled to their feet as Elsie's plodding footsteps made their way down the stairs.

'So,' Elsie said, pouring out the three cups of tea. 'We had quite a night of it after you left.'

Biddy looked at her friend now, thinking that she always looked different in the evenings – sort of younger when she was minus her pinny and her grey-flecked hair was out of its usual bun and tied back loosely.

'As I were just sayin', it were just as well our Eric had come over this evenin' or we'd have been in a right pickle, what with no lights and everythin'.'

'He did a good job,' Lloyd said, reaching for the sugar. He was almost afraid to look at Biddy after the madness that had just passed between them. 'He did a good job sorting out the fuses. I gave the fuse-box the once-over when I came in, and everythin' seems just fine.'

'To tell you the truth,' Elsie said, giving him a friendly smile, grateful that he'd come down on Eric's side, 'I don't know the first bleedin' thing about fuses, I don't – and God knows what I'd 'ave done without him, for there were none of the lodgers to be seen, with it being a Saturday.' She put a cup of tea in front of Biddy now. 'There's times as I could see him far enough – as Biddy well knows – but fair dues to him this evenin' – our Eric came up trumps!'

Biddy nodded her head. Even in her drink-befuddled mind, she was aware that Eric had averted a crisis and that Elsie was hitting the point home with a very big hammer.

'You'd have been fierce stuck without him tonight,' she agreed, speaking with some difficulty, 'and I wouldn't have been any good if I'd been here. Sure, I don't know one end of a fuse from another.' She glanced over at Lloyd, and gave a sad little smile. 'It was different when Ruby was here, wasn't it, Lloyd?' she slurred. 'When all you lads were here to see to things like fuses and bulbs.'

'Different times, flower,' Lloyd agreed, without meeting Biddy's eye. 'Different times.'

'As I say,' Elsie went on, checking the toast under the grill, 'our Eric's handy enough around the house when he's given the chance.' She lifted the three slices of toast on to a wooden board, buttered them lavishly, then cut each piece in two. 'I think he feels his nose has been pushed out of joint since our Anne's fella moved in. As though he's not given his rightful place as the man of the house, like.' She piled the hot toast on to a plate and brought it over to the table. 'But what can I do about it? You can't do right for doin' wrong with families.'

'Still,' Biddy said, her voice slurring, 'it's better to have them than to be without. An' it's me that knows all about not havin' a family.'

'That'll help yer stomach soak up some of the drink,' Elsie said, holding the plate out to Biddy. 'You won't feel so bad in the mornin' if you've had a cup of tea an' some toast inside you.'

Biddy took a piece of toast, nodding her head. She bit on it and then chewed it slowly, her mind a million miles away.

'It's only since Fred went into the hospital', Elsie whispered to Lloyd, 'that she's been hittin' the drink a bit hard. She didn't used to take more than a couple. When Fred comes back home, things'll sort themselves out then.'

'Yeah,' Lloyd said, casting a wary glance in Biddy's direction. 'Things will get back to normal just as soon as he gets back home.'

'An' if Biddy wants it,' Elsie said 'she'll have Eric holding the fort until he does. He'll be there for all the bits an' bobs that need doin' – and he's not the kind of lad to get in your way or owt like that. There's times you'd hardly know he was around.' She paused. 'He can be kind of deep in himself . . . not a great talker like. Exact same as his father was.'

They sat drinking their tea, drifting slowly into silence. Eventually Biddy dozed off, her head on her folded arms.

'It's her I feel sorry for,' Elsie told Lloyd, nodding in Biddy's direction. 'She's been through the mill with all this hospital business. Thank heavens he's gettin' better, because in the beginnin', straight after his accident like, poor Fred didn't know if it was Christmas Eve or rice puddin' half the time. It were no joke for Biddy tryin' to act as if everythin' was normal when he was like that.'

Lloyd nodded vaguely, wondering what time the early train left in the morning. He glanced at the kitchen clock – it was heading on for two o'clock. He wondered if maybe there was a milk train stopping at Stockport station around six o'clock that might be worth staying up a few hours for. If he gave the driver a few quid he might just let him on.

Elsie got up out of her chair and went over to take her coat and headscarf from the hook on the back door. 'I think it's time for me to head home,' she said. 'Things should be quiet back at the house at this hour.'

'Have you far to go?' Lloyd asked, finishing off his lukewarm tea.

'The next row of houses – just across the back entry,' Elsie told him. 'It's only two minutes' walk.'

Lloyd got up. 'I'll see you back home,' he said. 'It's not safe for a lady to be out on her own at this time of the night.'

Elsie put her coat and headscarf on. 'That's real good of you,' she said, 'but there's no need, like. I'm used to goin' home on me own.' Anyway, she thought to herself, what would she say to the neighbours if any of them saw her walking along the street at night with a *darkie*? Her good name, such as it was, would be tarnished for ever. But Lloyd wouldn't take no for an answer.

A short time later they reached her gate. 'Looks as though they're all in bed,' she said, indicating the darkened windows.

'I'll watch until you're safely inside,' Lloyd told her, turning up the collar of his jacket against the chilly breeze.

'Ta very much,' Elsie told him now, feeling guilty about her earlier thoughts regarding his dark colouring. 'It were right good of you to walk over here with me. You're a proper gentleman, you are.'

'My pleasure,' Lloyd replied, giving a little bow.

Elsie walked a few steps up the path then suddenly turned. 'You will put a good word in for our Eric, won't you? Because Biddy really needs a hand around the place – as you can see for yourself, things are getting on top of her a bit.'

'Yeah,' Lloyd said, digging his hands deep into his jacket pockets. 'She does need a bit of help.'

'You won't crack on to Biddy I said owt to you?' Elsie checked anxiously. 'It's just that it would help out all round . . . just until Fred gets back home.'

'No . . . no,' Lloyd reassured her. 'I won't say nothing about it.' He moved away from the gate. 'Goodnight.'

'Goodnight,' Elsie said, sticking her Yale key in the lock, 'and thanks again for bein' such a gentleman.' She went inside with a big smile on her face.

Lloyd walked back up the street towards Biddy's, wishing with all his heart that he was on the train back to London without having to face her again.

Biddy woke up as Lloyd was tiptoeing past the kitchen table. 'Has Elsie gone home?' she asked, still a bit of a slur in her voice.

'Yeah, yeah,' Lloyd said, clapping his hands together in an attempt to appear relaxed and casual. 'I saw her safely back to the house. She's a nice old girl.'

'I don't know what I'd do without her.' Biddy put her palms flat on the table and then pushed herself to stand up straight. 'I think it's time I headed upstairs to bed . . .'

Lloyd made towards the hallway, rubbing his hands together. 'I think I'll just kip down on the sofa, if that's

all right with you. I'm gonna head for the early train . . .
and it'll save waking anyone if I just nip out the front
door.'

'No,' Biddy said, 'you need a decent night's sleep, and
anyway, the trains aren't so regular on a Sunday.' She
moved towards him. 'You could be sitting in a freezing
waiting-room for hours waitin' for a train.'

'Well . . .' Lloyd said, moving steadily towards the
hall, 'I'll kip downstairs in the sitting room anyway, it
don't make any difference to me where I sleep.'

Biddy suddenly moved towards him. 'Come upstairs
with me, Lloyd . . . *please*,' she said taking hold of his
hand. 'Just for the company . . . I get ever so lonely on
me own.'

Lloyd shook his head. 'But it ain't right, Biddy . . .
you're a married woman, and Fred's a decent man.'

Biddy dropped her head. 'I don't mean us to *do*
anything . . . I don't want to be cheatin' on Fred, either.
I just feel so lonely up there every night . . . and then it's
runnin' around after the kids and the lodgers all day.'
She squeezed his hand tightly and looked up at him with
huge, tear-filled eyes. 'I just want you to hold me for a
while, and let me fall asleep in your arms – that's all I
want.'

'But that's easier said than done, darlin',' Lloyd said
in a low voice. 'Look what happened earlier when we
came through the door . . .'

'But we were both a bit drunk then,' she argued, a
tear sliding down her cheek. 'This time, we both have
our full fac – fac-ul-ties about us. We'll keep our clothes
on, and we'll just lie on top of the bed.' She pulled him
by the hand along the hallway to the bottom of the
stairs.

'Are you sure you know what you're doin', girl?'
Lloyd whispered, as they went up the stairs.

'I do,' Biddy whispered back. 'All I want is a bit of

76

manly company for a few hours.' She stopped and looked into his eyes. 'Sure, there's no harm in that . . . is there?'

Chapter Ten

TRAVELLING TO STOCKPORT

'Are you sure you're okay?' Tara checked anxiously. 'Are you sure you don't want to stop for a bit of a rest?' She'd noticed, first driving up to Dublin last night, and now on this leg of the journey from Holyhead, that Gabriel had seemed a bit on the weary side. Both of them had slept little in their cramped berth on the boat the previous night, and Tara knew that he must be tired.

'We'll stop and have something to eat soon,' he said, moving one hand from the steering-wheel to give hers a little squeeze. 'We'll be coming into Chester in about half an hour.'

'Grand,' Tara said, wrapping both her hands around his. She was relieved that he was going to have a break from the tedious drive. She checked the diamond-faced gold watch that he had given her last Christmas. 'It's after ten o'clock, so we should find a tea-room or a hotel open by the time we arrive.'

'Did ye say we're going to have a stop-off soon?' Angela's sleepy voice came from the back seat. 'Will there be any shops in the town?'

Tara rolled her green eyes to the roof of the car and smiled. 'There won't be any shops open in Chester on a *Sunday*,' she told her young half-sister, 'but I'm sure Biddy will be only too glad to have company to go shopping with in Stockport over the next few days. She was always a great one for the shops and the market.'

'Oooh . . .' Angela said in a high voice, sitting up straighter and looking around at the green countryside, 'I can't wait to get to the shops in England! I've heard they're far better than anythin' we have at home.'

Tara looked straight ahead, thinking how much Angela reminded her of Biddy at that age when they had made their first journey over to England. Of course, Angela wouldn't remember Biddy – she had been much too young when the girls left Ballygrace back then.

It had been the one and only journey across the Irish Sea for Biddy, because she'd never set foot in Ireland since.

They pulled up outside Ruby Sweeney's old boarding-house in Maple Terrace in the afternoon. Tara felt a little pang, as return visits to her first home in England always reminded her of the day she arrived in the strange country and town.

'There's houses everywhere!' Angela exclaimed excitedly, tossing back her heavy blond hair. She had been wide awake since Chester, drinking in every detail of all the villages and towns they'd passed through until reaching Stockport.

'Indeed there is, and you'll have to get used to it,' Gabriel said, amused at the girl's excitement. He lifted Angela's case from the car boot. 'Life is much busier here than it is in Ireland – you're going to find some big, big changes.'

'But you needn't worry, there are plenty of Irish people over here,' Tara said reassuringly, 'and you'll meet a lot of them at Mass on a Sunday.'

'What was the name of the place we went to Mass in this morning?' Angela asked, seemingly not in the slightest bit worried about anything. 'It had a fierce unusual name . . . what was it called now?'

'It was Welsh,' Tara said, lifting her hat and handbag from the car seat. 'I think it was—'

Just at that moment, the boarding-house door opened and a pale but smiling Biddy appeared at the top of the stairs. 'You're here!' she called in a delighted voice, coming down to greet them. 'And it's welcome you all are – heartily welcome.'

'You're looking great!' Tara told her old friend as they hugged. 'I can't believe you're looking so well after all you've been through.'

'Sure, I've hardly time to look in a mirror these days,' Biddy said, brushing away the compliment, but delighted at the same time. A compliment from the beautiful, elegant Tara was worth ten compliments from anybody else.

'We thought we'd stop off here first and get Angela settled in,' Tara said, motioning the smiling, but slightly hesitant young girl towards Biddy. 'She's amazed at all the houses and shops, and I'd say you won't have any worry about company for going into Stockport, or taking the children around the market.'

'Won't it be grand to have nice, young company?' Biddy said, stretching her hand out towards Angela. 'And my two will fairly keep you on your toes – they can be fierce wild when they start.'

Angela shook Biddy's hand, sensing immediately that they were going to get on – and silently thanking God she wasn't as stiff-necked and uppity as Tara was at times. This landlady who originally came from Ballygrace was of the same stock as herself. Ordinary, working stock. Yes, Angela thought with great relief, Biddy and herself would get on just grand.

'Come in, come in,' Biddy said, ushering them all up the stairs. 'I have a nice Sunday dinner waitin' for ye.'

'Oh, Biddy, you shouldn't have!' Tara told her. 'You have quite enough to do without cooking for us. We could easily have got something to eat in one of the hotels.'

'Indeed you will not!' Biddy said. 'And anyway, Elsie

came over early to give me a hand with the potatoes and vegetables, and her son Eric has been busy sorting fires and everything for me this morning.' She winked at Angela. 'You surely don't think I'd have a young Flynn over here all the way from Ireland, and not give them a bit of dinner? Wouldn't I be the talk of Tullamore?'

Angela grinned back, wondering how old Eric was.

'I believe Fred's continuing to make good progress?' Gabriel said, as they all sat down at the well-polished dining-table which, as Biddy said, was only used on high-days and holidays. Today, with her old friends around her, it was definitely a high-day.

Biddy hesitated for a moment. 'On the whole,' she said carefully, 'he is definitely making progress.'

Tara stretched behind her to put her beige leather handbag and cream and beige felt hat on a small side table. 'And how's his memory?' she asked gently.

'Improvin',' Biddy said, nodding her head, 'but he still has a bit to go.' There was a little pause. 'But he's walking an awful lot better,' she said, brightening up, 'an' he's eating well. He's startin' to put the weight back up again, so that's a good sign.'

'Definitely,' Gabriel agreed. 'That's a very good sign – very good indeed. Especially for a fit, well-built man like Fred.'

There was a little pause, then Elsie came knocking on the door to say that dinner was ready to be served. Biddy moved quickly to help her.

'Can I give a hand?' Angela asked, getting up from the table and starting to take off her coat.

'You can take your coat off and hang it out in the hall, and then you can sit yourself back down,' Biddy told her, 'because today you're a *guest*.' She laughed. 'Tomorrow it'll be a different matter altogether. Oh, indeed it will! Tomorrow you'll be the same as meself – running about like a scalded cat.'

A few minutes later they were all helping themselves to roast chicken, boiled potatoes, and a favourite Ballygrace mixture of carrots, swedes and turnips all mashed together with butter, salt and pepper, and thick slices of hot ham.

At one point Biddy leaned in close to her old friend, and Tara was taken aback by the smell of stale drink on her breath. The sort of smell that only lasted after a lot of drink was taken. A smell she recognised only too easily due to the heavy drinking bouts her father had indulged in when she was a young girl.

Later, as dishes of sherry trifle were being passed around, Biddy confirmed Tara's suspicions. 'Isn't it a great pity you missed Lloyd?' she said, looking sadly at her friend. 'He had to leave early this morning; he says his mother's not too well. After we visited Fred last night, he took me out for a nice meal and a few drinks, so we had a chance to catch up a bit on each other's news.'

'I'd love to have seen him,' Tara agreed. 'I don't think I've seen him since Ruby's funeral. Lloyd was one of the nicest lodgers she had. He was always polite and easy to talk to.'

Gabriel leaned across the table and gave her hand a little pat. From the details she had told him, life had not been easy in those first months in England. When she looked up at him he smiled encouragingly, and she knew exactly what he was thinking.

'You'd wonder what his mother looks like,' Biddy mused. 'I wonder if her skin is the same colour as Lloyd's?'

Angela's ears pricked up at the interesting conversation, but she decided not to join in until she was asked. One of the last things her mother had warned her about was not to be passing remarks on older people she knew nothing about.

Tara smiled. 'I can't say it's something I've ever given

any thought to. But he's not *very* dark himself, so I suppose one of them might well be English.'

'It makes you wonder, doesn't it?' Biddy said thoughtfully. Then her face brightened. 'Lloyd thinks the world of Fred – you should have seen him pushing the wheelchair through the ward last night.'

'He came all the way up from London to see Fred?' Tara said. 'That was very good of him, wasn't it?'

'He had some business over in Leeds or Liverpool or somewhere,' Biddy explained. 'He caught the train over to visit him, and afterwards took me out for a lovely meal.' Her eyes lit up at the memory. 'We had a grand night out – it's the first night I've really relaxed since Fred's accident. We had a lovely meal and a few drinks to go along with it.'

Tara nodded but said nothing. It was quite obvious by Biddy's red eyes and alcohol-smelling breath that she'd had more than a *few* drinks the previous night. Still, Tara thought, maybe a lot of women would take more than a few drinks if their husband was lying in a hospital bed, seriously ill.

After the meal, Angela got up from the table, insisting that she help clear up.

'You sit and talk to Tara and Gabriel,' she said to Biddy, 'and I'll help Elsie wash up.' She disappeared into the kitchen with a pile of dinner plates.

'Let her do it,' Tara said quietly, 'it'll help her to settle in.'

'And,' Gabriel said, 'it will give *you* a bit of a rest. You must be exhausted with looking after the children and running the boarding-house without Fred.' He leaned forward, touching his hand to Biddy's arm. 'You should be very proud of yourself – and I'm sure Fred will be, when he comes home and realises all the responsibility you carried so very well.'

Biddy looked up at him and smiled – then her eyes suddenly filled up with tears at the unexpected kindness.

She was suddenly reminded of this gentle, caring side of Gabriel – obviously one of the things that had attracted Tara to him.

Later, after several cups of tea, Biddy took Angela upstairs to see her room. Tara accompanied them, eager to see the young girl's reaction to having her own bedroom, because Angela still shared a room with one of her sisters at home. She was both surprised and pleased to see it was the old room she and Biddy had once shared.

'Fred decorated it over Easter,' Biddy said proudly, indicating the blue flowery wallpaper and the white skirting-boards. 'It was his first attempt at papering, and he took his time making sure he got any bubbles out of it, and that all the flowers were matching exactly. He was going to do our own room next . . .'

There was silence for a few moments, during which Angela scanned the room for any missed bubbles or mismatched flowers. 'It's lovely!' she declared, having found no obvious flaws in Fred's work. Her eyes now flitted from the double bed with the lovely blue candlewick bedspread with the pink and green carnations stitched on it, to the big oak wardrobe at the back wall. Not only had she never had her own room, but she'd always had to share a bed and wardrobe with one or other of her sisters. This newly decorated room was an unadulterated luxury for her.

'Fred made a fine job of it,' Tara said, touching her friend's arm. 'And in a few months he'll have your own bedroom papered and painted, too.' She paused, trying to think of something to cheer her friend up. 'When he's finished decorating here, I might ask him to do a bit of work for me up at the houses in Cale Green.'

'Oh, he'd love to do that for you,' Biddy beamed, 'he thinks the world of you, Tara, and he's always praising you for the way you keep those houses.'

An hour or so later, Tara and Gabriel offered their

thanks again for the lovely meal, and prepared to leave. Tara was still enjoying her old friend's company and chat, but she could see that the long boat journey and drive was now catching up on Gabriel, although he was doing his politest best not to show it.

'Don't be worryin' about me,' Angela told Tara as she waved the car off. 'Biddy and Elsie and myself are gettin' on just grand.'

Things were just as always at the house in Cale Green. Under the beady eye of Miss Vera Marshall – who took pride in being Tara's longest-staying resident – everything was clean, tidy and well-organised. She showed Tara and Gabriel up into their bedroom as though they were honoured guests.

'I made sure that Mrs Winterbottom aired your bed well before putting on the fresh bed-linen,' Miss Marshall said, 'and I've checked that she's kept your piano well polished, and I ensured that the piano tuner did a good job when he came for the annual tuning of it.' Although she was still only a boarder, the spinster teacher had taken on all these little extra responsibilities – unasked and unpaid – to ensure that standards were maintained in Tara's absence.

A picture of Frank Kennedy flew into Tara's mind at the mention of the piano – then equally as quickly she shut it out. After all the years of experience at it, she was an expert now at shutting certain pictures out of her mind.

'I'm very careful when I use the piano myself,' Vera Marshall went on, 'and I make sure that no visitors touch it . . . or anything like that.' Encouraged by the sight of a beautiful piano going to waste, the teacher had taken up lessons last year, and had told Tara that she planned to play Christmas carols for the school choir at the next concert.

'Thank you,' Gabriel said, putting their cases down

on the bed. 'We're both very grateful for all your attention.'

Vera Marshall blushed to the roots of her slightly greying hair. 'I'm only too delighted.'

'If you would say to anyone who calls or phones that we don't want to be disturbed,' Tara said, 'we'll have a rest now, as we've been travelling all night.'

'Certainly,' Miss Marshall said, 'I'll make sure no one disturbs you.'

Tara smiled broadly when the bedroom door eventually closed on the fussy schoolteacher. 'I think that nothing has been missed that could possibly have been missed.'

'You would think that woman had trained as a boarding-school matron, rather than a teacher,' Gabriel said, smiling back. 'Although it is very kind of her to keep an eye on things while we're not here.'

Tara took her coat off and hung it up in the big, heavy wardrobe. Then, noting the slump of his shoulders as he sank into the armchair by the window, she lifted her husband's coat from the bed and hung his up, too. 'I think a rest might do you good,' she said quietly. 'Shall I close the curtains?'

Gabriel looked up at her, his eyes crinkled up at the corners in a weary smile. 'Will you lie down beside me?' he said, holding out his hand.

Tara's heart lifted at his suggestion. She had a feeling that this just might be the right time of the month for her to conceive. She stretched her arms out towards him, and slowly pulled him to his feet, looking deep into his eyes.

He pulled her into his arms. 'If you don't mind us having a couple of hours' sleep just now,' he said quietly, 'I'm sure I'll feel more energetic this evening.'

Tara nodded and buried her disappointed face in his chest. 'Of course, of course,' she whispered. 'I'm tired myself.'

Chapter Eleven

STOCKPORT

It was strange waking up in Stockport the following morning to the background noise of the town traffic. Within a few moments, Tara had picked out the familiar drone of a milk float with its clinking glass bottles and the rumble of a heavy lorry as it deposited a ton of coal down a neighbour's cellar.

It was a quarter past eight on a Monday morning, and the weekly grind was already well underway. Everything was so different to life back in the fresh green fields of Ballygrace House. And yet, if Tara was asked to pick which location she preferred, she would be hard pushed to decide. There were good things about both places – the country life and the town life. And as she looked at the sunshine peeping round the edge of the curtains, she felt the familiar excitement of being in the middle of a busy town, with people rushing about with purpose, and all leading very different lives.

She could hear the murmur of voices downstairs in the kitchen where some of the residents were obviously having breakfast, and the sound of splashing water coming from the bathroom. Tara gently turned on to her side, to see if Gabriel was coming round at all. But there was no movement from him, apart from his chest moving up and down, signalling that he was still deep in sleep.

Quietly, Tara moved to the edge of the bed and slid

out. She padded over to the door and took her dressing gown from the hook and put it on, then after checking that there was still no movement from him, she silently opened the door and went downstairs. She stopped to look into the dining room on her way to the kitchen.

'Good morning, Tara,' Vera Marshall said in a high, surprised voice. 'I didn't expect to see you up and about so early after your journey yesterday.'

'Oh, I thought I'd come down and see how things are being run in my absence,' Tara replied with a broad smile.

'The same as always,' Vera said, adjusting her spectacles a little higher on the bridge of her nose, 'you'll be glad to hear. The faces change every so often, but the routine stays just the same.'

Tara sat at the end of the table and had a few words with the other two girls, who had recently moved into the house: Sarah, a newly qualified teacher from Miss Marshall's school, and Joan, a secretary – a bespectacled, plumpish, intense-looking girl in her mid-twenties.

The young teacher chatted enthusiastically about her job and her pupils, and sang Vera's praises about how hard she worked as deputy-principal of the school. Then the plump secretary, who had been listening but saying very little, suddenly turned to Tara. 'I've been asked to pass on the warmest of regards to you,' she said, then paused, almost theatrically, 'from an old friend of yours.'

Tara's brow raised in surprise. 'An old friend of mine?' she asked. She had never met this girl before, and couldn't imagine how they would have a mutual friend.

'A man who calls into the office, an Irishman.'

Tara's stomach muscles tightened. 'And where do you work?' she asked, her voice suddenly formal.

'Thornley's,' the girl said with a little gleam in her eye, 'Thornley's Estate Agents in Bramhall.'

'Ah,' Tara said, nodding. 'You'll know, of course, that I used to work there myself.' She swept her long, curly red hair back over her shoulder.

'It's Frank Kennedy,' Joan said, her eyes scanning Tara's face for her reaction. 'He's one of our best customers, he's—'

'I know perfectly well who he is,' Tara said, arching her eyebrows. 'He's a friend from a long time back.'

There was an awkward little pause.

Miss Marshall looked out of the window. 'It's a lovely morning,' she observed rather anxiously, knowing all about the relationship between Tara and Frank Kennedy. She had been around in the days when Frank Kennedy had turned up on the doorstep, only to be turned away by a stony-faced Tara. Eventually, he had got the message and ceased his pointless visits. 'Mr Fitzgerald and yourself should have a nice few days in Stockport if the weather keeps up.'

Tara smiled and nodded. 'Oh, I'm sure we'll have plenty to keep us busy whatever the weather.'

Vera gave a nervous little smile, and glanced anxiously from Tara to the secretary and back again, then poured herself another cup of tea.

Tara stood up. 'I'm just going to get myself a cup of coffee and some toast.'

'Oh, Mrs Winterbottom will happily sort you out with breakfast,' Vera said quickly.

Mrs Winterbottom, a thin, nervous woman, looked after all the housekeeping business and that of the house next door – a responsibility she took very seriously, especially when she knew that the owner of the houses was in residence. 'She knew you were due back yesterday, so she will probably have your favourite bread and marmalade in stock, as well as your usual coffee. I always remind her to check when you're due back.'

'You're so very good,' Tara said, putting a hand on

89

the spinster teacher's shoulder, 'and I appreciate it very much.'

'I have the morning papers here, if you'd like to read them over breakfast,' Vera said now, waving a copy of the *Guardian*. She knew that Joan wasn't due to leave for the office for another fifteen minutes yet, and thought that her elegant landlady might need a distraction from any more conversations about old friends.

'Lovely,' Tara said, disappearing in the direction of the kitchen and Mrs Winterbottom.

A few minutes later Tara reappeared, carrying a pot of coffee, with a flustered Mrs Winterbottom following behind with a full toast-rack and a pot of Old English thick marmalade.

There was more general chat about the increasing traffic on the roads and the weather, and then Miss Marshall checked her watch and pushed her chair back to stand up.

'Time we were moving,' she said to her young colleague. Sarah finished the last drop of her tea and then the two teachers left for work, leaving Tara and the secretary on their own.

'Do you come back to Stockport often?' Joan asked, her head to the side, studying Tara again.

Tara gave a little shrug. 'It varies,' she said in a slightly cool manner. This plain, plumpish girl for some reason was getting under her skin. Then, to veer the subject away from herself, she said, 'Where are you from yourself? Are you local?'

'Oh, no,' Joan said, 'I'm not from around here. I'm from Yorkshire, near Bradford.'

'Ah,' Tara said nodding, 'I suppose I should have known from the accent.' She smiled. 'I must still be tired from the travelling to have asked such a silly question, when I've been listening to your Yorkshire accent for the last ten minutes.'

'It's not as strong as it used to be,' the secretary said

defensively, 'and none of the customers have complained that they couldn't understand me.'

'I wasn't suggesting that for a moment,' Tara said, surprised that the girl would have taken her comment as a criticism.

'I have an aunt in Macclesfield,' Joan went on, 'and when I first moved over here, I travelled back and forth on the train and bus. Then when I was told there was a room available in the house here, I moved over to Stockport.'

Tara nodded, and took a sip of her coffee, wishing the girl would hurry up and go off to work like the others.

'It was Frank Kennedy who put me on to the house here,' Joan informed her, with a flutter of her lashes. 'He said he would make enquiries about any rooms he knew for rent, and then he came back into the office to give me this address. He said he thought I'd fit in very well here, with the other professional women.'

Tara felt her throat tightening at this information. *How dare Frank Kennedy interfere in her business!* And what would she do if Gabriel walked in right now and heard her having a discussion about Frank Kennedy with this gossipy girl?

'Look,' she said, leaning across the table towards the heavy secretary, 'I think you are under the misapprehension that I have some interest in Mr Kennedy, and I'd like to correct you on that matter.'

Joan suddenly slumped in her chair, shocked at the change in the landlady's manner. Tara took a deep breath to steady her voice. 'Frank Kennedy *used* to be a friend of mine some time ago . . . when I was a single girl.' She narrowed her eyes. 'As you are very well aware, I happen to be a married woman now, and have been for a number of years, so it's rather strange you think I would be interested in Frank Kennedy.'

The secretary sat up straighter now, trying to compose herself. 'There was no harm intended, I'm sure . . .' she said in a strangled voice. A very little voice for such a big, hefty girl.

'That's grand, then,' Tara said crisply. She looked at the clock on the mantelpiece pointedly. 'Don't let me keep you back – you wouldn't want to be late for work.'

A short while later, Tara sat at the end of the dining-room table with the newspaper spread out, finally enjoying her toast and coffee. Three of the four women in the house had now left for work, and the fourth – a nurse – was in bed after coming off nightshift in the local hospital.

Mrs Winterbottom was busy rattling dishes about in the kitchen when the phone rang. The cups she was drying were duly dropped and Tara could hear her footsteps as they came tapping out into the hall.

'Yes . . . yes,' the housekeeper said, 'I'll get her for you now.'

It was Biddy. She sounded much brighter than yesterday afternoon, and was singing Angela's praises. 'She's a grand girl,' Biddy enthused. 'Up with the lark this morning, and helping me and Elsie with the breakfast.'

'Oh, I'm glad it's working out fine,' Tara said, 'and I know she's a good worker from back at the house.'

'And you should have seen her with the lads,' Biddy said, her voice lower in case her new help overheard her. 'No sign of shyness *there* I can tell you!'

Tara suddenly remembered how Angela was with the delivery boys back at Ballygrace House. 'She's not being *too* familiar with them, is she?' she said, sounding slightly alarmed.

'Not at all,' Biddy said quickly, 'not a bit of it. Sure, I was only passing a light-hearted remark. She's a nice girl, and just being friendly with them. Just the very same way we all were with Ruby's lads and the young fellas back in Ireland.'

Tara definitely heard alarm bells now. Surely Biddy hadn't forgotten where all her friendliness had got her?

'It's just a bit of harmless banter,' Biddy rattled on, determined to allay her friend's concern. 'Sure, what's life if you can't have a bit of a laugh now and again? Isn't that what we're put on this earth for?'

'True, true,' Tara said, trying to keep the edge out of her voice. It was too early in the morning to start having words, although she could think of more important issues in life than 'having a laugh'. She'd had quite enough of strained conversations this morning, having to put the forward secretary in her place. If there were any problems with Angela, Biddy was perfectly capable of handling things. 'As long as you're happy,' she said, 'and feel that Angela's of some help to you, because that was the whole idea of her coming over.'

'She's a grand young one,' Biddy said, relieved that she seemed to have reassured Tara. 'And she's going down into Stockport this afternoon with Elsie and the children after they give me a hand changing all the beds.' For some reason, she decided it was best not to mention the fact that Elsie's Eric would be going down to Stockport with them as well. Or the fact that he and Angela had got on like a house on fire, sitting drinking tea and laughing away together, after the lads had all gone to work. In fact, she'd never seen Eric come out of his shell the way he had that morning. She'd never seen him really laughing before that morning either.

'Oh, that's grand,' Tara said, 'that'll make life a bit easier for you.'

'I'm having my hair done this afternoon while they're all out,' Biddy said, having definitely made up her mind about going blonde, 'and Angela says she'll keep an eye on the kids later in the evening to let me go in and see

Fred. It'll take the pressure off Elsie a bit, and give her a bit of a lift, too, for she never stops. She tells me she comes over to help me to get a break from home.'

'Gabriel and I will go into the hospital with you this evening, if that's all right,' Tara said. 'We're really looking forward to seeing Fred. We might take a drive into Manchester later on, so if there's anything he needs we can pick it up then.'

'Oh, you needn't be worryin' about bringing anything in to Fred except yourselves,' Biddy told her brightly. 'He has everything he needs. His family and all his old wrestling pals and the crowd from the hotel are in and out with bottles of Lucozade and bunches of grapes every other day.'

'What about some books or new pyjamas or something like that?' Tara suggested. Biddy thought for a moment. Books were definitely out as far as Fred was concerned. The daily newspaper – mainly the sports section – had always been his reading preference, and since his accident, he hadn't shown much interest in even that. 'Pyjamas might be handy,' she said. 'He gets through them quick enough with wearin' them night and day.'

'Grand,' Tara said, 'I'll pick him up a pair when we're out.'

'Make sure they're large,' Biddy said. 'Even though he's lost a bit of weight, he needs room in them for moving around.'

They chatted for a few more minutes, then, when Tara heard Gabriel come out of the room and go into the bathroom, she suddenly said in a low voice, 'Biddy . . . have you seen Frank Kennedy recently?'

There was a pause. 'Well, not *exactly* recently,' Biddy said. 'He called a few weeks ago to see how Fred was – and he drops into the hospital any time he's working in the area.' She bit her lip, then continued on, a small defensive note in her voice now. 'He knows Fred from the wrestlin' and from going in and out of the Grosvenor, long before you and me moved over to Stockport.'

'Did you know', Tara hissed, 'that he's been interfering in my business? That he's sent a young oddity of a secretary from Thornley's to look for a room in this house? And God knows what he's been telling her, because she was all familiar as if she knew the ins and outs of my whole life. The absolute cheek of him! I told him that I didn't want anything to do with him that time I met him at the restaurant, and I thought he'd got the message then.' She paused for a few seconds. 'Has he said anything about me to you?'

Biddy took a deep breath. She'd only just escaped Tara's wrath a few minutes ago over Angela, and she wasn't going to land herself in it now. How could she tell her friend that Frank *regularly* called around to the house to check up on Fred, and often called to check on young lads who were looking for lodgings?

And how could she tell Tara that at the end of every visit or phone call, he always finished with the same questions. 'Any word of our friend from Ballygrace? Any word of her next visit?'

'Nothing worth mentioning,' Biddy lied. 'He's not asked any more about you than he does about anybody else. Anyway, I hear he has a new lady friend.' Biddy hadn't heard anything of the kind, but she needed something that would make Tara drop this very heated subject.

Tara heard Gabriel come out of the bathroom now and head back into the bedroom. 'I haven't the slightest interest in anything that man does,' she said in a low voice, 'and I'd be grateful if he just keeps well out of my way.'

Mrs Winterbottom had reset the breakfast table with two places for Gabriel and Tara, and she was now bustling about in an efficient manner between kitchen and dining room with dishes of bacon and sausages and eggs, black pudding and fried mushrooms.

'This looks lovely as always,' Tara said warmly, sitting down to her second breakfast that morning at one of the places set. She was now bathed and dressed in tan fitted slacks and a fine cream sweater with a colourful silk scarf knotted loosely around her neck, and her hair tied back. It was an outfit suitable for almost any situation that might crop up during the day, because up until now, they had not planned anything specific.

Mrs Winterbottom placed a silver toast-rack filled with both brown and white toasted bread on the table. 'If you need anything else,' she stated, 'just ring the bell by the fire and I'll be straight through.'

Tara thanked her, and then gave Gabriel a big grin when the housekeeper closed the door behind her. 'Thank God for Biddy's cheery chat,' she whispered, as she reached across to help herself to a couple of slices of bacon.

Gabriel nodded in the direction of the high, ornate fireplace, where a small push-button bell was imbedded in the wood. 'It's just as quick to go into the kitchen,' he said, smiling broadly, 'as it is to walk across the room to press the button to bring poor Mrs Winterbottom scuttling in.'

'Ah, I'm too down-to-earth for all this servant business,' Tara said ruefully. 'If it wasn't for the fact that the house might end up burning down with some boarder who is ham-fisted with a frying-pan, I'd leave the girls to do things on their own. I'm sure they're perfectly capable of cooking for themselves.'

Gabriel raised his eyebrows in surprise.

'I know, I know,' Tara said, pre-empting his reply, 'but you've been brought up with servants all your life, darling.'

'And I have no complaints about it,' he said, buttering a piece of toast. 'It gives employment, and keeps things running smoothly in both houses when we're at home or away.'

'That's true,' Tara said, taking a sip of her coffee. 'It's just that I often feel this sense of guilt at having someone running after me . . .'

Gabriel reached across the table and patted her hand. 'I'm sure you could find far more sensible things to worry about,' he told her teasingly.

Then, before Tara had time to reply, the phone rang again, and Mrs Winterbottom could be heard rushing down the hallway.

'Mr Fitzgerald!' she called after a few minutes in a high-pitched voice. 'Phone for you!'

They both froze, looking at each other. Gabriel never got calls here, and nobody he knew had the number of Tara's house. They both rose up from the table together, slightly alarmed.

'Are you sure it's not for me?' Tara asked as Mrs Winterbottom came down the hallway towards them, the phone receiver lying on the polished table near the door. 'Mr Gabriel Fitzgerald,' the housekeeper repeated, 'is what the boy said.'

'The *boy*?' Gabriel said in a low voice to Tara, even more confused. He strode towards the phone. 'Yes?' he said quickly into the receiver, and then a few seconds later, his voice rose in surprise. '*William?* Is there anything wrong?'

'No . . . not actually *wrong*,' his younger brother's high-pitched voice echoed from London. 'I just thought I'd phone to ask you if you could come down to London sooner than you had planned.' There was a little pause. 'I wondered if you could come this week.'

'Why?' Gabriel said, shrugging his shoulders in Tara's direction.

'Well . . . it's Harry, actually,' William said, referring to his and Gabriel's stepfather.

'What about Harry?'

'He's got to go away to America on business . . . and he'd promised to take me to some of the open days at the boys' schools. And we were supposed to be going up to the city at the weekend since it's the beginning of the holidays.'

'Can't mother take you?' Gabriel checked.

'Well . . .' William said, 'I'd really rather have a man. I wanted some advice on the clubs I should join at the school. They have fencing and rugby and so on – and mother doesn't know anything about those things. That's why Harry had agreed to take me.'

There was a silence. 'Look, William,' Gabriel said now, 'give me a bit of time to think about it, and I'll ring you back.'

'OK,' William said, suddenly sounding very business-like and grown-up. 'I'll speak to you later.'

Chapter Twelve

'The peroxide's not stinging you too much, is it, Mrs Roberts?' the hairdresser checked, handing Biddy a cup of tea with a Penguin biscuit balanced on the saucer. 'Oh, thanks, love,' Biddy said, taking it from her. 'And no, it's not too bad at all. My scalp's not stinging anything like the time I had a perm.' Biddy settled down into the fake-fur-covered chair, carefully balancing the cup and saucer on her lap while she unwrapped the chocolate biscuit.

She really enjoyed coming to the hairdresser's. It was lovely being pampered and looked after by the girls, and then, when her hair was all done, it was even lovelier having them all crowd around her telling her how nice she looked. She knew they made a special fuss of her because Ruby Sweeney had gone to that particular hairdresser's for donkey's years, and she had been one of their favourite customers. She took her time enjoying the Penguin, then deposited the wrapping and the saucer on a ledge behind her, so she could sit comfortably finishing her cup of tea and reading *Woman's Own*. She thumbed through the pages, scanning the latest fashions and new hairstyles, and eventually settled down to read her favourite bit – the problem page. After reading the disappointingly trivial problems, she then came upon an article about a woman who confessed to having an affair with her husband's best friend.

As she read through the feature, a little knot tightened in her stomach. A knot of guilt and shame. Guilt about her silly teenage carry-on the other night with Lloyd. A hot, burning feeling moved from her chest up to her neck, then up to her face. What had she done? What had they both done together? The real problem was that she couldn't actually remember. She knew that they had been messing about a bit . . . more than a bit, for Lloyd had ended up spending the night in bed with her.

She vaguely remembered something about them arguing – well, Lloyd arguing that it wasn't right that he should be in her and Fred's room. And then the burning feeling turned into a feeling of nausea and complete shame, as Biddy realised that she had almost dragged the poor lad into the room along with her.

She was sure he had kept his clothes on, and she was almost certain that nothing terribly bad had happened. If something *really* bad had happened, surely he wouldn't have kept all his clothes on?

It was just that there were bits she couldn't quite remember. Bits that were complete blackouts. But surely she wouldn't have done anything wrong in her own house and not remember it? Surely she wouldn't have done anything while her two innocent children were asleep in the next room? What kind of mother would that have made her? Biddy bowed her head with the shame of it – even if it was just the possibility of something *nearly* happening – because nothing should have happened at all.

The drink would have to go, she decided. It would never have happened if it hadn't been for the drink. It obviously had a bad effect on her. That, and the loneliness.

'You OK, love?' the hairdresser asked. 'Are you sure that peroxide isn't irritating your skin? You're lookin' a bit red around the gills.'

'No . . . no, I'm grand,' Biddy said, looking flustered.

'Hot tea sometimes makes me go like that . . . I should have had a drop more milk in it.'

The hairdresser started checking Biddy's hair, lifting blue-coated strands to check how the bleaching process was progressing. 'I think another ten minutes should do it,' she said, patting the hair back in place. 'It seems to be takin' well.'

Half an hour later, Biddy was staring at a stranger in the mirrored wall: a blonde, with a new, shorter hairstyle. A blonde who looked very like a youngish Ruby Sweeney. A Ruby Sweeney in the whole of her health.

The hairdresser's eyes filled up with tears. 'You look the spittin' image of her,' she said, groping for a tissue in her nylon overall pocket. 'I wouldn't have believed it, if I hadn't seen it with me own eyes. You look completely different to the way you were with the brown hair.'

Biddy gazed at herself in the mirror, not quite sure what to think. Apart from the shorter, layered style being like Ruby's, it looked like somebody else looking back at her. When she stared hard at herself, it looked as though she was wearing a wig – as though it wasn't her own real hair at all.

'It's fabulous!' the young girl who had washed Biddy's hair said. 'It really suits you, Mrs Roberts.'

'Definitely,' the older hairdresser said. 'It looks dead modern on you, it does. It fair lifts you up – lifts your face up, like.'

Biddy looked in the mirror again and smiled, feeling more reassured. She wondered what Fred would have to say about it when she went into the hospital later. She wondered if he would prefer her blonde or whether he would say he preferred her with her hair brown.

A cold hand of fear clutched her, and she wondered if he would notice any difference at all.

'Oh, Biddy,' Angela gasped excitedly, when she saw her. 'You look like a film star! Like that Marilyn Monroe. You look real glamorous altogether!' She had to stop herself from clapping her hands together with delight, the way she did back home. This house, this whole area, and this married woman – who was more like a teenager than a grown-up – just made everything seem so exciting and unpredictable.

Chapter Thirteen

Tara came over and put her arm around her husband's shoulder. 'Do you want us to go straight down to London?' she ventured. 'Do you feel William really needs you?' Gabriel nodded, then ran a hand through his blond hair. 'I'm sure it's my mother,' he said quietly. 'He didn't say it in so many words – but I think William knows that she doesn't like having to deal with everything on her own when Harry's away.' He paused. 'If I went down, I could help him to sort out the school business and—'

'Then that's what we'll do,' Tara agreed. 'We can leave straight away. It won't take us long to repack.'

They moved back down the hallway towards the dining room. 'We still have things to do here in Stockport,' Gabriel said in a slightly distracted manner as they sat back down at the table. 'We haven't visited Fred yet, and you have things to sort out with the estate agents, and we have to check on Angela . . . we didn't imagine we would be leaving her on her own so soon.'

'She won't mind a bit, and Biddy will understand,' Tara reassured him. 'We can visit Fred when we come back up. His condition isn't going to change hugely while we're away.'

Mrs Winterbottom appeared at the door now with a steaming pot of coffee. 'I thought the other pot might have gone cold . . .'

'You're very good,' Tara said, giving her a grateful smile.

An hour later they were packed up and heading back down Shaw Heath towards Biddy's place. The lodging-house seemed a hive of activity compared to the house they had just left. The two children were running about excitedly when they saw the visitors, but were happy to be coaxed off out into the garden by Angela to see the small pup that Elsie's Eric had borrowed from a neighbour, and brought round and tied to the washing-pole. Biddy and Elsie were just sitting having a cup of tea before starting on the potatoes and vegetables for the evening meal.

The first few minutes were spent admiring Biddy's new hairstyle, although if Tara had been completely honest, she wasn't at all sure if she really liked her blonde. It was very different, but she decided not to say anything, as it might just take a bit of getting used to. Tara was relieved that there were no signs of drink on her friend, and she presumed that the earlier incident was just a bit of a weekend binge.

They told Biddy all about Gabriel's mother not being too well, and how they now needed to set off to London.

'Don't be worryin' about Fred,' Biddy reassured them. 'He has plenty of visitors, and you'll see him when you come back up from London.'

'We wondered if we might give the hospital a ring and check whether we could visit him before setting off?' Gabriel said. 'At least we would have done the most important thing.'

Biddy's face softened, delighted that they would have made her husband a priority when they had so many other things to think of. 'I'll ring now, if you like,' she said, moving out into the hall. She came back a few minutes later, her face beaming. 'They said we can go up for a few minutes, and they said they just got word that Fred has a place in one of those rehabilitation hospitals for people who need physiotherapy and things like that.'

'But that's wonderful news, Biddy!' Tara said coming over to hug her. 'That means that he's turned another corner in his recovery.'

'We don't know when exactly he'll be moved to Leeds,' Biddy said, her face growing red with delight, 'but it could be some time this week.'

While Biddy ran upstairs to get her handbag and touch up her lipstick and Gabriel went to make room in the back seat of the car for her, Tara went down the steps at the back door to explain to Angela about the change in their plans. The young girl listened carefully, keeping one eye on the two children and the puppy, and hoping that Eric wouldn't come back with the ice creams while Tara was still around. She was only being friendly with the boy, but she had a feeling that her older sister might not approve.

'Are you settling in OK?' Tara checked. 'Is there anything worrying you, or anything you need to ask me about?' She had a slightly anxious feeling about leaving the girl on her own so quickly – a feeling of responsibility towards her – although she knew that Tessie and her father would understand the circumstances.

'No, no,' Angela said airily, 'I've settled in just grand. You needn't be worrying about me at all.' She lifted young Helen up into her arms. 'The children are lovely, and Biddy's lovely.' She smiled broadly. 'And I like Stockport and all the shops – everythin's just grand. You can head off to London and don't be worryin' one bit about me. I'm havin' the time of me life.'

Tara reached into her handbag and gave Angela a ten-pound note. 'Take this,' she said quietly. 'You might need to buy yourself some bits and pieces before I come back. I don't know how Biddy's fixed for money . . . but this should keep you going for a while.'

'Oh, thanks, Tara.' The young girl beamed and

tucked the money into her skirt pocket. 'I promise you I won't go wastin' it or anything.' Her eyes flickered to the fence at the bottom of Biddy's garden. She was sure she had seen Eric's head bobbing along over the fence a few seconds ago. 'Anyway,' she said, moving to the steps at the back door, 'you go on and don't be worryin' about me. I'll be just grand here.'

Tara patted her half-sister on the shoulder and then ran up the steps and back into the house. She met Biddy in the hallway on her way out to give the children a kiss and to grab a packet of Fred's favourite Eccles cakes to have with his evening cup of tea.

'Everythin's working out grand,' Biddy told Fred as they all sat in the day room. Fred nodded and smiled around the little group. 'I have Elsie's lad doing the heavier jobs around the house, and now I have young Angela Flynn helpin' me out with the children.' She patted Fred's hand. 'It's givin' me more time to come and visit you, and it means I don't need to be relyin' on poor Elsie day and night.'

Fred nodded, and then his gaze focussed on Gabriel again, as he tried to remember what he worked at over in Ireland.

'Well,' Biddy said, leaning forward and taking Fred's hand now, 'I'm waitin' on the verdict.'

Fred turned his gaze towards his wife, a frown appearing on his face. 'The verdict?' he repeated.

'Me hair – you soft eedjit!' she said, waving their clasped hands around. 'Don't tell me you haven't noticed!'

There was a tense little silence as everyone watched for Fred's reaction. 'Your hair . . .' he repeated. 'You got it done . . . at the hairdresser's!'

Biddy nodded and beamed around everyone. 'Aren't you going to tell me if it suits me?' she prompted.

Fred suddenly brightened up – as if a light had just gone on. 'Lovely!' he stated. 'Your hair's just lovely!'

'Thank God for that,' Biddy said. She looked at Tara and Gabriel and shook her head. 'Nothing changes!' she said, trying to sound light-hearted. 'You have to drag the compliments out of him. He was the very same before the accident.'

'That's men for you,' Tara said, patting Gabriel on the knee.

Fred looked around them all, his gaze coming back to settle on Gabriel. Then, once again, his brow become furrowed as he tried to figure out who the strange fair-haired man was.

They passed around grapes and then sweets, which Fred eagerly accepted and took his time painstakingly unwrapping. Then, just as Tara and Gabriel were standing up to leave Fred and his wife alone for a few minutes, the day-room door opened and an awkward silence descended on the group.

'You have a full house, I see,' the voice came from the door. 'I needn't have bothered coming after all, and having to talk my way past the nurses.'

The sound of the familiar voice made Tara's whole body tense, and she suddenly felt her face flushing red-hot. Talking his way past nurses would have been no trouble to this particular visitor, she thought.

Frank Kennedy came over to the group, hand out-stretched in Fred's direction. As usual, he was immacu-lately dressed – on this occasion, in a pin-striped suit with a pristine sky-blue shirt and a subtly patterned tie. 'I was passing the hospital and had a few minutes to spare, so I thought I'd drop in on you.'

Tara felt her chest tighten, and she turned her head to gaze out of the window towards a yellow flowering bush in the hospital garden.

'Frank!' Fred said, almost breathless with delight. He

made a good attempt at a firm and enthusiastic handshake.

'Good man – and you're looking better again today,' Frank told the patient, being careful not to let Fred get carried away with the heavy handshake. He turned to the others now, and shook each one's hand in turn, noticing that Tara held her hand out reluctantly and only briefly allowed his hand to contact hers. 'Sorry for interrupting your visit – this is usually a time that you can depend on things to be quiet.'

'Indeed that's true, Frank,' Biddy said quickly, terrified that Tara might think she had arranged for Frank to turn up while they were at the hospital. 'It's rare that I get in to see him at this time of the day myself, with minding the children and everything . . .'

Gabriel stood up now and, reaching for Tara's hand, was surprised at how tightly she grasped it. 'We only came for a quick visit, as we're heading straight down to London,' he said, aiming his conversation at the room in general.

'I can give Bridget a lift back home,' Frank Kennedy suddenly offered. 'I'm going down that way, and it'll save you doubling back.'

'That would be grand,' Biddy said quickly, delighted to have a bit longer with her husband.

Tara moved to her feet now, still holding her husband's hand tightly. 'I'll ring you,' she said to Biddy in a low voice, 'and let you know how things are.'

'You've no idea when you'll be back up?' Biddy asked.

Tara moved towards the door of the day room. 'No,' she said, fiddling with the clasp on her handbag – desperate for anything that would keep her eyes away from Frank Kennedy. 'I've no idea when we'll be back.'

Biddy walked with them to the door, leaving Frank to sit and chat to Fred. 'I hope you didn't leave just because of—'

'Indeed we did not,' Tara replied briskly. 'There's no way I'd do anything on account of that man.'

Gabriel put his hand on Biddy's arm. 'We'll see you and Fred again soon,' he said quietly. 'And I'm so sorry we have to rush away on this occasion.'

As they walked towards the car, a small silence fell between Tara and Gabriel. 'That's the only thing I hate about coming to Stockport,' Tara suddenly blurted out. 'There's always the awful possibility of bumping into Frank Kennedy.'

'Don't let it upset you,' Gabriel said, opening the car door. 'There's nothing he can ever do to hurt or upset you.' They both got into the car now, and Gabriel leaned over and squeezed her hand reassuringly before kissing her tenderly on the lips. 'He's had no part in your life for an awfully long time now, and it's perfectly obvious to everyone that you and I are a very well-suited, very happily married couple.'

Tara smiled and squeezed his hand back. Gabriel knew nothing of the night in the restaurant with Kate – and he would be so upset if he knew. And he was quite right – she was very, very happily married. And maybe it was a good thing that Frank had seen them together today, holding hands in the way that only very close couples do. If he had any foolish notions about her, seeing her with Gabriel today should have completely dispelled them.

Chapter Fourteen

TULLAMORE

Shay and Tessie stood at the bottom of the narrow dark wooden staircase, looking upwards towards the bedrooms, and listening carefully for any more noise.

'There's nothing else for it,' Tessie Flynn whispered to her husband, 'I'm going to have to stay the night with her. She's not in any fit state to be left on her own.'

Shay nodded solemnly. 'I won't argue with you on that,' he said in a low voice. He ran a hand through his curly, slightly thinning hair. 'She could set fire to the place or anythin'. There's nothing she's not capable of doing when she's like this.'

They both stood silently for another few minutes, then Shay put his arm around his wife and they moved back into the little sitting room. 'I'll go back home and get your bits and pieces for the night,' he told her, lifting his jacket.

'No, Shay,' Tessie said firmly, '*you* stay here and I'll run back home.'

'But surely to God it's a woman she needs—' Shay started to argue.

'She's *your* auntie, don't forget,' Tessie reminded him, pulling on her coat, 'and anyway, you wouldn't know what I need – the last time you forgot me slippers and me curlers. I had a head on me like a bush the next day.' She made towards the door. 'I won't be long, I just want to check that Assumpta and Mary are in the house and have had their bit of supper, and that everything is fine.'

Shay looked up towards the ceiling and sighed. 'We'll have to get this sorted out. It's not fair that she's landed on us . . . we were never her favourite ones at any time, an' it's not us she'll be leavin' anythin' she has to when she goes.'

'Don't start that again,' Tessie warned him. 'May God forgive ye, Shay Flynn. Didn't Molly help to bring up your son? Didn't her and her poor sister put every penny they had into making sure he got all he needed for the priesthood? And don't I get paid a few pounds every week for looking after her?'

Shay opened his mouth to say something, then thought the better of it. 'You head off,' he said, lifting the newspaper from the table. 'I just pray to God she doesn't land down here and start all that oul' Cecil Smith shite again. There was never any man lived around here by the name of Cecil Smith.'

'God love her,' Tessie said, a little smile coming to her lips. 'The poor oul' cratur is all confused. It must be something she's heard on the radio or read in a book over the years, or something like that.' She paused. 'It could be a boyfriend we know nothing about . . . maybe it's somebody she met down at the church or the novenas . . .' It was the only thing that Tessie could think of, because neither Molly nor Maggie had ever gone to any social occasions where they were likely to meet men. Drinking and bingo nights were definitely not on the spinster sisters' agendas.

Shay rolled his eyes to the ceiling, and made a big palaver of turning to the sports section of the newspaper.

Tessie rubbed the top of Shay's black curly head in an affectionate manner, knowing that his hand would fly up in a moment to cover the growing bald spot she teased him about. 'That's the trouble with you, you have no romance in your soul.'

'Romance, me backside!' Shay scoffed. 'Romance indeed – an eighty-odd-year-old spinster goin' on about an old fella she met at the church. If there ever was a man called Cecil Smith, he'd be another oul' holy-willie like herself, that thinks it's a bit of a thrill dippin' their hands together in the holy water! I know what I would call it at their ages – an' it wouldn't be feckin' romance – it would be more like *madness*! Feckin' well madness.' He shook his head.

'There's nobody saying she ever had a boyfriend at the church,' Tessie said now, 'and I've asked around if anybody knows anything about Cecil Smith, but nobody has the foggiest idea who he is. Isn't it strange she keeps going on about that same name?'

'It's strange, all right,' Shay muttered. 'An' it's us that's landed with it all, while Tara an' Joe are off swanning around, mindin' their own business.' He shook the *Irish Independent* out viciously, attempting to get the double-spread sheet to fold in the middle. 'Ah, sure, it's the same oul' story,' he sighed. 'It's the oul' dog for the hard road as usual.'

'Will you go away out of that!' Tessie laughed. 'You should be countin' your lucky stars, Shay Flynn. Both Tara an' Joe are very good to us and to the children. You don't turn up your nose at the few pounds Tara gives you for tidying up the gardens in Ballygrace House, do you?'

'An' I do a good day's work for a good day's wages!' Shay retorted defensively.

'An' what about Tara taking Angela off our hands this summer? And she'll be well taken care of by both Tara and Biddy Hart in Stockport.'

A faraway look came into Shay's eyes at the mention of Stockport. It always had that effect on him – reminding him of the few intensely happy years he spent there. The happy years he wasn't entitled to, when he had a good wife and family back home in Ireland.

'Surely', Tessie went on, 'the least we can do is help poor oul' Molly until the doctors come down one way or another on what's to happen to her?'

'True enough,' Shay said quietly, all argument suddenly gone out of him. He had once again reminded himself of the promise he'd given Ruby on her deathbed. The promise that he would make the best of his life with his wife and children, and give back that little bit extra to make up for the years that he and Ruby had stolen from them. Besides, he well knew that he was a luckier man than most. He had experienced the love of two good women in his life – two hard-working, attractive women that many men would give their right arms for. Oh, Shay knew it well. It was just that he had a problem remembering it at times, especially at times like this when he felt he was under pressure.

'I suppose she's quiet enough for the minute,' Shay said now. 'Just hurry yerself on, an' be back as quick as you can.'

Tessie Flynn stepped out into the cool, clear evening. She walked quickly up Church Street and through Hayes' Cross and, a few minutes later, was back at their own house behind the garda station.

All was quiet enough inside; the two girls were listening to some show on the radio in the kitchen, having already eaten their supper. The place seemed much more peaceful now that Angela had left. Whatever was it that had got into her these last few months? She was forever sniping and arguing with her two older, quieter sisters, and the slightest things set her off. She was like a prickly briar at the best of times and almost unliveable with when her bad time of the month came around.

As Tessie bustled about now, sorting out her overnight necessities and making a quick supper of scrambled eggs and toast, she gave a silent thanks to Tara for sorting the problem out for the moment. If nothing else, having Angela out of the way for a bit gave herself and Shay some breathing space, and left them with a more settled frame of mind for tackling the current problem of poor old Auntie Molly.

Chapter Fifteen

LONDON

Elisha Fitzgerald – or Elisha Mortimer as she was now known – came out of the wisteria-covered doorway within moments of the car pulling up outside the large London townhouse. She had obviously been waiting at the window, watching for them. As usual, she was immaculately attired, in a pink short-sleeved dress and wine-coloured leather court shoes, and was wearing her customary double strand of pearls.

As she came towards the car, Tara noticed that she had changed her long, pinned-up hair for a softer, medium-length style, which looked much more modern on her. She then noticed that her mother-in-law looked older, and more lined around the eyes and mouth than the last time she had seen her.

Elisha was carrying Poppy – her small Yorkshire Terrier – in the crook of her arm.

'You're so good to come!' she told her son in a high, quivery voice that fell somewhere between an upper-crust Irish and London accent. She threw her free arm around him, and before he had a chance to reply, she quickly moved around the other side of the car to embrace her daughter-in-law.

'Tara, Tara,' she said in a faint, wispy voice. 'How good of you both to come when you have all the trouble with your friend's husband and everything.'

'How are things?' Tara asked. 'Are you both well?'

'Really, we're fine,' Elisha said, 'but it's so wonderful to have you both here. I'm afraid when William realised you were only a few hours' drive away, he badgered and badgered me into letting him phone you. He cleverly managed to get the number of the house from Ella back in Ballygrace House.' She lifted the little dog up higher, and led them up the white steps and into the house. 'I told him off for asking you to come down to London early – but I have to admit I was more than delighted myself when he said you were coming.'

Elisha led them into the drawing room, and before they even had a chance to sit down, a young maid appeared, dressed in a black dress with white apron and cap.

'Sherries to start, please, Lucy,' Elisha said in the manner of one used to servants all her life. She turned to her son, suddenly noticing his pale, tired face. 'Are you all right, Gabriel? Was the drive down very awful?'

'No, not at all,' he said, settling down into one of the large leather armchairs. 'The new car is very good, and Tara drove part of the way to give me a rest.'

Elisha gave her daughter-in-law a warm, grateful smile. 'You're so good, Tara,' she said in a low voice. 'There are times I wonder what our family would have done without you over the years.'

Tara felt her stomach muscles tighten at the compliment, although she knew without a shadow of a doubt that it was genuine. Elisha had expressed her gratitude more and more over the years for the friendship she had shown to Madeleine, her dead daughter who had been Tara's old Ballygrace schoolfriend. Poor Madeleine – beautiful, but at times deranged, and becoming even more so just before the terrible accident that had claimed both herself and her father, William.

Tara suddenly stood up – the usual panic gripping her when she thought of William Fitzgerald. She excused herself. 'I'll just go upstairs for a quick freshen-up,' she said.

Just at that point the young maid appeared with the decanter and sherry glasses, and Elisha was too distracted for the moment to wonder why Tara had suddenly disappeared in such a flustered manner.

Chapter Sixteen

CORK

'Well, Father?' the stocky, red-faced woman said. 'Didn't I tell you he was a fine-looking fella at one point?' She held a black and white photograph up. 'There he is again, looking as right as rain – before all the trouble started. Before he took to the bed permanently.' She gave a sigh – a very sorrowful sigh. 'That was on a day out to Bantry Bay with the whole eight of them. It was a parish trip . . . not the last curate, but the one before, used to organise them regularly.'

Joe stared at the array of photographs scattered on the highly polished dining-table in front of him. For a few moments they swam in front of his eyes, all mingling together into a lump, as opposed to little black and white squares. He realised then that he was tired. Tired and weary of listening to other people's problems. And especially tired and weary of not being able to help them.

This was the second parishioner who had turned up at the parochial house this evening, expecting him to sort out their family problems for them. *What exactly did they expect him to do?*

He, Father Joe Flynn, who had no experience of marital relations, who had no experience of a real family life . . . being cosseted by two elderly great-aunts had not given him the foggiest idea of what it was like to rear eight children in a two-roomed cottage without the benefits of running water or electricity.

The woman suddenly enlightened him as to how he might help. 'I was just wonderin' if you might call up at the house . . . and give him a bit of a fright, like.' She smiled up at the young, handsome priest. 'He would listen to *you* . . . and it might just make him buck his ideas up. Make him get up out of the bed, at least. It hasn't been changed these last six weeks.'

Joe fought back a little shudder at the last piece of information. 'The thing is, Mrs Doherty . . . if the poor man has not been well,' he said, moving the photographs around the table, and desperately hoping for some sort of inspiration, divine or otherwise, 'he just might not appreciate me calling up to the house and haranguing him.'

'Well, Father,' Mrs Doherty said, 'supposin' I was to tell him that you were goin' to come into the house to say a Mass for the sick?'

Joe looked up at her. 'Would you like to have a Mass said in the house?' he asked.

The woman's cheeks suddenly flushed pink. 'Lord, Father,' she said, 'wouldn't I be only too delighted to have a Mass in the house . . . if we could only get himself up out of the bed to get the place cleaned up.' She shook her head. 'I'd be ashamed of me life to have any of the neighbours in until we'd whitewashed the inside and outside of the house. It's like somethin' from the dark ages at the minute.'

Joe nodded. 'I'll drop up to the house in the next day or so and have a word with Mr Doherty. I'll see if there's anything at all I can do to help the poor man.'

The woman's eyes lit up. 'Oh, Father Flynn,' she whispered, 'I feel a weight has been lifted off me shoulders already . . . you don't know what it means to me to hear you say you'll speak to him.'

'I can't promise anything,' Joe said, 'but I'll bring some holy water and give him a blessing.'

Mrs Doherty started to gather all her photographs into a pile now, to put back into the faded, flower-bedecked chocolate-box. Her hand hovered over a photograph of a young couple smiling brightly for the camera. 'You wouldn't know that young woman, by any chance?' she asked in a strangely coy manner.

Joe took the photograph from her and studied the curly-headed young man in the suit and then the dark-haired girl with the small veiled hat and pale dress and jacket. His blank face gave her the answer.

'It's me,' she said, her eyes suddenly filling up with tears. 'Ten years ago, that was. Before I had the children – all nine of them . . . countin' the little one that died. It's no wonder you don't know me with all the weight I've put on and the way I've aged. Sure, I hardly know meself.' She put the photograph in the box on top of all the others, and then carefully tied the faded, frayed ribbon in a bow on top to secure it.

'Thanks, Father,' she said softly, 'you've been a great help . . . you've made me feel a bit lighter about it all.'

Joe smiled and nodded, feeling a complete fraud. He knew he had done very little to actually help the woman. If it had been within his power he would have done anything he possibly could.

He walked her out to the door of the parochial house, shook hands with her, and then just stood, staring off into the distance, long after the plodding Mrs Doherty had disappeared out of sight.

Some minutes later he went back into his study and sat down at his desk. His eyes flickered first to the clock on the mantelpiece, and then came to rest on the heavy black phone.

It was nearly half past nine. Around the time when Mary O'Connor's husband – a local solicitor – would be driving out to the local golf club for his nightcap of two large whiskies. And around the time the dark-haired, vivacious Mary would pick up the phone and once again tell Father Joe Flynn how he had saved her sanity and saved her life. She would then repeat how she didn't know how she could ever thank him for listening to her and advising her, when she couldn't have told her problems to a single person in the whole world.

And then she would go on to say how there was nothing she wouldn't do for the priest – absolutely *nothing*. She had emphasised that on every occasion they had spoken on the phone, and the conversations were becoming increasingly regular. On the last occasion she had suggested that maybe she could show her gratitude by taking him out for a nice meal in Cork City – some weekend that Mr O'Connor was away on one of his business trips. Or maybe they could even take a trip up to a quiet hotel in Dublin for the weekend. Not with any improper thoughts in mind, of course. Just two friends who would sit and enjoy each other's company in a place where no one would know them, where there would be no scandal.

The fact that the beautiful Mrs O'Connor's problems all stemmed from her marriage never having been consummated was a secret between her and the priest, a secret she had divulged to him in the confessional box to be sure of it never going any further. Joe stared at the phone again. There was always the chance that someone might need to get through to him for a sick call or even for the last rites – or for any number of problems that might occur.

It might even be his father on again to give him an update on Auntie Molly's condition, or to remind him about organising a phone to be installed in the old lady's house. Joe knew that other people's needs were a lot greater than his own, but lately – just lately – he felt he needed a little break from it all to recharge his batteries. Just a little time to distance himself from other people's problems, and to allow himself to get a fresh perspective on some of the problems he wasn't in the least qualified to help with. Even an hour to himself to listen to the radio or just to sit and read the American detective novel he had bought last month and hadn't had a chance to open yet. Even to just sit in the silence and stare into space.

He lifted the phone receiver from the cradle and placed it on the polished table.

Chapter Seventeen

STOCKPORT, JULY 1962

It had been two weeks since Tara and Gabriel had left for London, and Biddy's life had been turned upside down in the meantime. On the whole, things had changed for the better. The day-to-day running of the house had definitely improved, what with Eric taking over Fred's jobs, and Angela having taken some of the load from Elsie's shoulders.

But the main improvement was in the attention that the young Irish girl gave the two children. Little Michael's and Helen's routine had been severely disrupted since Fred's accident, with Elsie looking after them as much as Biddy. It hadn't been so bad when they were in school for most of the day, but the summer holidays meant that they needed entertaining from morning until night, and thank God that Angela had the energy to do that, because most of the time Biddy certainly didn't.

'Were they good for you?' she asked now, opening the kitchen door to let Angela and the quiff-haired Eric and the children in. She swept Michael up into her arms first, giving him a big kiss, and then Angela held up Helen for the same treatment.

'Grand,' Angela replied, sweeping her long blond hair behind her ear. 'We walked all around the water and fed the ducks, and then we had our picnic on one of the benches up at the big house.'

'Bramall Hall is a lovely old place, isn't it?' Biddy said, going back to the pot of home-made soup she had been thickening with a pile of grated carrots. The weather was actually a bit hot for soup, but she had leeks and leftover potatoes to use up and the lads loved soup at any time of the year. 'Tara and me used to go for walks there a lot when we first came to Stockport.' She paused. 'And me and Fred often took the kids there for walks on a Sunday.'

'They're a bit fussy up there, though . . .' Angela said, helping Helen out of her light hooded jacket. 'This oul' lad came over to tell Eric off for kicking a ball with the kids on the grass. He was a grumpy old bugger, wasn't he, Eric? You'd think he owned the place the way he went on.'

Eric confirmed with a grunting noise. 'He were a right little Hitler,' he said, sticking both hands deep into his black leather bomber jacket. 'Them places are public property, paid for by the people of Stockport. That old git has no more right to be there than anyone else.'

Biddy stirred the huge pot of soup with a wooden spoon. 'Well,' she said, picking her words carefully, 'I suppose if everyone did what they liked, the place would be in ruins in no time. We all have to abide by rules.'

'Eric soon told him,' Angela said, looking admiringly at her dour-faced companion. 'You should have seen his face when Eric said that he was a taxpayer and entitled to play football on the grass whenever he wanted.' She gave a giggle. 'The old lad went off in a rage, looking for somebody else to sort Eric out – but we decided it was time to head back home anyway.'

'They're probably still lookin' for us now, the stupid old sods,' Eric said gleefully.

Biddy put the spoon down and turned around. 'You need to be more careful,' she said to Eric. 'You've already been in serious trouble, and you don't need to go landin' yourself in any more.'

The grin slid from Eric's face to be replaced by his usual dour countenance.

'But that's not fair! Eric didn't do *anything* – he was completely innocent,' Angela said heatedly.

Biddy took a deep breath, suddenly feeling very flustered. If Shay Flynn or Tara were here listening to the way Angela was going on there would be war. There would probably be a bigger war if they saw how friendly she'd become with Elsie's Eric, because even Biddy herself was feeling a bit uneasy about their friendship. One part of her felt like taking the easy route, laughing and agreeing with them – but there was another, more sensible part telling her that she should be careful about what she agreed with. 'I'm not sayin' that Eric did do anything,' she stressed, 'but there are those that will believe he must have done *something* wrong to be locked up – and will be keeping a close eye on him because of it.' She patted the sullen Eric's shoulder now. 'Me and your mother don't want you to be gettin' into any more difficulties. Don't give those official types a chance to get at you – keep your nose clean and steer well away from any signs of trouble.'

Then, mercifully, Biddy was saved from any more aggravation when the window-cleaner came knocking at the back door for payment.

An hour later Biddy was sitting watching *Animal Magic* on television, with Michael tucked under one arm and little Helen in her lap, when Angela stuck her head through the door. 'The mince is cooked, d'you want me to put the potatoes on now?' she asked brightly.

Biddy glanced at the clock – she hated moving from the lovely comfortable position she was in with the children. It felt all cosy and nice – the way she used to feel, snuggled up watching the telly at night with Fred – but the first group of builders would be due home within the next half an hour. 'That would be grand,' she said. 'This thing will be over in ten minutes and I'll come in and sort out the vegetables.'

'I've done it already,' Angela said. 'I have three large tins of peas in the big pan on the cooker. I'll wait until the shepherd's pie is nearly ready before putting them on to heat with a knob of butter and some salt and pepper – the way you showed me last Monday.'

'You're a quick learner,' Biddy told her. 'The very same as I was myself at your age.'

Angela beamed at the compliment. 'Have we any dessert to fix for this evening?'

Biddy shook her head. 'The soup and bread and shepherd's pie will be tons. If they have any room left, there's Swiss roll and apple tart to have with their cup of tea.'

'They're well looked after,' the young girl said. 'Better looked after than they probably would be at home.'

'Well,' said Biddy, 'that's exactly what we try to do. Give them a home from home, like.' She shifted little Helen higher up on her knee. 'I learned that early on – if you play fair with the lads, then they'll play fair with you.'

As Angela went about her business in the kitchen, Biddy sat back to watch the last few minutes of *Animal Magic*. Having Angela around the place had also given her a bit more time to spend with the children, playing games or watching children's programmes on the telly with them. And now that Fred had been moved to the special unit in Leeds, it meant that she couldn't visit him every night, so that gave her the evenings to put them to bed herself instead of asking Elsie or Angela.

She felt bad about not seeing him every night as usual, but Fred didn't seem to mind. He was so easy-going about everything. He always had been, but he was even more so since his accident. Still, Biddy missed not seeing him every night, and even though she knew his own family visited regularly she was happier when she could see him every day.

The staff at the Grosvenor Hospital had been very good and had set up a rota for driving her over one or two nights during the week, but Biddy had insisted that she could make her own way by train and bus at the weekends when she had more time. Again, the afternoon visits on the Saturday and Sunday gave her and the kids an outing together, and they enjoyed the journeys there and back.

Frank Kennedy had been very good about lifts, and had insisted on driving them over to Leeds on Saturday. Biddy thought it was a pity the way that Tara went on about Frank, for he had been one of the best when it came to visiting Fred, and he made no great fuss of anything. Like the day he'd turned up at the hospital when she and Gabriel were there. Biddy was sure that Tara thought it was all planned, but there had been nothing planned about it whatsoever. Frank had just dropped in as he often did, out of the goodness of his heart.

Biddy had felt bad for him that day. She could tell by the look on his face that he wouldn't have come in if he'd known the Fitzgeralds were there – definitely not. He had been very subdued – very subdued altogether. Although she knew it might have been a different story if Tara had been on her own.

Biddy didn't know why Frank still bothered about Tara, because there wasn't a hope in hell of anything ever happening between them. Tara had changed and grown into a very different person from the girl he had known a number of years ago.

Biddy shrugged to herself. Sure, didn't everybody change at some point in life? Hadn't she changed herself? She looked around her nice family sitting room, at the lovely three-piece moquette suite with the polished wooden arms, and at the modern teak coffee-table in the middle of the floor with the shelf underneath for the papers and children's comics. Then her gaze took in the tall standard lamp with the flowery shade that almost matched the flowery wallpaper, and then the new black-and-white television the children were watching. Who would have believed just ten years ago that Biddy Hart from Ballygrace would live in a fancy place like this?

Biddy should have guessed that there was something coming. Angela had been too good to be true this evening. Not only had she cooked most of the dinner, but she had cleared up the table and washed and dried all the dishes when the meal was over. And now, Biddy suddenly realised, it was pay-back time.

'Please,' the young girl said, her hands joined together as though in prayer, 'I promise I won't be late . . . and Eric says he'll walk me back home after the film.'

Biddy took a deep breath, noting that Angela had washed her blond hair and had changed into her good black slacks and a fairly tight peach v-neck sweater that highlighted her more than adequate bust. 'I'm not sure about this at all, Angela. I don't know how your mother and father would feel about ye going out to the cinema with a lad. It's a bit quick. You're hardly here any length of time and you're already fixed up with a date.' She hesitated. 'Maybe I should give Tara a ring . . .'

'But it's only *Eric*,' Angela said, looking incredulous. 'It's Elsie's son . . . surely you must trust Eric when he's here helping you in the house and everything?'

Biddy pursed her lips. That was *exactly* the problem. She didn't know if she trusted Eric at all. So far there hadn't been anything to not trust him about – but there was something that made her wary of the lad. And it wasn't just the fact that he'd already been in serious trouble. She felt she was caught between a rock and a hard place with Eric being Elsie's son. 'What film are you going to see?' she asked.

'*Psycho*,' Angela said. 'It's supposed to be brilliant . . . although I'll likely be terrified. It's been out a while, but I never got the chance to see it before.' She waved her arms around the kitchen. 'Everything's done – I've even set the table for the breakfast in the morning.'

'I know,' Biddy said with a grateful smile. It wasn't the film that bothered her. It was the fact that she was going with a boy – and that the boy was Eric. Then she reminded herself that there was a time when *she* would have done anything to be allowed out with boys. And in fact had resorted to *very* ingenious ways of getting out with them. After all, she supposed, it was only human to want to mix with the opposite sex – but Biddy would have felt far more comfortable if Angela had been going with a girl.

'OK,' she said, 'you can go. Just so long as you come straight home when the film is over.'

'Oh, I will,' Angela said delightedly. 'You've nothing to worry about there.'

Biddy hoped with all her heart that she didn't have anything to worry about with Angela – because she already had more than enough to worry about with everything else.

Chapter Eighteen

LONDON

'Are you sure you don't mind going back on your own?'
Gabriel checked again. 'I would have preferred to drive
back up to Stockport with you . . . but with Harry still
in America, I feel that William really needs me here.
And I've promised to take him to see the Tower of
London and Madame Tussaud's this week.'

'Darling,' Tara said, coming over to the sofa to sit
beside him. She kissed him lightly on the forehead. 'I've
already told you I really don't mind going on my own.'

'But the journey . . .'

'Gabriel, the journey is nothing,' Tara reassured him.
She leaned her head on his shoulder, her long red curls
tumbling all over his chest. 'It's a straightforward
matter of catching the train from London up to
Stockport, then a taxi up to the house. I've not become
so used to a car that I can't manage on public transport.
I'm perfectly capable, you know. It's like having help
around the house – I would hate the day to come when I
couldn't manage to do things by my own wits as I've
always done.'

Gabriel shook his head, smiling, then reached out
with both hands to ruffle the curls. 'Oh, there's no fear
of the very modern-minded Tara Flynn ever becoming
dependent on anyone or anything. Or worse still – any
man!'

She gave him a little dig with her elbow, playfully pulling her hair out of his grasp.

'You're mocking me again,' she said.

He took her hand in his and kissed it. 'I'm not mocking you at all. In fact, that's one of the things I've always admired and liked about you,' he said in a low voice. 'You have always been an independent and adaptable woman, and I wouldn't have it any other way.'

'I'll ring Biddy and tell her what time the train is due in on Wednesday afternoon, then we might walk down to the station and pick up my train ticket. We could take William with us and buy him an ice cream or one of those knickerbocker glory things he likes in the Wimpy Bar. It might just perk him up a bit.'

Gabriel nodded and smiled. 'I think we might all have a knickerbocker glory to perk us up and, hopefully, the walk out might just liven me up a bit.'

'Are you OK?' Tara asked anxiously, scanning his face

'I'm *grand*,' he said quietly but definitely. 'It's just all the running around these past few months that's caused it.' There was a little pause. 'When we get over this difficult patch, things will get back to normal. In every way.'

Tara lowered her gaze, knowing he was referring to the previous night in bed. And the increasing number of other nights over the last few months when all he wanted to do in bed was sleep. Tara squeezed his hand now. 'Everything *will* be fine,' she whispered.

'I feel bad that you had actually planned to spend most of the month in Stockport giving Biddy support, and you've ended up spending a good bit of it down here helping out with my family instead.'

'Stop worrying about that,' Tara scolded him. 'The situation is much better than I expected, and I'm not as worried now that I've seen the improvement in Fred.

Who would have believed that he would be allowed home for a weekend soon? And Biddy said that the rehabilitation unit has made a huge difference to him. They have him walking around and even doing light exercises, although Biddy is adamant that he'll never set foot in a wrestling ring again.'

Gabriel suddenly turned to his wife and very gently took her face in his hands. 'You do know that I love you, Tara Flynn, with all my heart and soul? I know that I haven't always shown it recently . . .' There was a catch in his voice.

Tears sprung into Tara's eyes, and she buried her face in his neck so that he wouldn't see them. Whether they were tears of relief or tears of sadness she didn't quite know. All she knew was that more time had passed, and there was not the faintest hope yet that they were ever likely to become parents.

Chapter Nineteen

STOCKPORT

As always, Biddy was delighted that Tara was on her way back to Stockport. 'I think that we have everything more or less ready,' she said to Elsie, looking at the well-polished dining-room table, now set with rose-patterned china and silver cutlery and hand-embroidered napkins: the best china and cutlery that lived most of the time in the mahogany display cabinet in the sitting room, and the napkins were so little used that they had faint yellow marks on the lines where they had been folded and ironed. There was rarely a call for such items as napkins in the boarding-house, as most of the lads wouldn't have known how to use them.

'If she's yer friend,' Elsie said, a bit sniffily, 'she should be happy to take you as she finds you. The table couldn't look any better if it were the Queen of England herself that was comin', with all the work you've done and the way you've got yourself all dressed up in the middle of the afternoon.' She gestured now to Biddy's pastel blue and yellow twinset and blue skirt.

'But Tara's not *just* my friend,' Biddy stressed. 'She's my oldest and best friend, and I want to make a bit of an effort for her. It wouldn't be very welcoming to meet her at the door in my working overall and old trousers.' She halted, a lump suddenly coming into her throat. 'We've been through a lot together. We've been friends through thick and thin.'

'All the more reason for her to take you as she finds you,' Elsie repeated in a tight voice. 'No need to be standin' on ceremony when it's a good friend.' She lifted a teacup up, scrutinising the china stamp on the bottom.

A frown crossed Biddy's face. She didn't like Ruby's china being examined as though it was part of a stack being sold on a market stall. She knew the point the older woman was making, that she was trying too hard to put a show on for Tara – that she was trying too hard to impress her. It was a sore point with Biddy, because even Ruby used to tell her off for putting Tara on a pedestal in much the same way.

But neither Elsie nor Ruby had ever quite understood the bond that was there between the two Irish girls – a bond forged by all they had gone through back in Ireland, growing up as young girls without mothers. A bond that saw them through the dreadful times that had forced them to leave Ballygrace and start afresh in England. And it was important to Biddy that Tara knew she was grateful for the chances in life that coming to Stockport had given her – and how she would be grateful to her dying day that Tara had supported her when she'd had to give her illegitimate child up for adoption.

Biddy reached across the table now, checking that there was salt in the rose-patterned cruet set that matched the rest of the china. She would have to refill the container. If there was any salt it had obviously gone solid from lack of use. 'You should go off home now for a few hours,' she told the older woman, 'because you'll find it hard on your legs later tonight by the time you've sorted out the dinner and cleaned up.'

Elsie was irritating her no end at the moment. If the truth be told, both women were irritating each other. And it was all to do with the business between Eric and Angela. She'd had words with Elsie about it last night. In fact, they had both sat up till after midnight discussing it, and putting away most of a bottle of sherry as they did so. Biddy couldn't quite remember whether they had reached any agreement or not. The main thing she could recall was Elsie repeating over and over in a slurred tone, 'With our Eric, it's a case of givin' a dog a bad name before he even has a chance to prove himself.' And then when Biddy had tried to explain that Angela was naïve and ignorant in the ways of the world, Elsie had looked at her almost pityingly, shaking her head and saying things like, 'It takes two to tango', and 'If there was no bad women in the world, there'd be no bad men.'

Whatever Biddy had tried to say, and however carefully she had tried to say it, Elsie had taken it as a criticism of the much-maligned Eric.

But fact was fact – the girl was being led astray. Whatever way you looked at it, it just wasn't right that they had spent hours up in Eric's room listening to records yesterday afternoon, when Biddy was under the impression that they were still down shopping in Stockport for Elsie.

Biddy stifled a weary sigh now, for she knew that there was no avoiding the confrontation to come. She hated things like this, and unfortunately could see things from *everybody's* point of view. Well, maybe not everybody's – she found it difficult to see Eric's point of view.

But certainly she could see how, if she were Elsie, she would want to believe the best of her son, although Eric was definitely the sort of lad that only a mother could love. But then Biddy was a mother herself, and she could understand Elsie's feelings. If Michael or little Helen turned out to be like Eric, maybe she would feel she had to defend them the way poor Elsie did.

Biddy could also understand things from Angela's point of view. And at the end of the day, weren't young ones like Angela supposed to be out enjoying themselves to a certain extent? And there wasn't a thing wrong with that – as long as they didn't go *too* wild.

Then again, Biddy could also understand Tara's point of view – Tara, who was the one who would be held responsible for her young half-sister if anything went wrong. And God knows what could have gone wrong all those hours supposedly listening to records in Eric's bedroom. Biddy suddenly felt sick just at the thought, knowing quite easily what could have happened – and did happen to herself at that age.

Suddenly she knew she would have to speak to Angela as soon as the girl came in from the park with the children – and before Tara arrived. She would remind her in no uncertain terms that she was on a final warning. Any more carry-on between her and Eric and Biddy would report it to Tara, and leave her to deal with it. The thought that she might be packed off back to Ireland would probably be enough to make Angela toe the line.

Chapter Twenty

STOCKPORT

As she alighted from the train in Stockport, Tara realised that she had mixed feelings about this visit – both relief and guilt. She felt a weight had been lifted off her now that she didn't have to spend another afternoon and evening with Elisha Fitzgerald. In many ways Tara liked her mother-in-law, and still felt she had a lot to learn from the elegant older woman. But there were times she found it just a little bit much, sitting on her own with Elisha or with Elisha's sister or friends, while Gabriel spent most of his time with his younger brother.

As Tara queued outside Stockport station for a taxi, she was surprised at just how much she was looking forward to seeing Biddy again and listening to all her news. Even at the worst of times, Biddy managed to make things sound funny and full of life. Whether it was just relating stories about the builders lodging in the house, or recalling with delight the small steps forward that Fred was making. And then there were the children, who were always on the go and who helped lighten the conversation when things were not so good.

Tara also planned to catch up with her friend Kate Thornley this weekend, to do some shopping in Manchester, and maybe have a night out at the theatre or some new restaurant they hadn't tried. When Tara spoke to Kate on the phone earlier in the week, she was full of her new position of editing the fashion page in a women's magazine. She had also suggested that Tara might like to accompany her on an overnight trip to York City the following week.

'I'm covering a winter collection from a new designer,' she told Tara excitedly, 'so I'll be able to charge most of our hotel expenses and meals to the magazine, and we'll meet lots of interesting people.' Kate had then giggled. 'This will really put us ahead in the fashion stakes, knowing what's going to be "in" for next winter.'

'It sounds wonderful,' Tara had replied, 'but I'll have to see how things work out with Biddy and Fred first before giving a definite answer.'

'It'll do you good, Tara,' Kate said firmly. 'You need to spoil yourself a little. You've been busy looking after everyone else – it's time to look after yourself.'

'I'll see,' Tara had hedged, not at all sure how she felt about going off on a glamorous trip while poor Gabriel was still looking after his family down in London. She knew perfectly well that if she told him she was going off with Kate he would be delighted, but something held her back – something stopped her from making a commitment immediately.

'All in all,' Biddy said, holding her good rose-patterned china teapot high in the air, as she poured tea into Tara's cup, 'I think things are starting to look up. This special physiotherapy unit is really making a difference to Fred. They've said he might get a weekend home soon.' She put the teapot down on top of the fancy wrought-iron holder, then reached for the matching rosy milk-jug.

'Thank God,' Tara said, her green eyes lighting up. 'I desperately need some good news after all the tension down in London.' She took a sip of her tea. 'That's lovely, Biddy,' she said, giving a contented little sigh. She gave her friend a big smile. 'And now that I'm getting used to it, I really like your hair blond. It makes a lovely change.'

'D'you think so?' Biddy said, ruffling the back of her hair and beaming. 'I was worried that it made me look a bit . . . kind of cheap.'

'Not at all,' Tara said reassuringly. 'It's a nice shade of blond, it brightens you up for the summer and it looks lovely with your blue and yellow outfit. Did Fred like it?'

Biddy's gaze shifted away from her friend's eyes. 'I'm not too sure what he thought. Oh, he smiled and everything . . . but there's times it's hard to tell exactly what's sinking in with him.'

Tara put her teacup down and stretched her hand across to cover her friend's. 'It's early days yet, Biddy. He's made amazing progress so far.'

'Indeed,' Biddy said, nodding her head vigorously. 'Oh, there's no doubt – he's definitely made great progress since he first had the accident.'

They sat in companionable silence for a little while, drinking their tea with Danny Williams singing 'Moon River' on the radio in the background. Then Biddy held out a plate of fresh-cream cakes to Tara. 'Was London really bad?' she asked curiously. She always imagined that gentry like the Fitzgeralds had much easier, happier lives. Of course she knew that they had bad luck like everyone else, especially considering the tragic car accident that had killed poor Madeleine and her father, but she felt that their money and big fancy houses helped them to cope better than ordinary people like herself.

'Elisha has always been a bit highly strung,' Tara said with a sigh, 'and she finds it difficult to deal with the smallest things when Harry is away on business. Gabriel really went down to help William sort out things for his new school. It's not for a while yet, but apparently they have to put their names down early for the various things.'

'Oh, the poor woman,' Biddy said, her brow creased in sympathy. 'But then, she was always a bit light in the head, wasn't she?' She paused. 'In fact, when you think about it, that whole Fitzgerald family were all inclined that way. Poor Madeleine . . .'

'*Biddy* . . .' Tara said in a warning tone. 'Have you forgotten that I'm married to one of that Fitzgerald family?'

'Jesus!' Biddy said, her hand flying to cover her mouth. 'I'm really sorry! Now, Tara, you know I didn't mean it that way. There's not a single thing wrong with Gabriel – sure, you well know I think the world of him, and you know that Fred thinks the very same. I was just meaning – I was just thinkin' back to when we lived in Ballygrace.'

Tara reached over to the sugar bowl and spooned some sugar into her cup of tea. 'I know exactly what you were just meaning,' she said, trying not to show her amusement. She slowly stirred her tea and waited to see how her friend would extricate herself from this latest situation.

'Well,' Biddy said weakly, holding out a plate of perfectly cut egg and salad-cream sandwiches, 'I really just meant that Mrs Fitzgerald and Madeleine had a bit of trouble with their nerves . . . that's all that I meant. It wasn't meant in a bad way, or anything.'

Tara took two of the dainty sandwiches and placed them on her side plate, then spread her napkin out over her knees. 'I'm only codding you,' she said to her friend, 'I know you meant no harm, and you're perfectly correct.' She paused. 'Well, Elisha has Gabriel there for a few weeks and that should help her out with William, and hopefully give him a change from work, if not a complete rest.'

'And the change up here will do *you* good, Tara,'

Biddy said, giving her a big smile. 'It'll be like old times when we first came over. Now that I have Elsie and Angela helpin' out, and I'm not visitin' Fred every evening, I'll have a bit more time.' She halted, a guilty look coming over her face. 'That sounds fierce bad, doesn't it? As if I mind going to visit Fred . . . I don't a bit, I'm always delighted and relieved to see him. I just mean it gives me more time for the kids and to catch up on other things that I've got behind with.'

Tara nodded, swallowing the last mouthful of a sandwich. 'We'll go and visit Fred tonight, and then we can decide what to do over the next few days.'

'We can take walks into the shops in Stockport,' Biddy suggested, 'and maybe we could get tickets for one of those fancy concerts you like in Manchester.'

Tara paused for a moment, then her beautiful face lit up. 'I think, Biddy, that's just exactly the sort of thing I need!'

Biddy decided now that this wasn't the time to bring up Frank Kennedy's offer of a lift to the hospital to visit Fred tonight. Tara had enough on her plate just now, and she would only need to hear Frank's name mentioned to send her off again. She wouldn't chance spoiling things, and anyway, Tara would never believe that Frank hadn't known that she was back from London. She always thought the worst of him. Biddy decided that she would ring Frank as soon as Tara left to go back up to her own house, and tell him that she wasn't going over to the hospital this evening. She would tell him that one of the children was a bit off-colour and she didn't want to leave them.

It was a white lie, of course, but it was better than having to explain to him that Tara would rather travel any other way than travel with him. Better than seeing the wounded look on his face when he knew that Tara had snubbed him yet again. Besides, he wouldn't know any different. He was probably only being polite and would have better things to do on a Saturday night than to drive her all the way out to Leeds.

Tara had a rest on top of her bed for an hour and then, feeling revived, had a bath and dressed for her trip out with Biddy. She checked her appearance in the mirror, deciding she did like the newer, shorter length of her green-and-rust-striped dress. Every year skirt lengths were creeping up that little bit further, and Tara kept a watchful eye on what actually suited her as opposed to current fashions. Apart from the styles, she had to be very careful about colours and shades because of her red hair. She pulled on a matching rust cardigan, and then decided she'd better carry her Burberry raincoat just in case, because although it was warm, it was a dull and heavy evening that could go either way.

She came downstairs and made a quick phone call to Gabriel. They chatted for a few minutes, and Tara was delighted to hear that his day out in London with Elisha and young William had gone well. There was also an energy and brightness in his tone that she hadn't heard for a while.

'I'm missing you like mad already,' he told her in a quiet but urgent tone. 'But I'm going to enjoy the time I have with William. Poor kid, he needs the company – someone younger, with energy, to take him out and play games and things like that.' He paused. 'Spending time with William makes me realise just how much I'm looking forward to us having our own children . . .'

Tara's heart soared. 'Oh, Gabriel,' she whispered. 'I can't wait either . . . it's the one thing I really, really want . . .'

'When we get back to Ireland,' he promised, 'we'll make it a priority . . . I promise. I know I've not been too energetic recently, but the break away from work has really helped.' He paused. 'And you have been so patient, Tara. So very patient.'

'Gabriel,' Tara said, 'I have *you*, and that's the single most important thing in the whole world.'

'And you always will have me, darling,' he said emphatically. 'You always will.'

After hanging up the phone, Tara turned down the hallway towards the kitchen to make a quick cup of coffee before walking down to meet Biddy at the lodging house. She had just cut herself a slice of Mrs Winterbottom's cherry cake when the front door opened. Tara stuck her head around the kitchen door and saw the plump secretary from Thornley's Estate Agents. Her hackles rose slightly, remembering the forward way the girl had spoken to her a few weeks ago. The girl was ready to mount the stairs when she saw Tara.

'Hello,' Tara said. She was polite, but there was a small edge to her voice. 'How are you?'

The girl halted, and Tara noticed an embarrassed flush coming to her cheeks. 'Oh, Mrs Fitzgerald,' she said, coming down the hallway towards Tara, her voice slightly quivery and not at all as confident as she had been before, 'I have a message for you . . .'

Tara's eyebrows lifted and her body tensed. Surely this girl hadn't come with another message from Frank Kennedy? Surely she had got the message loud and clear last time they had a conversation? 'A message from whom?' she asked.

'Mr Pickford.'

Tara's face visibly relaxed.

'He said he would be grateful if you would call in at the office as soon as possible . . . he has some interesting news for you.' The girl paused. 'He said if you are too busy to drop in, maybe you could give him a ring. He said it was quite urgent.'

'Thank you for passing that on,' Tara said quietly, intrigued as to what her old boss could have to tell her that was so important. She had planned to call in at

Thornley's when she had first arrived in Stockport, but all the business with London had overtaken everything. Tara turned back into the kitchen now, looking for a small plate for her cake.

'Oh . . . and Mrs Fitzgerald,' the girl said now, her voice faltering, 'I think I may owe you an apology . . . I didn't realise that you actually *owned* these houses. I thought you were a long-standing boarder who kept the room on for when you were over in England. I think it was the fact that you look so young that I never considered you being the actual landlady.' She gave an anxious smile. 'Miss Marshall told me that you actually owned *both* these houses. I would never have been so chatty or forward if I'd known . . . if someone had explained to me . . .'

Tara's eyes narrowed. 'But that's hardly the point,' she said quietly. 'Whether I own a hundred houses or rent the smallest room in one of them, I should like to feel I have privacy and respect from the other boarders. The respect and privacy I've always given them.' There was a little silence. 'And the same goes for my *husband*,' Tara stressed. 'I wouldn't want to be involved in any kind of talk with friends or lodgers in this house that excluded him, or made him feel uncomfortable.' She was determined not to get into a conversation with this girl that even referred to Frank Kennedy, but she wanted the point driven home once and for all.

'Of course,' the girl said, nodding her head vigorously, 'and I'm so sorry if I came across as being rude . . .' Tears were now glistening at the corners of her eyes. 'I would hate Mr Pickford to – to get a bad impression of me.'

'That's OK,' Tara said, giving the girl a reassuring smile. The point had been made and she wasn't going to labour it any further. 'I don't think there's any need for Mr Pickford to be told of any conversations that have gone on in this house.' She motioned over to the cooker.

'The kettle has just boiled if you'd like to make yourself some tea or coffee.'

Tara turned away now and carried on with her business, assured that there would be no more unwanted messages passed through Thornley's naïve secretary.

Chapter Twenty-One

The train journey from Stockport to Leeds passed pleasantly with a weak summer sunshine streaming through the glass windows for most of it. The two women chatted and drank watery British Rail tea with small packets of shortbread biscuits. Tara had brought a couple of women's magazines with her from London, so they read them in silence for a while, then fell into more discussions over the latest fashions in them.

'D'you know, Tara,' Biddy said at one point, motioning towards her *Woman* magazine, 'this reminds me of the two of us reading your American comics in your granda's house back in Ballygrace. Do you remember when we used to churn the butter and collect the eggs?'

Tara nodded, her eyes suddenly moist as she conjured up a picture of the two young girls they had been all those years ago. 'We've travelled a long way since then,' she said, patting her friend's hand.

By the time they had boarded the bus that took them straight out to the hospital, the sun had disappeared behind dark clouds and rain was splattering hard against the windows. The friends swapped magazines and sat silently absorbed in them once again, totally relaxed in each other's company.

Biddy turned her head to look out of the bus window, and thought of the conversation she'd had earlier on that day with Frank Kennedy. He had been grand when she told him that she was cancelling Fred's visit tonight. She felt guilty lying, then immediately felt better when

Frank said that he actually had a late-afternoon business meeting out in Derbyshire, and might have found it a bit tight to make it for the hospital visiting time.

'We'll leave it for the time being, so,' said Biddy. 'Because I'm hopin' that he might be allowed home for an overnight visit this weekend.'

'Oh, that's a big step forward!' Frank said delightedly. 'I'll call down to the house and see him when I get a minute. I've managed to get hold of some light weights and some small gadgets that he can squeeze to exercise the muscles in his hands. I'll ring the hospital and check with the physiotherapy when he's allowed to start using them.'

'Oh, Frank, you've been so good to him . . . good to us both. You've been a real friend.'

'Fred's one of the few really decent men I've met in my whole life,' he said quietly, 'and if there's anything I can ever do to help him, I will. I know how we all felt when my young daughter was sick a few years ago . . .'

'If you're thinking of calling out to the house, ring first,' Biddy said quickly, 'in case he's sleeping or anything . . .' Whatever happened, she didn't want Tara to run into him on this visit.

'I will indeed,' Frank said. He paused. 'I hope he won't find the week too long without any visits.'

'Oh, he'll be grand,' Biddy said. 'He's never without visitors. His mother and father will be in and out with uncles and aunties and cousins. And any time it's quiet, they have the television room and radio and everything to keep them entertained – sure it's a home from home he has.' She laughed now, trying to make light of everything. 'When I rang yesterday, the nurses told me that Fred was even playing table-tennis and snooker the other afternoon. It's supposed to help with getting his coordination working again – at least that's what they tell me.'

'Are you sure it's a hospital that fellow's in?' Frank

said laughing. 'He sounds as if he's having a better time than the rest of us. I think we could all do with booking in for a few weeks!'

Biddy's face had lightened. That's what she liked about Frank – he could always see the cheery side of everything.

The bus the two women had boarded was a local one put on especially for the hospital visitors, and it stopped every so often to pick up passengers. As they drove along, Biddy pointed out various landmarks to Tara through the rain-splattered window.

At one stop a balding, middle-aged man boarded the bus with a Yorkshire Terrier tucked under his raincoat. He swayed down the aisle until he found a seat directly behind Tara and Biddy.

After a few minutes, the dog came out from under the wet coat to sit on the man's knee. It was a nervous, hairy little thing that cowered when the bus made a sudden movement or there was a loud noise. As the conductor approached them with his ticket machine making a whirring noise, the dog started to whine.

'The poor cratur!' Biddy said, turning around to the man. 'He seems terrified, doesn't he?'

'Terrified?' The man leaned forward, sending beer fumes in the direction of the two girls. 'It's me that should be bloody terrified, gettin' landed with a useless little rat of a thing.' He lifted the shivering little dog under the front legs so that it was forced to stand on its hind ones.

'The poor little cratur!' Biddy repeated, giving Tara a horrified glance.

'It were me sister's,' the man elaborated now, putting the dog back down. Then, with one hand, he swiped a long strand of hair that had escaped on to his shoulder back up to cover his bald patch. 'I've only come from buryin' her today, you know. Cissy, her name was.' His mouth turned down dolefully at either side. 'Hadn't seen her for years, mind. We never got on, the pair of us. Not even when we was kids.' He shook his head and another strand of hair fell down on his shoulder. 'I'm not a hypocrite, like . . . I call a spade a spade . . . even if it is me own sister.' He rolled his eyes. 'She were a right corker – would argue with her own bleedin' shadow, she would. But anyroads, I went to her funeral, just to show some respect, like. They can't say I never did me duty.'

'That was good of you,' Biddy said kindly, trying not to catch Tara's eye in case they both started laughing.

'Anyway,' the man went on, enjoying having an audience, 'just as I were coming out for the bus home, her bloody nosy-parker of a neighbour came runnin' to me with this ratty little get! Said there were no one else to look after it, and he had two big Alsatians of his own, so he couldn't have it. He soddin' well handed me the lead and walked off.' He prodded his finger on the bar of the girls' seat. 'He deliberately waited until he saw the bus comin' over the hill before comin' over to me. He knew that if I'd ran after him, I'd have missed me bus home.' He shook his head. 'And there wouldn't have been another for an hour.'

'That would have been terrible,' Biddy said, her lips twitching at the corners.

'Well, we're right lucky that the hospital buses pass right by both our front doors,' he stated. 'It's one of the few good things about this area – a decent bus service.' There was a pause while he tried to remember where he'd left off his story about the dog. 'Well,' he continued, 'what the hell could I do? Our Cissy had never got married, and she has no family to take it.' He looked down at the cowering animal. 'The wife's gonna go bloody mad when I turn up with this rat of a thing – she bleedin' well hates dogs, she does.' He caught the dog by the scruff of the neck and gave it a shake.

'Don't do that!' Tara suddenly snapped. 'You'll hurt the poor little thing.'

The man grinned. 'If it keeps that whinin' up when I'm tryin' to sleep tonight – I'll do more than bloody shake it. It'll feel the end of my toe up its—'

Just then the conductor came towards the man's seat looking for his fare. He moved the dog under one arm, and then under the other, trying to find some change for his ticket. 'Here!' he said. He stood up and suddenly thrust the dog in Tara's direction. 'Since you're so fond of it, you can hold it for a few minutes till I sort out me money.'

Tara's instinct was to pass the dog back to him, but when she felt the warm little body shaking in her hands, her heart went out to the animal, and she started to stroke it. 'I should charge you for havin' an animal on a public bus, you know,' the conductor said, eyeing the dog.

The man threw his head back and laughed. 'That would be the icin' on the bloody cake, that would!' Then he looked up at the conductor. 'Possession is nine tenths of the law – and since she's holdin' the soddin' thing – she can pay its fare!'

'You've got some nerve!' Biddy told him, handing the conductor the exact amount for both herself and Tara. 'No wonder your sister had nothing to do with you!'

'You wouldn't be sayin' that if you'd ever met her!' the man said, winking.

The conductor leaned over to the two girls. 'Who owns the dog?' he demanded.

'They do!' the man said, suddenly rising to his feet again, and squeezing out past the conductor. 'I'm gettin' off here – I need a few pints before headin' home.'

'No, you bloody well aren't!' Tara said, moving swiftly to her feet. As her arm shot out to grab the man, the dog let out a yelp, and then promptly did its business all over Tara's raincoat and dress.

'God almighty!' she gasped. 'My clothes are ruined!' She held the dog away from her with both hands to stop it doing any further damage.

The bus shuddered to a stop and before either of the girls had a chance to stop him, the man had staggered to the door and taken himself down the steps and off the bus.

'I still don't believe it!' Tara gasped, feeling the warm dampness penetrating through her lovely dress.

'Don't worry,' Biddy said in a quick, decisive voice, 'I'll keep the dog – the kids will love him.' She dug down into her handbag to find a packet of tissues to help dry Tara's coat and dress. 'They've been wantin' a dog for ages.'

Then, just to add insult to injury, as the bus slowly pulled away again, a bang came on the window beside Biddy. She and Tara looked round, wondering what new catastrophe was now about to befall them. The grinning face of the man came into view as he held up his thumb, shouting, 'Cheers, girls! Youse have saved me life!'

'It's spilling down! Thanks be to God we've brought raincoats and umbrellas,' Biddy said, as they stood up to get off the bus. 'We'll let everyone else go on ahead, then I'll go under your umbrella, Tara, so's I can carry the dog inside my coat. The poor little thing is still shivering.'

'I still don't believe this has happened!' Tara stated, as they scurried across from the bus-stop to the gates of the hospital. 'You know they won't let us in with this dog, don't you?'

'We'll think of something,' Biddy reassured her. They stopped to shake the rain off their coats and umbrella when they reached the shelter of the hospital building.

Then, just as they were heading for the main

entrance, a man dressed in a white hospital uniform came out.

'That looks like a porter,' Tara said, and they both rushed towards him.

'Excuse me askin',' Biddy said to the man, 'but you wouldn't know of any place we could put this little dog until after visiting hours?'

'A little Yorkshire, isn't it?' the porter said, smiling. 'They're toppin' little dogs, aren't they?'

And, within a few minutes of hearing how the girls came to have him, the dog was safely tucked up in a large cardboard box inside the boiler-house door.

'He won't come to any harm in there for an hour or so,' the porter said, waving away the half-a-crown that Tara tried to put in his pocket.

As soon as they got inside the hospital building, Tara made straight for a toilet and attempted to clean the dog's accident from her clothes. Between wet hankies and scrunched up Izal toilet paper and the tiny bar of hospital soap, they managed to eradicate the worst of the problem.

Eventually, they joined the throng of visitors and headed in the direction of Fred's room.

'Would you look at that?' Biddy gasped, when she saw the note pinned on his door, saying that he was in the games room, which was further along the corridor.

'Games room, indeed!' Tara said, nudging Biddy. 'It sounds as though he hardly has time for visiting in this new place.'

'Thank God,' Biddy replied. 'I don't feel so bad not coming every day when I know he's so busy. I used to feel fierce guilty missing a day when he was nearer home, even when I'd been up all night with the kids.'

When they arrived at the games room, Biddy tapped lightly on the swing door and then pushed it forward. She took a few tentative steps inside and then she suddenly froze – unable to believe her eyes. There was

Fred, standing beside the ping-pong table with his arms wrapped around the waist of a nurse. An older, middle-aged nurse, who was laughing up into Fred's face as he appeared to be trying to kiss her. Biddy turned towards Tara, her face as white as a sheet. And when she saw the same shocked look on her friend's face, she suddenly shouted, 'Fred! What the hell d'you think you're bloody well doin'?'

Immediately the nurse pulled away, pink-faced and flustered, and started to collect up the table-tennis bats and balls that were scattered around the table.

'What's going on here, Fred?' Biddy said in an ominous tone, advancing towards patient and nurse.

Fred gave his wife a huge, beaming, innocent smile. He then came towards her with outstretched arms. 'Biddy!' he said. 'You came to see me again.' He enveloped her now in a big bear hug that she furiously endured as opposed to enjoyed.

'We've just finished a game, and Fred won,' the nurse rushed to explain, smiling in a placating manner at Biddy. 'He just got a little bit overexcited . . . he didn't mean any harm.' She patted Fred's shoulder. 'The nurses here are well used to it . . . we're trained not to take any notice of it. It's all to do with missing their families and friends . . . and just feeling desperate for a little bit of physical contact.'

Biddy looked at Tara again, not sure what to make of the unsettling situation. Tara was frowning, but Biddy couldn't tell what she was thinking.

'I'm not too sure if I like Fred behavin' like that,' she said, her face dark with concern. 'I'm not sure if it's good for him . . . he'd never have gone on like that before.'

The nurse smiled again. 'As I said, it's all part of the recovery – and don't forget they recover in some areas quicker than others.' She stooped to pick up another ping-pong ball from the floor. 'I'll leave you to your visit now.'

As they walked back in the direction of Fred's room, he regaled them all about his scores that evening in table-tennis, his manner telling them that he was completely oblivious to the shock his behaviour with the nurse had caused.

He stopped outside a lavatory and indicated that he needed to go in, so Biddy and Tara walked over to sit on a bench in the corridor while they waited for him.

'What do you make of all *that*?' Biddy asked Tara as soon as they sat down.

There was a small pause. 'I'm not quite sure,' Tara said slowly.

'Well,' Biddy said, 'put it this way – would you be happy if you were to come upon Gabriel with his arms wrapped around another woman and kissing her like that?'

Tara shook her head, appalled at the very thought. 'No, of course not . . .' She hesitated. 'But as the nurse explained—'

'Never mind the bleedin' nurse!' Biddy said, her eyes blazing. 'She wasn't exactly struggling to get away from him, was she?'

Tara took a deep breath, not wanting to make the situation worse – but unable to lie.

'I think I agree with your feelings, Biddy . . . Fred might have had a serious accident, but I don't think they should be encouraging the men to behave like that. Fred's an . . .' She halted, getting the words right. It wouldn't do to make Biddy feel even worse. 'Fred's an attractive big fellow, and there's plenty of women who wouldn't mind having a kiss and a cuddle with him – even now, while he's still not a hundred per cent.'

'And she was a fair bit older than Fred – she must have been bleedin' forty if she was a day! A dry oul' thing that no man would give a second glance to,' Biddy

154

said, so agitated that she didn't even notice or care that she was swearing in front of Tara. 'I suppose it must brighten up her spinstery oul' day to have a fine-looking fella like Fred givin' her a kiss!' Biddy took a breath, unable to think of anything bad enough to say about the nurse.

'Do you want to have a quiet word with the ward sister?' Tara suggested. 'I can go down to the office and see if she's there while you wait for Fred.'

Biddy halted for a few moments, mulling the situation over. 'No,' she said slowly, 'I don't want to go causin' a big fuss . . . I suppose it might be best if we say nothin' on this occasion. I'll try to get it out of him later what really happened. Who started what.'

Tara thought there was a good improvement in Fred since she had last seen him, although he was still a little vague on certain things. She and Biddy sat in the visitors' chairs and Fred sat on the side of his bed, while they told him all about the Yorkshire Terrier and the terrible man who had dumped the little dog on them.

'So the dog will be there when you're allowed home at the weekend,' Biddy stated, handing Fred the Eccles cake she had unwrapped for him, 'and we'll have to pick a name out for it.'

Fred's head nodded up and down. 'Beltin'!' he said, breaking a piece of the cake. 'The kids will love havin' a dog.'

Tara stayed for the first half of the visit, then left Biddy and Fred on their own for a while to have a bit of privacy. When Biddy protested, Tara told her that she was going to check on the dog and that she fancied a bit of a walk now that the rain had died off.

'I'll leave my coat with you, and let the air dry my dress,' she said, laughing and rolling her eyes.

She was now feeling tired after the journey from London that morning and then their journey out to the hospital. And although good sense was telling her she shouldn't have any feelings about it, she was actually concerned about the little terrier.

But there was also another reason for wanting a little while on her own. Watching Biddy fussing over Fred and telling him all about what the children had been up to and all the things going on at the house had made Tara suddenly realise that she missed Gabriel already. That she missed him looking adoringly at her, listening carefully to everything she said, and checking that she was all right. Watching Biddy and Fred made her realise that she missed Gabriel very badly indeed.

She walked around the outside of the building now until she came to the door to the boiler-room. She opened it cautiously and peered inside into the semi-darkness – then she frowned. The box was lying on its side and completely empty. She slowly stepped inside, her eyes adjusting to the dark. Then, a little nervous whimper directed her to a corner, where she found the Yorkshire Terrier cowering amongst a pile of old newspapers and rags. She picked the little thing up and made her way back out of the boiler-room, but it was only when she was back out into the light that she realised the dog was covered in black oil from the rags.

'Holy God!' Tara said out loud, once again holding the dog away from her. But it was too late ... her hands and dress were now all smeared with oil. It was bad enough when the dog had done its business all over her but at least it hadn't left any obvious marks like this oil.

She dropped the dog to the ground, keeping a grip on the lead, and dipped very carefully into her cardigan pocket for a hanky, trying not to touch the garment with her oily fingers. She dabbed the hanky over the worst areas on the dress, but it made little difference – the damage had been done. Her new stripy dress was ruined – oil was notoriously difficult to remove. How on earth could she travel back on the bus and train looking like this?

Tears of frustration sprung into her eyes and, looking down, she shook her head at the Yorkshire Terrier. There was no point in being angry at the dog – it wasn't the poor little thing's fault. That stupid, ignorant, drunken man on the bus! If she could have got hold of him now, Tara would cheerfully have wrung his neck. No doubt he was sitting back in the pub, downing his pint of beer and telling anyone who would listen what a fast one he had pulled on two silly Irish girls.

She moved along the path now, trailing the terrified dog on the lead, and asking herself how on earth she and Biddy had got themselves into this ridiculous predicament. If she had been with Gabriel – sensible, practical Gabriel – none of this would have happened. Things like this only happened when she was with other people.

There was nothing else to do but to grit her teeth until Biddy came out, because she definitely wouldn't be allowed inside the hospital with the dog. Then they would have to see if some of the hospital staff could get them some cloths or cleaning materials to clean both herself and the dog up.

She decided that for the time being she would follow the path around the back of the hospital building, and give the dog a chance to do its business before they had to journey back to Stockport. She didn't need another doggy accident on her clothes.

After a bit, the dog had settled down and was walking along beside her in an easier manner, as though used to being taken out on a lead. They went around the building until they came to a car park, where thankfully there were no people to see the state of her and the dog.

Then, a car door opened in the row nearest to her and a tall figure got out. 'Tara?' a familiar, surprised voice said.

Tara's heart almost stopped. It was Frank Kennedy. She paused, stooping to gather the little dog up into her arms. He came striding across to her now, dressed in a dark suit, perfect as usual, and carrying a raincoat over one arm and some kind of package under the other.

Tara bent her head, giving her attention to the dog. She wanted to keep on walking, but she knew it would only lead to a big scene, since there were only the two of them around. She knew it would be giving Frank Kennedy more attention than he deserved.

'I didn't expect to see *you* here . . . I didn't expect to see anyone here this evening,' he said, his brow creased in confusion. 'I thought Fred would have no visitors . . . that's why I decided to drive out.' He halted. 'I presume Bridget is here, too? That she decided to come after all?'

The hesitant note in his voice told Tara that he was telling the truth. He hadn't expected to see Biddy or anyone else at the hospital, and he now felt very awkward. It also seemed fairly obvious that he had had a recent conversation with Biddy, during which she had said she wouldn't be coming to visit Fred tonight.

There was a silence. Eventually Tara lifted her eyes to look at him. 'I think there was something that Biddy needed to discuss with the doctors . . . she just decided to come at the last minute.'

'So I see.' He nodded slowly, but his dark eyes told her that he knew *exactly* what had happened. 'Do you think it would be all right if I went inside to see Fred for a few minutes?' He indicated the package. 'I have a few things for him.'

Tara suddenly felt very embarrassed. She knew he must have driven a good hour to get to the hospital and there was only a short while of the visiting hour left. 'There's just Biddy in with him,' she said more civilly, looking down at the small dog. 'I'm sure Fred will be delighted to see you.'

The look he gave her was sceptical. 'I can see there

was no need for me to come this evening – but since I'm here I may as well go and see him.'

The dog suddenly wriggled out of Tara's arms and jumped down on to the ground, revealing her stained dress in all its oily glory.

Frank Kennedy stared at the black-streaked cloth and then looked down at the dirty dog. He raised his eyebrows questioningly, but said nothing.

'We got landed with this little thing on the bus journey over,' she suddenly heard herself explaining. 'The drunken goat that had him would have ended up having him put down or something . . . I think Biddy's decided to keep him.'

'I'm not a bit surprised,' Frank Kennedy said. 'She has a big heart.' He paused for a moment. 'Misguided at times,' his eyes narrowed, 'but nobody can say she doesn't have a heart.'

Then he turned on his heel and walked off.

'It's OK,' Frank said, 'I know perfectly well why you said it.'

'I'm no good at telling lies,' Biddy said, her face beetroot-red with embarrassment. Her hands tightened around the paper bag that held the two pairs of Fred's pyjamas she was taking home to wash and iron. 'But it was either say I wasn't comin' tonight . . . or tell you that Tara wouldn't come to the hospital if she knew you were coming.' She shrugged. 'I was tryin' not to hurt your feelings . . .'

'It's OK,' Frank repeated. 'I know well she wouldn't want to meet up with me.' He stood up now, and put the visitors' chair back in the corner of the room. 'And I have to say that lately, I have no great wish to meet up with Tara Flynn either. She's not the same person she used to be.'

Biddy looked down at the brown-paper bag in her lap, as though searching for an answer that might make him feel better. She suddenly felt very, very weary. It had been a long and tiresome day.

By the time Biddy came out of the hospital building, Tara had already made up her mind that she would travel back to Stockport in Frank Kennedy's car.

'Are you sure?' Biddy checked, the wind completely taken out of her sails. She had come out unusually strident and almost prepared to have a stand-up row with Tara if she refused the offer of a lift home in Frank's car. It made absolutely no sense to do otherwise, especially with the little dog. And besides, Biddy now felt at the end of her tether and couldn't face the thought of the bus and train journey back home.

It had not been the best of evenings, even if the dog had given them a bit of a laugh at the beginning. The business with Fred and the nurse was still niggling away at her, and Biddy also felt bad about the state of Tara's clothes – almost guilty. And then, to crown everything, there was this terrible atmosphere between Tara and her old boyfriend.

Tara had known her friend long enough to read the situation – to know that Biddy was stretched to the limit. Plus, she was tired and weary herself. 'I'm not going to cut both our noses off just to spite Frank Kennedy. And anyway,' she said, looking down at the tiny Yorkshire Terrier asleep in her arms, 'I don't think it's fair on the poor little dog to have to go on the bus and train again.'

'Or fair on you to get peed on and covered in oil,' Biddy said, with a hint of a smile.

'Well,' Tara shrugged, 'there's no guarantee that the dog won't wet all over Frank's fancy car, is there? But if he insists on driving us back to Stockport . . .'

Biddy looked up and caught Tara's eye, and they both suddenly dissolved into fits of laughter. They laughed and laughed, pointing at the oily-haired dog and then at the streaks on Tara's dress.

'What', Biddy couldn't resist asking, 'did you say to Frank Kennedy about the state of your clothes?'

'Nothing,' Tara replied, shaking her curls. 'I was so annoyed when I saw him, I almost forgot what I looked like . . .'

'What was that drunken eedjit like on the bus?' Biddy suddenly giggled. 'With the hair swiped from one side of his head to cover the bald patch?' They both broke into peals of laughter again. 'Oh, don't!' Biddy said, crossing her legs. 'If we keep laughing I'm going to be as bad as the dog and wet myself!'

And at just that moment Frank Kennedy came out of the hospital entrance and found the two friends hanging on to each other, almost hysterical with laughter. He looked from one to the other, then at the grubby little dog, and shook his head in confusion. He had been dreading seeing Tara's tight, uppity face, and the guilty, strained look that Biddy had worn back in the hospital. What on earth had brought all this hysterical laughter on, he wondered.

'We'd love a lift back to Stockport, Frank – if that's OK?' Biddy managed to struggle out between giggles.

'I'll keep the dog on my knee in the back,' Tara reassured him, her face dead serious again as it always was when she was forced to talk to him. 'I'll make sure it won't do anything on the upholstery.'

Chapter Twenty-Two

TULLAMORE

Tessie woke with a start. She lay in the dark for a few moments, listening. Then the sound of the front door banging jolted her into action. 'Jesus!' she said aloud, reaching across to the bedside table and groping for the switch on the small lamp. She took a few seconds for her eyes to adjust to the brightness, and then she threw the bedcovers back and in a few moments had her feet in her slippers and was wrapping her dressing-gown around her. She could now see the upstairs hall light streaming in under the bedroom door, and when she opened it she checked the time on her watch. It was half past two in the morning.

'Surely not the same damned thing again tonight?' she muttered to herself as she made her way carefully down the stairs and along the little hallway to the front door. The position of the bolt on the top of the door and the hanging thick chain that Shay had put on only last week told the story she didn't want to hear.

Molly had escaped from the house once again.

Taking the small Chubb key from the brass holder on the wall, she went out the door, pulling it closed behind her. The cool night air hit her as soon as she stepped on to the street, making Tessie pull her dressing-gown belt tighter. 'Jesus Christ!' she said again to herself as she looked first one way up the street and then the other. There was not a soul in sight. She shook her head, unable to believe that it had happened yet again – not after the latest lock and chain going on. She moved a few feet to the left, which would take her in the direction of the town centre, then she changed her mind and moved in the opposite direction. *Which way should I go?* And then suddenly, her slippered feet were taking her down to the bottom of the street and in the direction of the canal.

The further along she got – and not a sign of Molly – the more anxious Tessie grew. Surely she couldn't have got this far? For all the elderly spinster was sprightly and relatively sure on her feet, she was still in her eighties. She couldn't go *that* fast, could she? Then, as she turned the corner with the canal bank in view, Tessie realised that she had made the wrong choice of direction.

Quickly she turned and, as fast as her thin-soled-slippered feet would go, she started to retrace her steps, her eyes scanning every corner and building.

Tessie's breath was coming quickly now, and she could feel a tightness in her chest – caused by her hurried steps and her mounting anxiety. Within a few minutes, she was back where she started – and still no sign of her charge. She stood outside the house, looking this way and that, unsure of what to do. There was no point in going back into the house because Molly could not have let herself in. There was only the one key kept on the rack, and that was the one that Tessie had safely tucked in her dressing-gown pocket.

As she started walking in the direction of the town centre, Tessie came to the conclusion that when this latest incident was over, she was going to have to insist that Shay talk to Joe and Tara about getting a phone put in. There was no avoiding it any more. If there had been a phone in the house, then Tessie could have picked it up and phoned the garda station.

If she didn't come across Molly soon, she was going

to have to walk to the station at the top of the town and get the guards to look for the old woman. And then she would have to nip back to her own house to waken Shay and tell him that he could get out of his nice cosy bed and go and join in the search for Molly.

After all, she was Shay's auntie – as she was fed up reminding him – and more his responsibility than his wife's.

Tessie came to Hayes' Cross now and halted for a few moments to look in all directions, but again there was not a single person or a car in sight. In one way she was relieved, for what would she have done meeting anyone, dressed as she was in her slippers and dressing-gown? And what kind of people might be roaming the town at this hour of the morning? The fearful thought set her moving again, in the direction of the garda barracks.

She pushed the heavy door open, to see a bangarda on a bench and there, sitting beside her, wrapped in an old blanket, was the absconding Molly. The old lady looked up at her nephew's wife, with absolutely no sign of recognition.

'Thanks be to God!' Tessie said, rushing towards them. 'Thanks be to God and his blessed mother! I've been all over the place looking for her!' Her legs now felt weak with relief.

'She's grand now – aren't you?' the bangarda said kindly, putting her arm around the old lady. 'She was a bit cold when they brought her in, so we put the blanket on her, and Sergeant Power has gone to make her a nice cup of tea.' She patted Molly's shoulder.

Tessie sank down on the bench beside them. 'She's my husband's aunt,' she started to explain breathlessly, 'and we're tryin' our best to mind her . . .'

The bangarda nodded understandingly. 'She hasn't been here long at all. Luckily enough, one of the guards spotted her tearing up the road, and he brought her straight to the barracks.'

'Thanks be to God!' Tessie said again. 'If he hadn't found her she could have caught her death of cold dressed only in her night attire. Thank God she had at least a cardigan over the nightdress.' She took Molly's hand and rubbed it between both of hers. 'You could have caught your death of cold, couldn't you?'

Molly looked at her vaguely, then her eyes suddenly lit up and she nodded her head as though Tessie's words had finally sunk in. 'Did you see Cecil Smith?'

'Cecil Smith?' Tessie gasped. 'Were you out looking for him again?'

'We're still looking for him,' the guard said, winking. 'We'll let you know when we find him.'

Molly nodded, a satisfied look on her face now.

Tessie sighed and looked at the guard. 'Don't tell me she was going on about *him* again?'

The guard nodded, rolling her eyes.

'I wouldn't hold your breath about findin' him,' Tessie said quietly. 'Cecil Smith is a mystery man that nobody's ever heard tell of.'

A quarter of an hour later, Molly and Tessie were taken in the squad car, and deposited safe and sound back at the house.

'Thank God there's nobody around to see us in our nightwear,' Tessie said to the guard wryly.

'Take my advice and keep the house-key well out of her reach in future,' the guard advised. He paused, adjusting his hat. 'We've had a few of these cases over the years, and I'm sorry to say it, but they never get better – only worse.'

Tessie bit her lip. 'I don't know what we're going to do about it . . . but something will definitely have to be done.'

Chapter Twenty-Three

STOCKPORT

Tara woke late the following morning, having sat longer than she should have done, chatting with Biddy and helping to sort out a sleeping place for the new addition to the Roberts family. Angela had been very helpful, and had gone running across to Elsie's house to see if they could locate an old wooden crate or box for the dog's bed. Shortly afterwards, Elsie's son Eric had appeared back with Angela with a couple of fruit boxes, and they had spent a good hour outside nailing the boxes together and then finding an old blanket and cushion to make the little dog comfortable.

Tara was amazed at how settled Angela had become in Stockport in the few weeks she had been down in London. The young Irish girl was now very familiar with Biddy and the children – almost like one of the family – and was on friendly terms with all the boarders as well as with Elsie and her rather strange son.

Although Tara was pleased to see her half-sister so pleasant and helpful to Biddy, there was something about the young girl's naïve manner that made Tara feel slightly concerned.

She bathed and dressed now, leaving her long hair drying while she had a quick breakfast, and then she phoned Mr Pickford.

'Ah, Tara!' Her old boss's voice came on the line,

warm and delighted to hear from her. 'I hear you're back in our neck of the woods again.'

'Indeed,' Tara said. 'I had been hoping to drop in on you this week.'

'Good,' he said, 'because I have a property that's just come on the market ... something you might well be interested in.'

'A property?' Tara said, surprised. 'To be honest, I have no notion of buying anything else over in England.'

'The lodging businesses have done very well for you, haven't they?'

'Yes, indeed they have,' Tara confirmed. 'I'm absolutely delighted with them. Apart from the fact that they've more than covered the mortgages, they've definitely increased in value over the time – just as you said they would. They were an excellent buy.'

'Oh, I keep a close eye on everything while you're across the Irish Sea!' he joked. 'I believe we even have one of our staff installed there on a lodging basis.' There was a pause. 'Now, about this other property—'

'In all honesty,' Tara said, 'I would really be wasting your time even discussing another house. Is there a particular reason for you telling me about it?'

'Well,' Mr Pickford said, 'it's the fact that it was built by Bardsley – the same man who built both your houses for his own family.' He paused, and Tara could hear a rustle of papers as he checked out the details. 'It was built to a very high standard at the time ... but obviously it might need some maintenance work or modernisation carried out now.'

'Go on,' Tara said, smiling to herself and running her fingers through her damp hair to help it to dry. 'I suppose it won't do any harm to hear about it.'

'Well,' Mr Pickford's voice dropped a little, 'it's actually a small hotel ...'

'A *hotel*?' Her high, astonished tone immediately told him her thoughts on the matter.

'Hear me out now, Tara,' he said quickly. 'The main thing about it is that it's fairly close to where your houses are now, and it's not a great deal bigger than some houses. In fact, it's probably comparable size-wise with your house back in Ireland.' He gave a little officious cough. 'Why don't you drop into the office and have a look at the details? That can't do any harm.'

'Why', Tara probed, 'did you think I might be interested in a hotel of all things?'

'Timing and intuition,' he said. 'The fact you happen to be back over in Stockport the very week that it came on the market, and just a feeling I got about it . . . probably because of the building connection with your own houses.' He paused. 'It's an unusual little place at a good price, and with a lot of potential. If I was younger myself and had the confidence and courage that you have . . .'

'Mr Pickford!' Tara said, laughing. 'I think with me it was more a case of naïvety and good luck.'

'And the help and advice of your Irish builder friend at the time,' Mr Pickford reminded her. 'Mr Kennedy had enough confidence for everyone.'

There was a little silence. Tara knew that the estate agent was not aware of the details of their relationship, and had no idea that he was putting his foot in it. 'The hotel does sound interesting,' Tara agreed, 'but I'm afraid it's just not for me. Apart from the money, I have neither the time nor the interest to devote to such a project. My life is now based back in Ireland with Gabriel and Ballygrace House, and it wouldn't be fair or sensible to take on something like this from a distance. I have a lot of commitments back there . . .'

'Well,' he said now, 'I thought it was worth mentioning to you before it was extensively advertised . . . I just thought it might be a bit of a challenge to a business-woman like yourself.'

Tara smiled at the description. A *businesswoman*. It reminded her of the high aspirations she'd had all those years back when she was saving for her first house. To have been described in such a way would have thrilled her. But not now. Her life had changed in so many ways since then. Gabriel and starting a family were her first priorities.

But Mr Pickford had sown a little idea in her mind. Perhaps it would do no harm to look at the hotel. Perhaps it would do no harm to remind herself of the successful businesswoman she had once dreamed of becoming.

Chapter Twenty-Four

On Friday afternoon, Tara found herself standing outside the old Victorian building, with Mr Pickford smiling and explaining how just a bit of pointing here and a new weather-board there would make all the difference to the front of the Cale Green Hotel.

Earlier on when they met up for lunch, Tara told him that she was doing a check on both her houses for any maintenance work that needed doing. He had kindly offered to come back and inspect the houses with her, and had been very helpful noticing some small points that she would otherwise have overlooked.

After all his help, Tara felt it would have been ungracious and churlish to refuse his invitation to come and look at the hotel, which was only a short walk away from her own house.

In a few minutes, they were walking through the weed-strewn alleyway at the side of the hotel, and Mr Pickford was enthusiastically pointing out the flower-beds and rockeries that only needed a bit of reorganising and replanting to look good within a matter of weeks.

And then they turned a corner and they were faced with the back view of the hotel. Tara's hand flew to her mouth when she saw the neglected gardens with the rusting wrought-iron furniture and the crumbling window-sills and brickwork. Her heart sank even further when she saw the dilapidated, sad-looking conservatory that was barely propped up.

'A good builder . . .' Mr Pickford started.

'The amount of work,' Tara interrupted, shaking her head and sending her auburn curls rippling over her shoulders. 'Not in a million years could I consider even looking at this . . . it's not worth stepping inside!'

Mr Pickford pressed a finger to his lips thoughtfully. Then, he strode towards the back entrance to the side of the conservatory, searching for the key in his jacket pocket.

'Since we're here, I wouldn't mind a brief look inside . . . I'm curious.' After a few moments trying out the various keys for size, he got the right one and the heavy wooden and glass door creaked open.

Tara stood her ground outside, arms folded, kicking a stone here and a bit of broken glass there. What was the point of going inside such a place? It was probably no better inside than out, and anyway, she had no more interest in buying it than flying in the air.

'Tara?' Mr Pickford's voice called from somewhere in the building. 'I think you might find this interesting.'

After a few moments' silent debate, Tara allowed her good manners and fondness for her old boss to overtake her and she followed him inside. The first thing that hit her was the musty, closed-up building smell – just exactly as she expected. Then of course there was the lack of light. Where they could be seen, the windows were filthy and fly-strewn, and the heavy red velvet curtains were either half-pulled across or hanging down. Tara went over to the windows and pulled the curtains back, immediately allowing light to flood into the large reception hall, then she walked across to the tall, dark fireplace where Mr Pickford was standing.

'I know what you're thinking,' he said, smiling, 'but you've got to look beyond the obvious flaws. Just that few seconds' effort of opening the curtains has literally shed a new light on the place.' He gestured to the ornate fireplace. 'Can you imagine this on a cold winter's evening with a blazing fire? When the place is renovated and decorated, of course . . .'

Tara looked at the fireplace, at the flowers and leaves carved into the wood, and then she studied the dusty but beautiful mirror that hung over it. It was indeed impressive and a perfect first focal point for guests being brought into the function room.

'The thing is,' Mr Pickford said, heading out into the hallway, 'I know you're a young woman who appreciates the more traditional type of building, and I think that would be a huge advantage to the buyer of this place. Restoring and maintaining what's already there would be considerably cheaper than ripping everything out to modernise and obliterate the original features.' He turned back to Tara. 'The few people who have viewed it have all said it would cost too much to "do it up" or to "gut it out". Not one person has appreciated the faded beauty that could be restored quickly and cheaply.'

Tara raised her eyebrows and smiled, but she said nothing. She followed him through a door leading to the front of the hotel and into a wide corridor, her eyes taking in the original Victorian patterned floor tiles and the studded walls and low-beamed ceilings. They looked in at the two rooms on either side of the corridor – one big enough for a wedding reception and the other a restaurant and a bar – and they both told the same sad, neglected story as did the reception hall.

They moved up the black wrought-iron staircase with the polished wooden handrail to the hall upstairs, and then into the bedrooms. By the time they had viewed all fourteen bedrooms and several bathrooms, Tara knew that Mr Pickford had been right about the small hotel.

It had great potential – for the right person.

But that person most definitely was *not* Tara Fitzgerald.

*

When Gabriel phoned that evening, Tara was in two minds whether or not she should tell him about her visit to the hotel with Mr Pickford that afternoon. She felt slightly uneasy about mentioning it, although she wasn't really sure why. It had something to do with Gabriel worrying that maybe life back in Ballygrace House wasn't as exciting as Tara would like.

Tara wasn't exactly unhappy with life back in Ireland ... but there was definitely something missing – a feeling of excitement and challenge. Every day more or less followed the exact same pattern – and that was the problem. She needed more of a focus and a goal in her life – something to fill the gap when Gabriel wasn't there. The gap that a baby would have filled perfectly.

'My mother has brightened up considerably,' Gabriel told her. 'We've sorted out all the school business for William for next year, which was the main issue. And she's talked over business worries that she had – and half of the things she needn't have worried about at all. She's still living in the days when my father kept everything from her, and then they would suddenly find themselves in deep trouble. By this time she should realise that Harry has everything organised down to the last detail.' He paused. 'But that's my mother for you; if she hasn't anything to worry about – then she'll find something.'

'But she is much happier?' Tara checked.

'Definitely,' Gabriel reassured her. 'A friend of Harry's went on holiday and left them the key to their swimming-pool, so we've gone over most days and I've taught William how to swim. Mother's absolutely delighted; it's one less thing for her to worry about.' He gave a low laugh. 'Now she only has to worry about him being killed crossing the road or being struck down by lightning. We've been playing tennis in the evening, so he might even get hit by a flying tennis ball.'

'You're awful,' Tara laughed, relieved that things

sounded so much better now. 'You sound as though you've been very energetic yourself – swimming and playing tennis and everything.'

'I'm not too bad at all,' he told her. 'I got this tonic from the chemist and it seems to have pepped me up a bit. Anyway, enough about my news – how are things up in Stockport? How is Fred progressing?'

'Still improving, thank God,' Tara said, a picture of Fred wrapped around the nurse suddenly flashing into her mind. 'The physiotherapy is definitely helping, he's walking better on his own and his speech is better – all round there seems to be an improvement. He's coming home for the weekend, so that will be a big step forward.'

'That's wonderful news,' Gabriel said. His voice lowered then. 'Is he improving mentally, at all? Because that's really the big thing, isn't it?'

'Yes,' Tara said, 'it is *the* big thing.' She halted, grateful she could be honest about Fred with her husband at least. 'He's still not completely right yet, Gabriel . . . and we don't know if he ever will be. Biddy said the doctors are delighted with his progress, but that they can't give any guarantees about the future.'

She could hear Gabriel taking a deep breath. 'Maybe in time . . .'

'Yes,' Tara agreed. 'Hopefully, it's just a matter of time.'

'Now,' Gabriel said, brightening up, 'I was just thinking that after we've spent all our energy on trying to sort out other people's problems, perhaps you and I could do with a little break away on our own.'

'Really?' Tara said. 'Can you take any more time off from work?'

'I'm sure I can sort something.'

'Had you anything particular in mind?' she asked, a mixture of excitement and curiosity taking over now.

'How does Paris appeal to you? I was in a travel

agent's this morning, and we can get flights over from London.'

'Paris?' Tara was really excited now. 'I absolutely adore Paris, and I would love to go . . . but when?'

'Why not next week? While we're over in England it's easier to travel over to France. I'll have done my duty down here, and you'll have sorted out all your business in Stockport. You've already said that Fred's improving, and we can stop off in Stockport again for a few days on our way home.' He paused. 'You haven't made any arrangements with anyone for next week?'

'No, no,' she said, 'nothing of any great importance.' Tara thought fleetingly of her friend Kate and the fashion magazine trip to York. Trips like that would come around again, and Kate would understand. Besides, she hadn't actually committed herself to anything. Paris *now* with Gabriel was much higher on her list of priorities than any other plans, with anyone else.

'Good,' he said, 'that makes it much easier if the decks are clear for both of us.'

'What about our passports?' Tara suddenly thought. 'We would need to have them for France.'

'All organised! I have them with me,' he told her. 'Something made me lift them when we were packing . . . I think I must have had this idea at the back of my mind.'

'Oh, Gabriel! What a brilliant idea! I would really, really love to go to Paris.'

'I'll get back to the travel agent first thing in the morning,' he told her, 'and I'll see what can be organised for early next week. Harry will be back, and that will give you time to sort out any work that needs doing to the houses.' He lowered his voice. 'I'm going to ask the travel agent to book us something right in the centre of the city – an old, romantic Parisian hotel with a very romantic bedroom with a balcony.'

'Oh, Gabriel . . .' Tara gasped, 'I am so, so excited!

I'm going to go straight down into Stockport tomorrow and buy a guide book and a French phrase book. I might even buy some new outfits ... the weather is bound to be hotter over there, isn't it?'

'Just so long as you promise not to load us down with too many cases,' he joked. 'Actually, Tara, I've got some other news as well ... very good news.'

'What is it?' Tara asked.

'Some property my mother is signing over to me ... a very substantial house in London that my grandmother apparently owned. I don't want to say too much now. I'll tell you all about it when we're in Paris.'

'OK,' she agreed, 'but it certainly is good news.'

'I've got to go now, I've promised William that I would take him for a game of tennis before dinner. He's a real livewire and gives me quite a run over the court. *Au revoir*, darling, and I love you very much.'

'*Au revoir*, Gabriel,' Tara whispered, suddenly feeling very emotional. 'I miss you and I love you with all my heart.'

Maybe, just maybe, she thought, holding the receiver to her cheek after he'd gone, *maybe this was the time when their child would be conceived!* The child she so desperately wanted. The child that would fill all the little gaps in her life. Maybe this very special, first child would be conceived in the wonderfully romantic city of Paris. It was only when Tara was halfway up the stairs that she realised in the midst of all their talk about Paris she had forgotten to mention Mr Pickford and the visit to the Cale Green Hotel.

She shrugged to herself. Discussing romantic nights in a beautiful hotel in Paris was much more exciting than discussing a dusty, broken-down hotel that she wasn't in the least bit interested in.

Chapter Twenty-Five

CORK

Joe hesitated outside the large stone-built house, gathering his thoughts together before passing through the high iron gates and pressing the bell. He felt most uneasy about this particular pastoral visit – but knew he couldn't put it off any longer. Ridiculously, he hadn't even been sure what to wear for it. Instead of going straight from his Legion of Mary meeting, wearing his casual black-ribbed sweater over his clerical collar and shirt, he had gone back to the presbytery for the protection of his formal black jacket.

Although he had never been inside it, he knew the house well. It was one of the finest and most prestigious houses in the parish. He was well-used to Mary O'Connor speaking to him on the phone, and calling into the church office after Mass, but he had never been summoned to their home before by Eamonn O'Connor.

Mary had invited him over to the house on numerous occasions, but he had always found a plausible excuse not to be anywhere on his own with the solicitor's wife. His gut reaction and the way the dark-haired, attractive woman looked deep into his eyes, had been enough warning.

But this visit tonight was different. He had received a phone call that afternoon from Eamonn O'Connor to join him and Mary for supper and a drink.

'I'm not too sure now . . .' Joe had hedged, fumbling

for his church appointments book. 'I think I have a Legion of Mary meeting around seven o'clock.'

'It doesn't matter how late,' Eamonn had said, in his rich Kerry accent. 'We're not early-bedders.'

Joe had felt his heart sink. He wondered if Mary had told her husband that the curate knew about their unconsummated marriage – or even if she had told him about the long phone conversations she often had with Joe. This determined, businesslike manner definitely made Joe feel that there was something that the solicitor needed to discuss with him – and he was determined to discuss it tonight.

At exactly nine o'clock, Joe pressed the doorbell and stood back, unconsciously squaring his shoulders, for he was only of above-average height and build, while Eamonn O'Connor was a good six feet tall, a former rugby player some ten years older than his wife.

Within seconds the door was answered by a red-lipsticked and fragrant-smelling Mary, and Joe found himself being ushered into an elaborately decorated marble hallway which was dominated by a striking central wrought-iron staircase. Mary guided the priest into a large room to the left of the hallway.

Eamonn O'Connor was standing with his back to a white marble fireplace, in which was lit a very small fire on account of the mild summer night. The room was tastefully decorated with a greenish floral William Morris wallpaper and a pristine cream paint. A highly polished walnut cabinet filled most of the back wall, and small lacquered tables with glass and cream ornaments were dotted around the room, along with a matching collection of expensive-looking stained-glass lamps.

'Good of you to fit us in,' Eamonn said, stepping forward to shake Joe's hand.

'Not at all,' Joe replied, since it was really the only polite thing he could say.

'Over here, Father,' Mary said, motioning him to a high-backed floral chair that blended in perfectly with the wallpaper.

'Whiskey? Brandy? Port?' Eamonn said, going over to the walnut cabinet. He opened a door to reveal a wide selection of spirits.

'Umm . . . a whiskey would be just fine, thank you,' Joe said, running a finger around the inside of his stiff white collar.

Mary fluttered across to another door in the polished cabinet, her dark wavy hair and her yellow summer dress swishing past Joe as she went. She took two crystal whiskey glasses from the cupboard and handed them to her husband and then went back for a large brandy glass. 'And I think I'll have a brandy and lemonade, please, Eamonn.'

'We wanted to ask your advice,' Mary said, when they were all sitting down with their drinks in front of the fire – the men in the two armchairs on either side of the fire, and she perched in the middle of the sofa. She looked across at her husband.

'To come straight to the point,' Eamonn said, 'Mary has a proposition she would like to put to you.'

Joe, suddenly feeling alarmed, took a large mouthful of his whiskey. 'Indeed?'

'Lourdes, Father,' Eamonn said. 'She'd like to organise a church trip for families in need – and maybe get involved in fund-raising.'

Joe raised his eyebrows in interest.

'The thing is,' Mary said, moving to the end of the sofa that was nearer to Joe, 'I'm bored to death rattling around this big house all day, and I'd like to do something *useful*.'

'A job, maybe?' Joe suggested, looking from one to the other.

'No, no,' Eamonn said, looking at his wristwatch. 'It's much too restricting for her, we've been through that already. She worked as a schoolteacher before we were married – but she found it too draining and time-consuming.'

'I thought that some sort of charity work would be a good start,' Mary said, spreading out the yellow skirt of her dress on the sofa. 'Something for the less fortunate in the church. I feel in many ways I've been very lucky in my life, and I'd like to give something back.' She smiled across at her husband.

'Well,' Joe said, running his fingers through the back of his hair, 'I'm sure that Father O'Leary would find your offer very welcome. There are definitely families in need of a pilgrimage to Lourdes.'

'We thought that if the suggestion were to come from *you*, Father Flynn,' Eamonn said, 'he might take it more seriously. Also – Mary thought you and she might work together on this.' He took a gulp of his whiskey. 'You're younger and more energetic than Father O'Leary.' He motioned to the room. 'You could hold your meetings here . . . I'm out most evenings and you would have the place to yourselves.'

'Yes,' Mary said, smiling broadly at Joe now. 'We wouldn't be disturbed at all.'

There was a small silence. 'I'm sure we needn't worry about where to have meetings,' Joe said, the feeling of alarm suddenly rising inside him again.

There was a small tap on the door, and a young maid came in, pushing a gold-coloured tea trolley which held a large platter of delicately made sandwiches and a variety of home-made cakes, plus tea and coffee pots.

'That's lovely, Nora,' Mary O'Connor said, smiling at the girl. 'You can head off home now. We can see to the washing-up in the morning.'

The next half-hour or so passed with the very pleasant supper and chat about books and golfing, and the parts of Offaly where the O'Connors had relatives. Eventually, the talk came back to Lourdes.

'I thought we could start the fund-raising off immediately,' Mary said, 'with a garden party in the church grounds, with tombolas and a raffle, and that kind of thing.'

Eamonn looked at his watch again, and suddenly got to his feet. 'Have to go now,' he said, putting his cup and saucer on the trolley. 'I've arranged to meet a fellow down at the golf club.'

Joe put his own cup and saucer down now, too, and got to his feet. 'I must be going myself.'

'Not at all, Father,' Eamonn said, putting his hands on Joe's shoulders to guide him back into the chair. 'Stay and have another drink with Mary. She so enjoys your company and you have so much to sort out with all this Lourdes business.'

Joe sat back in his chair most uneasily. 'It all depends on Father O'Leary, of course,' he heard himself say rather lamely. And, as the front door closed behind Eamonn O'Connor, Joe Flynn had a definite sense of foreboding.

'I have some ideas written down already,' Mary said, going over to a small desk. 'It was really a friend of mine from Dublin who gave me the idea. She's organised several very successful pilgrimages.' She took out a notepad and came back to sit on the edge of the sofa, close to the curate.

'I think', Joe said suddenly, 'that it would give rise to gossip if we were to meet regularly in your house. You're a young, attractive married woman.'

Mary O'Connor lowered her head. 'But surely if my husband approves ... then no one else could find anything wrong in our relationship.'

Joe leaned forward in his chair, his hands clasped together. 'Can I ask you something, Mary?'

'Of course,' she said, smiling.

'Has the situation improved between yourselves ... the marital situation?'

There was a silence. 'Not really,' Mary eventually admitted. 'And I don't think it ever will. It's some kind of medical problem.'

'And how do you feel about it?' Joe said. 'Knowing that your marriage will be in name only?'

Mary shrugged. 'What can I do about it?' Tears suddenly sprung into her eyes. 'I love Eamonn in spite of it, and I know he loves me. It just means that we have to resign ourselves to a marriage without the physical side of things.'

'And what about children?' Joe asked, suddenly curious.

She took a hanky from her dress pocket. 'Thankfully, it's not something that I've been very desperate about . . . it's more the closeness that I miss between myself and Eamonn. I think that's why he felt the fund-raising idea might be a good idea.' She took a deep breath. 'He felt that you and I might make a good team – since we're in the same sort of boat.'

'Exactly what did he mean?' Joe asked, the picture suddenly becoming all too clear.

'The celibacy thing,' she whispered. 'He thought that perhaps you and I might just meet up every now and again . . .'

Joe stood up now. 'I'm sorry, Mrs O'Connor, but I don't think I can help you . . . When I took my religious vows, I took them with the intention of keeping them. I'd advise you to do the same with your marital vows.'

Mary O'Connor got quickly to her feet now, her face flushed and embarrassed. 'I think you might be misunderstanding me . . .'

'I don't think I am,' he said, walking out of the room, 'and I don't think there's any more to be said.'

He walked down the elaborate marble hallway and out of the front door.

Chapter Twenty-Six

STOCKPORT

'You'll be sure and be careful?' Biddy checked.

'Oh, we'll be grand,' Angela reassured her, a slight hint of impatience in her voice, 'we'll be absolutely grand. The walk around the park and a few goes on the swings and slides will tire them out and they'll be ready for their beds by the time we get back.'

Biddy and Elsie stood watching, arms folded, as Angela negotiated the front steps very carefully, taking Michael by one hand and little Helen by the other. Eric was waiting for them at the bottom of the steps, having come out of the back gate and around the front with Lucky, the Yorkshire Terrier, on a lead. He had been working on the dog that morning in between his household chores, and was now proudly showing how he could already get it to sit and give a paw.

'Aw . . .' Elsie whispered proudly, 'how many of the young lads nowadays would take the time to teach a dog good manners?' She pursed her lips. 'Meetin' Angela has been the makin' of our Eric . . . he's comin' right out of his shell. I can see a difference in him by the day.' She nodded approvingly. 'And I think it's done *her* the world of good an' all, bein' over here and gettin' in with a nice young fella like Eric. From what you've told me about yer own experiences, life in Ireland seems very backward to me. Very backward altogether. It don't seem a right kind of place for young girls at all.'

'I'm not too sure *where* would be the best place for young girls at all,' Biddy said thoughtfully. She had a lot on her mind at the minute, especially with Fred due home for his first weekend visit the following morning. She had worked double-hard the last few days getting ahead with all the domestic chores, so that she could devote as much of her time as possible to her husband.

'Well,' Elsie said sniffily, disappointed that Biddy hadn't joined in with the praising of Eric over the dog, 'it sounds to me as though there's nowt there for them back there at all. It sounds to me as though everythin' in Ireland in still in the Dark Ages. At least in Stockport they can hop on a bus or a train, and there's plenty of decent jobs goin'.'

'That's true,' Biddy agreed, wondering if it had dawned on Elsie how come if there were so many decent jobs going that Eric hadn't managed to find himself one yet. Elsie talked of nothing else but Eric having interviews here and interviews there, and was constantly asking Biddy if she knew if anyone like Frank Kennedy might be looking for a good, strong worker like Eric.

But in all these weeks, and having attended numerous interviews without any luck, Eric seemed quite happy spending most of his days and evenings over in the boarding-house, chatting to Angela or the younger lodgers.

Biddy watched the little group disappear around the corner now, the Yorkshire Terrier's tail distinctly tucked between his legs. Having heard how their mother had come to have the dog, the children had immediately christened him 'Lucky' – but Biddy hadn't been so sure of the name when she had come downstairs that morning to face the puddles he had left on the kitchen floor. She wasn't too happy about this at all, as the dog was a few years old and she thought it was only puppies that had accidents. Everyone had assured her that it was because the dog was in a strange, new environment and the accidents would stop when Lucky regained his confidence. Biddy certainly hoped this was the case, because if he kept having accidents like this, he might not find himself so lucky after all.

Biddy and Elsie weren't back inside the house two minutes when Tara arrived at the front door. Biddy ushered her friend into the sitting room, then asked Elsie to put the kettle on for them.

'I met Angela and the children walking with the dog to Cale Green Park,' Tara told Biddy breathlessly, having rushed down to tell her all the news about Paris. Then, when she espied Biddy's help through the crack in the door, something made her add, 'The young fellow who helps you was with them – Elsie's son. Isn't it good of him to help Angela with the dog, when she has her hands full with the children?' She took her jacket off. 'Herself and him were chatting away as if they'd known each other all their lives.'

'Oh, he's a lovely lad,' Biddy said quickly, glancing at the door as she heard footsteps approaching.

'Is it the good china cups you'll be wantin' again?' Elsie said dourly, coming in through the sitting-room door.

Biddy got to her feet, her face reddening. 'No . . . not at all. The ordinary cups and saucers will do us fine, won't they, Tara?'

'Did you think I was expecting to be wined and dined *twice* in the same week?' Tara joked. 'Of course the ordinary cups will be fine.'

'I won't be a minute,' Biddy said, following the older woman out to the kitchen.

'You go on home now,' she said to Elsie. 'There's nothing more to be done here for the time being.' She gestured around the tidy sink and spotless worktops. 'There's only the things to set for breakfast and a quick mop over the floor later tonight.' She reached into a cupboard for the large bottle of Camp coffee that she kept in especially for Tara. Then she lifted down the cake tin.

'I thought you'd be bringin' out the best china and napkins since it's your fancy Irish friend,' Elsie commented, lifting her duster coat from the back of the door.

'That was only to welcome her back from London,' Biddy said evenly, determined not to let the older woman get under her skin. 'She'd do the very same for me, if it was me visitin' her at her house in Ireland.' She set the two pink cups out on top of the two matching saucers. 'If you were to go away for a while, Elsie, then you would get the same treatment, too. It's just about making a little bit of an occasion of things now and again . . . If you can't be nice to your friends, who can you be nice to?'

Elsie's eyes narrowed. 'You've never visited her at her posh house in Ireland, have you?' She did up the top two buttons on her coat.

'No,' Biddy said, carefully measuring a teaspoon of the black liquid coffee into one of the cups. 'But that's my own fault . . . Tara and Gabriel have asked me over on numerous occasions. It's me that just hasn't got around to organisin' it.' She put the top back on the bottle, trying not to let Elsie know the raw nerve she had touched, for the mere thought of revisiting Ballygrace filled her with dread. 'You never know,' she said, forcing herelf to sound chirpy, 'when Fred's back in the whole of his health, we might take a trip over to Ireland with the kids.'

Elsie's eyebrows shot up in surprise, but she said nothing.

'So I'll be seeing you in the morning at the usual time?' Biddy checked.

'Oh, you will,' said Elsie, opening the back door, 'you will.'

'And don't forget,' Biddy reminded her, 'there's no cookin' tomorrow night. It's the chippy for the whole house!'

'Fair's fair,' Biddy said, taking a sip of her tea. She and Tara were now sitting comfortably in armchairs on either side of the gas fire. 'Frank Kennedy made no fuss when the dog wet on the blanket, and he never said a word out of place, in my hearing, anyway.'

There was a pause. 'OK,' Tara agreed reluctantly, 'he was fine on *this* occasion.'

'I really think he's learned his lesson,' Biddy said. 'And he's not been asking about you this long time. Not the way he used to ask about you, anyway.'

'Long time' was a slight exaggeration, but it was true that Frank Kennedy had toned down his interest in Tara in the few weeks since he had turned up at the hospital when Tara and Gabriel had been there. The reception he'd got from Tara seemed to have cooled his interest.

'I sincerely hope he *has* stopped asking about me,' Tara said briskly, 'because it's been an awful long time since our . . . our . . .'

'Romance,' Biddy filled in.

'Talking of *romance*,' Tara said, cleverly changing the subject, 'guess where I'm going next week?'

'Where?' Biddy asked, all ears.

'The city of romance itself,' Tara laughed, 'Paris!'

'Oh, my God!' Biddy said, her eyes lighting up. 'You lucky thing! I'd love to go there. I've always wanted to see Notre Dame, ever since seeing that film, *The Hunchback of Notre Dame.*'

Tara shook her red curls despairingly. 'Trust you to pick the one thing completely unromantic about the place!'

Biddy's eyes danced with delight. 'Maybe Paris will be where it will happen! Maybe you'll fall for a little French baby!' Then she suddenly went serious. 'You're not due your . . . "you-know-whats" when you're over there, are you? Don't tell me that it's the wrong time?'

'No,' Tara said, her voice a little lower. 'I was working it out . . . and it could just be the right time.'

'Oh, my God!' Biddy said again, delighted. 'Wouldn't it just be brilliant if you came home expectin'? Wouldn't it?'

'At this minute in time,' Tara said, 'it's the only thing in the world I really, really want to happen. I'm saying prayers and lighting candles every time I pass a church.'

'Isn't life funny,' Biddy said, her face serious again. 'I was just thinkin' about havin' Fred home tomorrow, and what I'm goin' to do.'

'What d'you mean?' Tara asked.

'Well . . . about *sex*,' Biddy said, looking awkward. 'I don't know what I should do if Fred makes any moves in that direction.' She paused. 'I wouldn't like to deprive him, especially after seeing that funny business with the nurse.' She paused again, not used to talking in such a very personal way with Tara. Not really used to talking in such a personal way to anyone since Ruby died. Even with Elsie, she found herself keeping a bit of distance where Fred was concerned.

'He's always had a very healthy appetite in that direction . . . *very* healthy, if you get me. I'm just wonderin' if he'll be the same when he comes home . . . or whether we should take it more carefully. I had thought of mentioning it at the hospital, but I didn't like to . . . especially after what that nurse told us.'

A red flush came over Tara's neck. 'I think you should just take it a step at a time,' she advised. 'You'll know yourself when it's all right . . . you'll be able to tell.'

'True,' Biddy said, nodding, 'that's true, right enough.'

Tara took a sip of her coffee now, wishing she could offer Biddy better advice, because it was indeed a tricky situation. And there was a part of her that wanted to unburden herself to Biddy about the worries she had in that department herself. But she couldn't. To talk about Gabriel in such a personal way would make her feel that she was betraying him – and that was the last thing she wanted to do.

Just then, the front door burst open as the children, the dog, Angela and Eric all came trooping in. Little Helen came rushing over to climb up on Tara's knee, while Michael went straight to his mother to show her some stones he'd found in the park.

'Oh, Tara,' Angela said airily, sticking her blond head through the sitting-room door, 'one of the women down at your house caught me as we were passing the gate, and said to tell you that you had a phone call from London, and that you'd to phone straight back.'

'Was it Gabriel?' Tara said, bouncing the little girl up and down on her knee.

'Don't know,' Angela called, heading down into the kitchen with Eric and Lucky. 'She just said you've to ring straight away.'

'Go on,' Biddy gestured excitedly to the phone in the hall, 'give him a ring back. It's probably to tell you all the news about *gay Paree*!'

Tara put Helen down on the floor, and reached for her jacket. 'I'll walk back to the house and phone,' she said. 'It's too expensive to put it on your phone bill.'

'You will not walk back,' Biddy told her. 'Go and phone Gabriel right now! I want to hear all the details.'

'OK, OK!' Tara laughed. 'I think it might be easier to bring you along with us so you don't miss anything.'

'I don't think I dare,' Biddy giggled. 'I'll have enough of that on my hands when Fred comes home for the weekend!'

Tara rolled her eyes to the ceiling. 'You get worse instead of better, Biddy Roberts!'

Elisha Mortimer's number rang and rang with no

answer. Tara hung up and tried again, to make sure she had dialled the correct number – but still there was no answer. She went into the kitchen to join the little crowd there.

'No luck?' Biddy asked.

'No answer,' Tara replied. 'I'll try again in a few minutes.' She stood now, as Lucky performed his new tricks of sitting and lying down when the serious-faced Eric gave him the appropriate command. Tara wasn't entirely impressed, as she guessed that the dog had already been taught all these things by its previous owner. Nerves at being in a new environment with new people had probably made him too frightened to obey Biddy's commands the previous night.

'Good lad, Eric!' Biddy said, clapping her hands. 'You've worked wonders with him in a few hours.'

'Oh, he's brilliant with animals, aren't you, Eric?' Angela said, looking up into his face.

Everyone gave Lucky and Eric a clap now, and Tara noticed Angela sliding her hand into Eric's and giving it a squeeze. It was just for a second – but it was long enough to tell Tara all she needed to know about their friendship. She would have to have a word with Biddy about it later, and see what her thoughts were on the subject. Not that Angela wasn't old enough to have a boyfriend or anything like that – but, given the fact she was only going to be staying a few weeks, it might be worth warning the girl not to be getting too friendly with anyone. In any case, there was something about Eric that made Tara feel that maybe he wasn't the sort of lad Angela should be getting too friendly with.

Her thoughts were interrupted when the phone rang in the hall.

'I'll get it,' Biddy said, making her way out of the kitchen door. She stood for a moment, then Tara heard her saying, 'Yes . . . this is Bridget Roberts's house.' There was a small pause, then Biddy asked: 'What hospital did you say you were phoning from?' She went quiet for a moment, then she held out the receiver to Tara, her brow creased in confusion. 'I think it's for you . . .'

Tara took the phone from her. 'Yes?' she said, her voice high with surprise at receiving a call at the boarding-house.

'Tara?' a vaguely recognisable voice said. 'Is that you, Tara?'

'Yes, it's me,' she said, knowing she should recognise the voice.

'It's Elisha . . . I've been trying to locate you for the last hour.'

'Elisha?' Tara repeated, a tight little knot coming into her throat. 'Is there something wrong?'

'It's Gabriel . . .' Elisha whispered, her voice fading away. 'It's Gabriel . . .'

'What about Gabriel? Is there something wrong with him?'

'He was playing tennis . . . and he collapsed.'

'Is he OK?' Tara asked, the knot in her throat starting to strangle her.

'The hospital,' Elisha choked, 'have just informed me that he died . . . he died . . . ten minutes ago.'

Part Two

Walls have been built against us,
but we are always fighting to tear them down,
and in fighting,
we grow,
we find new strength,
new scope.

ESLANDA GODE ROBESON

Chapter Twenty-Seven

LONDON

Tara would never forget that interminable, dark train trip down to London as long as she lived. She had sat resolutely silent for most of it, and had spent the rest of the time in the awful, claustrophobic train toilet being sick. Twice she attempted to drink cups of tea or coffee, but her throat kept closing over. Nothing that Kate Thornley could say or do helped.

Nothing that *anyone* could say or do would ever help.

As far as Tara was concerned, the whole world had just crashed in on top of her. When she had eventually taken in the dreadful, nightmarish information that Elisha had struggled to impart, she had withdrawn into herself, unable to feel or to think straight.

She had waved away offers of brandy or whiskey for the shock. Finally, she had accepted a cup of hot, sweet tea. All the while she'd felt she was dying inside.

Eventually, Biddy had guided her into some sort of action, and had taken over the arrangements. 'Tell me your friend Kate's phone number,' Biddy had gently urged, and Tara had wordlessly reached into her bag and found her small, leather-covered address book.

An hour later, a pale-faced Kate was at the boarding-house with a weekend case already packed.

'You'd be better going down to London with her than me . . .' Biddy had whispered to Kate out in the hall.

She waved her hand around. 'I have all this to see to, and Fred is due home from hospital in the mornin' . . . and anyway, I think you might get a better reception than me from Gabriel's mother . . .' She bit her lip. 'As soon as you know any news about – about the arrangements, give me a ring.'

'Of course I'll go with her,' Kate said, 'but if you want to come, if you can sort things out here, then I don't see why you shouldn't. After all, you're Tara's oldest friend.'

Biddy gave Kate a teary-eyed but grateful look. 'I don't think so . . . I don't think there would be much of a welcome for me from Mrs Fitzgerald. She never had any time for the ordinary girls in Ballygrace like me.'

'Well, you and I could book into a hotel or a bed-and-breakfast,' Kate suggested. She didn't know Biddy very well, but she knew how highly Tara thought of her.

'No,' Biddy said, her voice decisive. 'It's best if you go down with her. As soon as you let me know what's happening, then I'll make my own arrangements.'

Tara and Kate took a black taxi straight to the hospital. There the nightmare just intensified when Tara met the two doctors who had been attending to Gabriel. She was told that Elisha had had to be sent home and sedated, and that Gabriel's body would have to stay in the hospital until they completed a post-mortem in the morning.

'I'm so sorry,' the doctor had told Tara. 'But with him being so young . . .'

'*What*,' Tara whispered, her face chalk-white, '*what* could possibly have happened? He's only thirty-two years old.'

The doctor had pursed his lips, finding it difficult to meet her darkened eyes. 'Early signs', he said, 'indicate some kind of heart problem.' He paused. 'Had he any symptoms recently? Anything unusual?'

Tara shook her head. 'He was a bit run-down . . . more tired than normal. That's all.' Then her face suddenly tightened. 'Last year he had pneumonia. He took a while to recover from it . . .' Tara suddenly felt sick, the memories flooding back now. 'There was something about his heart having been weakened at the time . . . but we were told he had made a full recovery.'

The doctor nodded and patted her shoulder, an automatic gesture he was used to making with bereaved relatives. 'Hopefully, we should have some answers tomorrow.'

'Can I . . . can I see Gabriel?' Tara asked. Kate moved forward to take Tara's arm.

'Yes . . . yes, indeed,' the doctor said. 'If that's what you wish. He's across the grounds in the low, white building . . . the hospital mortuary.'

Tara's legs buckled under her at the word *mortuary*, and only Kate's firm grip and the outstretched arms of the doctor saved her from dropping like a stone on to the tiled floor.

After a few minutes she composed herself again, and began the journey down a series of corridors, out into the fresh night air, and over to the mortuary building.

The doctor left the two girls in a small waiting-room, and a short time later, Tara was brought into a large, white-painted room. There was a high bed on wheels covered in white sheets.

The doctor moved to the head of the bed to fold down the top of the sheet. Tara stepped forward to the other side, and saw the familiar blond hair of her beloved husband. The same blond hair he had shared with his sister, Madeleine.

Tara looked at his unlined face and closed eyes. He looked just as he did when he was sleeping in bed beside her.

Tentatively, she touched his cheek with a shaky hand, and gasped aloud at the marble-cool stillness of him. It was in that instant – that touch – that she suddenly realised.

The man she had loved since she was a young, naïve girl was quite, quite dead.

Chapter Twenty-Eight

STOCKPORT

'We're jinxed,' Biddy said with wide eyes. 'Me an' Tara ... we're bloody well *jinxed*!' Her face was red and swollen from all the crying she'd done over the last few hours. But it was only now, with the kids gone to bed and the lodgers gone to their Friday-night dancing in Manchester, that she could really let go and give vent to her feelings.

'Come on now, Biddy,' Elsie said, filling her boss's glass halfway up with brandy and then topping it up with dry ginger. 'You'll need to get a grip on yourself, love. This in't doin' you any good. It in't doin' you any good at all.'

Biddy shook her head, staring off into the distance. She had been sitting in the armchair, her feet tucked under her, for the last half-hour, unable to find the slightest bit of sense in all of this. 'First Fred ... and now Gabriel.' Then her hand flew to her mouth. 'An' even before that ... there was poor Madeleine! Did I ever tell you about Madeleine, Elsie? Did I tell you about the terrible car accident that killed her and Gabriel's father?'

'You did,' Elsie confirmed, 'you did. You told me it more than once before. Now, take a good mouthful of that brandy.' She poured herself another stiff one too. 'They say brandy's good for shock – and you've had one helluva shock tonight, you have. No two ways about it.'

Elsie had had a bit of a shock herself. Especially after the tense atmosphere that had been between herself and Biddy earlier on over Tara. But how was she supposed to know that only a few hours later Tara's husband was going to drop down dead? How was anyone supposed to know that?

Biddy took a drink from the glass. Just like the last one she downed, it was warm and comforting. Hopefully, it would eventually numb things and make them easier to bear. 'Poor, poor Gabriel,' she moaned, her face crumpling up again. 'He was only a young fella . . . never even had a chance to become a father . . .'

'Was they hopin' for a baby, like?' Elsie asked, curious.

Biddy nodded her head, tears dripping down her face. 'They were supposed to be going to Paris next week . . . a nice romantic holiday. Tara was hopin' that she might fall for a baby, like . . . while she was there.'

'Dear, dear . . .' Elsie said, at a loss for anything more comforting to say. 'It's a rum do altogether . . .' She took a mouthful of brandy, hoping it might help her to find the right and proper thing to say to her employer.

'The thing is,' Biddy went on, wiping the sleeve of her Fair Isle cardigan across her eyes, 'you don't expect things like this to happen to somebody like Gabriel. He was mostly a healthy kind of a fella – he did all the right things. Never smoked, didn't really drink . . . the odd glass of wine.'

'That goes for nowt, love,' Elsie said, shaking her head vehemently. 'It goes for nowt at all. If your number's up – your number's up. It's as plain and simple as that. Whether you drink or smoke, or eat or . . .' She paused now, searching for a suitable word. 'Whether you eat or sleep – if your number's up, your number's up. Plain and simple.'

'Poor, poor Gabriel!' Biddy wailed again, shaking her head. 'An' how will poor Tara cope with this?' She looked at Elsie. 'He was the love of her life . . . the one and only man she ever loved.' She paused and her face softened for a moment. 'They were like two film stars, her beautiful and him handsome. And it was like a fairy tale . . . her just an ordinary girl . . . and him one of the quality.' She nodded her head, the tears spilling again. 'Oh, there's no doubt about it – they were definitely a love-match.'

'And what about that other feller?' Elsie suddenly thought. 'That Frank Kennedy chap that often calls to the house . . . didn't you say she used to go out with him?'

'Oh, *Frank*!' Biddy wailed, suddenly moving to her feet. She lifted the glass of brandy from the table. 'I never thought to ring him . . . I'd better ring him straight away. He met Gabriel a couple of times . . . I'll have to let him know.'

Frank Kennedy wasn't stupid or completely insensitive. This was one Irish funeral he would not attend. He knew that under no circumstances would his presence be welcome or even tolerated.

'I'll do whatever I can to help out,' he told Biddy quietly. 'I'll drive you to the airport and I'll go in and out to the hospital to see Fred while you're away. And if there's anything at all you can think of that might just make things a bit easier for Tara – then I'd be more than happy to do it.'

'Oh, you're very good, Frank,' Biddy told him, her voice trembling. 'You're always there when we need you.'

'Do you think it might be received well if I sent a wreath or some flowers?'

'And why wouldn't it?' Biddy said. She took a quick gulp of brandy. 'In fact, I'll get a wreath for you in Tullamore when I'm getting my own.' She actually had no idea how Tara would react to flowers or any other kind of contact from Frank Kennedy, but there was no point in worrying about it now. She would judge the situation when she got over there.

'How is Tara coping?' Frank asked.

'God alone knows,' Biddy told him, tears welling up in her eyes again. 'She was in the most desperate state when she left here – didn't know what had hit her. None of us did.' She took another mouthful from the glass. 'He was only a young fellow – he'd hardly lived any life.' She paused. 'Do *you* think we're jinxed, Frank? Me and Tara?'

Frank hesitated for a moment. 'No,' he said quietly. 'You've both just had terrible things happen to you at this time of your lives. We all have to face these things sometime or other.' He halted, thinking back to when Tara had left him and his whole world had come crashing down, remembering how she'd taken away the final shred of hope he'd clung to when she married the young, handsome Gabriel Fitzgerald – the man who had died only hours ago. He reached over and patted Biddy's shoulder.

'Things will improve . . . the way Fred is improving. It might not seem like it now, but better days will come again.'

'Do you think so, Frank?' Biddy whispered, not sure about it at all. 'Do you really think so?'

'I don't think so,' Frank replied, 'I *know* so.'

Chapter Twenty-Nine

In the wake of Gabriel's death, the big event of Fred coming home for the weekend turned out to be more of a problem than a celebration. Most of it was caused by Biddy sitting up half the night, long after Elsie had gone home and Angela had gone to bed. She had made herself some strong tea to help take away the worst effects of the brandy, and then, feeling the need for someone to talk to, she got her phone book out. She thumbed through the pages, thinking of the people whom she knew kept late hours and wouldn't mind her calling at this time. She put the book down, deciding that her first port of call would be Lloyd, whose number she knew by heart. She hadn't heard from him in a while. In fact, she hadn't heard from him since that awkward weekend a short while ago. The memory of that visit still brought a hot flush of embarrassment to her face and neck, and she hadn't managed to pluck up the courage to phone him since.

But she had more than a good reason to phone him now. Not that he'd known Gabriel as such – but he certainly knew Tara. He wouldn't be expected to go over for the funeral or anything, but he might want the address in Ireland to send a sympathy card or a wreath to. Whatever his situation, she knew Lloyd would want to know about Gabriel having died.

She dialled his number now – but there was no answer.

After about five minutes of constantly redialling the

number, she gave up and decided to make herself a hot brandy to help her sleep. And then, just as she was heading up the stairs, some of the lads came back in from the dance. Seeing the drink in her hand, they insisted she came back downstairs to join them, as they had a few bottles of beer they would drink to keep her company.

With the drink they had already taken, the whole group became quite maudlin, talking of young people they knew who had died in all kinds of ways. They recounted drowning incidents, motorbike accidents, talked in hushed tones about known suicides, and then gradually moved on to talk in slurred tones about death and the meaning of life in general.

As a result, Biddy found herself rushing about like a headless chicken the next morning, with the ambulance and Fred due at the door at twelve o'clock.

'I was right worried when you didn't answer the back door,' Elsie said, bustling in through the front door now, holding a pint of milk in each hand, which she'd picked up from the front doorstep. 'Lucky was barking his bleedin' head off, an' I knew if you were in the kitchen you'd have heard him . . . so I thought I'd better come around to the front door and give the bell a good long ring.'

'Thank God you did!' Biddy told her, stopping now to take the time to tie her pink quilted dressing-gown properly. 'It's nearly nine o'clock and there's not a movement in the whole house, not even a sound from the kids.'

'You all right?' Elsie said, looking closely at her.

Biddy shook her head, and immediately wished she hadn't, because it made her feel dizzy. 'I couldn't get to sleep at all last night.' They both started to move down the hallway towards the kitchen. 'I kept goin' over and over everything in my mind. Picturing poor Gabriel lying in his coffin . . .' Her voice cracked a little now.

'Now, don't be thinkin' like that again this morning,' Elsie told her, putting the milk bottles down on the table. She went over to the sink to fill the kettle to make them both a cup of tea. 'Today's meant to be a happy day in this house. Fred is comin' home and it's the best thing that's happened in a long time.' The older woman's face broadened into a smile. 'Oh, can you imagine how the two little 'uns will be when they see their dad comin' through the door?' She clapped her hands. 'I can't wait to see the looks on their little faces, I can't! It's been a fair exciting week for them, gettin' a new little dog, an' now their dad comin' home from hospital.'

And then, right on cue, Lucky started his high-pitched barking, making Biddy hold her hands over her ears.

'Shall I get him some of them dog biscuits to shut him up?' Elsie suggested.

'Please,' Biddy said, reaching across the table for two of the cups and saucers that Angela had set for the breakfast the previous night. 'My head's killin' me, Elsie,' she said. 'I had a hot brandy after you left, meanin' to go straight to bed, and then some of the lads came in, and I think I might have had another one too many . . .'

Elsie patted her arm, then opened the back door and threw a handful of the biscuits in Lucky's direction. 'It's no wonder,' the older woman said sympathetically, 'with all you've had to put up with. It's no wonder you would need a little drink to help you to relax.' She lifted the battery-operated igniter for the gas cooker, and after a few clicks lit the grill.

'But that's the trouble,' Biddy said, taking two slices of Mother's Pride from the bread bin. 'It didn't help me to sleep. I lay awake until it was light goin' over and over everythin' in my mind.'

'You'll feel better once you've had a nice cup of tea

an' a slice of toast an' a couple of aspirins,' Elsie told her. 'You'll feel as right as rain after it.'

Twenty minutes and two cups of tea later, Biddy felt a little bit more human and, leaving Elsie to start sorting out the breakfast things, she took herself back upstairs to get washed and dressed. She looked in her wardrobe and quickly decided on a pair of blue stretch slacks and the short-sleeved jumper from the blue and yellow twinset. It was always easier to work about the house with short sleeves, and it was a nice bright outfit to welcome Fred home with. She sat at her dressing-table mirror to tidy up her hair and put on a bit of make-up. The sight that met her eyes in the mirror was not encouraging.

Her face was blotchy and puffy, and her eyes were vaguely bloodshot. Definitely not the way she wanted Fred to see her for his first homecoming in months. She reached into her make-up bag for the Pan Stick foundation that hid a multitude of sins. Ruby had introduced her to it back in the days when Biddy suffered from the odd lingering teenage spot, and she had used it ever since.

She mechanically dotted circles of the honey-beige foundation on her forehead, chin and cheeks, and then carefully rubbed it in with the tips of her fingers to cover the blotchy tiredness. Then she finished off with a layer of a creamy-coloured face powder to set it all. Within a few minutes she looked a good deal better on the outside than she felt on the inside. A few strokes of mascara and a quick slick of pink lipstick and she was ready.

As she gave herself a final once-over in the full-length mirror, her gaze came to rest on her hair – or more precisely the dark roots that were starting to show through the blond. She lifted her fringe to check how bad it looked, and she could see it was going to be very bad. Her own blackish-brown hair was a very obvious contrast to the Marilyn Monroe lookalike. And that was after only a few weeks. She was going to have to find the time to get the roots touched up soon, as Ruby used to do every three or four weeks.

Ruby, however, had only had herself to look after. She hadn't had any kids running about or regular visits to the hospital to fit in, the way that Biddy now had. Biddy's eyes narrowed as she stared at herself in the mirror. How could she go back to Ballygrace village sporting peroxide-blond hair with dark roots? She'd be the talk of the place. Well, she was probably going to be the talk of the place in any case – but there was no point in drawing more attention to herself than was necessary. She now looked herself straight in the eye in the mirror, and made a decision.

The blonde would have to go.

'There we are now,' Elsie said, folding the red and white checked tea towel and putting it over the bar of the cooker, 'sausages and bacon and black an' white pudding keepin' warm in the oven, and a loaf of pan bread all buttered and covered on the table. All that's left to do is fry the eggs when we hear any of the lads movin' upstairs.' She lifted the tea towel from the cooker, shook it out and folded it all over again. She looked around the kitchen. 'That's everythin' more or less done and dusted before Fred arrives.' She smiled. 'Didn't I tell you that we'd get everything put to rights in a half an hour?'

Biddy smiled gratefully. 'Thanks, Elsie, you're a saint – I couldn't have faced frying bacon and sausage this morning, far less sit and eat it. It would just have turned my stomach.'

'Have the aspirins started to work on you yet?' the older woman enquired.

'I think so,' Biddy said. 'My head certainly doesn't feel as bad as it did earlier . . . but I'll go easy on the fry myself. I think I might just stick to plain toast for the morning. I'm still a bit queasy.'

After her own breakfast, Biddy tidied around and then, finding it hard to settle, took Lucky for a quick walk around Cale Green Park. Her mind was so weary and tired with thinking about Gabriel and Tara that it was easier to do something than to sit and think.

All the little pleasantries that Biddy usually enjoyed in the park totally escaped her this morning. The trees and flowers gave her no pleasure and she didn't even think to glance at the nice big houses to see what colour their doors were painted or what kind of blinds they had. Her heart was too heavy with sadness and worry to notice such trivial things.

When she got back, she checked on Michael and Helen, and, seeing they were still asleep, she went back downstairs to phone for an appointment about her hair.

'Why don't you come down right now?' the hairdresser suggested. 'We've had a wedding crowd cancelled at the last minute, so we're empty.' Her voice dropped. 'It seems the groom did a runner – went off with the bride's mate last week and with all the carry-on they forgot to let us know until this morning.'

'Oh, my God!' Biddy said.

'There was a bit of a note scribbled and pushed through the shop door,' the hairdresser went on, 'so we're left high an' dry with no customers for the first few hours.'

'How long would it take to colour my hair back to brown?'

'Back to *brown*?' the hairdresser repeated in a shocked voice. 'But the blond suits you lovely – it gives you a bit of a lift, like.'

'I've made up me mind,' Biddy told her firmly. 'And I have a funeral to go to over in Ireland and I want to be back to my old self for it.'

'Okey-dokey,' the hairdresser said, in a none-too-impressed voice. 'I have to say that I thought the blond gave your face a real lift . . . but it's your hair after all.' There was a pause. 'How long will it take you to get down?'

'Ten minutes,' Biddy said, a relieved smile on her face.

As luck would have it, the two children suddenly appeared at the top of the stairs in their pyjamas, all excited and talking about their daddy coming home. Biddy set to, organising boiled eggs for their breakfast and checking that Angela was up and about to dress and entertain them until she came back.

Twenty minutes later she rushed into the hairdresser's shop. 'I came as quick as I could,' she said breathlessly, taking off her light coat, 'but it's been one of those days from the beginning, and it can only get worse. The only good thing is that there was a bus waiting at the stop so at least I didn't have to stand and wait.'

'I have the colour all mixed for you,' the girl said, 'and we'll have you back to your old self before you know it, an' out of the place in under an hour.' She held a pink, grubby-looking nylon gown out for Biddy to put her arms into. 'Sorry about the state of the gown, but we're still waitin' on that bleedin' useless commercial traveller to bring our new ones.' She pointed to a black stain on the front. 'It's only hair dye, but it looks shockin' bad, don't it? And washin' don't make a bit of difference once the dye gets a hold – I've used everythin' on them.' She tied the gown in a bow at the back of Biddy's neck. 'An' it's tea with milk and two sugars, if I remember correctly?'

'Oh, lovely!' Biddy said, giving the girl a grateful smile. 'The way I'm feelin' now, I could just do with an hour of sitting down and being looked after.'

The hairdresser put a small towel over her customer's shoulders and tucked it in around the neck. 'You said it was a funeral you were going to?'

'Yes,' Biddy said, the smile sliding from her face. 'A lad I know from back in Ireland . . . the husband of my best friend.' Her voice dropped. 'I'm really dreadin' the funeral . . .'

The hairdresser clucked her tongue and shook her head. 'Oh, it's a right bad do when it's a younger person, isn't it?'

Biddy nodded, tears coming into her eyes.

'It's bad news all round this mornin',' the hairdresser said, lifting a rather battered-looking *Woman's Weekly* from the pile on a nearby chair and giving it to Biddy. 'First the weddin' being cancelled due to that bastard of a groom and a bitch of a friend – an' now this news about your funeral.' She patted Biddy on the shoulder. 'I don't know what the world's comin' to lately, I don't.'

The hairdresser was true to her word. Biddy was out and rushing up the hill for the bus back home in less than an hour. She glanced in the shop windows every so often, checking her hair and feeling exactly the same as she'd felt when she'd first gone blonde. It was as though it was a stranger looking back at her and not her own reflection. She hadn't realised how used to the light hair she'd actually got.

Well, she thought, she'd just have to get used to it being brown again, for that was the way it was going to stay from now on.

As she walked along, she wondered if Fred would notice any difference in her hair this time, because she hadn't been at all sure if he'd noticed when she'd gone blonde. Then she wondered what Lloyd would think, were he to see it. She was sure he had preferred her blonde. Suddenly, Biddy felt overwhelmingly guilty for thinking all these silly, trivial things about her hair when poor Gabriel was lying dead in a coffin down in London. Tears came rushing into her eyes at the thought of him, and of how terrible a person she must be to be thinking of her hair colour.

She was distracted from her thoughts when a 92 bus came over the hill. Biddy took a deep breath, tucked her handbag under her arm, and ran hell for leather to catch it.

Chapter Thirty
LONDON

Tara lay staring into the last dregs of darkness, wondering how she was going to face the new day that lay ahead. How she was going to face *all* the new days that lay ahead without Gabriel for the rest of her life.

She turned her face back into the pillow, still damp from her tears from several hours ago. Her head ached from all the thinking and all the crying. Days and days of it, years and years of it to come . . . and she had to face it all without her precious Gabriel.

Several hours later, there was a knock at her bedroom door, and it was only when she woke with a start that Tara realised she had actually slept. The bedroom was now streaming with light, and she was startled when she looked at the clock and saw that it was nearly nine o'clock.

'Tara?' a young, hesitant voice called from outside the door.

'Yes?' she called back.

'It's me – William. Can I come in, please?'

Tara pulled herself to a sitting position in the bed, checked that her white cotton nightdress was buttoned up to the neck, then pulled the bedclothes up high under her arms.

'Come in, William,' she called in the thin, broken voice she had been left with since Gabriel's death.

Her young brother-in-law opened the door and then stood, unsure of what to do. Since his older brother had died, the world he was used to and confident in had suddenly changed. Now he was unsure of everything.

'It's OK,' Tara said, sensing his awkwardness, 'you can come right in.'

'I wondered', he said, coming to stand at the foot of the heavy wooden bed, 'if I could travel to Ireland with you in Gabriel's car?'

Tara suddenly sat bolt upright. 'Gabriel's car?' she repeated, her brain struggling to make sense of what the boy was asking.

'For the . . . funeral,' he said quietly. 'I wondered if I could travel with *you* to the funeral.'

A mixture of emotions flooded through Tara at the mention of that awful word, *funeral*. Anger was the thing she felt most strongly. It was the emotion she was becoming much too familiar with as the hours and days passed. She took a deep breath and, for the boy's sake, fought the feelings back. 'I'm not really sure how I'm going to be travelling to Ireland,' she told him truthfully. 'I haven't really thought about it.'

The boy looked at her with dark-ringed eyes. Eyes that looked much older than his ten years. 'I guessed you might want to take the car back to Ireland with you, with it being a special edition and everything. Gabriel said it would be hard to get another one the same.' The two brothers had often talked about cars and motorcycles – Gabriel always trying to fill the gap that an interested father would have filled. Harry tried, and made a good stepfather, but it wasn't the same as a real, blood relation.

Tara nodded her head, vaguely realising that she would have to start making decisions about what was going to happen next in this awful sequence of events. Then, her mind automatically flitted away from the terrible darkness, and she found herself staring at the young boy, searching his face for traces of Gabriel. Little familiar bits of her husband that she might comfort herself with. But there was precious little of Gabriel physically in the boy, and, with the same dark hair, much more of an unsettling resemblance to his father. The father whose obsession with Tara had nearly ruined her life.

William did, however, have some of Gabriel's mannerisms and, for a young boy, his eyes had that same contemplative look that reminded her so much of his brother.

'Are you all right, Tara?' William whispered in a low voice, feeling a bit weird with the way his sister-in-law was looking at him. 'Are you feeling all right?'

'I'm grand,' she said, running her hands over her hair. 'I was just thinking how late it is . . . and how I should be up and about. I have so many things to do.' She paused, and forced her lips into something resembling a smile. 'I'll let you know about the car, William . . . as soon as I've had time to think about it.'

'Thanks, Tara.' Then a thought occurred to him, and he suddenly brightened up. 'Maybe we'll all be going on a plane – I hadn't thought of that. It would be much quicker, wouldn't it?'

Tara clenched her teeth tightly together, reminding herself that he was only a child, and one she was very fond of. His innocent chatter about cars and aeroplanes was harmless. This was his way of coping with it all. And wasn't it merciful that he could find something new and exciting in the midst of his only brother's death? 'I'll chat to you about it all later,' she told him now as visions of dark-wooden coffins being lifted into a plane slithered into her mind. 'When I feel I'm . . . brave enough to think about it all.'

William turned towards the door. He paused with his hand on the doorknob. 'It's very hard for me to know

I'll never see Gabriel again. But I think it's even worse for you, Tara . . . isn't it?'

Tears flooded into her eyes once again and a terrible weakness washed over her. She suddenly felt much too tired to face what lay in front of her today.

'Yes,' she said simply, tears now coursing down her cheeks. 'Yes, William – it's very, very hard indeed.'

Chapter Thirty-One

BALLYGRACE

The lawns of Ballygrace House were clipped as short as Shay Flynn could get the new and very modern lawnmower to manage. The hedges had been given yet another trim, even though Shay and Mick had cut them the previous week. Every bed in the house had been made up with the best freshly ironed linen sheets that Tessie and Kitty could lay their hands on. There wasn't a table or ornament in the house that hadn't been washed or polished, and the grand piano had such a high sheen on it that you could see your face in it.

The larder was stocked to capacity. The fresh meats and the cooked meats and the loaves of thin sliced bread for sandwiches would be delivered from the shops as soon as they were needed. Everything was left as late as possible to make sure it was at its very freshest for Tara and the crowd arriving from England in the next day or so. Anything that could be done to make things easier for her had been done. But even as they sweated over ovens of soda bread and struggled to push lawnmowers against the grain uphill – they knew nothing would make a damn bit of difference. They knew there was not a single thing they could do to bring Gabriel Fitzgerald back.

After waving Mick and Kitty off to pick up fresh milk and cream, Shay and Tessie sat down for a well-earned cup of tea and a bite to eat in the large kitchen of Ballygrace House.

'Well, the one bit of good news in all this terrible business', Tessie Flynn said, 'is that we'll have Angela back home faster than we expected. I didn't expect to miss her as much as I do.' She finished the last mouthful of tea left in the cup. 'She'll be a great help during this terrible time.'

'Poor feckin' consolation,' Shay said, walking over to put his empty cup in the sink. 'A young man in the prime of his life dead, an' all you can say is that it'll be nice havin' Angela back home for the funeral.' He gave a loud sigh, then folded his *Irish Independent* in half and threw it down on the kitchen table.

'That's some way to be talkin' about your daughter, isn't it?' said Tessie. 'That's a nice way to be goin' on! You'd think you'd be glad to see her back safe and well at home with all the bad things that are goin' on in the world.'

'We'd have seen her soon enough, and anyway, you were glad enough to see the back of her, the way she was carrying on,' Shay reminded his wife. 'She was like a bag of cats before she went – she was like a feckin' prickly briar.'

'There's no need to exaggerate,' Tessie said, sweeping the milk jug and sugar bowl up from the table and into the pantry. 'Angela's not the worst.' She rinsed a dishcloth under the tap, wrung it out hard and then came back to wash over the brown-checked oilcloth on the table.

There was a small silence as Tessie viciously swished the cloth back and forth.

'It's gettin' to the point', Shay eventually said, his voice suddenly cracked and weary, 'where you can't be sure of anythin' or anyone anymore. Who would have expected this to happen to Gabriel? Not a sign of bad health about the man, and then he suddenly goes and drops down dead.'

Tessie halted her cleaning and sat down on one of the chairs. 'It's terrible,' she whispered, 'I can't believe it . . . a fine fellow like Gabriel Fitzgerald. Poor Tara . . .'

'But I don't understand the feckin' *meaning* of it all!' Shay stated, his voice rising with agitation. 'Here we are strugglin' with an oul' woman of over eighty years of age who's lost all sense and knowledge, but who is hale an' hearty – and there's a young, fit man snuffed out like a candle. Just like that!' He clicked his fingers. 'Where's the meanin' in all of that, I ask you?'

'Well,' Tessie said slowly, 'I suppose when we can't find any answers, then that's where we have to turn to our religion and the Church.'

'Religion and the Church?' Shay repeated incredulously. 'Religion and the Church? Don't make me laugh! Since when did the Church ever have the answer to feckin' anythin'?' His lips tightened as though he had a bad taste in his mouth.

'Shay Flynn!' Tessie said, her face aghast. 'How can you say such a thing? And you with a son in the priesthood.'

Shay pointed towards the door. 'Go down,' he said, 'go down the road there to Father Purcell and ask him if he has any answers to all of this. Go down and ask him and see what he says – see what feckin' rubbish about God he'll try to palm you off with, because he doesn't know the answers himself.'

'Things like this are a test of our faith,' Tessie said, her voice low and fearful. She had never ever heard Shay coming out with this kind of talk about his religion before. She knew he wasn't the best Catholic going, but she'd always thought he was a long way from the worst.

'A test, you say?' Shay came back with, up on his feet and pacing the floor now. 'A test? More like a torture –

a feckin' hell on earth! What kind of God would allow the terrible things to happen that we've seen over the years? What kind of God would let what happened to poor Fred Roberts over in Stockport happen?'

'Shay—' Tessie tried to interrupt, but there was no stopping him.

'Don't talk to me about God,' he went on. 'If you ask me, God's the biggest feckin' cod of them all!' Then suddenly there were tears streaming down his face – a thing Tessie had never witnessed in all their married years. 'How many more people are we going to have to bury before their time?' he demanded. 'Sure, the whole Fitzgerald family have nearly been wiped out – for all we know, it could be Tara next!'

'For God's sake, Shay!' Tessie, now alarmed, came over to put her arms around him. 'Don't let things get in on you like this . . . don't be—'

Suddenly Shay's head was in his hands, and his shoulders were heaving up and down with racking sobs. Tessie pulled him against her and rocked him in her arms like a child. 'I know,' she whispered into his grey-flecked, curly hair, 'I know what you're thinkin'. I know all this business with Gabriel must have started you rememberin' your poor young mother and your poor young first wife.' She kissed the top of his head as she used to kiss the children when they were younger. 'I know you must be remembering two women who died young in your life, your mother and Joe and Tara's mother who died before their time.'

For the next ten minutes Shay Flynn let all the anger and frustration seep out of his body, until he was silent.

Silent with the memories of all those women that Tessie had just mentioned. And heartbroken with the memory of the one she never knew about. Ruby Sweeney – the woman Shay would mourn until the day he died.

Shay was back weeding and raking around outside when Mick and Kitty returned from the shops. Mick lifted the bags inside and left the two women sorting things out while he went outside to join his brother.

'I had the strangest thing happen while ye were away,' Tessie said in a low voice to her sister-in-law. 'Shay broke down in bits over Gabriel Fitzgerald.'

'Did he, God love him?' Kitty asked, her brows knitted in concern.

'Not a bit like him,' Tessie said, taking the milk and cream and putting it in the door compartment of the big fridge. 'Not a bit like him at all.' She wiped her damp hands on the blue and white striped apron.

'Ah, sure, it's hitting everybody,' Kitty sighed, sitting down at the big kitchen table. 'We don't know whether we're coming or going, none of us – and God alone knows what Tara's going to be like.' Her eyes filled up, and she searched in the pocket of her pink cardigan for a tissue. 'She's lost everything now . . .'

'The only consolation', Tessie said, checking that the kettle had enough boiled water in it for a pot of tea, 'is that she's young enough to start all over again.'

Kitty pursed her lips. 'She'll never find another man like Gabriel Fitzgerald.'

'No . . . no,' Tessie hastily agreed, feeling that she'd just put her foot in it. 'We all know that Gabriel was the finest . . . I was only meanin' . . . I was just tryin' to find somethin' hopeful to say.' She scalded the teapot now with boiling water, and then put three spoons of tea leaves into it.

'I don't know if it's better or worse that they have no family,' Kitty said in a low voice. 'I only know from my own experience. I'd no family and I felt very, very lonely when my first husband died.'

'There's no better way,' Tessie sighed. 'When ye have childer you do nothing but worry about them when you're on your own.' She paused. 'But I suppose it does give ye less time for broodin' over things.'

A fresh rush of tears suddenly came into Kitty's eyes. 'Poor Tara – she was fierce desperate for her and Gabriel to have a child, and now it'll never happen . . .'

'I didn't know,' Tessie said. 'I often wondered if they were ever going to have a family . . . but it wasn't the sort of thing I would ever have spoken to her about.'

'In the last year or so, she had great hopes,' Kitty confirmed, 'but it just never happened. It wasn't meant to be.' She dabbed her eyes now, deciding she'd said enough. She'd said more than she really should have said to Tessie, and to reveal the rest of Tara's circumstances would have been to break her confidence completely.

Chapter Thirty-Two

STOCKPORT

A hush descended upon the little crowd gathered outside the boarding-house in Maple Terrace as the ambulance driver and his attendant got out and opened the back doors. Then, with Helen gripped firmly by one hand and Michael by the other, Biddy stepped forward to welcome her husband home.

Very slowly, the slimmed-down figure of Fred appeared at the doors, and then the two ambulance men moved to either side of him to take an arm each. The man who had once danced around the wrestling ring slowly plodded, one step at a time, down the metal steps.

'Thank God!' Biddy said, letting go of the children's hands to put her arms around her husband's neck. 'Thank God you're home at last.' And as his arms tightened around her, she could feel his heart thumping and his body trembling just a little, and she realised what a big ordeal this was for him, too.

'You're different again,' he said, stepping back to get a better look at her. Biddy held her breath, and waited to see if he could work out what it was. His eyes narrowed in concentration. 'Your *hair*!' he said. 'It's gone brown again . . . am I right?'

'Do you like it?' she asked anxiously, holding out a strand.

'Like it?' he said, his eyes shining. 'I love it!' His arms

wrapped round her again. 'But then I love *everything* about you.'

Biddy clung tightly on to him. It was fine – everything was grand now. She could cope. Fred's brain was coming back to normal – the hair proved it. She buried her face in his neck. She would be able to manage the funeral and helping Tara and everything – now that Fred was getting back to normal.

After a few moments, they let go of each other, and then Fred very carefully stooped to let the children give him a hug and a kiss too. Michael was all over his father with great excitement, testing him with friendly punches and finally coming to a halt wrapped around his legs. Little Helen seemed less sure – as though she didn't quite remember who this man was who looked a bit like her daddy in hospital.

Elsie sent a reluctant, embarrassed Angela down to bring the children into the house, to let Biddy and Fred take their own time coming up the steps. Angela felt awkward because she'd never met Fred before his accident, and she didn't know what to do or say. The children ran to take her hand, and the minute she saw Fred's beaming, friendly face she knew they were going to get on just fine.

In spite of the bad start to the day, Biddy had everything ready and waiting for Fred's visit. The dining-table had been pulled from under the window into the centre of the sitting room, and was laden with all Fred's favourite things for an afternoon tea. There were warmed-up sausage rolls and fresh barmcakes filled with roast pork or sliced cheese and thin slivers of fresh onion, and a cake stand filled with French fancies, fresh-cream chocolate éclairs and vanilla-cream slices. All the nice creamy things he loved, and the things that would help to restore him to the big, burly man that Biddy had got used to cuddling into at night.

Before his accident she had worried about Fred getting too heavy, because apart from all his muscles, he had to keep a certain weight on to be any good in the ring, and he had always bordered on being described as fat. She couldn't wait to get him back to his old, fighting weight. He could get as fat as he liked for all Biddy cared now – just as long as he was her same old Fred.

'Tara's husband . . .' Fred said, his head nodding slowly. 'The blond Irish fellow, you say?'

'The fellow that came to visit you with Tara a few weeks ago in hospital,' Biddy reminded him. 'The time that Frank Kennedy dropped in unannounced.'

He took a drink from the pint glass of weak lager shandy that Biddy had made. He had always enjoyed a pint or two of lager in the evenings, and Biddy wanted everything about their Saturday nights in to be like the old Saturday nights in.

There was a little pause. 'And how did you say he died?'

Biddy shrugged her shoulders. 'Just dropped dead.' She clicked her fingers. 'Just like that! Seemingly, he had some sort of heart complaint that nobody knew anything about.' She paused. 'Although I think Tara knew there was something wrong – she was worried about him being unusually tired.'

'It's a bad do, isn't it?' Fred said thoughtfully. 'It's a right bad do when somebody of our age dies . . . especially if you know them.'

'Shockin',' Biddy said, taking a sip of her sherry. 'Desperate shockin' altogether.'

'And you say you and the blondey fellow went to school together?' he checked. 'Back in Ireland, was it?'

Biddy bit her lip. 'Yes,' she said quietly, 'it was back in Ireland.' She raised her sherry glass and finished it off in one mouthful, telling herself not to worry about Fred not remembering Gabriel again. After all, it wasn't as if he had known him very well in the first place.

Chapter Thirty-Three

LONDON

Who had made the arrangements, and how most of them had come to be made, Tara could never really remember. There were all sorts of people involved including Elisha's sister and close friends in London and the family solicitor. Then of course Harry had flown back early from America to quietly organise things, help throw a cloak of calmness on everything, and soak up the worst of Elisha's hysteria. All she knew was that it was decided that Gabriel would be flown home to Ireland the following week for burial back in Ballygrace cemetery.

During the first few days following Gabriel's death, Tara discovered that up until now she had been shielded from the awful but practical details that had to be addressed after the death of a loved family member.

There was the matter of the coffin. What type of wood was required? What type of casket lining? What inscription should go on the brass plate on the top of the coffin? How would she like the deceased to be attired in the funeral? And the question that was asked in a bare whisper – what price would she like to pay?

Every time she thought of the polished wooden coffin, her mind would go haywire. How could her living, breathing, wonderful Gabriel be put in this and then taken away from her for ever?

And then her mind would start repeating over and

over again: *Gabriel, Gabriel! Where are you? Where are you? Come back! Come back and help me . . . tell me that this is all a big mistake. Come and help me to make some sense of all of this.* But all too quickly she had come to realise that there would be no answer. Just a big, empty black silence. The biggest silence that she would ever feel in her life.

Tara was almost horror-struck, never realising that all these dreadful, dreadful details were part and parcel of the burial process. That in the middle of trying to make some sense of this terrible nightmare, she was to be plagued by decisions about all these ghoulish but necessary things.

As a young girl, she had never given a thought to all the practical details when her granda had died. Up until now she had known nothing whatsoever about them. She thought back and remembered that all the arrangements had been made by her Uncle Mick and her father. But that was different – *very* different. Whilst at the time she'd been devastated, she now realised it was because it was the first time death had visited her. Her mother had died when Tara was a baby, so there was nothing to remember there.

And suddenly *now*, she could appreciate the fact that her granda was an old man who had come to the end of a full life. She could see now that everything had been in the natural order of things. But that was definitely not the case with her beloved Gabriel.

There was another vivid memory that stood out in her mind, of arguing with Elisha about exactly *where* in Ballygrace cemetery Gabriel would be buried.

'But *surely*,' Elisha had said, holding her head in her hands, 'Gabriel should be buried with his father and sister? Surely that would be the right thing to do?'

'No,' Tara had said emphatically, 'I do not agree. Gabriel is my husband, and I want a new plot for him – one that I can join him in, when the time comes.'

After a long and painful battle with her mother-in-law, Tara had eventually won her point on this. She had no problem with him being buried beside poor Madeleine, but under no circumstances would her beloved Gabriel be buried anywhere near his father.

Chapter Thirty-Four

STOCKPORT

On Monday morning, Biddy lay in bed reflecting over the weekend. It had been the busiest one she could ever remember since she'd been running the boarding-house on her own. And it had been one of the saddest weekends she could remember with the dark cloud of Gabriel's death hanging over them.

But in spite of it all, there had been good bits amongst the bad. The children had been delighted to have their father back, and after being initially wary of Fred, little Helen had ended up falling asleep in his lap on Saturday night. Biddy hadn't let him carry her upstairs or anything like that, but it was another sign of family life returning to normal.

And then there had been the best bit of the weekend – their first night back together in their own bed. Definite proof of Fred's recovery.

Biddy blushed every time she thought of it. As soon as they were alone in the bedroom, Fred couldn't keep his hands off her. And his hands knew exactly where they wanted to go, and he wasn't taking no for an answer. Not that there was any reluctance on Biddy's part – far from it. She had gone months without any kind of manly comfort – and she had sorely missed it.

She had helped him to undo the buttons on his shirt and then unbuckle his belt, and had thanked God inwardly for Fred's easy-going nature. Most men she knew would have been very frustrated at not being able to do the simplest task, such as fastening clothes or cutting an even slice of bread by themselves – but not Fred. He just smiled and kept plugging away until he mastered it or got someone to do it for him. If anything, he was even more placid than he had been before the accident.

Biddy thought back to Saturday night and smiled. No woman would have described Fred as *placid* when they eventually got him undressed and into bed. He had made loud appreciative noises at Biddy's black brassiere and knickers set with the embroidered red roses placed exactly over her nipples. And he had held her at arm's length to examine the same red rose that adorned the front of her knickers. And then he had slipped his hand down inside.

Within minutes Biddy knew that, physically, Fred was every bit the man he had always been. A little slower maybe, a little clumsier – but more than capable of performing his duties as a man. He had given her several great performances over that weekend. Each one better than the last.

It was with a sweeter temperament and an unusual feeling of contentment that she had waved Fred off at six o'clock on the Sunday evening. All the tension and the vague aches and pains she had felt since his accident had faded away. And there was a great difference in the children: they had slowed their constant running and trotting down to their father's pace, and had spent a great deal of time taking turns at sitting on Fred's knee. Then, to save argument, he had got Biddy to lift them up and place one on each knee.

But the highlight of the weekend had come on the Sunday afternoon, just before they sat down to their roast dinner, when Fred had lifted Helen up in his arms to look at herself in the mirror over the mantelpiece. Witnessing the same little routine he had carried out since both children were babies had made Biddy rush for her camera, to capture the precious image for ever.

There were various episodes over the weekend that had warmed Biddy's heart. The way Fred had sat quite comfortably with the lads over breakfast on the Sunday, and the way he had nodded his head at the right times even when he didn't know the people or places they were talking about.

But there were also one or two little incidents which had disturbed Biddy. She had presumed that Fred and Angela would hit it off well, but she hadn't reckoned on them getting on quite as well as they did.

'Oh, he's the grandest fella,' Angela had giggled, as she came into the kitchen after the dinner on Sunday. She had joined Biddy at the sink, carrying the empty trifle dishes, her cheeks pink with laughter. 'I'd no idea he was so funny, the way he carries on.'

Biddy's eyebrows had shot up. 'What d'you mean? What carry-on are you talking about?'

Angela's face had suddenly straightened. 'Well . . . nothing, really. Just . . . the way he was going on with the children . . . messing about.'

Biddy pointed to the dishes. 'It would suit you far better, young lady,' she said, her eyes narrowing, 'if you kept your messing about to the sink and the things you're asked to do.' She dried her hands on the striped towel by the cooker. 'Making free with married men is a dangerous game. If Tara knew the half of what you've been getting up to while she was away!'

'I wasn't making free with anyone,' Angela said, her eyes wide with shock. 'I haven't done anything wrong – I haven't done anything that would annoy Tara.'

'Well,' Biddy said, taking off her fancy lace pinny that she'd worn for Fred coming home, 'make sure you don't do anything that would annoy her *or* me. Just make sure you know your place.'

They'd had a pleasant hour watching cartoons with

the children, and then it was Fred's time to head back to the rehabilitation centre.

'Now remember,' Biddy had whispered as he waited for the ambulance men to help him up the steps, 'tell the doctors you feel well enough to come home for good . . . and keep well away from those nurses.' She prodded his chest at this point. 'Tell them if any of them lays a hand on you, they'll have me to answer to!'

'Don't be goin' on about things like that,' Fred had said, his brows down. 'The nurses are only doing their job . . . they're only doing their job.'

'I've no problems with them doing *their* job,' Biddy stated, 'but I have a problem when oul' ones like that nurse in the table-tennis room start to think they can do *my* job as well as their own!'

Chapter Thirty-Five

'Do I really need to go back over to Ireland for the funeral?' Angela asked in a low, hesitant voice.

'Do you need to go back for the funeral?' Biddy repeated, her voice high with astonishment. 'Indeed and you *do* need to go back! For one thing, the plane tickets are bought and paid for, and Frank Kennedy's pickin' us up at eight o'clock tomorrow morning.' She sucked her breath in. 'Isn't it your half-sister's husband? *Gabriel* – the same man who brought you over from Ireland only a few weeks ago?' Biddy closed her eyes, shielding off what she presumed was a pre-period headache.

She had enough on her mind without all this nonsense from Angela, and was finding it hard to adopt her usually patient and understanding manner – plus, she still wasn't sure if she liked her hair back so dark. 'What a question to be askin'! Of course you will have to go back for the funeral. You and me will both have to go back. Can you imagine how Tara would feel if she thought we couldn't make the effort to attend Gabriel's funeral? Christ almighty, Angela, what's goin' on in your head at all?'

'It's not anything to do with Tara and Gabriel,' the young girl said quickly, 'it's just that I hate funerals . . . they make me feel all peculiar and depressed. And I'm terrified of the thought of goin' up in one of those aeroplanes.' She put the salt and pepper on the table for the meal that evening.

'Well, that makes two of us, then,' Biddy told her. 'I'm scared to death at the thought of flyin' myself, so we may just get the rosary beads out and say our prayers like everybody else.'

Angela's gaze slid to the floor. 'Don't you think I'd be better off here, lookin' after Michael and little Helen? And then there's all the cookin' and cleanin' for the lads.'

'Never mind the feckin' lads!' Biddy snapped. 'Elsie can manage – she'll be well paid for the time I'm away. She's more than capable of managing on her own, and she has Eric here for the heavy jobs, and a friend comin' in to help with the breakfast and dinners.' She gave a heavy sigh. 'Anyway, the lads know what's happened, and they won't be expectin' too much while I'm gone. As long as they have a bit of breakfast in the mornin' and something plain and filling in the evenin' they'll be fine.'

'I still think—' Angela said, turning towards the kitchen door.

'Well, *don't*!' Biddy almost screeched at her. 'Just go about your business, and don't be thinkin' at all!' She reached for her purse and took out two pound notes. 'Here,' she said, handing the girl the money. 'Take the children down to the market and get two pairs of black stockings for us for the funeral. Then go to the holy shop on Petersgate and see if you can get two black mantillas – I don't want to be wearin' a black hat all the time when I'm over.' She rolled her eyes. 'Helen has my own mantilla ruined by tying it around Lucky's head for a headscarf.'

'Do you need anything else?' Angela asked, suddenly brightening up.

Biddy thought for a moment. 'Maybe some of those hard dog biscuits they sell in the market, in case they run out while we're away, and a couple of Swiss rolls.'

Angela took a few steps out into the hall and called

upstairs to the children. 'Michael! Helen! Get your shoes on, we're going down to Stockport.' Then she returned to Biddy. 'I'll take Lucky with us,' she said, all full of business, 'it'll give him his walk for the day.'

Biddy raised her eyebrows. 'And no doubt you'll be callin' for Eric on your way past the house?'

'I hadn't really thought . . .' Angela said lamely, her face reddening at being caught out. 'But it would be a help if he took the dog when we're crossin' the main roads . . .'

'No doubt,' Biddy said sceptically. 'No doubt at all that Eric would be a great help to you.'

The clatter of footsteps coming down the stairs now heralded the arrival of the two children. Angela busied herself buckling Helen's summer sandals and tying the laces on Michael's newly whitened plimsolls, and in a few minutes they were gone out of the back door to collect Lucky.

Biddy stifled an irritated sigh and turned towards the sink. One of these days she just might get the better of Angela. So far, the girl was always a good few steps ahead, plotting and planning to make sure she got her own way, and the sullen Eric was usually involved somewhere in her plans.

Biddy was finding all the business with the funeral bad enough without having to argue about it with Angela. The fact that her oldest and closest friend had lost her husband was a catastrophe to Biddy, and the fact that Gabriel had grown up in Ballygrace and gone to the same school as herself made it seem even worse. But – and she was totally ashamed to admit it even to herself – the biggest catastrophe of all was the fact that she was now being forced to return to Ballygrace. The village she had left in complete disgrace years ago, as a pregnant unmarried girl. And the thought of returning filled her with the most awful, awful dread, for she knew it would be like facing a judge and jury. All her old sins from when she was a girl would be brought out and aired again in houses up and down the village. And every inch of the successful woman she was now would be put under the microscope and scrutinised – and definitely found wanting. She knew it only too well. Hadn't she been brought up by the most vicious old witch of them all, Lizzie Lawless? It was her worst nightmare come true. And there was no way out of it.

Half an hour later, Biddy felt a bit better. Instead of going to the cupboard in the sitting room for the sherry bottle that kept coming into her mind, she had gone upstairs and finished packing her brand-new case. Then, on an impulse, she had rushed into the bathroom and shampooed her hair again, giving it a really good scrub to get the worst of the new dark dye out of it. Then, with the towel around her head, she had lifted her black coat out of the wardrobe, taken the mothballs out of the pockets, and gone over it with a damp cloth to remove any bits of lint that might have stuck to it.

Happy that the coat now looked perfect, she hung it outside the wardrobe to air for a while and to get rid of the cloying mothball smell, while she dried her hair off with a hairdryer and then set it in big rollers. The ringing of the phone interrupted her train of thought and she came tearing down the stairs to answer it.

'Biddy?' A low, barely recognisable voice came on the line.

'Is that you, Tara?' Biddy asked, tears welling up in her eyes at the sound of her friend's voice. 'How are you . . . are you all right?'

'Yes . . . I'm grand,' Tara replied, not sounding in any way normal or grand. 'How's Fred? How did his visit home go at the weekend?'

Biddy took a deep breath. How could Tara even think of her and Fred at a time like this? 'It went fine,

Tara,' she said, 'and it's good of you to ask.' There was a pause. 'How are things there?'

'We're leaving shortly now for the airport . . . Gabriel should have arrived there by now. They're flying him over with us.'

'I have me tickets booked,' Biddy cut in quickly, afraid that talking about funeral arrangements would start her off wailing and crying again like the last time they'd spoken, 'and I've spoken to Mick and Kitty, and they said I can stay at the cottage with them. They said I can have your old room—'

'No, Biddy,' Tara said, her voice sounding a little stronger, 'I don't want you to stay with Mick and Kitty . . . I want you to stay at Ballygrace House with me and Gabriel.' She paused. 'You were always promising to come and stay with us . . . and this is the last chance you'll ever have to stay in the house with Gabriel.'

Biddy opened her mouth but nothing came out. The words were all in a big tangle in her head. Eventually, she struggled to say, 'But Mick and Kitty—'

'I'll sort it out with Mick and Kitty,' Tara told her, 'so you don't need to worry about offending them. They'll understand perfectly.'

'But won't Mrs Fitzgerald and her new husband and the young lad be staying in the house?' She paused. 'And maybe some of their relatives?'

'There's room for them all,' Tara said quietly. 'It was the Fitzgeralds' home for a lot longer than it was mine. Their family and friends have a right to be there. And they'll all be there comforting Elisha . . .'

Biddy suddenly understood. 'I'll be there, Tara,' she heard herself saying. 'Don't you worry your head about it, I'll be there . . . an' I'll have my proper funeral clothes on and a black hat and everything. I have the blond all gone, and my hair's back like Jackie Kennedy.'

'I don't care what your hair looks like, Biddy,' Tara whispered, in a thin, frail voice. 'But I'd be really, really grateful if you stayed with me at Ballygrace House . . .'

'You'll have Kate Thornley there, too,' Biddy added, 'and she'll fit in far better with the Fitzgeralds than me . . .'

'That's different,' Tara said, sounding very, very weary. 'She's a very nice person, and she's been a great help down here consoling Gabriel's mother and William . . . but she doesn't know me the way you know me. Kate doesn't know anything about Ballygrace.'

Biddy's heart soared. Imagine her being put in front of someone like *Kate Thornley*! And Tara telling her she needed her.

'I feel I could just about cope if you came – you understand the way things are back in Ireland.'

'I'll be there, Tara,' Biddy said, her voice suddenly sounding confident and strong. Strong enough to face anything that might come her way back in Ireland. Strong enough to face all the gossips and the backbiters and the people who never knew the truth of the terrible things that had happened to her. Strong enough to be Tara Flynn's oldest and truest friend. 'You an' me will be together back in Ballygrace . . . I'll be with you every step of the way.'

A few minutes later, Biddy hung the phone up and laid her head in her hands. When she had composed herself again, she walked straight from the hall into the sitting room and opened the cupboard that housed the sherry bottle which she now so desperately needed.

Chapter Thirty-Six

Biddy didn't feel too great as she prepared the dinner for the lodgers that evening. Her head was tight and sore and the strong smell of the smoked haddock was turning her stomach. She was kicking herself now for giving in and having the two schooners of sherry she'd drunk earlier on. She'd felt perfectly fine after drinking them, but it was probably the reason she was feeling so bad now. What had she been thinking of?

Drinking in the evening was one thing, but drinking in the afternoon was another matter entirely. And especially drinking on her *own*. It was a well-known fact that drinking all on your own was a danger sign. A sign of somebody developing a problem. Of course Biddy well knew that she could take the drink or leave it – it was just that these last few months had been the most desperate in her life. And anyway – who could blame her for having a drink – on her own or not – after the sad conversation she'd just had with her oldest and best friend?

She shook her head. The quicker Fred Roberts came back home the better. There would be no need for the comfort of afternoon sherries when she had her husband back where he belonged.

It was the worst possible evening for her to feel in bad form: as luck would have it, Elsie was having the evening off to visit her sister out in Macclesfield, so she'd had to call Angela away from reading to the children to finish off cooking the fish. 'The mashed potatoes and peas are all ready in the oven,' she told the young girl, 'so you can just serve them up as soon as the haddock has finished frying.' Even the mention of the fish was making her feel queasy. 'I'm just goin' upstairs to have a lie down on the bed – I've got a splittin' headache. I just don't feel meself at all.'

'Will I put Michael and Helen to bed for you when I've cleared up the dinner dishes?' Angela offered, trying to get back on a better footing with her.

Biddy hesitated. Even though she'd been angry with the girl earlier on, she didn't want to look as though she was taking advantage of her being in the dog-house. Then the smell of the haddock wafted over to where they were standing and her stomach churned. 'That would be grand,' she said, managing a weak, grateful smile. 'And Angela – I'm sorry if I was short with you earlier . . . it's just that I've got an awful lot on my plate at the minute. The thought of goin' over to Ireland for this funeral is nearly killing me . . .'

'I know,' Angela said. 'And don't be worryin' – I'm all packed and ready to go over with you in the morning.' She lowered her head. 'And I'm really, really sorry for anythin' I shouldn't have said or done.'

'There's no need for all that – I know you're a good girl,' Biddy said, touching the girl's cheek in an affectionate manner, 'it's just that I don't want to see you going the wrong way. It's easy how things happen. I know all about it – nobody could understand better. I was a young, innocent girl just like yourself and I had some narrow escapes.' She paused. 'Very narrow indeed. But I would never forgive meself if anythin' untoward happened to you while you were under my roof.'

Biddy had cause to remember her words to Angela in the early hours of the following morning when she was awakened by the sound of the girl retching violently in the bathroom. She jumped out of bed and rushed along the landing, meeting Angela on her way back to her room.

'What's wrong?' Biddy asked anxiously. 'Have you been sick or somethin'?'

'I'm not at all well,' Angela snuffled. 'I must have ate something that didn't agree with me . . . I've got the most terrible sickness and diarrhoea.'

'Oh, dear God!' Biddy said, taking her arm and guiding her into her room. 'And us going over to Ireland in the mornin'. What a time for this to happen!'

'Don't worry,' Angela said in a faint voice. 'I'll be grand in the mornin' . . . I'll be grand now I've brought it all up.'

'It's half-past one,' Biddy said, checking her watch. 'If you get another five or six hours you might feel back to normal.'

But when Biddy went to look in on her charge in the morning, it was obvious that she did not feel at all back to normal, and apparently had visited the bathroom several more times during the night.

'I'll bring you up a tumbler of Andrews' liver salts,' Biddy told her, 'and see if that'll help you.'

'Are you sure that won't make me worse?' Angela whispered. 'I'm sure my father takes that when he hasn't been able to go to the toilet for a couple of days.'

Biddy pursed her lips together, thinking. 'I'll go down and read what it says on the tin—' Before she could say another word, Angela had thrown the bedclothes back and, with her hand cupped over her mouth, made a dash out of the room for the toilet.

'Christ almighty, this is all I need,' Biddy muttered to herself as she went back downstairs to help Elsie with the lads' breakfasts. Whatever it was, the girl was obviously not well and probably not fit enough to make the plane journey over to Ireland. In fact, if Biddy allowed herself to dwell on it, she wasn't feeling the brightest herself. She still couldn't get rid of the lingering smell of that damned smoked haddock from the kitchen, and the fresh bacon and sausage smell of breakfast wasn't doing a lot for her stomach either.

Whatever it was, Angela must have a worse dose of it than herself.

'Now d'you see what I mean about us being jinxed?' Biddy said to Frank as they drove through Cheadle Hulme and out towards Manchester airport. 'There was two of us supposed to be here this morning, and now there's only one.'

'Well,' Frank said, picking up a bit of speed now they were on a straight road, 'these things happen. You said the other day she was anxious about the flying and the thoughts of attending the funeral, so maybe she got herself into a bit of a state about it all.'

'I never thought of that,' Biddy said, rooting in her handbag for a packet of Murray mints, 'and I hope to goodness that's not the real reason she's not here, because her plane ticket wasn't cheap.'

'Don't worry about it,' Frank said. 'We'll have a word with them at the airport and maybe they'll be able to sort something out with the travel agent.'

'Oh, it's not the money,' Biddy explained, counting out four mints and putting the rest back in her handbag. 'At a time like this money doesn't come into it. I would just have felt better if Angela was along with me. Apart from the fact that I don't like travelling on me own, I just don't feel happy leaving her back at the house unchaperoned.'

'Has she been giving you any trouble?' Frank asked.

Biddy hesitated for a moment, resting the sweets in her lap. 'Not as such,' she replied cautiously. 'But let's put it this way, there's more of Shay Flynn in her than there is of Tara Flynn.'

Frank suddenly laughed. 'I think that tells me everything I need to know! God, will you ever forget the time that Shay turned up at Cale Green looking for her and caused havoc with all the snooty teachers?'

Biddy started to laugh at the memory. 'Tara nearly had a bad turn! And then when he got in with Ruby, that really put the tin hat on it.' Biddy wiped her eyes with the back of her hand. 'Oh, God,' she spluttered. 'We might have had some bad times, but we've had some good laughs along the way as well. Mind you, I don't think Tara could laugh about that even now, but I'll tell you something – that Angela could give Shay a run for his money any day. She can be just as determined as Tara, but in a very different way.'

'I don't think there's too many young girls like Tara Flynn around,' Frank said now, the joviality gone out of his voice. 'She's a one-off. She takes life very seriously, and I'd say she was the same even when she was a teenager – am I right?'

'Yes,' Biddy said, nodding in agreement. 'She was always old for her years when we were at school – always more sensible than the rest of us put together.'

Frank cleared his throat. 'She has very high principles, doesn't she?' he said, in a low voice. 'When she makes her mind up about something, she seems to stick to it – come hell or high water.'

Biddy looked out of the car window now, suddenly feeling uncomfortable with the turn the conversation had taken. 'That's not going to be of any help to her now, is it, God help her.'

She unwrapped two mints and put them on the dashboard for Frank, then unwrapped another and put it into her mouth. A small wave of nausea hit her, but thankfully it soon subsided.

Frank put the car radio on and they both sat with their own thoughts while the music covered up the silence.

Frank's question about Angela had sown a little seed of suspicion in Biddy. It had fleetingly crossed her mind that it was strange that there'd been no sign of evidence of Angela's sickness or diarrhoea. She didn't like to be too crude about it, but she had followed the girl into the bathroom on two occasions – literally passing her in the doorway – and on neither occasion was there any smell to suggest a severe bout of gastroenteritis.

Biddy had wondered about this, because last year a couple of the lads had gone down with it, and she was constantly using air-freshener and opening the windows wide to keep the place smelling decent. But there had been no bad smells at all – in fact, on the second occasion they had collided, Biddy had actually smelled a sweetish perfume off Angela, and had wondered at her putting scent or talc on when she wasn't feeling well. The very thought of the smells were now making Biddy feel like heaving again herself.

No, she thought to herself, she shouldn't be so nasty and suspicious. Sure, the girl was packed and everything was ready for travelling, and hadn't she been a bit green around the gills herself since yesterday?

'Are you sure about getting the wreath for me?' Frank Kennedy asked as the airport buildings loomed into view. 'I have money on me now . . .' He kept one hand on the steering wheel and reached into an inside pocket with the other.

'You can put that money back in your pocket!' Biddy told him. 'As if I'm going to take money off you for a wreath after all the things you've done for me and Fred Roberts.'

'You're very good,' Frank said graciously, halting now for a car to pull out from a perfect parking space just up from the airport entrance. As soon as the other car moved off, he slid his own black, shiny new car into its place.

They both got out, and Frank retrieved Biddy's case and black hat from the boot.

'Give her my regards,' Frank said, putting the case down on the ground in front of Biddy. 'And tell her I'm genuinely sorry for what's happened to her husband and that I'll have a Mass said for him in the next few days. You'll be sure and tell her now, won't you?'

'I'll tell her,' Biddy said, lifting the case. 'And thanks, Frank – you're one of the best.'

Chapter Thirty-Seven

BALLYGRACE

When Mick Flynn pulled up outside Ballygrace House he warned Biddy: 'Be prepared now, for she's taken it very bad. She's not at all herself . . .'

'If you don't mind, I'd rather go around the back way,' Biddy said quickly, terrified that they might have to go up the front steps.

'Same as meself,' he said quietly. 'Especially now the real head-woman is back from England.' And as they turned and walked round the path to the kitchen entrance, he added: 'Years ago, the likes of us would have been shot before they would have let us in the front door of this place.'

Kitty was in the kitchen, and she gave Biddy a tearful but enthusiastic greeting. 'You're heartily, heartily welcome,' she said, putting her arms around the prosperous-looking woman she had known as a young orphan girl.

'Thanks, Kitty,' Biddy said quietly. She was struggling now, desperately trying to control the quiver in her voice that was now moving to her knees. Everything from the flight over, the drive through Ballygrace Village, and now her entrance into Ballygrace House, was starting to overwhelm her. And she still had to face Mrs Fitzgerald and all the other toffs staying in the house. And she still had to face Tara, and see the heartbreak staring out of her eyes.

'She's having a lie-down at the minute,' Kitty said in a low voice, 'she's not been sleeping properly since she came back, so if you don't mind, I'll leave her for a while longer.' Then Kitty suddenly took Biddy's hand, stepping back to admire her. 'I don't believe what a fine-looking woman you've turned into. Well, fair play to you!' She waved Biddy's hand from side to side, then turned to her husband. 'Would you have believed it, Mick? The young girl who left here – how many years ago, is it now?'

Biddy closed her eyes, calculating. 'I suppose it must be eleven or twelve years . . .'

'And I believe you have a husband and two children and a fine big house – a boarding-house, isn't it?' She paused, her face becoming serious. 'And you haven't had it too easy yourself, your poor husband . . .'

'Oh, Fred's grand now,' Biddy reassured her. 'He was home last weekend and he's in great oul' form, thanks be to God.'

'I'm glad to hear it,' Kitty said, 'for it's no joke trying to look after somebody when you have two young children. And I hear you have young Angela over there, helping out at the minute? She didn't come back with you?'

'Well,' Biddy began, 'she was supposed to, but early this morning she had the most terrible oul' bug.' She lowered her voice. 'Vomiting and diarrhoea. I wasn't sure how serious it was . . . I didn't know what to do, but you couldn't take a chance. Not when you're travelling on planes and everything.'

'Indeed not,' Kitty agreed. 'But wasn't it an awful pity? I'd say Shay and Tessie would have been delighted to see her, even under the circumstances.'

They talked for a while about the children and Fred and things in Stockport, then Mick left to go back into Tullamore to pick up Tessie and the two girls.

'Shay said he would come out on the bike when Mick

offered to bring them all out,' Kitty said, pouring boiling water from the kettle into the teapot, 'but I don't know where he's got to, for there's not been a sign of him yet.' She looked towards the back door, then her voice dropped. 'He's not been himself lately, since all this happened . . . it seems to have knocked the wind right out of him, and poor Tessie's at her wits' end, what with Auntie Molly getting worse by the day.'

'That's desperate . . . I'm sorry to hear it,' Biddy said. 'What about Father Joe? Has he arrived yet?'

'On his way,' Kitty confirmed, getting two cups and saucers from a side table. She and Tessie and a few other local women had sorted out the china and cutlery and all the domestic things necessary for the constant flow of mourners. 'And you won't believe it, he's staying in with Auntie Molly. He said it's only fair to take his turn for the few nights he's here.'

Biddy raised her eyebrows now as she took her cup and saucer from Kitty. 'That's decent of him. There's not too many priests who would do that. I was sure he'd be stayin' here in the house. To tell you the truth, I feel he'd be more suited to stayin' here than the likes of me, but Tara insisted on it.'

'She insisted that you stay out here with her,' Kitty said, pouring the tea into Biddy's cup, 'because I told her that myself and Mick would have been delighted to have you out at our place.'

Biddy looked first at the door to the hall and then at the back door. 'I'm not looking forward to stayin' here one little bit,' she confided in a low voice. 'And I'm dreadin' seeing Mrs Fitzgerald . . . I can't remember her ever giving me the time of day.'

'Don't be worrying,' Kitty reassured her. 'Sure, I was the very same meself, and d'you know something? She's been as nice as pie to me. Quiet, of course – but that's only natural under the circumstances.'

Biddy looked at her watch anxiously, then asked

what the arrangements were for the funeral the following day, and what was happening that evening.

'Everything is being held here,' Kitty said in a low voice. 'Neither Tara nor Mrs Fitzgerald are up to travelling to hotels or anything like that for functions. There's a delivery of bread and cold meats and things arriving any time now, and Ella Keating is coming to organise a group of us making sandwiches for this evening.'

Just then, the kitchen door opened and both women halted as Tara came in.

'Biddy . . .' she said, standing in the doorway, 'I thought I heard a car and I wondered . . .'

Biddy looked at her, shocked that a few days could cause such a drastic change in a person. The vibrant, laughing woman who had been sharing her plans for Paris last week was now a shadow of herself. She stood, dressed from head to foot in black, and her glorious red hair was dragged back off her colourless face. In the space of those days, not just her face but her whole appearance was altered. She had turned from being slim and pretty to being bony-white and gaunt.

Biddy moved across the kitchen to embrace her friend. 'I don't know what to say . . . I can't—'

'You don't have to say anything,' Tara whispered, holding her tightly. 'You came back to Ballygrace for me and Gabriel – and I know what that took.'

Tara led Biddy up to one of the guest bedrooms, then the two friends sat on the bed as Tara related the whole story of Gabriel's death all over again while Biddy held her in her arms. Then, when there was nothing more to say, they went down together to stand and pray beside Gabriel's coffin, which stood in the middle of the candlelit drawing room.

'I can't believe it, Biddy,' Tara whispered, time and time again, as they stood looking at the closed, polished box that held her husband's body. 'I can't believe he's gone for ever.'

After a while, young William came in to stand beside Tara, and then Biddy held her breath as Elisha Fitzgerald – supported on one side by her husband and on the other by her sister – came into the room. She went straight to the head of the coffin and just stood there.

Eventually, Biddy forced herself to look up at the older woman, and she suddenly realised she had nothing to be afraid of. Nothing to be afraid of at all. The sophisticated, confident woman she had last seen when Gabriel and Madeleine were teenagers had long gone. In front of her now stood an older, broken woman whose life had taken a difficult path the day she married William Fitzgerald. A woman whose life's blood had drained away with the son and daughter she had borne and loved. Both of whom were now dead.

Kate Thornley came downstairs a few minutes later, and came over to sit with the younger women. She was very quiet in herself, and even though she talked posh like the Fitzgeralds and their friends, Biddy thought she seemed a bit out of place as well. Maybe she had found the last few days difficult, what with travelling over from London and then trying to console both Tara and her mother-in-law. She looked at Kate's bobbed red hair and her sharply contrasting pale face and suddenly felt sorry for her. She was in a strange house and in a strange country, and she probably didn't know what to do any more than Biddy did herself. And Kate Thornley wouldn't feel as easy with Kitty and Tessie and Shay and all their family as someone like herself.

The undertakers and the parish priest arrived shortly afterwards, and people began coming to pay their respects, so Tara was swept along in a sea of practicalities, leaving Biddy to seek comfort in the depths of the kitchen among the ordinary women like herself.

Chapter Thirty-Eight

Father Joe Flynn had had a difficult journey. The black Ford car that, to his surprise and delight, the parish priest had loaned him had caused him nothing but trouble on the long journey up from Cork. Supposedly far more comfortable and reliable than his own old car, it had started overheating after the first fifty miles, and after a stop to top up with water and oil, it had continued to overheat every half an hour, which meant that Joe had to pull off the road each time it happened to let it cool down again.

It had frustrated him so much that the third time it happened the Lord's name had reverberated around the inside of the car so violently that he had forced himself to take his prayer book from out of the glove compartment and then sat in silence, calming himself down by reading his favourite psalms and asking God to help him to accept the things he could not change.

Things like the criticisms of his cantankerous parish priest, Father O'Leary, the unwanted attentions of both Mrs O'Connor and Mrs Doherty – to name only the worst of that kind of female parishioner – the terrible affliction that had taken a grip on Auntie Molly, and the untimely death of his brother-in-law.

And above all, at this critical point in time, he prayed to God to help him accept the flaws in the engine of the parish priest's car and to help him to keep his temper with the damned bloody vehicle.

Eventually, the treacherous car limped into Offaly a

good two hours later than he had planned. Realising that time was against him, Joe abandoned his original plan of going to Auntie Molly's for a cup of tea, and decided to head straight out to Ballygrace House.

To Ballygrace House and the sadness and loss that now resided in it.

The dignified but emotional welcome he was given by his father and uncle when he arrived at the house quickly dissolved any frustrations that Joe had felt over the car. At least it had got him to his destination, and for that he was duly thankful. The two men were sitting on a bench at the side of the house, both dressed in dark suits and black ties, watching for any cars that might need guiding into suitable parking places.

They were particularly watching out for the hearse that was due to arrive in the next hour or so to carry Gabriel Fitzgerald to Ballygrace church, where he would spend his last night before burial.

Joe shook hands with them solemnly, then stood chatting quietly with them for a few minutes, trying to find that middle ground where a member of the clergy could keep pace with members of his own family. A family he'd never really known.

Then, all three men walked around to the front, and had a short debate about the best place he should park his car so that he wouldn't get boxed in. On the advice of Mick and Shay, Joe got back into Father O'Leary's car and turned it around so that it was facing back down the drive.

'That's the finest now; you'll have no trouble getting back out later,' Shay told him, patting the bonnet of the car. 'Jesus Christ!' he suddenly cried, moving his hand quickly off the hot metal. 'I think your oul' engine is burning up.'

Joe stifled a huge, weary sigh – a sigh built up from the long, torturous journey. This was the last thing he needed – a post-mortem on the parish priest's car. And it was just the very thing that his father and uncle needed, to distract them from the terrible tragedy that lay inside the house. 'It'll cool down,' he told them. 'It's inclined to overheat when it's been driven for a long period.'

'A car of its age shouldn't be burning oil like that,' Mick stated, taking off his jacket and rolling up his sleeves. Shay did likewise, a renewed energy appearing in his eyes. It wasn't often he got the chance to be of service to his son.

Then, ignoring all priestly protestations, the two men quickly had the bonnet of the car up and were peering inside to see exactly what the cause of the overheating was. Joe stood back and breathed in the fresh Bally-grace air while the men debated the intricacies of the engine.

'It'll be grand when it's had a chance to cool down,' he told them at one point. 'You needn't be spending your time this evening on it, when you have so many other things to attend to.'

'Ah, sure, it's a bit of a break for us,' Shay said. 'It's not often we get the chance to tinker about with a fine big car like this.'

After a while, another car could be heard coming up the drive, and the young priest took his chance and left Shay and Mick to attend to their mechanics, while he made his way around the back to the kitchen.

He took a deep breath, knocked on the door, and then walked in.

'Oh, Father Joe!' Kitty Flynn exclaimed, coming through the crowd of busy women to greet him. 'What on earth are you doing, coming around the back way?' She took his arm, guiding him over to a quiet corner. 'Sure, that's no way for a priest to be entering the house! You should have come in the front way. Mrs

Fitzgerald's husband is there to greet all the gentry – and people like yourself.'

'I'm happy coming in the back way,' he said quietly. He signalled a greeting over to Tessie and to the dark-haired woman with her, whom he vaguely recognised as a friend of Tara's.

'Did you come straight here?' Kitty asked. 'Or have you been out to Tullamore?'

'I came straight here,' Joe said, running a finger around the inside of his clerical collar. 'I'd a bit of a problem with the car.'

'It's always at times like these – the worst times – that things happen. Could Mick have a look at it for you? He's quite handy with engines.'

'He was under the bonnet when I left him outside.'

'He's never happier than when he's tinkering away with something,' Kitty said. 'Now, can I get you a cup of tea or a drink or anything? You must be starving after that long car journey up from Cork.'

Joe's eyes flickered over to the array of bottles at the side. 'I'll have a drop of brandy, if you don't mind,' he said in a low voice. He wasn't a big alcohol drinker, but it might just be the only thing that would help him over the ordeal of facing Tara now.

'*Mind?*' Kitty echoed. 'Indeed we don't. It's all there to be used, and Tara would be only too delighted to see you having a drink after that long journey. Would you like water, lemonade or dry ginger with it?'

'Lemonade,' Joe said, hoping that the sweet mixer might help it slip down more easily.

Kitty bustled over to the sideboard to look for a nice-sized brandy glass that would befit a priest.

Joe felt a hand on his shoulder. 'Father Joe,' Tessie Flynn said to her stepson, 'I have an old friend of Tara's here, come all the way over from Stockport in England.'

Joe turned now to the dark-haired woman whom he had vaguely recognised when he'd come in. The penny suddenly dropped. 'Biddy Hart!' he said, with as warm a smile as he felt the occasion would allow. 'Good Lord! How many years is it since I've seen you?'

'An awful lot . . .' Biddy said, her throat drying up and an embarrassed flush coming to her cheeks. She hadn't really known Joe that well, in fact, she'd only met him a few times, but Tara had kept her up to date with her brother's news. The thing that worried Biddy was that even if Tara hadn't kept Joe up to date on her own news over the intervening years, there were other people in Ballygrace who would have been happy to keep the priest up to date. And her life before marrying Fred wasn't exactly the sort of details that a priest would like to hear.

Kitty made her way back to them with Joe's drink. She'd also had a word with the group of women who were filling plates with sandwiches, and had asked them to sort out a decent plate of meat and salad for the priest.

'Are you sure you won't have a drink, Biddy?' Kitty asked now. 'Maybe a small sherry or something?'

Biddy looked longingly at the large brandy glass in Joe's hand. 'No, thanks,' she replied. 'I'll have another cup of tea in a few minutes.' She would have loved a brandy or a sherry, but she had promised herself that she wouldn't go near the drink while she was in Ballygrace. She wanted to keep her wits about her, so that she wouldn't end up saying the wrong thing to Mrs Fitzgerald, or letting her guard down and getting too involved with any gossipy locals who might touch a raw nerve.

Biddy was also wary of letting anything slip to Tessie and Shay about the little difficulties she was having with Angela. When Tessie had first cornered her to chat about her daughter, Biddy had concentrated on the girl's finer points and had made a great show of praising her patience with Michael and little Helen, and saying what a good worker she was around the house.

With all these little minefields to negotiate back in Ballygrace, it was much safer to avoid the drink. And in any case, whether it was the same bug that Angela seemed to have, or whether it was nerves at the whole situation, her stomach still wasn't a hundred per cent.

She cleared her throat now. 'Isn't this a shockin' bad thing to have happened? Who would believe it, Gabriel Fitzgerald of all people?'

Joe took a gulp of the brandy that his aunt had just thrust into his hand. It was comfortingly strong. 'No words to describe it,' he said in a low voice. There was a little silence, while he took another drink. 'How is Tara?' he asked, his brow furrowed. 'Is she bearing up well?'

'She's doing and saying all the right things,' Biddy said quietly, 'but inside she's in bits . . . there's no other way of describin' it. Her heart is completely broken. She'll never be the same girl again.'

Joe pursed his lips together and nodded his head. Of course Tara was in bits – how else could she be? He lifted his glass and took three big gulps one after the other to finish the brandy off. Then, when he could put it off no longer, he negotiated his way out to the front of the house in search of his sister.

Ballygrace church was hushed and shocked to its very foundation stones. Terrible things like this didn't happen to families like the Fitzgeralds. Especially not *twice* in a few years – not to the gentry.

But it *had* happened, and the people of Ballygrace and Tullamore, and the surrounding villages and towns, found themselves wondering that if something so awful as this could befall the *Fitzgeralds*, what terrible things might lie in wait for the more ordinary families? And that fearful thought brought them to the church in droves to pay their respects and pray for their own souls.

And of course there were the other reasons that brought the crowds out in full force to Ballygrace church. Reasons that had nothing whatsoever to do with spiritual matters. Reasons that had more to do with an unusually quiet summer in the village – a summer during which very little of interest or gossip was happening. The activity centred around Ballygrace House was enough to warrant great attention, because it was now full of people who would never have seen inside of it in Rosie Scully's day. The Fitzgerald family's old housekeeper had always tried her best to ensure that the high standards were upheld, and had been successful for many years. Up until the arrival of Tara Flynn.

And from the first day that the young brat had arrived, talking and walking around the place as though she was as good as the gentry, things had never been the same. In Rosie's feeble old age now, she told anybody that would listen that Tara Flynn had put a curse on Ballygrace House. What else would explain all the tragic, untimely deaths that had occurred since she had started visiting the house? She had certainly put a curse on Rosie Scully, for her life had gone downhill from the minute the girl had entered the house. And it had completely ended when Mrs Fitzgerald departed for England, closing the old house up. And from the very minute the housekeeper had heard that Gabriel had married the Flynn one in England and was bringing her back to be the mistress of Ballygrace House, she knew that no good would come of it.

Housebound now, her legs having finally given out on her the previous year, she had been unable to attend Ballygrace House or the church to pay her respects to the man she had looked after as a child, but she had people who would come back to her house that night and give her a full account of everyone who had been there and everything that had gone on. And she would remind them of all the things she had forecast when Gabriel had sealed his fate by taking up with Tara Flynn.

She knew that her prophetic words would ring in a good many ears tonight in the church. People only had to look at the expensive wooden coffin at the altar rails for proof.

Chapter Thirty-Nine

STOCKPORT

Angela couldn't believe her luck! She couldn't believe that things had worked out so well with Biddy. After their row on Sunday, she had seen no way out of going back to Ireland. She knew without a doubt that if her feet touched the ground back in Tullamore she would end up staying there. From her mother's last letter she well knew that she wanted her back home to help mind Auntie Molly – and there was no way that Angela was going to bury herself in a dark little house with a deranged, cantankerous old woman. Especially when there was still so much life she hadn't yet sampled in Stockport.

As late as yesterday evening she had given up all hope of getting out of the trip back home. She had even made it up with Biddy after the row because, apart from the fact that she was very fond of her, she didn't want to travel back for the funeral with an atmosphere between them.

And then – as if it had been handed to her on a plate – she suddenly had the most genuine excuse not to go to Ireland. Her stomach had been feeling off, like it usually did before her 'monthlies', and she really felt she couldn't face the thought of the aeroplane. When Biddy said she was suddenly feeling sick herself, it had given Angela the perfect opportunity to pretend she had gone down with the same thing. It had worked like a treat and, given the fact that she really didn't feel all that well, she didn't feel too guilty about exaggerating. In fact, she'd had a great day yesterday, with Elsie running up and down the stairs with hot-water bottles for her stomach and aspirins for the slight aches and pains which had now completely gone. Her period was often unreliable – some months she got pains, and others she didn't – and she wouldn't be surprised if it arrived any time now. She'd spent the whole day in bed, catching up on her sleep and reading magazines. And then later in the afternoon, when Elsie took the children into town to pick a birthday present for her daughter Anne, she had had a visit from Eric.

Not wishing to give anything away, she had made out to Eric that she was worse than she really was. She wanted to see how he would react to her when she wasn't her usual perky self. Surprisingly, Eric came up trumps. He had brought her a bunch of grapes and a bottle of Lucozade, and had been as sympathetic as he possibly could have been. The only trouble had been when he wanted to lie on top of the bed beside her, and Angela had given him short shrift over that idea after he had made a joke about her high-necked, 'granny-style' nightdress.

'But we never get any time on our own,' Eric had moaned. 'An' then you go an' get sick the first time we have the house to ourselves.'

'I'll be fine by tomorrow,' Angela promised, and then, before she knew it, she had agreed to Eric's suggestion that he come over early in the morning before everyone was up.

The following morning Angela was awake a good half-hour before she heard the back gate bang, quickly followed by Lucky barking a welcome. She glanced at the alarm clock on the bedside cabinet: it was still only six o'clock, and there wouldn't be anyone moving in the house for at least another half an hour. Smiling, she threw the bedclothes back and then grabbed the black nylon dressing gown with the leopard-print trim from the hook on the door, and slipped it over the matching nightdress. She had borrowed both items from the extensive shelf of underwear and nightwear in Biddy's wardrobe the previous night.

Apart from the fact that she liked nice feminine things, she wanted to give Eric a bit of a jolt when he saw her this morning. Last night he had been teasing her again about her nightdress and about being 'a little Irish Catholic virgin', and telling her she was behind the times compared to the girls in Stockport.

'I don't care,' she had told him with a toss of her long blond hair, 'I'd rather be behind the times than have a bad name like some of the girls I know back home.' But even as she said it, deep down Angela knew that she did care. She cared very much what Eric and other lads thought about her.

'But you're not back home,' he'd told her, pulling her close to him. 'And anythin' that happens will only be between you and me.'

'I'm waitin' until I get married to give myself to my husband on my wedding night,' she had said, testing out his reaction.

Eric's brow arranged itself into deep furrows, as his mind decided which tack to take with her. 'You could die long before that,' he told her in a solemn tone, 'and then you would die wonderin' what it was all about.'

'Well, in that case,' she'd told him smartly, 'you'd never miss what you never had.'

Angela smiled to herself now, thinking back on their conversation. Lads were such awful fools at times. As if she was going to agree to go to bed with him like that! There was a long road that Eric was going to travel before he got what he wanted. But there was no harm in whetting his appetite while he waited, and it was a nice way to test out what kind of sex appeal she had for men in general.

She lifted the small perfume bottle from the dressing-table and gave a quick spray of Californian Poppy to both her wrists and either side of her neck. Rubbing one of the damp, scented wrists well down into her cleavage, she crossed the room to lift the pair of pink furry mules that were standing by the wardrobe and then tiptoed barefoot out of the bedroom and downstairs to let Eric in.

She paused at the bottom of the stairs to slip the mules on and to check her appearance in the hall mirror. Very glamorous, she thought. And even if she did say it herself, the fancy nightie and dressing gown looked far better on her petite slim figure than they did on Biddy's bigger frame

'Come on!' Eric's impatient voice came from outside the door.

Angela slid back the bolts on the door and then opened it wide to give her visitor a good view of the front of her outfit before turning and walking across the kitchen to give him a lingering view of the back.

'Bloody hell!' he hissed, moving across to grab her around the waist. 'You look absolutely gorgeous – and dead sexy!'

'You weren't saying that yesterday when I was lying in me sick bed, were you?'

Eric gave a leery grin. 'Well, you weren't wearin' a get-up like that in bed yesterday, were you? If you had, I might not have been able to control myself!' He pulled her round to face him now, and planted his lips roughly on hers. They stood kissing passionately for several minutes, then Eric's hand moved down to the hem of her nightie and started to travel up her thigh.

'No ... no!' Angela whispered, suddenly feeling alarmed. She had only really meant to show off to him – get a few appreciative compliments – not to get him going in a way she couldn't handle. 'What if your mother was to come in now, and catch me dressed like this?' she pointed out. 'She'd tell Biddy an' I'd be straight out that front door – an' me father would kill me. I could never go home again.'

'My mother weren't even up when I left,' Eric said impatiently. 'We've loads of time before she comes.' He paused, his gaze centred on the low, lacy neckline that revealed the soft curves of her breasts. 'We could go into the sitting room and have a lie-down on the sofa.'

'But what about the lodgers?' Angela argued in a hushed tone, terrified now of what she had done by wearing Biddy's sexy outfit, terrified she'd unleashed an Eric she might not recognise – or even worse, one she couldn't control. 'What if one of them comes in and catches us? They'll definitely tell Biddy, especially if it's one of the older ones.'

'I've got an idea,' Eric said, suddenly grabbing her by the hand. 'We'll go upstairs – into yer bedroom. Nobody would dare go in there, an' when we hear me mam or anyone comin', I'll nip into the bathroom an' make out I've just come in from walkin' the dog.' He leaned down and kissed her full on the lips again, his tongue searching deep into her mouth.

'But what if we get caught?' Angela whispered, half excited and half frightened by his kissing.

Eric caught her hand and moved it over the zip on his trousers. He pressed his hand down on top of hers and suddenly she could feel a bulging stiffness growing even harder as she touched it. For a few seconds, her hand tightened around it as she tried to gauge exactly what it was that lay under the rough denim material, for none of the women's magazines she often sneaked from Biddy gave any indication of situations like this.

'We won't get caught,' Eric assured her, his breath coming more quickly now at the pressure of her touch.

Angela suddenly pulled her hand away, less certain of

things now. 'What if somebody caught us?' she repeated.

'None of them builders would dare to come into yer bedroom, would they?'

'Indeed and they wouldn't!' Angela said, appalled at the very thought. 'They'd get the heel of my shoe over their head if they so much as tried!'

'Right!' he said, leading her by the hand out into the hallway. 'We'd better get a move on up them stairs.'

As they mounted the stairs, Angela knew with a sickening feeling that she was making a big mistake. While she liked and fancied Eric, he had already started to move far too fast for her. And she wasn't at all sure how she was going to handle things. Something told her that once Eric got inside the bedroom with her, things might happen that she had no experience or idea of.

Things that Eric professed to know plenty about.

He had divulged to her the other night about an affair he had had with an older woman, just before he'd gone into the remand centre. 'Two kids, she had,' he told Angela, 'and both with different lads.'

'And where did you meet the likes of her?' Angela had demanded, her forehead creased disapprovingly.

'In the pub,' Eric said, 'and she weren't bad-lookin' for twenty-five. She weren't bad-looking at all.'

'And did you . . . ?' Her voice dropped. 'Did you?'

'Did I what?'

'Did you – *you* know?' Her voice was a hiss now – the Angela of old back arguing with her sisters.

Eric suddenly gave a lop-sided, embarrassed grin. He wasn't used to getting tackled like this – he only had to raise his voice at home and his mam and his sister caved in straight away. ''Course I did – what lad in his right mind wouldn't? I'm only flesh an' blood, aren't I?' He paused, deliberating on the way the conversation was going. 'An' anyway, she knew I wasn't the type that would go braggin' about it. She knew I weren't gonna go around talkin' about her. I wouldn't do that to any girl – not me.'

There was a silence. 'Have you been with many girls?' Angela asked quietly, her arms folded high across her chest.

A dark, defensive look crossed the youth's face. 'Enough to know what to do,' he said, 'but I've not been with *that* many.'

Angela had turned away from him. 'I thought you were a decent lad,' she'd said. 'I thought you and me were the same kind . . . I didn't think you were only after women for one thing.'

Then Eric's hand had tightened on her arm. 'What d'you mean? Are you sayin' I'm not a decent fella? What's that supposed to mean?'

Angela swiftly pulled out of his grip. 'I told you before, I'm saving myself,' she told him, her gaze directed away from him in disapproval. 'I'm saving myself till I get married . . . an' I would hope my husband would do the same.'

Eric stared at her for a few long moments, then he shook his dark head. 'You're livin' in cloud-cuckoo-land, you are,' he told her. 'There's not a lad alive who wouldn't take it if it were offered to him on a plate – and anyone that says any different is lyin' his head off!'

'Maybe I'd have preferred not to know – maybe I don't want pictures of you and other girls doing things in me mind. I don't want to know about things being offered on a plate – because you're not goin' to be offered anythin' on a plate by me.'

Then he'd taken her by the arm again – more gently this time – and turned her towards him. 'I could have fuckin' lied. I could have told you what you wanted to hear – I'm not stupid, you know. I could have played along the minute I knew you didn't like it, but I told you the *truth*.' His face had softened, and his hand came to touch her under the chin. 'Don't that mean something to you? Doesn't it tell you that I think a lot of you?'

At last Angela's eyes had lifted. She had got what she wanted. She looked at him now through thick brown lashes. 'I'm not like any of those other girls, so don't go thinking I am.'

'An' that's *exactly* what I like about you,' he said, intensity written all over his face. 'I've never bothered with any other girl before . . .'

'Well then,' Angela had said, 'we both know where we stand.'

And here they were now, on the way upstairs to her bedroom at six o'clock the following morning and her dressed in a short, skimpy dressing gown. Just to let Eric know that she had everything those other girls had – and more.

But she wasn't going to let him have it. Not now – maybe not ever. It would all depend.

She came to a sudden halt midway up the stairs, dragging Eric to a standstill as well.

'What's that?' she whispered dramatically, pulling the dressing gown tight over her exposed cleavage.

'What?' Eric said, his eyes as wide as saucers. 'What you on about?'

'That noise . . . downstairs.'

'I never heard owt,' Eric said, looking over the banister suspiciously.

'The back gate,' she said, pulling out of his reach, 'I'm sure I heard the latch going on the back gate.'

They listened in silence for a few moments. 'It's only your imagination . . .'

And then, mercifully, Lucky gave a low howl and started yelping. Angela moved to push Eric back down the stairs. This was her opportunity to reverse the tide. 'It'll be your mam,' she whispered heatedly. 'You'd better go . . . say you were looking for the dog lead.'

'Fuckin' shit!' Eric said, almost missing his footing on the step. 'What a waste of a mornin'—'

'See you later,' Angela said, disappearing up the stairs.

Then, just as she reached the top, she heard a crash and a thud. She held her breath, listening, and when she heard Eric mutter *'Fucking plant'* to himself, she deduced that he had fallen foul of Biddy's maidenhair fern which trailed from a fancy Japanese-style stand she had got in Stockport market.

She heard Eric cursing as he put the plant pot back up on the stand again, and she quietly closed the bedroom door and locked it securely. Then she heard footsteps moving on the attic floor above, and realised that the noise must have woken one of the builders. She tiptoed back across the cold linoleum floor and got straight into bed. She didn't care what Eric did now – nothing would make her open the door again to him this morning. She had tested him to the very limit, and had been lucky to escape untarnished. And apart from having a narrow escape, she had learned a very valuable lesson.

She heard the back gate banging and then the dog started to bark and whine again, thanks to the vicious kick that Eric had just delivered in retribution for Lucky having spoiled his early-morning plan. On his way out, he detoured to the small planted area that gave decoration to the perimeter of the concrete yard, and tramped heavily on six pink busy Lizzies and several magnificent purple petunias.

Completely unaware of the devastation that her suitor had caused in the back yard, Angela settled back into her bed and fell into a deep sleep. An hour and a half later an irate Elsie came banging on her door, telling her that she was needed down in the kitchen.

Later, after the lodgers had gone to work and they were sitting down having a well-earned cup of tea, Elsie told

Angela of the mess she had seen as she had arrived that morning.

'It were bloody disgraceful,' she said. She went on to tell her that one of the lodgers must have knocked over the good Japanese plant stand, and hadn't even had the bleedin' decency to clean up the soil. Then, just to cap it all, some friggin' hooligan had come in the yard during the night and ruined half of poor Biddy's plants. Angela had sat there, mouth open at the stories. 'Never mind,' she had said to Elsie, 'I'll walk up to that flower shop in Davenport this afternoon, and I'll buy some new plants that we can stick in before Biddy comes back.'

Elsie's face had softened. 'You're just like meself, you know – all heart when it comes to things like that.'

Angela had smiled back, privately sniggering to herself at the thought of being anything like Elsie.

'You're not a bit like your sister, you know,' the older woman said now, studying Angela's face carefully. 'No offence intended, or anythin', and I'm very sorry and all about her husband, but in my opinion – only in *my* opinion, mind – Tara's a little bit uppity in herself.' She tipped the end of her nose with her finger several times. 'A little bit snooty, some might say.' She leaned forward, her voice low and conspiratorial, her finger prodding on the kitchen table. 'As I were sayin', it's only my opinion – and I know you won't repeat it to anyone – but I find it very hard, myself, to understand what her and Biddy really have in common. Oh, I know they grew up together in the same little Irish village and everythin', but you'd wonder what *keeps* them friends nowadays when they're so different.'

Angela listened to all Elsie had to say with great interest, because, amazingly, she had been thinking along the very same lines since she'd come to Stockport. But something held her back from agreeing aloud – from actually committing herself. She knew that Elsie was waiting to see what side of the fence she was going to come down on – and it could well have consequences if it was the wrong one.

'Well,' she said cagily, 'there's times I've wondered what they have in common, too, because they do seem awful different to me as well.'

Elsie's broad smile and the way she sat back in the chair with her arms folded told Angela she was on the right track.

'The way I look at it,' the young Irish girl continued, 'is that Biddy seems to be a good judge of character, and she must be able to talk to Tara in a way that people like us can't, for them to be friends.'

A quizzical look crossed Elsie's face. 'Say that again – I'm not quite sure that I get what you're actually tryin' to say. And slow down a bit, sometimes that Irish accent goes a bit fast for me an' I can't make out a word you're saying. Biddy Roberts is the very same at times, when she's excited – all worked-up like, or maybe when she's had a few too many. Then I find it hard to make head or tail of what she says.'

'Well,' Angela said, suddenly self-conscious of her accent, 'I'd definitely say that Biddy is a good judge of character, and that she wouldn't be friends with someone like Tara unless she thought she was a nice person.' She gave the older woman a big smile now. 'She thinks the world of *you*, you know – it's always Elsie this and Elsie that. She's always sayin' "I'll have to see what Elsie thinks about that".'

'Oh, get away!' Elsie said, giving her a beaming smile that took a good five years off her normal expression. 'Does she really talk like that about me? I can't imagine what I've ever said that's been that useful – although I try me best, when she's lookin' for advice, like.'

'She says you've been like a second mother to her,' Angela added for good measure. She couldn't remember if Biddy had actually said that, but it sounded good and, by the look on Elsie's face, it was definitely the sort of thing she liked hearing.

'Oh, well,' Elsie said, getting up to her feet now, 'much as I'd like to, I can't sit here chatting all day. Talkin' never did a day's work in its life – did you ever hear that expression before? Do they use that one in Ireland?'

'No,' Angela said, shaking her head, 'I've never heard it in Ireland or anywhere else.'

'That's because it's one I made up meself!' Elsie said, laughing now at her own little joke. 'Oh, dear,' she said, 'it's worse I'm gettin', instead of better.' She halted, finger to her lips. 'I think it was the attic bedrooms that Biddy said wanted changin' today. She meant to do it before she went, but with not feelin' the best she never got round to it.' She looked out of the window now, checking how the weather was for drying bed-linen. 'I'll make a start on them, if you finish clearing up down here.'

Chapter Forty

BALLYGRACE

The new young doctor from the village had to be called to Ballygrace House early on the morning of the funeral. Elisha Mortimer had lain awake most of the night, and then finally fallen asleep just before five o'clock. When she woke again at around half past six, she felt as though a heavy weight was pinning her down, and she could only manage the shallowest of breaths.

Realising that the situation was serious, Harry had rushed downstairs in his dressing gown and rifled through the phone book until he found the doctor's number in Tara's neat handwriting.

In just over ten minutes, a car had scrunched into the driveway, and Harry had opened the door and ushered a very fresh-faced young doctor up the staircase and into their room – the room Elisha had shared with William, her first husband.

Harry Mortimer was relieved to see Elisha now sitting up in bed. She still looked ghastly, but at least she was sitting up and taking sips of water from a glass held to her lips. Her sister Frances – whom Harry had called to sit with her while he phoned the doctor – had somehow calmed her down, and she was now coaxing her with the drink.

The doctor wasted no time. After checking her heart with his stethoscope, he took her blood pressure, then did several more routine checks to rule out any obvious causes for her distress. Then, deducing that her symptoms were the result of pure grief, he gave her an injection, and within minutes she was breathing more easily. A short while later, she fell into a heavy, noiseless sleep.

'I would leave her sleeping until the last possible minute before the funeral,' the doctor told Harry out on the landing. 'The medication should see her through the best part of the day.' He gave Harry a small dark brown bottle of tablets. 'Give her one of these if it starts up again, and don't worry if she's a bit dopey – it's either that or she might go into another of these attacks.'

Harry paid the doctor and thanked him for coming out so quickly, and then saw him downstairs and out of the house. After he closed the door, he stood for a moment at the foot of the staircase, examining the little bottle.

It was just as he thought. The pills were similar to the ones the doctor back in London had given her last year when she had been going through one of her bad patches. Hopefully, these were even stronger. Strong enough to get her through the next few days.

Ballygrace church was awash with men in black ties and women in black lace on the sunny autumn day that Gabriel Fitzgerald was buried. The main female mourners had all opted to cover their heads and faces with mantillas or black hats with a piece of black lace coming down over their eyes.

One funeral custom had been completely dispensed with – the women going to one side of the church and the men to the other. Harry Mortimer, not being a member of any particular church, found no need to stick to such rituals, and insisted on sitting beside Elisha, to keep a close eye on her should the ceremony become too much for her.

A couple of men from the village who performed such stalwart tasks as handing around the collection baskets at Sunday Mass and lighting the church candles, hovered nervously around the front pews, wondering whether they should say something. But when Father Joe Flynn came down from the altar to shake hands with all the close family, with Harry and the young Fitzgerald boy seated amongst the women, they decided to say nothing. If the seating arrangements suited a priest – who were they to question it?

William had walked side by side with Tara into the church, and he had automatically moved in to sit in the first pew between her and Harry.

Nobody really spoke, and when the five priests who concelebrated the Mass came on to the altar, the whole congregation just swung into the familiar pattern of standing, kneeling and saying all the Latin words they said every Sunday.

Tara Fitzgerald kept a ramrod-straight back throughout all the proceedings, her head held erect, her face as white and as still as the statue of Our Lady on the altar. She wore a plain black coat with a black hat trimmed with heavy lace that covered her eyes. She had bought the sober outfit last year for the funeral of one of her old bosses in the office she had worked in as a girl, little realising that she would wear it to her own husband's funeral.

Her luxuriant hair was dressed the same way she'd worn it for the past week – tied in a ponytail by a thin black velvet ribbon. She stood up when she was supposed to and sat down when everyone else did. But the Mass could have been in double Dutch for all the words meant, because they offered her no hope or consolation.

She had no time for God or the Word of God any more.

Gabriel's young brother stood small amidst all the

adults, his dark gaze moving from the priests to the polished coffin with the brass handles, then to his mother. At least she had Harry there; at least William didn't feel responsible for her today.

Occasionally, he slipped his hand into Tara's hand, knowing that she would give it a little squeeze of encouragement, even though she didn't look down at him. But that little acknowledgement was enough.

Biddy Hart sat in the row behind the immediate family with Kate Thornley and Tessie and Kitty. Like Tara, she looked neither to the left nor right – but for different reasons. She was afraid of who might catch her eye, and in that wordless look remind her of all the reasons she had left Ballygrace and all the reasons she had never come back. She kept her gaze firmly focussed on the altar – as she relived her young years growing up in Ballygrace with Lizzie Lawless.

As she fell in with the chanting of prayers and the standing and kneeling, pictures of people like Nora – Lizzie's other orphan who disappeared and was never seen again – and Dinny the lodger and Father Daly flitted in and out of her mind. When those pictures went, pictures of the little baby son she had left behind twelve years ago in the Dublin hospital took their place . . . bits of memories, like torn-up photographs that had been tossed up and scattered to the wind . . . bits of her life that she rarely dared look at.

Shay and Mick had done the correct and traditional thing and had stood in the first pew of the men's side. Both men felt uncomfortable in that prime position, as they would normally have slunk into a seat nearer the back of the church. But there was no slinking away from anything today.

Final blessings were performed over the coffin, and the final prayers said for Gabriel Fitzgerald's soul – and then the black-robed crowd emerged from the church. Tara Fitzgerald and the rest of the family, then the other mourners, fell into their allotted places walking behind the hearse. They walked the half-mile out to Ballygrace cemetery – their footsteps beating a mantra all the way – to where Gabriel Fitzgerald would be laid in his final resting-place. Quite near – but quite separate from – his father and sister, in a newly dug grave.

Chapter Forty-One

STOCKPORT

Biddy returned from Ireland on the Thursday evening. She came out of the airport building, phoned home to say she was on her way, and joined the queue for a taxi. When Frank Kennedy had dropped her off on the previous Monday, she had promised him that she would ring him for a lift back home, but she decided against it.

As she sat in the back of the black cab, holding on to her bag of presents for Michael and Helen and the carrier bag of duty-free whiskey and sherry and cigarettes, she kept picturing Tara's stricken face. It was a picture she'd never get out of her mind. Biddy knew she would never, ever forget the feeling of sadness and despair that had rattled through the beautiful rooms in Ballygrace House. All happiness and life had departed from the house as if never to return. Lying in the old-fashioned brass bed with the satin-covered bolster and quilt, Biddy had thought that it was the saddest house she had ever been in. Far worse than Lizzie Lawless's old cottage, and that had been bad.

If pieces of stone could have feelings, Biddy thought, then heartbroken is exactly what Ballygrace House was feeling.

The welcome she received from the children brought tears to Biddy's eyes, and she watched in delight as Helen unwrapped a fully dressed baby doll with a dummy in its mouth, and Michael opened a box that held a Lego castle. She had a bottle of whiskey and a box of chocolates for Elsie, and had brought back a few bits and pieces Tessie had sent for Angela.

While the children played with their new toys on the floor at her feet, she and Elsie sat with cups of tea and corned beef and HP Sauce sandwiches and caught up with each other's news.

'So Angela made a quick recovery after I left?' Biddy said, raising her eyebrows suspiciously. 'Do you think she was only dodgin' the funeral?'

Elsie shrugged. 'Well . . . I wouldn't really like to say.' She took a drink of her tea. 'She had the day in bed after you went off, and she were as right as rain the next day . . . an' that's all as I'm sayin' on the matter.'

Biddy lifted a sandwich and went to take a bite out of it, then stopped, not sure if she could stomach the sauce she usually liked. 'If I thought for a minute that she was pullin' the wool over our eyes . . .' she said, putting the sandwich back on the plate. 'Where is she now?'

'She's out,' Elsie told her, with a slight edge to her voice. 'Said she was goin' to the library and wouldn't be long.' She shook her head. 'These young ones, you couldn't be up to them.' She took a good-sized bite out of her sandwich.

'The *library*?' Biddy repeated, her voice high with surprise. Angela had recently started taking the children to the library on a Saturday afternoon, but she'd never known her to go there in the evening. 'Did she go with Eric?'

'I shouldn't think so,' Elsie said. 'I don't think you'd get our Eric inside the door of a library. The sight of all them books would be torture to him. He had enough of books at school to last him a lifetime.' She tilted her head to the side, thinking. 'D'you know, when he were around eleven year old, I once caught him burnin' a pile of schoolbooks in the bin outside. After I gave him a good hidin' for it, he told me that he was going to take the half-burned books to school and say we'd had a chip-pan fire in the house an' he couldn't do his homework!'

Biddy laughed heartily. 'He deserved to get off with the homework for thinkin' that one up! That definitely showed brains.'

Elsie shook her head. 'You don't know the half of it . . . but as I say, I'm sure you'd never get him inside the door of a library.' She lowered her voice. 'Anyroads, between you an' me, I think they've had a bit of a fallin' out – him and Angela.'

'What about?' Biddy asked.

Elsie waved her hand. 'I haven't gorra clue . . . I've learned to switch off when I hear rowin' goin' on in the house. It doesn't do to get involved. They was upstairs in Eric's room the other evenin', listenin' to records as usual, and then the next thing I could hear the raised voices, and the bangin' and the thumpin' around in the room.'

'What were they arguing about?' Biddy asked, alarmed on two counts. What was Angela doing up in Eric's bedroom again, when she'd been warned about it only last week? And what was all the banging and thumping about?

'Don't ask me – I know nowt about it,' Elsie said grimly. 'As I said, it doesn't do to get involved, for they're fighting and arguin' one minute, and the next minute they're back the best of friends – and suddenly I'm the bad one for interferin'. Oh, I had enough of it with our Anne an' her fella. I could write a book about it, and that's no word of a lie. And even though I'm his mother, I'm the first to admit that our Eric can be very pig-headed when he doesn't get his own way. He takes after his father, he does – and don't get me started on about *that* bastard . . .' She crammed the rest of the corned-beef sandwich into her mouth, and washed it down with a gulp of her tea.

'Well,' Biddy said, 'he might have met his match with Angela, for she's the very lady that likes to get her own way as well.'

She wondered again about Angela's convenient one-day illness, and hoped with all her heart that it had been genuine. If she thought for a minute that the young girl would do such a terrible thing as to fake an illness when she should have been at a family funeral, then she definitely wouldn't want her here in the house. She put it to the back of her mind for the time being, as she had firmly assured Tara that she would look after Angela. Besides, she would need her help with the kids when Fred came home from hospital.

'You've not touched yer sandwiches,' Elsie said, reaching for another one.

'My appetite's not great,' Biddy sighed, 'what with the flying and being in a strange house and everything.'

'What was it like being back home?' Elsie asked curiously. 'Apart from the sadness of the funeral, like?'

Biddy tilted her head to the side, thinking. 'Different,' she said. 'I don't think Ballygrace has changed that much . . . but I think maybe I have.'

Elsie nodded. 'That's life, that is,' she said philosophically. 'And what was it like, staying in the big posh house? I bet it were lovely.'

'Very nice . . . it's a beautiful house . . . although a bit more old-fashioned than the sort of furniture and everythin' we would like.' Biddy's eyes narrowed in thought, trying to picture the hallway and the bedroom she'd slept in. 'It's still got a lot of the furniture that the Fitzgeralds brought from Dublin, things that Gabriel's mother got from her own family. Very dark wood . . . the kind that's got flowers carved in it and bits of marble on top. As I say, it's more on the old-fashioned lines than the kind of things me and you would like.'

'Old-fashioned?' Elsie said, her voice high with surprise. 'I would have thought Tara would have had the best of everything. I would have thought she'd have had all up-to-the-minute furniture . . . right modern, like.' She finished off her tea, and put her cup back on the saucer. 'Now, you do surprise me there, I wouldn't have put her down as the kind that would have been happy to put up with old stuff. I would have thought she would have put her foot down and told her husband that she wanted the same as everybody else. Don't they have furniture shops in Ireland that sell the new, modern stuff?'

'Well,' Biddy said, tiring of the subject now, 'I think it's the sort of thing that Tara and Gabriel preferred . . . the sort of thing that the gentry in Ireland have – you know, the toffs. Come to think of it, she must like it – because it's the same kind of furniture as she bought for her house up in Cale Green.'

'Oooh . . .' Elsie said, lost for words. 'As I say, people are all different, aren't they? And did they look after you in this big, posh house? Did you get lots of fancy meals?'

Biddy gave her a brief rundown on her few days in Ireland, and then they moved on to discuss the funeral.

'A right sad do, by the sound of it,' Elsie said, clucking her tongue.

'Well,' Biddy sighed, taking her shoes off and putting her feet up on the small wooden stool, 'thanks be to God it's all over and done with. I was glad to get back to Stockport, I couldn't have taken another day of it all.'

'And what did they think of your hair?' Elsie asked. 'Did they notice you'd got it dyed back to brown?'

'No,' she said vaguely, 'and to tell you the truth, I forgot what colour it was myself.'

Elsie then gave Biddy a blow-by-blow account of all she'd done in the boarding-house since she'd been away.

She told her about all the meals she'd cooked for the lodgers, how she'd watered the plants every day, and how she'd Brasso'd all the bathroom taps and the knocker and the letterbox for her coming home. She decided not to mention the plants that the hooligan had killed the other night – poor Biddy was too tired to cope with news like that. It could wait until later. Then Elsie told her about all the work that her friend June had done as well.

'Some people think of her as bein' a bit rough, like,' Elsie said, 'but she's had a hard life. Brought four kids up on her own, she has.'

Biddy nodded sympathetically, always one for a hard-luck story.

'She worked like a Trojan,' Elsie elaborated, 'and she got on great with the lads and the kids . . . she's a bit of a rum'un when it comes to lads, but she means no harm. It's just her way – seeing as she never got out much when she was younger, on account of the kids. She's a good-lookin' girl – a bit like yourself when you had the blonde hair.'

Biddy smiled, delighted with the compliment.

'An' you'd never guess she was nigh on forty – especially when you think of the life she's lived.' Elsie gave a cackly laugh. 'Oh, some of the stories June's told me – about what she's had to do to put food on the table – it would make your hair curl, it would! I'm not a real prude, as you know – but it took my breath away.'

Before Biddy had a chance to hear any more of her friend's lurid tales, the kitchen door sounded and Angela's voice could be heard. Michael and Helen ran out into the hallway to greet her.

'I'll be off,' Elsie said, getting up quickly. 'I'll drop over after ten this evenin' and we can finish our little chat then.'

Biddy got up now, too. 'I've a small present I brought

you back from the duty-free.' She gave a laugh. 'We'll open it when you come around later.'

Then, just as Elsie went out, Angela appeared in the doorway, and the smile slid from Biddy's face.

'Well,' Biddy said, 'what's the story? I hear you were up and running about not long after I was gone.'

Angela came to sit on the edge of the sofa, taking Helen up on her knee. 'I wasn't myself for a few days . . . I was still running back and forth to the toilet, but I didn't want to be moaning to Elsie about it all the time.'

'I still have my doubts,' Biddy told her bluntly. 'It was very convenient that you were too ill to travel over to Ireland, when the previous day you were trying to get out of going . . .'

'I really wasn't well, Biddy,' the girl said, then she blessed herself, 'and that's as true as God. I wouldn't go telling lies over something like a funeral . . . I'd never do anything as terrible as that.'

'I'll have to take your word for it, then,' Biddy said, 'and just hope that nothing like that ever happens again.'

There was a small, awkward silence. 'Did everything go off OK?'

'Oh, it went off all right,' Biddy sighed, 'if you can call buryin' a young man all right.'

'How was Tara?' Angela said, stroking the child's hair so she wouldn't have to look directly at Biddy.

'In bits,' Biddy stated baldly. 'She's not herself at all. And as for Gabriel's mother, I wouldn't be at all surprised if they end up burying her next, the poor cratur. She was like a corpse herself in the church – white as a sheet and hardly able to string two words together. But how else could she be, burying her son only years after her husband and daughter?' She shook her head. 'It affected everyone real bad – even your father. Your mother was saying that he's not sleepin' well at night at all since it happened.'

'That's not like him,' Angela said in a quiet voice. 'Usually, you would never know what he was thinkin'.' She started fiddling with Helen's hair, fixing it into a plait now. 'How was Mammy and the rest of the family?'

'They were all asking for you,' Biddy said, 'and there's a bag over there in the corner with some bits that your mother sent over for you.' She looked on now as Angela set the child back down on her feet and went to investigate what her mother had sent.

'Oh, lovely! It's a barmbrack,' Angela said, holding up her favourite fruit loaf. The other well-wrapped packages revealed a long black pudding and a horseshoe-shaped white pudding. There was also a small container of perfumed talcum powder. 'Oh, that was fierce good of her to send them over,' Angela said, smiling now. 'When I wrote to her a few weeks ago, I mentioned that I was missing some of the things from back home, so she's sent them over to me!'

'I think they could be doin' with you back over in Tullamore,' Biddy said, watching for the girl's reaction. 'I think they're finding Auntie Molly a bit of a handful . . .'

Angela looked up from the bag, alarm written all over her face. 'Did Mammy say I *had* to come home?'

'Well,' Biddy said, 'they said for the time being that it was up to me . . .'

Angela's eyes suddenly filled up with tears. 'And are you goin' to send me home? Are you not happy with the way things have been going?'

Biddy shrugged. 'I'm not sure what to do for the best, now that Tara's gone back to Ireland . . . this arrangement was only supposed to be for the summer.'

'D'you not think I've been working hard enough?' Angela said, her voice quivering now. 'I can start getting up earlier, if that's what you want.'

'It's the responsibility,' Biddy said in a firm tone. 'I

have Fred coming home soon, and I'll have enough on my plate worrying about him, without worrying about you as well.' She shook her head. 'It was different when Tara was here . . . now there's all this business with Eric.'

'What d'you mean?' Angela said, suddenly alarmed. 'What business are you talking about?' Had Biddy found out about Eric being in the house? She was sure that his mother didn't even know about that.

'Elsie tells me that the pair of you have been havin' rows,' Biddy stated, now beginning to feel weary with the subject, 'and she told me about you being up in Eric's bedroom again. I just don't think it's the kind of carry-on that anybody back home would approve of.'

'I wasn't in it long,' Angela said. 'I was only up to collect an Elvis Presley record of mine that he has—'

'I don't care what your reason is for being up in Eric's room,' Biddy stated, 'it's the fact you were in the room at all that bothers me. It looks very bad for a young girl being up in a lad's bedroom . . . anythin' could be goin' on, for all I know.' She leaned down to slide a piece of Michael's Lego castle back over to him. 'In fact, I was just thinkin' about how this could all look for me . . .'

'In what way?' Angela asked, her face stricken.

'Allowing this type of behaviour to go on, when you're living in my house. It could look as if we have no morals in our house.'

'But I'm not doing *anything*!' Angela suddenly protested. She got to her feet now, gathering her packages as she did so. 'I've *never* done anything that I shouldn't have, and I'm not going to sit here and be accused of it.' Her face was now red with indignation. 'If it makes you feel any happier, I've actually finished with Eric . . . I'd gone off him in any case. I didn't think we were really suited.'

'Indeed,' said Biddy, trying not to show her surprise.

'Well, maybe that's no bad thing . . .' She motioned little Helen to bring her doll over to her.

'I'm going to put these puddings in the fridge, if that's OK,' Angela said in a wounded tone, 'and then I'm going upstairs to tidy my room.'

'That's grand,' Biddy said, fastening up the back of the doll's romper suit. Then, a few moments later, as the girl was on her way upstairs, Biddy called out, 'Where are the library books you got this afternoon?'

Angela halted and turned back towards the room. 'I didn't get any today,' she said, a flush coming over her neck. 'The book I ordered hadn't come in.'

Biddy nodded, knowing full well that the girl had been nowhere near the library.

Chapter Forty-Two

TULLAMORE

Father Joe Flynn's dark head was bent over his aunt in the rocking-chair, helping her to wind her white pearl rosary beads around her fingers.

'Ah, sure, you're a grand lad,' she told him, 'coming all this way to see your poor oul' aunties. There's not many like you ... there's not many young men these days who'd be bothered.' She turned around to the door. 'I don't know where that Maggie's got to ... she's always saying that she won't be long, and then she's gone for hours. You can never find her anywhere these days. I hope she hasn't gone cycling out to Ballygrace or Daingean again.'

'I think,' Joe said, 'that we'll just go on with the rosary without her. She won't mind.' There was no point in reminding Molly that her sister was long gone from this world – and hadn't cycled for many years before she departed – because it only upset her. And in any case, as Joe knew from experience, what he would painfully explain would only be forgotten a few minutes later. He was just grateful that she wasn't wondering where her mother and father were tonight or where Cecil Smith had got to. He lifted his own dark brown rosary beads from the table, and started to bless himself with the cross. 'In the name of the Father, and of the Son and of the Holy Ghost.' They said their usual opening prayers then moved on to the rosary. 'The first

Joyful Mystery, the Annunciation . . .' And then, as he knew she would, she just slid into the old, ritualised words which she had recited every day of her life. They recited the five Joyful Mysteries with all the intervening Our Fathers and Glory Be's.

As Joe led her through each of the prayers, he offered them up to God for his Auntie Molly's health and asked also that he might just bestow a little bit more patience on a priest, who was after all only human, who was trying his best.

So far, Molly Flynn still had bits of her memory that worked, and that allowed her to maintain some of the small routines of her life, and for that Tessie and the rest of the family were well and truly grateful. All the prayers Molly had learned as a young girl growing up were so deeply ingrained in her mind that she only had to hear the first few words for her to continue with the whole prayer, word perfect.

After they finished the rosary, Joe went out to the kitchen and got a small tumbler of water. Next he opened the drawer that housed the medicines and got out one of her sleeping tablets. He came back into the small parlour and held both out to her. Wordlessly, Molly popped the pill into her mouth and took a good gulp of the water to wash it down.

Thank God, Joe thought, *at least she doesn't argue about taking it.* He knew an old lady in his parish in Cork – with the same condition as his aunt – who made her family's life hell by knocking everything they tried to give her out of their hands, convinced that they were trying to poison her.

The priest then went back into the kitchen and boiled up some milk and made them each a mug of Horlicks, sweetened with a spoonful of sugar – although Molly's mug was filled only halfway up to prevent her from spilling it. He carried the mugs into the sitting room on a tray, along with four small, shop-bought pancakes on a plate, the butter-dish, a knife and the toasting-fork.

He gave Molly her mug – which she grasped carefully, as she was told – and then he put one of the pancakes on the fork and held it close to the bright flames in the open fire. Molly sat sipping her drink, and watching what her nephew did with great interest, as though she had never seen anything like it before. When the first pancake was lightly browned on both sides, he buttered it sparingly so that it wouldn't drip, and then he handed it to his aunt. He took a drink of his Horlicks and then he continued toasting the rest of the pancakes.

By the time they had finished their supper, it was time for the nine o'clock news on the radio, and then the music programme that his aunts had listened to since he was a young boy. After about ten minutes, Molly's eyelids started to flutter, and a short while later they closed.

Joe looked across the hearth towards his aunt, and a sadness clutched at his heart. This could only get worse instead of better – and there was nothing he could do to help things. Three nights he had spent with her in this little house, in which he had grown up. Three nights of sitting with her, trying to fill the long hours with a string of nothingness. And tomorrow he would depart for his parish in Cork again, guilt-ridden for leaving the burden of the frail old lady on the rest of the Flynn family.

Very gently, Joe woke her and guided her upstairs by the elbow. He waited outside while she used the bathroom and then he walked her into her bedroom. He put her little bedside lamp on and then lifted her nightdress and dressing-gown from the hook on the back of the door.

'You'll be grand now,' he told her. 'Goodnight and God bless.'

'Good . . . God bless . . .' Molly said, the tablets obviously having started to work on her.

Then Joe went out and closed the bedroom door firmly behind him – hoping that he wouldn't hear another sound from his aunt until the morning. And praying that she wouldn't come wandering into his bedroom – half-undressed – in the middle of the night.

Chapter Forty-Three

BALLYGRACE

Two days after the funeral, Elisha, Harry, young William and the rest of the group that had travelled over from London were packed up and ready to head back home. Tara's housekeeper had prepared the usual fried Irish breakfast, with kippers and porridge and a variety of white and brown breads, to fortify them on their journey. The coming and going of dishes being brought from the kitchen to the dining room helped to give a façade of normality to Ballygrace House. And the passing of dishes up and down the dining-table gave some semblance of social activity amongst the assembled group.

'Are you coming back to London with us, Tara?' William asked, as he buttered a piece of toast.

There was a silence while all eyes looked at her.

'*Tara?*' the boy said loudly, and when she turned towards him he repeated his question.

'No . . .' she said quietly, her face pale and drawn. 'I can't, William . . . I have things to do here.'

Harry suddenly got up and went to the sideboard behind the table to switch on the radio. An upbeat Glenn Miller tune filled the sad, weary silence in the room and gave everyone a break from trying to find something to talk about.

Kate Thornley, who was seated across from Tara, passed a plate of bread to her.

'Are you sure you don't want me to stay on for a few more days?' she said in a low voice. 'I can easily arrange—'

'No,' Tara said quickly, taking the smallest slice of white soda bread from the plate. 'No, thank you, Kate.' She tried to smile, but couldn't. 'You've been so, so good . . . coming down to London with me last week, and then coming over to Ireland as well. But I have a lot to do – business things of Gabriel's to sort out.'

'OK,' Kate said quietly, 'but if you need me, just phone or write and I'll be here.'

'I will,' Tara promised. She reached out for the teapot and poured herself a cup of tea. The bread and piece of bacon she had put on her plate remained untouched. As she lifted the china cup to her lips, Tara's fingers clasped it so tightly that the knuckles turned from pink to a shiny white.

After breakfast the luggage was brought down to the cars and Tara came out to see her guests off. She stood pale-faced and with folded arms at the top of the steps as the men went in and out with the cases.

'I don't know which house makes me feel worse,' Elisha said, coming to stand beside her daughter-in-law. 'All the memories here in Ballygrace House . . . or going back to London to where it happened. If only I hadn't asked him to come down . . . if only I'd been stronger and had coped on my own, maybe this would never have happened.' She pressed her handkerchief to her mouth and closed her eyes.

Tara moved to put a hand on her mother-in-law's shoulder. 'Try not to think about it,' she said quietly. 'The doctor told us it would have happened sooner or later.'

'I just can't stop blaming myself,' Elisha said. 'Why didn't we notice that he had that problem? How could my own son have had a heart condition all his life, and his own mother know nothing about it? How could it be possible?' She dabbed the handkerchief to her eyes. 'With his father and Madeleine . . .'

Tara's throat tightened, and she felt she was almost choking.

'. . . When they died,' Elisha went on, 'I knew it was an accident . . . it was unpreventable. But with Gabriel, I keep thinking that I should have *known*.'

Then Harry appeared with William. He came over and took his wife gently by the elbow. 'Time to go, my dear,' he told her, 'or we'll miss the plane.'

'Think about coming over to London soon, Tara,' Elisha said in a high, strained voice. 'Maybe it would be best to get away from here for a while. When the winter weather arrives, the wet, dripping trees around Ballygrace are very depressing – I couldn't bear to look at them some mornings. I used to feel they were closing in on me.' She squeezed Tara's hand. 'There's much more in London to keep us busy. We could all be together – help each other.'

'I'm sorry,' Tara said in a low voice, 'but I really don't feel it would be the right thing to do.' The circumstances Tara now found herself in were tragic enough, but the thought of going back to Elisha's house in London where Gabriel had actually died was just too awful to contemplate. And she knew that Elisha would lean very heavily on her as she had done even before Gabriel had died. Tara did not have the strength for that just now.

'Will you come soon?' William asked, his eyes wide and pleading. 'Gabriel's car is in our garage – he wouldn't want it to be left to rust. He loved that car, he was so proud of it.'

Tara nodded, a faraway look in her eyes. If anything at all could have touched her heart it would have been the young boy. 'Later,' she heard herself saying, 'maybe later . . . when things have been sorted out.'

Chapter Forty-Four

STOCKPORT

The week after the funeral, Biddy got a call from the hospital in Leeds to say that Fred was being discharged the following Friday. They explained that he would now continue his physiotherapy twice a week at the hospital in Stockport.

'I can't believe it!' she told Elsie as they sat over their mid-morning tea break. 'Back home for good . . . it's been so long, I never thought it would come. I can't believe we're going to be a proper family again.'

'Well,' Elsie said, unwrapping a Wagon Wheel biscuit, 'you can start believin' it, for it's definitely happening.' She gave a cackly laugh. 'It'll be like yer honeymoon all over again, after the length of time you've been apart . . . I hope that mattress is up to it.'

Biddy started to laugh. 'You're not too far off the mark there,' she said, going pink in the face. 'Even last weekend when he was home, you could tell that he'd been missing what he's entitled to. And he was nearly as bad when I was in the hospital visiting him at the weekend. He was closing the door and trying to get me on the bed with him!'

'That's friggin' men for you,' Elsie said knowingly. 'It's all they can think of. Me laddo was the very same.' She took a bite of her biscuit and munched on it thoughtfully for a few moments. 'Havin' said that, it was the only thing I missed about him when he finally went. We always had a good physical life, like.' She sighed. 'Of course, I'm past all that now.'

'Go away with you! There's still life in the old dog yet,' Biddy said, secretly finding it hard to imagine Elsie ever having had sex with anyone.

They both stopped as they heard the latch on the back gate and Lucky barking.

'That's them back,' Biddy said, looking out of the window. A frown came on her face. 'Angela doesn't look too happy. I wonder what's wrong with her now?' She watched as the girl tried to get the dog to settle down quietly enough to let her put his chain on.

Elsie got up from the table. 'I'll get out of the way. I'll go and finish them front steps now,' she said, going out into the hall, 'and then I'll give the doorknocker and the letterbox a bit of a polish.'

Biddy opened the back door and the two children came rushing in past her. 'Angela was shouting at Eric, and then he kicked Lucky!' Michael said excitedly. Then he spotted the open biscuit tin. 'I'm starving, Mam, can I have a Wagon Wheel?'

Biddy quickly gave them a biscuit each and then shooed them into the sitting room. Then she went down the few steps into the small back yard where Angela was still struggling with the dog's lead.

'What's the matter?' she asked in a concerned voice. 'Did something happen at the park?'

Angela kept her back half turned to Biddy as she finally got the hook from the chain on to Lucky's collar. She walked over to the steps and then said in a low whisper, 'Is Elsie around?'

Instinctively, Biddy pulled the door closed so they could talk privately. 'She's out the front doing the steps . . . why? What's wrong?'

'It's Eric,' Angela said, her lip suddenly quivering. 'He just won't leave me alone. He's started following me everywhere. He's watching me from his bedroom

294

window, and when he sees me going out, he's right out behind me.' Her head drooped now. 'And when he's around the house, if he sees me talkin' to any of the lodgers, he's in a right mood for hours. I'm nearly afraid of him, Biddy . . .'

Biddy's brow deepened. 'Has he tried to hurt you or anything?'

'No,' Angela said quickly, 'but one minute he's being all nice and trying to get me to go out with him, and the next minute he's really nasty.'

Biddy gave a deep sigh. 'I warned you,' she told the girl. 'Didn't I tell you not to get involved with him?'

Angela's gaze moved to the ground, and she started twisting the dog lead between her hands. 'I thought he was nice at first . . . and I didn't know anyone else when I came here.'

Biddy's eyes narrowed. 'And do you know anyone else *now*?' she asked. 'Is that the reason you've lost interest in Eric? Is there another lad on the scene?'

Angela shook her head. She definitely couldn't mention Philip that she'd met down at the library now – the lad with whom she'd met up a few times for a cup of tea. She was sure that Biddy would approve of him. He was a nice decent lad – a lot friendlier and more open than Eric – and he was a Catholic. He definitely would never have kicked a poor animal the way Eric had kicked Lucky this afternoon in the park. Angela decided she wouldn't mention Philip for the time being. Biddy wasn't in the best of moods since she'd come back from the funeral, and she knew that she would only eat her alive if she mentioned another lad just now.

'Well, this is a nice how-do-you-do you've got us all into,' Biddy said, pursing her lips in exasperation, 'an' it would have to be with that damned Eric. D'you not realise the awkwardness it's goin' to cause between me and Elsie if Eric starts kicking up trouble at home on account of you?'

Angela bit her lip. She'd known since that morning last week that she'd made one big mistake getting involved with Eric. Everything had just seemed so exciting when she first arrived, and Eric had been part of all that. But there was something about him now that frightened her, and she knew she was out of her depth with him.

'I'm sorry, Biddy,' Angela said, her eyes filled with tears. 'I was only being friends with him . . . and I wish I'd listened to you in the first place.'

Biddy's face softened. Something about the girl had suddenly reminded her of the way she had been with P.J. Murphy all those years ago – and she hadn't listened to what anyone had told her at the time either. 'Aw . . . don't worry,' she said, putting her arm around her. 'It'll all work itself out—'

The back door suddenly opened and Elsie stuck her head out. 'It's for you,' she called. 'I think they said somethin' about a doctor.'

Biddy stiffened now. She wondered whether it was the hospital phoning about Fred, or whether it was her own doctor up at the surgery. She turned back towards Angela.

'Forget about all this nonsense now, and just go in and make a start on the potatoes,' she said, before going quickly up the stairs and into the house.

'Mrs Roberts?' the voice on the phone checked.

'Yes,' Biddy said. 'It's Bridget Roberts here.'

'I'm just putting Dr Phillips on the line to you now.'

A few seconds later another female voice came on the line. 'Good afternoon, Mrs Roberts, it's Dr Phillips here . . . I have the results of your test back from the hospital.'

'Yes?' Biddy said, holding her breath.

'It's positive.'

'You mean . . .' Biddy started.

'Yes,' the doctor said, 'you're definitely pregnant.'

'Thank you,' she said, 'thank you for letting me know.' She put the phone back in its cradle and walked straight upstairs and into her bedroom. She closed the door behind her and lay down on the bed. She needed a few minutes to herself to take in the news. Although it shouldn't have been any surprise. She was a good bit late. She'd guessed far quicker than she had with Michael and Helen, but with everything that had happened recently, she'd just put it to the back of her mind. But last week when she'd suddenly realised that the nausea she had been feeling had never passed, she had twigged that it might be this.

Well, there was nothing else to do now, but to get on with it.

Chapter Forty-Five

BALLYGRACE

Ella tapped on Tara's bedroom door for the second time, then she opened it very slightly. 'I've some post for you, Tara. Shall I bring it in?'

Tara pulled herself into a sitting position in the bed. 'Just leave it on the chest of drawers, thank you, Ella.'

'Would you like me to bring you up some breakfast?' the housekeeper asked, putting a small pile of white and brown envelopes on the white marble top. 'I could do you a nice—'

'A cup of tea would be lovely,' Tara interrupted. 'I'm not ready to eat anything just now.'

When the bedroom door closed again, Tara sank back on to the pillows. After a while, she got out of bed and went across to the chest of drawers. She leafed through the mail, ignoring the handwritten white envelopes that came in relentlessly, day after day, containing Mass cards and sympathy cards.

She picked three of the larger brown envelopes and went back over to her bed with them. The first two she opened and just slid the paper out to read the heading on the notepaper. It was business stuff that she would give to the managers in the offices. When she saw the solicitor's name and address on the last document, she pulled it completely out of the envelope. Her eyes scanned the covering letter, then she turned over the pages, her eyes growing wider in shock as she read.

This can't be true! she thought, her hand flying up to cover her mouth. She went over the letter again, reading each line carefully and trying to take in all the legal jargon. Then she went back to the pages of columns and figures. She stared and stared at the paper until the lines were all blurred into a black and white mass.

How could this happen to her *now*?

After all she had been through ... how could she suddenly have all the things she had longed for since she was a young girl? The things she had dreamed about for years. She looked back at the letter now – the letter that she wished had never, ever come. The letter that told her Gabriel had left her a final gift. He had left her more money and property than she would ever need for the rest of her life.

Chapter Forty-Six

The waitress came over to the table. 'Meat and potato pie and chips?' she said, looking from one to the other.

'The meat and tatoe pie is mine, love,' Elsie said, moving her knife and fork to let the girl put the hot plate down on the table mat, 'and I've some bread and butter to come with that, too.' She smiled benignly at the young girl. She liked eating in the Co-op restaurant, as it was that bit more refined than the fish and chip shop.

'And the chicken and chips?' the girl checked, coming around the table to Biddy.

'And two lemonades to go with the meal, please,' Biddy said, making room for her plate now, 'and we'll have the cups of tea afterwards.'

'This is a right lovely treat,' Elsie said, lifting a chip with her fingers, 'and it's good and hot. You can always depend on them in here to do it right.'

Biddy nodded, unable to speak because she had a hot chip in her mouth. She swallowed it, then immediately regretted it as she felt it burning all the way down her gullet. She reached for the vinegar bottle, hoping that a good sprinkling might cool it all down. 'It's nice to get out for our lunch now and again,' she said, 'because we might not make it out too often when Fred comes home.'

'Oh, it'll be lovely havin' him back,' Elsie said,

putting circles of salt on her steaming pie. 'You'll be a proper little family again, won't you?'

'We will,' Biddy said, smiling, 'and this time next year there will be five of us instead of four.'

'You're not – are you? I knew it!'

Biddy nodded. 'Next April . . . it must have been when he came home that weekend.'

'I knew it!' Elsie repeated delightedly. 'I could see it in yer face . . . mind you, I didn't like to say. But I can always tell when women are pregnant, they have a certain look – and it crossed my mind last week that you might be expectin'. Have you told Fred yet?'

Biddy shook her head. 'No, sure I only found out for definite the other day . . . I'd been feeling a bit squeamish and generally off-colour. I don't know how it didn't dawn on me, I suppose it was with everything going on.'

'You've had a lot on your mind,' Elsie said sympathetically.

'You can say that again,' Biddy said, nodding. 'You're the first one I've told.'

'Am I?' Elsie said, smiling and going pink with delight at being singled out as her boss's confidante. 'And how d'you feel?' she asked. 'Are you happy enough about it?'

Biddy gave a little shrug. 'I'm not too sure how I feel this time – it was a real shock. With Michael and Helen I was delighted. I suppose when you have a boy first you're desperate for a girl next . . . but I've never really thought about it since.'

There was an unaccustomed silence for a while as they both ate their meals. 'I'm not going to say anythin' about the baby to anyone else for a few weeks . . . even Angela,' Biddy said now. 'I'll feel better mentioning it when I'm further on . . . you just never know.'

'Well, you know I wouldn't say a word about it,' Elsie reassured her.

Biddy cut into her chicken breast. 'As long as Fred is all right ... the way things have been since his accident ...'

'Why?' Elsie asked. 'D'you think he won't be happy about havin' another baby?'

'Oh, there's no problem about the baby,' Biddy explained. 'He'll be delighted about that. What I meant is, as long as Fred's recovery keeps goin'. I mean, they've said to me at the hospital that he might need a wheelchair if we were goin' any long distances. An' with him not bein' able to drive for a while, it might be a bit awkward trying to manage everything.'

'Well, you know our Eric is always there if you need him,' Elsie reminded her. 'Because you can't have Fred lifting and doing things just yet – he's not going to be fit to do *anything* around the house until he gets the all-clear from the hospital.'

Biddy took a deep breath, dreading what she was going to have to say next – the whole reason she'd suggested that she treat Elsie to lunch. The reason that she'd also given Elsie the news first, because she knew from past experience that to criticise Eric was to criticise his mother. Biddy knew that she would have to really soften her friend up to broach the subject.

'The thing is, Elsie, I'm not too sure about Eric helping in the house any more,' Biddy said hesitantly. 'Not that I've any complaints about him – far from it, he's been a great help. But there's a bit of an atmosphere when him and Angela are together ... and it's getting' worse.' Then, when she saw Elsie's mouth tightening, she rushed on. 'It's not just me that's noticed it, the kids have said several times that they were arguing, and one of the lodgers said he heard them fightin' out in the back entry.' She paused. 'It's just that Fred wouldn't like any kind of an atmosphere in the house – and it wouldn't be good for him. The hospital says he needs peace and quiet.'

'Well,' Elsie said, in a much calmer tone than Biddy had expected, 'I hate to say it, but there's only one answer to the problem.' She took a drink of her lemonade. Biddy felt a wave of relief rush over her – thank God Elsie understood.

'What answer's that?' she asked, not wanting to make her relief seem too obvious.

'You'll have to get rid of her,' Elsie said in an even tone. 'You'll just have to send Angela packing back home to Ireland.'

Angela stood behind the curtain in one of the top-floor bedrooms, looking down into the backyard of the houses across the way, to see if there was any sign of Eric around. She was due to walk down to the school to pick up Michael and Helen, and she definitely didn't want to run into him again today. He had been really awkward with her this morning when she had been hoovering the sitting room and he'd been clearing the fire out, pestering her and asking her to go for a walk with him so that they could talk things out.

As far as Angela was concerned, there was nothing else to talk about. After that morning when he had got too carried away, she had told him she didn't want to get serious with anybody just now. She realised that she had made a big mistake, and that she had given Eric the wrong impression about her. There was no way she was ready to get into a physical relationship with any lad – and she certainly didn't want to run the risk of getting caught with a baby.

That was definitely the last thing she wanted. She felt her skin crawl with embarrassment now when she thought of the way she had carried on with him. *How could I have been so stupid?* she constantly asked herself. But she knew that she'd only done it to show him that she was every bit as sexy as those girls he had been bragging about, not realising that it was the worst thing she could possibly have done. After she had refused him, he had started calling her terrible names like 'prick-teaser' and 'frigid-Brigid', and he hadn't let up since. Then he had changed his tune when she told him she only wanted to be friends with him – he had made every promise under the sun about keeping his hands to himself, as long as they could still go out. 'Me and you are suited to one another,' he had told her this morning as he was putting the ashes from the fire into the bucket.

'I'm sure you'll find plenty of girls that are more suited to you,' Angela had replied, 'and anyway, I'll have to go back to Ireland soon enough – so there's no point in us getting too fond of each other.' Not that she had any intentions of going home in the near future, but she just wanted him to leave her alone. Since meeting Philip in the library, she realised that she had no feelings of fondness left for Eric. In fact, she couldn't even imagine what she had ever seen in him at all.

Philip was much more suited to her. He wasn't quite as with it as Eric, but he was good-looking, in his own way, and he had a much nicer, gentler manner about him.

'But I like talking to you,' Eric had persisted. 'I never talked to any of the other girls . . . not the way I talk to you. You're special.'

But Angela didn't want to feel special to Eric, and she wasn't interested in talking or doing anything else with him anymore either. There was nothing else for him to do but to accept it.

Reassured that there was no sign of him now, Angela slid the curtain back in place and went quickly downstairs. She quickly checked around the kitchen – turning off the wireless as she went – and then she glanced around the sitting room. She moved a few of the ornaments on the mantelpiece, straightened up a few cushions, and then headed out the front door. She had made sure she had done everything that Biddy had asked her to do, and had left downstairs completely tidy in case the two women were back before her. Biddy was a bit snappy at the moment, and Angela didn't want to risk doing anything that might provoke her bad humour – provoke her enough to send Angela home.

It turned out to be a very busy evening for Biddy, considering it was only an ordinary Wednesday. She and Angela had done the clearing and washing-up when the lodgers had finished their meal, and she had then sat down with a cup of tea and a digestive biscuit. After that she'd had to go and change into a decent blouse and skirt and put a bit of lipstick on to go down to a meeting at the children's school about some new reading books they were introducing.

When she saw Biddy rushing about, Angela had offered to get the children washed and ready for bed, and said she would make a start on the basket of ironing that was steadily piling up. Biddy was grateful for the help, but there was something about the girl's face that made her look into the sitting room on her way out.

'Has Eric been behaving himself?' she asked in a concerned voice. 'Or has he been annoying you again?'

'I haven't seen him since this morning,' Angela said, her face flushing. 'I'm hoping he's got the message by now.'

'We're all hoping that he's got the message,' Biddy said grimly, 'because it would be a shame if he spoiled things here for you – because you've been a great help to me when you've put your mind to it.'

The meeting at the school had gone on for an hour and a half, and after Biddy had stopped and chatted to some of the other mothers, it was well after nine by the time she got back home. As she turned the corner, she was surprised to see two cars outside the house. One, she knew, was Frank Kennedy's, and the other – a shiny blue Beetle – she didn't recognise. The Volkswagen was parked awkwardly and Biddy noticed that it had a dent on the bumper.

As she walked into the house, she kept looking back at the Beetle, vaguely remembering someone talking about that particular make of car when she was over in Ireland.

When she reached the sitting-room door, Biddy could hear Frank's low, rich tones and a well-cultured voice she recognised instantly. It was Kate Thornley. A small wave of panic hit her, and she silently moved down the hallway, fishing into her handbag for her comb and compact. Then the kitchen door opened and Angela came out.

'You have visitors,' she said in a low whisper. 'I put them into the sitting room. They haven't been here long.'

'Grand,' Biddy whispered. 'Did the kids settle down all right for you?'

Angela nodded. 'I read them a few stories and then they went off to sleep.' She pointed to the sitting-room door. 'D'you want me to bring some tea in?'

Biddy hesitated. 'Give me a few minutes and I'll let you know.' Hopefully, she thought, they might have a drink instead.

'I'm listening to a pop show on the radio,' Angela said, turning back towards the kitchen.

Biddy went to the hall mirror and after a quick comb of her hair she dabbed some powder over her face and then reapplied her deep pink lipstick. Whilst Frank was easygoing and complimentary however she looked, Kate Thornley was not the type of person Biddy wanted to meet when she looked a mess. She gave silent thanks now that she had been dressed for her school meeting in a neat black flared skirt and a modern-style grey and pink striped blouse.

She paused outside the sitting-room door, took a deep breath, then went in to her guests. Frank looked very comfortable sitting in the middle of the sofa, his arms spread out over the back of it. Kate Thornley sat in one of the armchairs opposite him, looking much more glamorous than she had over in Ireland for the funeral. As she glanced at her, Biddy immediately felt envious of Kate's newly cut, very modern red hair, which was set off by the cream sweater-dress that stopped dead on her slim knee. Her face was perfectly made up with the latest fashion of dark-ringed eyes and pale lips.

'Bridget!' Frank said, standing up to give her a kiss. 'I visited Fred last evening, and I thought I'd drop out and give you a report on how he's doing.'

'I hope he's behavin' himself,' Biddy said, hardly able to take her eyes off Kate. She suddenly felt really frumpy and old-fashioned, and wished she'd gone to a more modern hairdresser's in Manchester like she was sure Kate had.

'I see a great improvement in him altogether,' Frank said, giving her an encouraging pat on the arm. 'He's almost back to his old self, and chomping at the bit to be home. He tells me if all goes well, he should be out next week.'

Biddy nodded. 'There should be nothin' to hold him back now, please God.'

'Well, it seems I wasn't the only one thinking of you this evening,' he said, his eyes warm and smiling, 'because this young lady literally bumped into me a few minutes after I pulled up outside.'

Kate stood up now, smiling, but looking slightly awkward. 'I hope you don't mind me calling out,' she said, leaning forward to squeeze Biddy's hands, 'but I was on my way out to Macclesfield, and I just wondered if you'd heard anything from Tara.'

Biddy took her coat off, and put it on the back of a chair. 'No,' she said. 'I did ring when I got home last week, but I only spoke to the girl that helps her. She said Tara was lying down.' Biddy came to sit in the other armchair. 'Have you heard nothing yourself?'

'I've phoned twice,' Kate replied, her face slightly anxious now, 'and I obviously got the same message that you did. To be honest, I'm a bit worried.' Then she quickly added, 'Not that anyone could expect her to be her old self, but . . .'

Frank sat up straighter, listening intently, and face serious.

Biddy bit her lip. 'It's going to take her a long time to get over this . . . an awful long time.' There was a little silence, then Biddy got to her feet again. 'Will you have a drink? There's a few bottles of beer or there's whiskey or sherry . . .'

'Go on then,' Frank said, smiling, 'you've twisted my arm. I'll have a whiskey and water.'

'Kate?' Biddy asked, delighted that she now had the excuse of being able to have a social drink herself.

'I'll have a sherry, please, Bridget,' Kate said, adopting the same name for Biddy as Frank had used.

'Grand,' Biddy said, going over to the cabinet that held the bottles and the glasses. As she poured the whiskey and the two glasses of sherry, she suddenly thought that she would quite like to be called Bridget all the time. It sounded far better than *Biddy*. People over in Stockport always looked at her a bit strangely when she told them her name, because it was one you never heard of here. She'd never really thought about changing to her proper name before, because apart from the teachers in school and the nuns when she was in the convent in Dublin, no one had ever used her proper name in conversation.

But listening to the way Frank, and now Kate, had said it, *Bridget* was definitely much more sophisticated.

Yes, she thought now as she turned to bring the

drinks to the others, she might just start calling herself Bridget from now on.

'So that's where you got the bump on your car!' Biddy said, her eyes wide with surprise. 'I noticed the nice new car when I was comin' in, and then I noticed the bump at the front. Oh, Lord! Isn't that fierce bad luck, havin' that happen to your lovely car!' Her second sherry was really loosening her up, and she was now thoroughly enjoying the chat with Kate and Frank. She was back to feeling as comfortable and confident with Kate as she had at the funeral.

'I feel so stupid,' Kate said, laughing and covering her face. 'I was just trying to get a bit closer to the kerb, and I thought I'd put my foot on the brake – but I'd hit the accelerator instead.'

'And went straight into the back of my car!' Frank said, laughing. 'Women drivers – what more can you expect?'

'Oh, don't! I feel bad enough,' Kate said, shaking her head now. 'You'll have to put it in to a garage to be fixed, and I'll pay the bill.'

'You'll do no such thing,' Frank told her. 'Sure, it's only a bit of a dent on the bumper. It won't cost much to have that repaired.'

'No, no,' Kate said, 'I insist on paying for it . . . I feel absolutely dreadful doing that to your beautiful car. It's different with my own, it's only a little Beetle . . .'

Biddy sat with a smile on her face, enjoying the banter between them. Then there was a knock at the door and Angela stuck her head around it.

'I'm goin' off up to bed,' she said. 'I'll see you in the morning.' She looked over at Frank and Kate. 'It was nice to meet you . . . goodnight now.'

They both said goodnight to her, and after she went off upstairs, Frank said, 'Has she settled down a bit better now?'

Biddy held her hands up. 'Don't ask me, Frank. It's grand one day and then something could happen the next. She's a lovely girl, but it's a big responsibility having her here . . . you know what they're like at that age.' She shrugged. 'I only wish Tara was here, she'd have a better idea of what would be the best thing for her.'

Kate nodded her head. 'It is a responsibility,' she agreed. She looked at her watch now. 'I think I'd better get going – my mother will wonder where on earth I've been.'

'Why don't you give her a ring?' Biddy suggested. 'The phone's out in the hall.'

The minute Kate left the room, Frank turned to Biddy. 'So, Tara's not too grand?' he said in a low voice. 'Has she taken it all very badly?'

'She has,' Biddy confirmed in a definite tone. 'He wasn't just her husband, Frank, she'd known him from the time she started school . . . sure, she was best friends with his sister.' She took a drink from her sherry. 'It's a tragedy what's happened to that whole family . . . nothin' short of a tragedy.'

'What do you think she'll do now – now that it's all over?' Frank asked, his eyes fixing on hers determinedly. 'Do you think she might move over here permanently? Maybe come back to the house in Cale Green? Did you get any idea of what her plans might be . . . surely she's not going to bury herself over in Offaly?'

'I have no idea, Frank,' she told him coolly, 'no idea at all.' She paused to take another little sip of her sherry, determined not to be led into any more discussion about her friend. 'Now, tell me, what was the news at the hospital – what's that husband of mine getting up to?'

Shortly after Kate came off the phone, Biddy heard someone coughing upstairs and went up to investigate, in case it was one of the children. She stood in the hall upstairs listening, and then quickly deduced that it was coming from one of the lads' rooms on the top floor.

When she came back downstairs, the door was half ajar and she could hear Frank and Kate chatting quite loudly. She paused for a moment, not wanting to interrupt them, and then suddenly felt awkward when she realised she could hear their conversation.

'I'll have to give you something towards the car, Frank,' Kate said. 'I feel really, really awful about it.'

'Forget it,' Frank said, his voice warm and friendly. 'It was an accident, and a small one. It's due to go in for a service in the next couple of weeks and I'll get them to sort the bumper out then. It's only a five-minute job.'

'I'll have to do something,' she insisted. 'Look . . . why don't I take you out for a meal or get tickets for the theatre or something like that?'

Biddy could hear Frank laughing. 'Grand!' he said, as though striking a bargain. 'If it makes you feel better, then that's what we'll do.'

'When?' she checked.

There was a silence, during which Frank was obviously thinking. 'I'm not sure whether I'll be here or travelling around over the next few weeks,' he said. 'You might be best to give me a ring on that.'

'OK,' Kate told him. 'Write your phone number down there, and I'll give you a call as soon as I sort something out. You don't mind what we do?'

'Mind?' he said, his voice low and velvety. 'I should think not. I'm delighted to be taken out by a beautiful woman like yourself. In fact, I will be looking forward to it.'

'Good,' Kate said, 'and I'll look forward to it as well. I'll try and find something nice to surprise you.'

'Bring yourself,' Frank told her, 'and that'll be more than enough.'

Biddy decided it was safe to come back into the room now, and she was surprised to see that Kate had joined

Frank on the sofa, and that they both seemed very relaxed with each other.

Later, after she'd waved them both off, Biddy wondered if there was any chance of a romance starting up between them. Frank was a free man now, and Kate was a single woman in her late twenties, or perhaps thirty already. And a very attractive woman she was. Thinking about how they looked sitting together tonight, Biddy suddenly thought that they would make a very handsome couple, and they had a lot in common.

She wondered if there was a chance that Frank Kennedy might just be interested in another woman.

Chapter Forty-Seven
BALLYGRACE HOUSE, OCTOBER

Tara came down the steps of Ballygrace House, a brown leather hold-all in one hand and her cream Burberry raincoat in the other, and then stopped to stare out over the gardens and the fields beyond. The chill of the misty late-October morning signalled that the fine autumn days were drawing in, and the sudden yellowing of the trees underscored the same message.

This morning she had risen earlier and filled a hot bath, and then had washed her long, luxuriant red hair. A glance out of the window at the cool, damp start to the day was enough to shake her into a decision about choosing suitable clothes for the changing weather. Up until now she had existed mainly indoors, and had simply recycled a few basic outfits of trousers and a blouse, and when it got colder in the evenings she put on a cardigan or sweater. Her bare feet were slipped into plain brown leather loafers that neither clashed with, nor complemented her clothes. She had scarcely glanced in a mirror for weeks, as she restrained her glorious hair in a tight ponytail and left her face naked of any make-up.

But this morning was different. She knew the time had come to venture beyond Ballygrace House, and it required her making a bit of the effort she always had done with her appearance. She had stood looking in at the shelves and hangers in her mahogany wardrobe for a few minutes, and eventually emerged with a camel cashmere sweater, tan slacks and dark suede boots. Her only concession to jewellery was her watch and a pair of discreet diamond earrings that Gabriel had given her as a birthday present. Her morning rituals of applying perfume and hand-cream no longer crossed her mind.

Tara moved from the front of the house towards the garage, where the car engine was already running. She had come out a quarter of an hour earlier to warm the car up as Mick was constantly reminding her to do.

She now went to the back of the car and threw her bag and coat into the boot alongside the wrapped bottles of red and white wine she had placed there earlier. She had packed very little – really only another similar outfit to the one she was wearing, plus essential toiletries – as she presumed her visit would only last a couple of days at most.

As she had lain awake the previous night in the empty, desolate bed that she had shared with Gabriel, Tara knew that she needed to talk to someone about the massive changes that had suddenly been wrought in her life. For one thing, she needed to air her feelings about living in Ballygrace House without Gabriel. It felt desperately empty without him, and it felt wrong that she should now be the sole owner of the house that had belonged to the Fitzgerald family. While she couldn't face the thought of any legal or financial discussions, and had been studiously avoiding them, she suddenly felt the need to talk over her feelings about just *being* in Ballygrace House.

Tara also felt an overwhelming need to talk to someone, and to ask for guidance, on her sudden lack of faith. Religion had never been a subject that had caused her any real anguish before. She knew exactly where she stood with regards to all the main issues. She followed the Church in the things she felt comfortable with, and listened to her own conscience for all the rest. So far, it had worked out fine. She had attended Sunday Masses in Ballygrace and in Stockport, she and Gabriel had married in church, and any children they might have had would most certainly have been baptised in the Catholic Church. But she was no longer certain of God or religion. Over the last few weeks, Tara had come to feel that God had deserted her. And when she lay awake in the long dark hours that gave no hope of dawn, she felt no sign of his existence. Just a big, empty silence. All the signs showed that God – if he existed at all – had given up on Tara Fitzgerald.

The road out to Portlaoise was quiet as always, and then it was a case of following the signs leading to Cork for the next four or five hours. It was a long, long way to drive to look for answers to some very difficult questions. Answers that might not even be found. Tara wasn't even sure that she was going to the right person, but after weeks of unanswered questions going round and round in her head, she had suddenly thought of Joe. Joe, her brother. Father Joseph Flynn, the priest. Who better to ask?

Who else could she trust to give her honest answers?

Joe's parish was a couple of miles outside the city centre, and as she drove out past the big old buildings in the afternoon sunshine, she felt a stab of sadness that she hadn't made the journey down here with Gabriel. Visiting Joe was another of the things that she had been putting off. Another of the things that she would never now do with Gabriel.

Just as Joe had described it, she came across the old stone church first, then took the left-hand turn immediately after it, and saw the big Victorian red-brick house with the stained-glass porch. She pulled up outside it, and then sat for a few minutes, gathering her thoughts.

She walked up to the door, past the neat pink and

blue hydrangea bushes and the last of the summer pansies and purple fuchsias that bordered the path.

A thin, pinch-nosed woman, whom Tara took to be the housekeeper, answered the door to her. She looked Tara up and down suspiciously, and after quizzing her about which priest she wanted to see, and what her business was, she eventually went off to find the curate.

'Tara!' Joe's eyes lit up when he saw his sister standing on the presbytery doorstep, the paleness of her cheeks and the hollowness of her eyes hitting him immediately.

'I hope you didn't mind me ringing this morning to invite myself down?'

'Mind?' he said, putting his arms around her. 'I should think not – I'm delighted! I think it's a very good thing that you decided to have a little break, and I'm even more delighted that you chose to come down to Cork.' He led her into the dark, wood-panelled hallway with the shining, mosaic-tiled floor and the long sideboard with an elaborately carved mirror and legs. A huge vase of white lilies, sitting high up on a mahogany plant-stand, brightened up a corner.

Tara followed her brother into the sitting room, which was equally graciously furnished with a wine-coloured velvet Chesterfield sofa and chairs, several bookcases, and a welcoming fire burning in the white marble fireplace.

'A drink?' Joe suggested, taking off his white clerical collar and putting it down on a small side table. Then he opened the top button of his long black robe. 'Maybe we could have a sherry before we eat?'

'Actually,' Tara said, standing up, 'I have a couple of bottles of wine I brought for you in the car . . .'

'That's very kind of you,' Joe said, smiling. 'We can get them later. If you'd prefer wine to drink now, we have white wine cooling in the fridge and some red in the drinks cabinet.' He laughed. 'Father O'Leary keeps the house well stocked up. He reckons it's his one little indulgence of the flesh. I can take it or leave it, although it's nice to have the odd drink on a social occasion like this.'

'I'd love a glass of white wine, please,' Tara said, hoping with all her heart that it just might relax her a little and help her to find the right words.

The parish priest joined them for a formal dinner in the beautifully furnished dining room at six o'clock. The severe-looking housekeeper – who had been so dismissive of Tara earlier on – was now the essence of civility, and it dawned on Tara that it was obvious that either Joe or the parish priest had alerted the woman to her recent bereavement. Father O'Leary was quiet and solemn to start with, offering Tara his condolences about the loss of her husband and telling her of young men he had buried before their time over the years. After his second glass of Burgundy, he came out of himself more and began to chat more generally. He asked Tara about various priests he knew in the Offaly area, and then went on to regale them both with stories from his seminary days in Dublin.

Tara finished half of her bowl of chicken and vegetable soup, which she'd taken without any bread, and then did her best with the main course of sliced beef and potatoes and mixed vegetables. Had she been at home, she would have found the soup alone was enough, with her reduced appetite, but she forced herself to eat a reasonable amount, since she was dining with company.

'Do you mind me asking?' Joe said later when they were drinking coffee in the sitting room. 'What was the reason that brought you down to Cork?'

Tara looked down into her half-empty coffee cup. 'To be honest . . . I felt I needed to talk to someone about . . .' She hesitated, not sure where to start. And then, before she could get any further, the doorbell chimed.

Joe looked at his watch, and then suddenly remembered. 'The Walshes . . .' He got to his feet and reached for his dog collar. 'A family . . . they're having a bit of trouble with their two teenagers,' he explained, slotting the collar in place. 'I forgot all about them.'

Hearing the housekeeper bring the people in, Tara got to her feet, feeling slightly flustered. 'Do you want to bring them in here?'

'No, no,' Joe said. He went to the mirror above the fireplace to check that his collar was sitting properly. 'We have an office we use for this kind of thing.' He held his hands out in apology. 'Do you mind? I promise, I'll be as quick with them as I can . . .'

'I don't mind at all,' Tara said, smiling. She went over to the largest of the bookcases that held Joe's collection of novels and poetry. 'I'm sure I'll find something here to keep me entertained.'

Much later than he anticipated, Joe came rushing back into the sitting room to find Tara staring into the orangey embers of the fire, a Thomas Hardy book open on her lap. 'I can only apologise . . . but they had a lot of problems they needed to talk out. It seems one of the boys has been expelled from school, and the other has been caught stealing.' He ran his fingers through his dark curly hair, then once again took his stiff white collar off and opened the top button of his soutane. 'Tea, coffee, a drink?' he said, almost breathlessly.

'Do you have parishioners calling for advice regularly?' Tara asked when they had settled down with a glass of wine and some crackers and cheese.

Joe nodded, taking a deep drink of his wine. 'It's a part of the job I hadn't really bargained on,' he confided. 'It takes up a huge amount of time – almost as much time as the church services, my youth work and visiting the sick.' He shrugged. 'The pastoral work eats into a big chunk of my evenings, the time when I should be preparing my Sunday sermons or reading over parish documents.'

'I'd no idea you were so incredibly busy,' Tara said, in a surprised tone. 'You must feel as though you are pulled in all directions.'

'It's not always just as hectic as I'm making it sound,' Joe said, smiling. 'I do manage occasionally to take some time for reading or – God forbid – the odd bit of socialising!'

'Well, I'm glad to hear that you make some time for yourself,' Tara said, 'because you obviously give the biggest part of your life to other people.'

'Not as much as I'd like to,' he told her, cutting himself a piece of red Cheddar and putting it on a water biscuit. 'The need in the big cities is so great. There are people living under enormous pressures with no one to turn to, whether it's money problems, alcohol problems, marital problems, sickness – you name it, and it's out there.' He handed Tara the cheese-board now. She left it on the table in front of her, untouched.

'But you must feel a great sense of satisfaction,' Tara said, 'knowing that you've helped these people. Knowing that you've been able to have some influence on their lives and their problems.'

'But that', Joe said, 'is the biggest fallacy about priests. Take the most common problem of all – marital problems.' He prodded his chest. 'Just what do *I* know about marital problems? Me, a single man who has never been in an intimate relationship with a woman.'

Tara shrugged, feeling slightly uncomfortable with the turn the conversation had taken. 'I'm sure you must have had some training for these things in the seminary . . .'

'Of course,' Joe said, taking a sip of his red wine, 'I've certainly studied the theory of these things – but what about the practical aspects? Just what experience have I in family life? I left home at ten or eleven years of age, and even then it wasn't a conventional family situation that I'd been living in.' He shook his head. 'Two very kindly maiden aunts who constantly pampered and praised me to make up for the fact that I had no mother or father's influence in my life.'

'I still think you must be of more help to people than you think,' Tara stated. 'Just having someone to listen makes a huge difference to people – and you're obviously good at that, otherwise you wouldn't have so many people coming for advice.'

'Maybe . . .' Joe didn't sound convinced.

'Actually,' Tara said, her face starting to flush a little, 'I drove down here to ask you for some advice myself . . .'

Joe sat forward in his chair now, his hands clasped in front of him, waiting. 'If there is anything I can do to help . . .'

'God,' Tara stated without any preamble. 'How do you help people who have lost all faith in him?'

Tara emerged from the red-brick house the following afternoon with her brother. The October sky was overcast, but so far it had remained dry. They had had lunch together in a lovely hotel restaurant, and had continued their conversation from the previous night.

'I'm so sorry about that late-night visit,' Joe said with a sigh. 'It was very inhospitable of me not to get back in time to say goodnight to you. It seems that every time we got into serious mode, something else cropped up.'

'A call to the sick is much more important than us having a chat,' Tara told him. 'And anyway, we picked up our conversation after Mass and again at lunch.'

'I hope you found something worthwhile and of comfort in your visit,' he said gently, lifting her bag into the boot of the car for her. 'I wish I could have been of more help to you . . .'

'You were very helpful, Joe,' Tara told him, as they walked around to the front of the car. 'You listened to me and you gave me any answers you had.'

His face brightened up. 'I have no problems advising you about Ballygrace House. I would simply say "wait". Make no decisions until after Christmas – or even further into next year. Don't make any hasty changes, like selling up or moving away. Take your time over things.' His voice had dropped. 'Getting over bereavement is the biggest challenge God can send us, but I promise you that you *will* get over it – in the fullness of time.'

Tara nodded, but she turned from his gaze. Joe placed his hands on Tara's shoulders, bringing her back round to face him.

'And remember what I said about your religious questions – it's all down to faith, Tara,' he told her gently. 'That's all the answer there is. For those of us who are fortunate enough to have that kind of faith, it's easy enough . . . but it's very, very difficult to find it – especially after what you've been through. Losing a wonderful husband and friend like Gabriel is an understandable blow to anyone's faith.'

'I'd do anything to get comfort from my religion,' Tara said quietly. 'I'd do anything to get comfort from anywhere now. And I really have tried . . .'

'Give it time, Tara,' he told her. 'Be kind to yourself. The fact that you've come all the way down here, searching for answers, proves that you want to feel something. Eventually, with time, it will come.'

Tara nodded slowly, then she put her arms around her brother's neck and hugged him. 'You're doing a wonderful job down here, Father Joseph Flynn,' she told him. 'You're a true example of what a priest should be, and I'm proud to have you as my brother.'

As she drove out through Cork City and started on the long road for home, Tara gradually let the tears and the bitter disappointment surface. At one point, it so overwhelmed her that she pulled over to the side of the road and cried aloud in the privacy of the car.

Joe had been her one and only hope. If Joe couldn't help her, then nobody could.

Chapter Forty-Eight

Biddy's heart had lifted when she'd heard Tara's voice on the line one Thursday afternoon. It was definitely a good sign. A sign that Tara was no longer hiding away from everyone. Up until now, Ella or Kitty had always answered the phone, apologetically saying that she was lying down or that she had a bit of a headache and would phone back when she felt up to it.

They spoke for a while, and though Biddy would have liked to have heard a little more life in her friend's voice, she knew that was asking for too much too soon.

'I'm glad to hear you've been out and about,' Biddy said. 'A trip down to Cork will have done you the world of good, and Joe's such a lovely fella, not a bit like a priest.'

'It was lovely seeing him,' Tara said, her flat voice belying her words.

'Did you go to Mass when he was serving?' Biddy asked, trying to imagine what it would be like staying in the priest's house, and what sort of conversations they would have. Probably highbrow stuff about books and obviously a lot of talk about God.

'Yes,' Tara said, 'he asked me to come the morning I was there. It was kind of strange, seeing my own brother up there on the altar in his priest's vestments.'

Biddy stopped herself from reminding Tara that they had both seen him on the altar before, at Gabriel's funeral. There was no point in adding sad reminders and making the conversation more difficult.

'How is Fred?' Tara asked. 'Has he settled back in at home?'

'Oh, he's grand,' Biddy said, 'you'd think he'd never been away.'

'It must be lovely having him back with you all . . .'

'Oh, he's there, getting under my feet as usual,' Biddy joked, but all the time thinking how painful it must be for her friend, knowing that her husband would never, ever come home again.

They talked about the children, how they were getting on in school and various other practical things, and then Tara brought the conversation around to Angela.

'Is she OK?' Tara asked, her voice sounding hoarse now, as though the conversation was starting to drain her. 'Tessie has been telling me about the letters she's written home, saying how much she loves Stockport, and how she's getting on great with you all in the house. She really seems to have settled well.'

Biddy bit her lip. This was not the time to burden Tara with more problems – and maybe problems she would think were trivial in comparison to what she was enduring herself.

'She's grand,' she said. 'Although I wouldn't be surprised if Christmas tells a different story. All young ones want to be at home for Christmas, don't they?'

'You'll know best,' Tara told her. 'But if she's helping you there with Fred and the children, then I'm sure Tessie and my father will be happy enough with that.'

'Oh, she's a good little worker around the house,' Biddy said, 'and Michael and Helen love her . . .'

There was a little pause. 'I shouldn't really say this,' Tara confided, 'but I think she has more of a life with you over in Stockport than she would if she were to come home. If she comes home I have a feeling that she'll be back where she was, helping to look after Molly.'

'That's no joke for a young girl,' Biddy said.

'It's no joke for anyone,' Tara agreed. 'I've gone in to stay with her a few times myself, and it's getting harder all the time.'

'And how are you in yourself, Tara?' Biddy asked. 'Are you finding things any easier? You sound a small bit brighter.'

There was a silence. 'I'm grand,' Tara said. 'Now, what's your news? Tell me more.'

Biddy then went on to tell her about the expected addition to the family. She had thought long and hard about whether or not to tell Tara, remembering the conversation they'd had about children the very day that Tara had got the news about Gabriel. Eventually, she had decided to tell her friend, and continue acting the very same way she had when the other two children were on the way.

'I'm delighted for you, Biddy,' Tara said. 'I'm delighted for you and Fred.' Then she added, 'And make sure you get a bit of a rest now and again, especially when you have Angela there to help you.'

They spoke for a little while longer, then Tara suddenly said, 'I'm really sorry, Biddy, but I'm expecting an important phone call from London. I promise I'll write to you when I have more time.'

Biddy got off the phone feeling much easier about her friend, not realising that Tara had taken her phone call by mistake. Ella had shouted to her that there was a call from England, and Tara had presumed that it was the call she was waiting for from London.

'Damn it! I never got a chance to ask Tara about me changin' my name,' Biddy muttered to herself as she came back into the kitchen. 'She went off in a fierce hurry before I could mention it.'

'Changing your name?' Fred said, sounding confused.

'Remember? Going back to my real name?' Biddy said, smiling encouragingly at him. 'Calling myself Bridget from now on, instead of Biddy?'

Fred nodded. 'Whatever you like, love,' he said, 'but Biddy sounds all right to me. I've got used to it now.'

'I told her our good news,' she said, 'about the baby.' Biddy had got used to having to spell things out to Fred because of his memory. And any time she started to get irritated by it, she reminded herself how desperately lonely she had been all those months when he'd been in hospital. She came over to where he was sitting, and wound her arm around his neck and planted a kiss on his forehead. 'D'you want tea or coffee, love?'

Fred pulled her on to his lap and started to kiss her passionately, his hand moving up under her jumper.

'Fre – ed!' she said, giggling. 'It's the middle of the bleedin' day! The kids will be home from school any—'

Then, just at that very minute, the front door suddenly burst open – banging against the wall – and Michael and Helen came running in crying, with Angela following, shouting 'Biddy, Biddy!' The children ran straight to their father, jostling with each other to get up on his knee.

'What the hell's goin' on?' Biddy demanded, coming out to the hall.

'Call the guards!' Angela screeched hysterically, pointing to the phone and then running back to the front door. 'Call the police! He's going to kill Philip!'

'What's going on?' Biddy repeated, grabbing the girl by her arm. 'Who the hell's Philip – and who's goin' to kill him?'

Fred came out to the hall now, having calmed the children down with packets of sweets. 'What's to do?' he said, looking at the hysterical Angela.

'Eric!' Angela cried. 'Eric's gone stone mad! He saw me walkin' up the road with Philip, and he came runnin' over and knocked him on to the ground – and started kickin' him. Philip got up and then he hit Eric, and now they're killin' each other. There's blood everywhere! I ran on with the kids because I was afraid anythin' might happen to them – and to get you to phone the police.'

'Where are they now?' Biddy said, going to the front door. She was reluctant to start involving the police if it was only a bit of a scrap, but if it was really serious, she knew it needed stopping.

'Just around the corner!' Angela sobbed, covering her eyes with her hands. 'Eric must have been waiting for me at the top of the entry – and he must have seen me sayin' goodbye to Philip.'

At that point, Fred suddenly pushed past Biddy and Angela. 'I'll sort the bastards out!' he said. 'I'm not havin' them frightening my kids like that.'

'No, Fred!' Biddy called, coming out after him. 'You're not fit to get involved – go back into the house.'

But Fred wasn't listening. The thought of anyone hurting his children had resurrected the old wrestling blood in him, and he was now acting on sheer instinct. He went down the front stairs of the boarding-house, momentum keeping his legs the steadiest they'd been since the accident.

Then suddenly a young, well-dressed lad came running into view, with blood pouring out of a gash in his head. 'He's got a knife!' the young lad called in a refined accent, looking back over his shoulder. 'He's trying to stab me!'

The racket now brought neighbours to their windows, some coming out to stand on their front steps. Maple Grove was a decent area and, despite the fact that there was a boarding-house with a motley crew of builders coming and going in it, they got very little trouble.

Just as the boy reached Biddy and Fred, Eric came

tearing around the corner with a good-sized penknife dramatically held aloft – as a villain would do in a farcical comedy.

'Get inside!' Fred said in a strangely calm voice to Biddy and the boy. He started moving towards Eric. 'I'll soon sort this little bastard out!'

'Hurry, Philip – hurry!' Angela called from the front door.

Philip didn't need to be told twice and, rubbing his sleeve over his dirty, blood-stained face, he ran up the stairs two at a time to the waiting arms of Angela.

'Fred! Fred!' Biddy shouted, pulling at the back of her husband's shirt to restrain him. 'Don't get involved – we'll call the police to come and sort him out!'

'Get inside!' Fred repeated, his voice a hiss this time and his eyes dark and calculating. 'I'll have this sorted out in no time.'

Eric came to a breathless, skidding halt a few yards from Fred and Biddy. Then he started moving from side to side like a boxer in the ring, waving a penknife with a skull and crossbones on it. 'This is nowt to fucking do with you!' he yelled, his eyes darting to the front door.

Fred moved his feet into a fighting stance now, and started to roll up his shirtsleeves.

'You come around here, frightening my kids and my wife, and you tell me it's got *nothing* to do with me?' he said in a low, dangerous voice. 'I'll soon show you what it's got to do with me!'

Suddenly taken aback, Eric retreated a few paces, his mind racing. He had never encountered this side of Fred before. Even before his accident, the wrestler had always come across as a big, easygoing kind of bloke. Eric had never imagined what Fred would look like riled and ready to fight. 'I said it's got nowt to do with *you*, half-a-brain,' the boy repeated in a low growl. 'It's that two-timin' little Irish bitch and her fancy boyfriend that I want to see.'

'Give me that knife!' Fred said now, advancing towards him. 'Give me that stupid-looking penknife, or I'll break your fucking arm!'

'Fred! Stop it – stop it!' Biddy said, grabbing him by the belt this time, as a group started to gather further along the street. She suddenly had visions of Fred being led away by the police for killing Eric.

Eric seemed to hesitate for a moment, as though weighing up the situation – then suddenly he spotted Angela at the door with Philip. 'I'll get you!' he yelled up at them, his rage renewed. 'You little Irish prick-teaser!' he called. 'You'll not make a fuckin' fool out of me – I'll kill the fucking pair of you!'

'You'll have to get past me first,' Fred warned him, making a grab for the skull-and-crossbones knife.

His eyes wild now, Eric started to dance in a circle around Fred. 'I'm not scared of you, you brain-damaged moron! I'll take you on any time!' He waved the penknife close to Fred's face. 'Let's see how good your wrestlin' skills are now, Mr Meathead!'

Enraged, Fred lunged forward again and grabbed Eric by the arm. In a few seconds he had his arm twisted up his back in a wrestling lock. Smiling now, as he always did when he had the upper hand over his opponent, Fred threw Eric on to the ground and pinned him down by sitting on him.

'What the bloody hell's all this goin' on?' a female voice shrieked, and then Elsie suddenly came running down Biddy's front steps. 'Get off him!' she yelled at Fred. 'Get bloody well off him – he's only a bit of a lad, and you'll smother him to death!' She tore over to Fred now, hitting him and pulling on his arm to get him off of Eric.

'Jesus, Mary and Joseph!' Biddy called. 'There's the police car – we're all going to be for it now!' She started pulling on Fred's other arm to get him off Eric, so that he wouldn't look as though he was the one doing the attacking.

As Fred moved up on to his feet again, he made one of the most basic mistakes that a wrestler can make. He underestimated his opponent. He then made a second lethal mistake – he forgot that this was not a fight taking place in the wrestling ring, where moves were rehearsed and rules were obeyed.

Before Fred was fully on his feet – and as the police came running towards them – an enraged, agile Eric leapt up from the ground and plunged the penknife high up into Fred's back.

Chapter Forty-Nine

'There's no two ways about it,' Elsie said, dabbing her eyes with the large white hanky she'd been carrying around with her since the terrible incident several days ago. 'He is me son – but facts is facts. He did the crime – now he'll do his time. Then nobody can say he didn't pay for what he did.'

Biddy stared at the older woman, amazed that she could come out with such a stupid rhyme at a time like this. 'He could have *killed* Fred,' she said now in a cold voice. 'Eric has got something seriously wrong with him when he could do that to poor Fred – he's got an evil streak in him.' She shook her head wearily. 'Another quarter of an inch and Fred could have been killed – or he could have been completely paralysed, if it had touched his spinal cord. It was only sheer luck that it didn't do any lasting damage.'

Elsie nodded her head. 'As I say, they'll make him pay for it now. They're keepin' him on remand until his court case comes up – they're not gonna give him bail or owt like that.' She looked up at her boss with red-rimmed eyes. 'He's very sorry for what he did to Fred – he says he didn't mean for any of it to happen. You know he appreciated all you both did for him – givin' him the job here and everythin'.'

'If I'd known where it would all lead, I'd never have let him through the door,' Biddy stated. 'And all the terrible things he said to Fred – all the terrible names he called him . . . I wouldn't have believed he would have done such a terrible thing.'

'Nor me,' said Elsie, forlornly, 'an' I'm his own mother.'

'He's a danger, Elsie,' Biddy said, her eyes blazing with anger. 'I'm sorry to say it, because I think the world of you – but your son has got something seriously wrong with him to go and do a thing like that.' She shook her head. 'That young lad that he attacked, that Philip – he'd never even seen him before. He'd never even spoken to him, and yet he went for him with a knife!'

Elsie wiped her eyes again with the big hanky. 'When I went up to see the doctor yesterday evenin' – to get something for me nerves, like – I told him all about what had happened, and I asked him what would make a young lad flip like that, an' the doctor said it were a crime of passion.' She took a deep, shuddering breath. 'He said something must have just snapped in Eric's brain, because he was so besotted with that Angela – seeing her with another lad just made him uncontrollable.'

'But they hadn't really been *that* serious,' Biddy said. 'It wasn't as if they were engaged or anything like that – and she hadn't been out with him for weeks.'

'I think there were more to it than we knew,' Elsie said defensively. 'That Angela isn't as innocent as she lets on – not by a long chalk. When I was visitin' him in the remand centre, Eric told me a few things about her that opened my eyes.'

'What sort of things?' Biddy asked, her brow furrowing. Things were bad enough with what had gone on so far – surely there wasn't anything else?

'Well,' Elsie said, folding her hanky into small squares, 'that time when you were over at the funeral in Ireland – that time she was supposed to be sick – it seems they were gettin' up to no good.'

A hot, angry flush came up over Biddy's neck now. 'What d'you mean?'

'You *know*,' Elsie said, 'hanky-panky . . . it seems that Angela was lettin' him into the house early in the mornin' and they were up in the bedroom and every-thin'.'

Biddy's face stiffened. 'I don't believe it! D'you mean they were carryin' on together – when Tara's husband was bein' buried?'

Elsie held her hands up. 'I don't know how far they went – but all I know is that Eric said she was teasin' him, and goin' around wearin' a fancy black nightdress with that sexy leopard-print stuff on it.'

Warning-bells went off in Biddy's head. 'A sexy black nightdress?' she said in a low, strangled voice, knowing exactly where Angela had got that from. The special nightwear that she'd bought for Fred's weekend home from hospital.

'So Eric said,' Elsie confirmed. 'An' there must have been some truth in him bein' in the house early in the mornin', because he were fit to tell me that he'd knocked over the plant-stand at the bottom of the stairs on his way out.' She pursed her lips, her head nodding in agitation. 'I know all about it, for it were me that had to clean the mess up.' Her eyes narrowed. 'And I remember mentionin' it to Angela that very mornin' – and her sittin' like butter wouldn't melt in her mouth, while I blamed one of the builders for knockin' it over.'

Biddy's blood ran cold as she listened to Elsie. Instinctively, although the story had come via Eric, she knew it was the truth. Angela had really let her down. She had really played her for a fool. And now she would pay for it.

'You can pack your bags,' Biddy said with a finality that brooked no argument. She'd summoned Angela down to the sitting room to confront her with all the things that Elsie had told her. 'You can take yourself back off to Ireland where you belong. I'll not have you stayin' here a minute longer. I won't have a liar in the house, a liar who put Fred's life at risk.'

Angela hung her head. 'I really don't want to go back home . . . I love being here with you and the kids . . .' Her voice broke off and tears started to trickle down her cheeks. 'I didn't mean to tell lies . . . it was a stupid, stupid thing. I don't know how I got myself into all that with Eric . . . but I'm really, really sorry.'

Biddy looked at the girl with cold, narrowed eyes. 'You're sorry you've been found out – that's all you're sorry about.' She shook her head. 'You took me for a complete feckin' fool. Me over in Ireland at the funeral, tellin' everybody that you weren't well, and you back here hopping into bed with that lunatic, Eric.'

'I didn't, Biddy! I promise I didn't do anything with him, apart from kissing him.'

'And what about all that disgraceful business when you had the feckin' cheek to go into my bedroom – then into my wardrobe – and take my nightdress and dressing gown out?'

Angela's shoulders started to heave now in racking sobs. 'I'm sorry – it was stupid – it was just because he was teasing me about bein' old-fashioned. I was just tryin' to impress him – and then I got scared.' She reached for Biddy's hand now but Biddy stepped back, unwilling to give her any comfort.

'You've caused trouble with me and Elsie as well,' Biddy went on. 'How d'you think I felt when Elsie could tell me all about the carry-on in the house while I was away?'

'As true as God – and on my mother's life – I did *not* do anything wrong with Eric.' She looked up at Biddy now, her face a picture of misery. 'I've been stupid and I've done things I shouldn't – but I've learned my lesson. I promise you – I'll never let you down again.'

'I don't feel I could ever trust you again,' Biddy said. 'All those lies about that other lad as well – saying you were going to the library.'

'I *was* in the library,' Angela said adamantly. 'I met Philip there . . . he's doing a course at night-school, and he goes in there to study some evenings.'

Biddy stared at Angela now, her eyes cold and unflinching. 'You nearly got Fred killed, you could have made me lose the baby – and you frightened the life out of the kids.' She turned away now, her face stony. 'I can't just be expected to forget all that and carry on as if it had never happened – so if I were you, I'd get me bags packed and head back home to Ireland.'

'But I love it here! I want to stay in Stockport.'

'If you want to stay in Stockport,' Biddy said coldly, 'then you'd better get in touch with your father and mother and check that it's OK to stay over here, as you're not living with me anymore. Then you'd better find yourself a job and somewhere else to live.'

'I met Angela on the stairs,' Fred said, 'and she was crying. When I asked what the matter was, she said she was leavin' to find somewhere else to live . . .'

'That's right,' Biddy said, staring into the fire. 'I've told her she'll have to go back to Ireland.'

'Why?' Fred asked. 'She's a lovely young girl, and she were right smashin' with the kids. They think the world of her.'

Biddy turned to face her husband. 'You still think she's a *lovely* young girl?' she said. 'After all that Angela's gone and done? After all the trouble she's brought to our door?' She was irked now at Fred's description. She didn't like him complimenting other women, and she still couldn't get the picture out of her head of that time he had kissed that nurse. 'I don't know how you can call her *lovely* after she nearly got

335

you killed and has given the kids nightmares because of what's happened!'

Fred sat down on the end of the sofa. 'I'm fine now,' he told Biddy. 'It were really only a bit of a scratch—'

'*A bit of a scratch?*' Biddy repeated, her voice high with indignation. 'It was more than a bloody scratch – you don't get six stitches for a scratch. You were damned lucky it wasn't a bit deeper or nearer the middle – for if it was, you wouldn't be standin' here today.'

'It weren't her fault, Biddy . . . she made a stupid mistake gettin' involved with that evil bastard, Eric – but she's learned her lesson. She got a fright from him herself.' He paused, thinking. 'And that young lad, Philip – he got a right beltin' off him, an' all.'

'His parents aren't a bit happy with him gettin' mixed up in a court case,' Biddy reminded her husband. She folded her arms over her small bulge. 'Anyway, I've made up me mind – if she doesn't want to go back to Ireland, I've told her she has to find herself another job and another place to live.'

'Aw, Biddy!' Fred said, shaking his head. 'You can't do that to the girl! And don't forget – it was you and Elsie that organised for him to come to work in the boarding-house in the first place. She'd never have met Eric if he hadn't been around the house so much.'

'Be that as it may,' Biddy said defensively, 'she's not my responsibility, Fred, and I'm not prepared to put up with her lyin' nonsense. She's not a young teenager anymore. She's a twenty-year-old woman. I was out on my own at eighteen with nobody lookin' out for me.' She lowered her voice. 'If she stayed here any longer, the next thing we'd know would be that she'd be expectin', and it would be us who'd get the blame for not mindin' her properly.' She shook her head. 'I won't throw her

336

out in the street – but I've made up me mind. If she won't go back to Ireland, she's goin' just as soon as she finds another job and another place to live.'

Chapter Fifty

The tram rattled to a halt and the passengers got off and started to disperse in different directions. Angela waited until everyone had gone, and then she walked slowly to the corner of the street and stood looking up at the tall, soot-streaked cotton-mill buildings. At least she presumed they were all cotton mills. Cotton was all anyone had talked about, and she wouldn't have had the foggiest idea what other things mills would have made.

She opened her black handbag and fished out the piece of paper with the directions. She had to find the Goyt Mill. There was no difficulty there, because according to the instructions it was the very first one, which meant she was standing right outside the entrance.

As she looked up at the small windows and the towering chimneys, her heart sank to the bottom of her stomach at the thought of having to walk through the tall iron gates and then into the building to find the office. She looked down at her high-heeled black court shoes, checking that they were still as clean and shiny as when she had left the house. Then she smoothed down the skirt of her suit and took a few deep breaths to calm herself down, knowing that if she got flustered and embarrassed, no one would understand a single word she said. Angela had had this happen to her on numerous occasions and, whenever she remembered, she now tried to adopt a bit of a Stockport twang to cover her strong Irish accent.

Eventually, she steeled herself to walk down the few yards and in through the high, forbidding iron gates. A few moments later, she pushed open the heavy front doors and stepped into a bustling corridor and a rattling, busy new world.

A group of men standing smoking around a steaming tea-urn trolley all turned to look when the doors creaked open. A small bald-headed man in a brown overall stepped forward, cigarette held discreetly behind his back. 'Can I help you, love?' he asked. Then one of the younger men gave a long, low wolf whistle, making Angela blush to the roots of her hair.

'I was looking . . .' she started, wishing she could just run back out the door, 'I was just wondering . . . where the office is?'

'Have you come for an interview, love?' the man asked, winking back at the others.

'Yes,' she confirmed, fishing the piece of paper with the details from her handbag. 'I've to see – a Mrs Tenby.'

'Well, you've come to the right place,' he said, taking her arm and pointing to a door at the bottom of the corridor. Straight past the men who were all staring her up and down. 'It's that door at the very end you want, love.'

Angela took a deep breath. 'Thanks very much.' Then, clutching the piece of paper between both hands, she held her head high and walked as quickly as her high heels would allow past the tea-trolley and all the men.

'See you, love!' one voice called, and 'Nice face an' even nicer legs!' called another as she strode along, praying she wouldn't trip over her stilettos.

Ten minutes later, Angela was back out in the corridor, this time accompanied by an officious-looking Mrs

Tenby. Thankfully, the tea break was over and there was no sign of any of the whistling, leering men.

'I'll take you to look at the winding-room now,' the manageress said, patting a hand to her bun to check that all the hairgrips were still in place, 'and then you'll know where to go first thing when you start on Monday.' She gave the young girl a sideways glance. 'You picked the right place to come to, with you being Irish.'

'And why's that?' Angela enquired, trying to sound bright and interested.

'Some of the other places aren't too keen on the Irish at all, you know,' Mrs Tenby informed her, 'but we take all kinds here. We don't make any difference whether you're Irish or black, as long as you can do the job properly and quickly. That's all that counts as far as the Goyt Mill is concerned – we believe in giving everyone a proper chance.'

Angela nodded, Elsie's dire warning about people's attitudes to the Irish ringing in her ears. 'What time do we start?' she asked anxiously as they approached the door of the winding-room.

'Seven o'clock on the dot,' Mrs Tenby said, 'and you're docked money if you're late. Have you far to come? D'you live nearby?'

'Well,' Angela explained, 'I'm in Shaw Heath at the moment, but I'm looking to find somewhere nearer the mill.'

'I'll introduce you to Mona Kelly before you leave, then,' the older woman said. 'A few of the girls board with her, and she's Irish, too. She's only up the road from here in Hillgate – it's only five minutes on the tram.'

Angela's face lightened – it would be grand now if she could get somewhere quick and handy for work – and somewhere she could move into straight away. 'That would be grand,' she said, 'especially if some of the other workers are livin' in the same house.' Angela was still living at Biddy's boarding-house, but she couldn't wait to get away from it now, the way things were. She had no intentions of returning to Ireland just yet, and fancied a little more freedom now that she wouldn't have Biddy watching over her all the time. And anyway, it was getting a bit boring working in the boarding-house with the same old routine. In a way, Angela felt quite excited about having a fresh start and making her own decisions. She had told Biddy that she would write to her parents and Tara and explain what had happened, but she hadn't done it just yet. She thought she would wait until she was settled in her new place and her new job. She would find a way of explaining why she'd left the boarding-house without mentioning anything about the trouble with Eric.

'Well,' Mrs Tenby said, putting her shoulder against a set of heavy swing-doors, 'we'll see . . .' and then the rest of her words were swallowed up by the horrendous clatter and rattle of heavy mill machinery.

Half an hour later Angela emerged from the noisy factory and out into the bright daylight – half delighted with herself for getting the job and half dazed with fear at the thought of having to go back into that place again in only three days' time.

She had a list of things to do before going back in. She had to sort out a dark working skirt and a couple of jumpers and an overall.

'Short-sleeved jumpers would be best,' Mrs Tenby had suggested, 'because they're more comfortable under the overalls.' She then went on to tell Angela where she could buy a suitable overall from a place up in Hillgate. As they walked along, Mrs Tenby suddenly threw a disapproving eye at Angela's feet. 'You wouldn't last an hour in those shoes,' she warned, 'and they would be dangerous on the factory floor.'

'Oh, these were only for the interview,' Angela had rushed to assure her. 'I'll buy good strong work shoes for Monday.'

Mrs Tenby had nodded her head in approval and smiled encouragingly. This was exactly the type of worker she liked – co-operative and willing. 'And you'll need an enamel mug and plate for break times. The tea-trolley comes around three times a day, and you bring your own lunch.' Her eyebrow shot up in a disapproving manner. 'Although some of the girls prefer a walk out to a fish and chip shop in the hope of meeting lads.'

'Oh, I'll be happy to bring my own lunch with me,' Angela said.

'And don't forget your hairnets,' Mrs Tenby finished off. 'As you saw in the winding-room, there's a lot of cotton and dust everywhere.'

Angela followed the stumpy figure of Mona Kelly into the dim and fusty-smelling hallway, one wall of which was taken up with numerous coats and jackets on hooks, all adding to the odour. As they walked the short distance down into the kitchen, the smell became more specific – that of yesterday's cabbage leaves left swimming in the greasy bacon-water. Angela held her breath, trying to become accustomed to the airless house and desperately trying to imagine herself actually living in it.

'It's not as you would call a lodging-house, really,' Mona said in her half-Stockport, half-Galway accent, 'because it's on the small side, and everyone is expected to pitch in with the cooking and the cleaning.'

From what Angela could detect, there wasn't too much of either going on. It was nowhere near as clean as Biddy's boarding-house. There was no comparison. But it would do for a start. If she liked the job, she could always think of moving to a better place in the near future.

'Dinner's as soon as it's ready, straight after work,'

Mona informed her when they reached the upstairs landing. 'First in starts it off, and thems that's last does the washing-up. And you do for yersel' the rest of the time. If you want a bit of breakfast, then it's up to yersel' to sort it out.' She came to a halt outside a bedroom door. 'An' there's a chip shop across the road from the factory that most of the girls use at lunchtime, or you can buy yersel' a couple of barmcakes and make them up the night before.'

Angela nodded, her heart sinking at the thought of all the responsibilities that were now part of her new independent life. No more cosy fried breakfasts in the warm kitchen with Biddy and Elsie, no more fancy cakes and biscuits in the afternoon. But at least she wouldn't have anyone watching every move she made.

The Galway woman threw open the door to reveal a medium-sized bedroom with a small window and two double beds taking up most of the floor space. The beds were old and saggy, with dubious-looking bedclothes, and each topped with greyish-coloured old quilts that had long lost any colour or embroidered pattern.

A chest of drawers, a rickety-looking wardrobe, and a dressing-table with a green-stained, mottled mirror took up the rest of the room.

All in all, a depressing sight.

'You're lucky,' Mona Kelly informed her now, 'because you'll have a bed to yersel' until we get another new starter at the factory. We often have two girls in each of the beds. Last year we were so full up that I had three girls in each of those beds for a fortnight. A bit of a squash, but we managed.' She gave Angela a smile. 'I wouldn't see any poor girl out on the street with nowhere to go. There's some that would, but Mona Kelly's not like that. Especially when it comes to Irish girls. I know what it was like to leave home and come to a strange country – an' I count my blessings every day for the good job an' the fine house that God saw fit to grant me.' She blessed herself now. 'Mind you, I've worked hard for it – you get nothin' in this life for nothin'.' She prodded Angela on the arm. 'As I say – ye get nothin' for nothin' in this life, and don't ever forget it. It's the best advice anyone can give a young girl in your position.'

Angela nodded, trying to blink back the tears that were threatening.

'Now,' Mona said, throwing open another door to reveal a grim-looking bathroom, painted from floor to ceiling in a depressing shade of sludgy green. Green gloss paint, normally used for skirting-boards and windows, had been liberally sloshed over numerous layers of ancient, peeling wallpaper, giving the walls a mummified effect.

'Like everything else in the house,' the landlady said, 'it's first come, first served in the bathroom in the morning.' She grinned. 'It could be worse, in some places it's first up, best dressed!'

When Angela emerged out of the dank, dark house, she was almost afraid that she had lost for ever the normal world she had taken for granted. The world she had become used to since coming to Stockport. A world of clean beds and nice food, and afternoon trips out to flower-filled parks with Lucky or down to Stockport with the chidren. Evenings spent sitting chatting to Biddy or going to the pictures with a nice lad like Philip. Now she would spend her sunny mornings and after-noons shut up inside the thundering factory mill, and her evenings would be spent in Mona Kelly's cabbage-smelling boarding-house with all the other mill workers. And she would have to work hard to make enough wages to cover her board and lodgings before she could even think of money for clothes or money for going out.

And then it hit her like a ton of bricks. She had thrown it all away! She had thrown away a nice home with a nice woman and nice things – all over that stupid eedjit, Eric. Angela Flynn now realised that she had thrown away the best opportunity of her life.

Chapter Fifty-One

TULLAMORE – LATE NOVEMBER

Shay handed his wife the letter and she put it back into the envelope. Then he went back to his newspaper.

'Well?' Tessie urged, a worried frown on her forehead. 'What do you think?'

Shay shrugged, turning to look at the sports section in the paper. 'Well, if she's looking for more money, I suppose the mills are better paid than working in a boarding-house.'

'I'm not a bit happy about it,' Tessie said, coming to stand in front of the fireplace, her arms folded across her heavy bosom. 'Angela was only supposed to be over there for a month or so staying at Biddy Hart's, and then we thought she would be back here at home.'

'She's twenty years old, Tessie,' Shay reminded his wife. 'Don't forget that Tara was gone from home when she was even younger. It'll do her no harm to get out into the world, and to see what it's like to do a hard day's work like the rest of us.'

'It's different,' Tessie said, shaking her head. 'She's a different girl from Tara . . . a different girl altogether. She's never been as sensible.'

Shay sighed. 'I don't know what you want me to say, Tessie – do you want me to go over to Stockport and bring her back home? Is that what you're saying?'

'Indeed it's not,' Tessie said, her voice high with indignation. 'We don't need you takin' time off from work to go chasing over to England after Angela; you're more needed here at home.'

'Well then,' he said, going back to the paper. 'I can't be in two places at once, can I?'

'I think we should write back to her straight away,' Tessie said, going over to get her belted blue raincoat from the row of hooks at the back door. 'I think we should write and say that we're not happy with her moving out of the boarding-house without asking us or Tara first, and that we want to know if she's behavin' herself and goin' to Mass every Sunday.'

Shay nodded, looking at the football results. He still kept up to date with the English teams he'd followed when he was over in Stockport. 'Poor Tara has more on her mind at the minute than to be bothered with what Angela's gettin' up to.'

'She was never meant to stay this long,' Tessie repeated, knowing that Shay was only half listening. 'If we don't get her home soon, she'll settle over there and we'll never get her back.'

'She's grand,' Shay said, 'leave the girl alone. And anyway, didn't Tara come back home eventually? She didn't stay over in England for ever.'

'And I suppose you think she's grand, too?' Tessie snapped now. 'She's out there rattlin' around in that big house on her own. What kind of life is that for a young woman?'

Shay threw the paper down on the floor now, exasperated. 'What d'you want me to do, Tessie?' he said. 'I go back and forth to Ballygrace House every other day to keep an eye on her.' He shook his head. 'I can't bring Gabriel Fitzgerald back from the dead – if I could, believe me, I would. I'd bring him back tomorrow – and a lot of other people along with him. My life would be a lot richer today if people I knew hadn't died.'

'And who's askin' you to perform miracles?' Tessie

347

said defensively, suddenly wondering if Shay was alluding to his first wife – Joe and Tara's mother. 'All I'm sayin' is that we need to check up on this situation with Angela. Anything could happen to her over there in England, and for all I like Biddy Hart, we know full well the kind of things that have happened to her.'

'Biddy's the finest,' Shay countered. 'She was an unfortunate girl that was taken advantage of, and she's learned about life the hard way. Sure, she's a respected businesswoman over there – she runs one of the best boarding-houses in Stockport.'

He prodded a finger on the arm of his chair. 'And I'm givin' you facts here – don't forget, it was me that stayed in the place when I was over in England sweatin' blood to send money back to keep you all.'

Tessie shook her head. 'I'll be off,' she said, lifting her headscarf from the back of a chair and stuffing Angela's letter in her coat pocket. 'That neighbour of Molly's will be wonderin' where I've got to.'

It was only after she read the letter for the second time, later in the day, that it dawned on Tessie that Angela had never mentioned Biddy Hart. There wasn't a word in the letter about why she had decided to move out of the boarding-house, or any mention of little Michael and Helen.

She wondered now if they'd had some kind of a falling-out. When she was up at Ballygrace House again, she must see if she could find out anything from Tara.

Part Three

*Faith
is the bird
that feels the light
when the dawn
is still dark.*

RABINDRANATH TAGORE

Chapter Fifty-Two

BALLYGRACE, DECEMBER 1962

'Tara?' the young, eager voice said on the phone. 'It's me – William.'

Tara took a deep breath. She had managed to avoid the phone calls from Elisha over the last few weeks, but this was the third time that William had called that Sunday, and she suddenly felt worried in case something was wrong. 'Hello, William,' she said, lifting her voice. 'And how are you?'

'I'm very well, thank you,' he said. 'I phoned you twice earlier today, but you weren't in.'

'Oh, I'm sorry,' Tara said, 'I've been very busy.'

'I'm *phoning* to check if you're coming to stay with us for Christmas.'

'*Christmas?*' Tara repeated, startled.

'Yes,' he said quickly. 'I thought we might go to a pantomime, and maybe into London to see Father Christmas . . . you know, like we did last year.'

'Oh, William,' she said quickly, 'I'm afraid I won't be coming this year . . .' Her mind raced now, searching for a solid excuse that would crush any more suggestions of this kind. 'My aunt – an old lady – is very ill, and I'm helping to take care of her.'

'Can't you come for a few days?' he said, his voice beseeching now. 'It would be so different if you could come . . . we could do things that Mother and Harry are too old to do.' There was a little pause. 'Before . . .

Gabriel said that if you came this Christmas we might go ice-skating. There's a new rink opened quite near us.'

Tara closed her eyes. 'I'm really, really sorry, William,' she told him, 'but I have to stay in Ireland this Christmas – I just can't come.'

'You still haven't collected Gabriel's car,' he reminded her. 'You said you would come for it soon.'

'Maybe sometime after Christmas,' she hedged. 'When I know what's happening to Auntie Molly.'

'Mother's not been very well,' he told her now. 'She has to lie down a lot – and Harry is very busy at work.'

You're not on your own?' Tara checked.

'No,' he said, 'Mrs Saunders is here. She looks after me most of the time, and she always makes me nice things to eat.'

'Well, then,' Tara said, 'isn't that lovely?'

There was another little silence.

'You're sure you can't come to London for Christmas?' William checked again. 'Even for a few days?'

'No, William,' she told him. 'Definitely not – I couldn't possibly come this year.'

Two days later, Tara found a letter from Biddy in the post in amongst all the serious brown envelopes that she dreaded opening. It was a chatty letter, bringing her up to date on all the family news – Fred's health, which continued to improve, how the children were both doing at school, what a great little reader Michael was, and how Biddy's morning sickness had more or less gone now.

The letter went on to ask Tara if she'd like to come over for Christmas, and to invite her to a special evening that the Grosvenor Hotel were putting on, and where Fred would be the guest of honour. Apparently they were running some kind of sports event, with a dinner dance, and the men wearing bow ties and everything, and they wanted Fred there to receive a special award from the Wrestling Association. The sporting function was to be held on the twelfth of December, and Biddy had been asked if she'd like to bring a table of guests along. She went on to tell Tara about who else would be there, including Fred's family and some people that they knew from when they'd both worked in the Grosvenor Hotel. She said she thought it would do Tara good to get away for a while from Ballygrace House, and she would be amongst friends. She pointed out that if she came for Fred's award night, she could stay on and have Christmas in Stockport as well.

Tara looked at the letter and then put it back down on the hall table. How could she go to a Christmas dinner-dance without Gabriel? How could she go amongst people all dressed up, wish them 'Happy Christmas'?

She would have to write back to Biddy and thank her for the kind invitation, and say that she hoped her friend would understand that she would prefer a quiet Christmas at home this year.

She wouldn't spoil Biddy's festivities by telling her that this Christmas – and all Christmases to come – would not exist for her.

Tara sat staring down at the documents on the dining-room table, and then suddenly got to her feet and went over to stand by the large bay window. She knew she couldn't avoid signing them any longer, as she had already received two reminders from the solicitor over the last few weeks. But she also realised that as soon as she signed them and set the legal wheels in motion, she would then have to start making decisions about the property that Gabriel had left her.

She found it difficult to react to the houses and the money he had willed to her. She swung from feeling grateful that Gabriel had left her this wonderful gift that was the means to propel her into a new life – to feeling that she had paid the highest, cruellest price for bricks and mortar.

It was ironic that she should feel such indifference to all this money – this huge fortune that Gabriel had left her. All her life she had strived for the security and sense of achievement that money and property would give her. And yet now she would give every penny she had ever earned, if only she could have Gabriel back.

Chapter Fifty-Three

Angela was wide awake and listening to the rain rattling on the roof for a long time before getting up. She called to Nancy and Alice – the two other mill-workers she shared the room with – that it was time to get up. She swung her legs out of bed, giving a tiny gasp as her feet touched the cold linoleum floor. She was thankful that she had a nice warm pair of turquoise winceyette pyjamas on, because the temperature in the house in the morning was nearly unbearable. She felt for her slippers under the bed, and went quickly out into the hall and knocked on the landlady's door, waiting until she heard a grunt that told her she was awake. Then she ran quickly into the bathroom before any of the other girls got a chance to beat her to it.

The sludgey-green-painted bathroom was cold and miserable, but at least it was reasonably fresh at this time of the morning. If you were last in the queue, the chances were that the floor would be wet and the smell none too fragrant. When that happened, Angela always opened the window wide, but this windy, wet morning was not conducive to opening windows.

After washing her face and hands, and under her arms, in the warmish water, Angela came out to meet Nancy, who was shivering outside the bathroom door in a cotton nightie, her arms wrapped around herself. 'I'm goin' to get meself a pair of nice warm pyjamas like yours off the market tomorrow,' she told Angela, as she slid in past her, her badly permed hair like an unruly bush. 'This place is like a bleedin' fridge in the mornin'.'

Angela hurriedly brushed her blond hair and tied it back with a blue ribbon, then dressed in the navy woollen skirt and navy short-sleeved jumper that she'd laid out on the back of a chair the night before. She fastened her thick black work-stockings on to her suspenders, and headed downstairs to put the kettle on the gas stove.

While she waited for it to boil, she got the teapot and put four scoops of Tetley's tea leaves in it, and left it on an unlit ring. She would fill the teapot to the brim, and that would save Móna and the other girls having to make their own when they came down. Some of the girls were selfish and just boiled half a kettle to make enough tea for themselves.

Angela got out her small packet of butter from the larder, and her sliced corned beef, wrapped in grease-proof paper and marked with her initials in pencil. Mona had advised her to put her name on everything, as it saved arguments. She stretched on her tiptoes into a high kitchen cupboard to reach the brown-paper bag of barmcakes that she had brought in with her yesterday evening. She took two from the bag, then wrapped the other two tightly for the next day.

Angela cursed silently to herself as she struggled to butter the two barmcakes, because the butter was in a solid block. When she eventually managed to roughly spread the lumps of butter, she put a slice of corned beef on each. One for breakfast and one for morning break time. She didn't need anything for her lunch, because today she was joining a group of the girls to walk down to the chippy at lunchtime.

She smiled now at the thought, because she had spent the first few weeks sitting on the edge of a group of older women each lunchtime, eating her sandwiches. The younger girls all had their own little cliques of friends, coming and going to work, walking along and linking arms with each other. But yesterday she had been asked by Nancy, her room-mate, if she wanted to go to the chippy for lunch with her group today. They always went to the chippy on a Friday.

It meant, at last, that things were looking up, that she was starting to be accepted by the other girls her own age. Mona Kelly had warned her that it took a while to break into the tight little groups in the mill, and that it was best to wait until you were asked. Yes, Angela thought, this was definitely going to be a good day, because Friday was also pay-day, and after work tonight she was going to meet Philip.

The day got off to a good start with Angela catching the early tram, which was quieter, and meant that she didn't get pushed and shoved as much as she would have done on the later one. It was always the same problem at the beginning and the end of each day, the pushing and the shoving.

She had solved the morning problem by getting up sharp and running for the early tram, but there was nothing she could do about the heaving snake-like crowds that spilled from the mill when work was over. She was now part of that working mob and was having to learn to push and shove her way on to the packed trams. Unfamiliar, alien territory for a girl who had grown up in a small farming town, and who had never had to push or shove her way on to any kind of vehicle before.

It was great not having to queue at the clocking-in machine as well, and as Angela checked her card in, she thought how much better she was getting at everything. She was finding the machines easier to use, and was becoming quicker at them. She was also able to tolerate the noise levels now, and had learned how to mouth words to the other women, and how to use the basic mill sign language.

Things at the lodging-house were working out better, too. It still wasn't a nice place to live, but Angela was getting used to it – and getting used to the way Mona Kelly liked things done.

She made sure she did her share of cooking the evening meals and washing up afterwards, and she tried to get back to the house as quick as she could after work. Mona liked the meal – usually something quickly organised like pie and chips or sausages and mash – over and done with and out of the way. She had a man-friend who called in the evenings, and they often sat drinking bottles of beer in the kitchen and listening to the radio or having a game of cards.

Angela had also been helping out with the weekend cleaning in the house, and didn't moan like the other girls, because she didn't want Mona to find any fault with her. She took charge of the cleaning and bleaching in the bathroom, even giving it a rub over on a Wednesday night as well. Biddy had drummed into her that the kitchen and bathroom were the most important places in a house to have clean, and Angela had come to appreciate this. She was determined that she wouldn't do anything that would cross Mona Kelly – she'd done that once before, and look where it had got her. The thought of having to start all over again was just too much – it was the thing that would send her back to Tullamore.

Angela hung her coat up, then headed into the winding-room, towards her own machine. There were only a few workers in, none of whom she really knew, so she sat down and started checking that all the bobbins were in place and that she was ready to start as soon as the machines were switched on. Then, hearing footsteps approaching, she turned and saw a dark-headed lad around her own age coming towards her with a carrier bag in his hand. She recognised him as one of the group of lads that Nancy was always talking about, as he sometimes came down to the winding-room to clean the cotton fluff off the dusty machines. She was glad that she hadn't put her hairnet on yet, as she felt really silly wearing it, especially when there were any lads around.

'D'you fancy a brew?' he asked, giving her an embarrassed grin. He held out a brown-paper bag. 'I've got a full flask wi' me, and it'll only go to waste. Me mam makes it up for me every mornin'.'

Angela smiled back at him. 'That would be grand,' she said, noticing his starched, spotless shirt and the fancy diamond-patterned tie under his brown overall. He looked a lot smarter than some of the other mill lads, and even though he had a bit of a Brylcreemed quiff in his hair like Eric had, you could tell that he wasn't a rough type. 'I'll go and get me mug.'

'Ye're all right,' he told her, taking the green and white flask out of its wrapping. 'There's two cups on the top of this. By the way,' he said, opening the flask up now, 'me name's Colin – Colin Wright.'

'And I'm Angela Flynn.'

'Well, pleased to meet you, Angela.' He gave Angela the outside cup with the handle, and sat the handleless mug on a ledge of the machine for himself. 'There's plenty of condensed milk and sugar in it already,' he informed her, pouring the steaming liquid into her mug.

Angela took a drink of the tea, and had to stop herself from grimacing, because it was so sweet. On the second mouthful, it didn't taste quite so bad, and it seemed to soothe her throat a bit. 'That's lovely,' she said, smiling, thinking how nice it was that she was making more friends in the mill.

'You don't come from round here,' he said, giving her a sidelong look, 'do you? Not with that accent.'

'Well,' she said, taking another sip of the tea, 'I'm actually from Ireland.'

'Gerraway!' he said, laughing. 'I thought you were gonna say you were from Wales or Scotland!'

Angela blushed, conscious of her accent again.

'How long you bin over here, then?' he asked, more serious now. 'An' where are you livin'?'

She narrowed her blue eyes, calculating. 'I've been here since the beginning of the summer, and I'm livin' up in Mona Kelly's lodging-house, for the time being.'

He nodded, lifting the white plastic cup to his lips. 'Mona Kelly . . . does she work here, like?'

'Yes,' Angela said. 'A few of the other girls who work in the mill live there, too.' She paused. 'I think you know Nancy and Alice – they work in this part of the mill, too.'

He stuck his lip out, thinking. 'Alice an' Nancy . . .' He shrugged. 'Can't say as I know the names. I might well know their faces – to see, like. But I can't say as I know the names.' He smiled. 'D'you go out much at the weekends? Into Stockport or anythin'?'

'Sometimes . . .' she said, looking away shyly.

'D'you like the flicks? You know, the pictures?'

Angela nodded, then had to stop herself shuddering when she remembered she'd only been to them with Eric. She looked over to the door now, as a crowd of the girls came in, all chattering and laughing – obviously off the later tram – and she spotted Nancy's curly head in the middle of them. They all stopped when they saw Angela and Colin – and then just stood, staring.

'There's two good films on this week,' Colin continued, oblivious to the staring girls. 'D'you like Elvis?'

'Yes,' Angela said, 'I've seen a few of his films.'

'He's crackin', in't he? They're showin' *GI Blues* at the Plaza . . .'

Angela nodded, only half listening. Nancy and one of her friends, the one with the long dark hair, had come over to stand next to them, arms folded, and making it obvious that they were listening in to the conversation. They hadn't changed into their green mill overalls yet, and Nancy's friend was sporting an outfit of a tight red sweater and a black pencil skirt that was far too good to be wearing to work. Nancy was more suitably dressed in her usual heavy grey skirt and a short-sleeved dark sweater.

'Or if you don't fancy Elvis, we could go to one of the other cinemas,' Colin went on. 'I can look it up in the *Manchester Evening News* later on, like – if you fancy goin' some evenin'?'

There was a silence, and to cover her embarrassment, Angela lifted the plastic mug to her lips and drained the remainder of the now-lukewarm, sweet tea.

'So, d'you fancy it, like?' Colin said, finishing his tea off, too. 'D'you fancy us goin' to the cinema some evenin' then?'

'I don't know,' Angela replied in a low, hesitant voice, acutely conscious of the two whispering girls at her elbow. 'I'm not really sure what I'm doin' . . .'

The mill machinery suddenly rattled into life, drowning everything else out and killing all conversation. Colin put all the bits of his flask back together, and then touched Angela's arm. 'I'll see you later,' he mouthed, giving her a big wink.

As soon as he had moved away from the machine, Nancy and her friend came to stand in front of her – hands on hips and faces like thunder.

'What bleedin' game d'you think you're playing?' Nancy mouthed, her permed curls flying as she tossed her head indignantly.

'What?' Angela said, her brows knotted in confusion. 'I don't know what you're talking about . . .'

Both girls looked at each other and made scornful faces, indicating their disbelief. Nancy suddenly leaned forward and poked Angela viciously in the chest, sending her flying back against the machine. 'I'll – see – you – later!' she enunciated slowly.

A flame of anger shot through Angela and her immediate instinct was to give Nancy a hard slap across the face – but when she saw the supervisor coming through the swing-doors she thought the better of it.

Angela worked through the morning with her heart in her mouth and a sick feeling in her stomach – dreading the morning tea break. She knew by now what she'd done – albeit unintentionally. Quite obviously, either Nancy or her friend fancied Colin. Or maybe Colin had been lying, and one of them was his girlfriend or ex-girlfriend. Whatever it was, she had made a big mistake encouraging him and drinking his tea.

As soon as the machines cranked to a halt for the break, Nancy was over to her like a shot out of a gun, while her friends stood in a huddle over by the wall, watching.

'What's your bloody game?' she said, poking Angela again, this time in the shoulder.

'I don't know what you're talking about,' Angela said, her eyes flaring. She had grown up in Tullamore with the rough and tumble of a large family, her sisters thumping and hitting each other, and her immediate instinct was to fight back. She pushed Nancy's hand away very firmly. 'And you can just stop poking me right now!'

Nancy took a step back, not quite so sure of her ground. She glanced back at her friends, looking for a bit of support. 'That Colin Wright – he's supposed to be goin' to a party at the weekend wi' me mate, Shirley. That's the girl that were with me this mornin' in the red jumper.'

'Well?' Angela demanded. 'What's that got to do with me?'

'You've just been makin' plans to go to the pictures with him,' Nancy said, glancing over her shoulder, to see if Shirley and the rest of her friends were still watching.

'I made no such plans with him,' Angela stated, 'and you *know* that, because you were standin' right next to me listenin' to every single word.'

'You didn't exactly say "no", did you?' Nancy demanded, feeling braver now that her friends had started moving towards them. 'You weren't exactly fightin' him off, were you?'

'I've no intentions of going out with him to the pictures,' Angela said indignantly, 'because I already have a boyfriend – as you well know. I told you that the first night I moved into Mona's.'

'Well,' Nancy said, 'it wouldn't be the first time a girl's gone out with two fellas.' Angela looked over Nancy's shoulder, and could see Shirley watching them closely. She looked far less glamorous now in her green mill overall and a hairnet down over her forehead. 'You can tell your friend', Angela said, turning away now, 'that I have no intentions of goin' out with that lad – none at all.'

'That's fine, then,' Nancy said. She paused. 'I think we'd better forget about the chippy today – I don't think Shirley's gonna feel too happy about you comin' with us after this has happened. Colin usually goes to the chippy on a Friday, an' she'd go mad if he started chattin' you up again.'

'That's grand by me,' Angela snapped. 'I'm quite happy stayin' here for my lunch.' She would just have to keep the barmcake and corned beef for the afternoon, and make do with a cup of tea now at the break.

The rest of the day crept along very slowly and, just to add to her misery, Angela suddenly felt she had the startings of a sore throat coming on. The lunch break was the usual tedious affair, listening to the older women moaning about their husbands and children when they got fed up moaning about the supervisors.

Thankfully, Nancy and Shirley just ignored her when they came back after lunch, and there was no sign of Colin Wright.

Angela heaved a sigh of relief that the incident seemed to have blown over, and just kept her head down, doing her reeling and winding and wishing the afternoon away. Her throat was now very raw, and every time she swallowed it gave her a funny feeling down around the side of her face and ears.

By the time the hooter went off, the only thing she felt like doing that evening was climbing into her bed.

'What the bleedin' hell happened to you?' Mona demanded, as she swept past Angela with a tray of fish fingers in one hand and a large jar of beetroot in the other. She set them down in the middle of the table, then turned back to the big, smoking chip-pan. She was obviously in a great rush tonight as she hadn't even taken her heavy woollen coat and scarf off yet. 'Did you conveniently forget that you were supposed to peel the spuds for the chips tonight?'

Angela shook her head, the movement making her feel dizzy. 'No, I didn't forget,' she said hoarsely. 'I couldn't get on a tram for ages . . . I'm not feelin' the best. I think I'll have to go to bed for the rest of the evenin'.'

'Well, you can just bleedin' well hang on and do the washin'-up before you disappear off to your bed,' Mona stated, lifting the chip-basket out of the hot fat. 'I'm not a bleedin' skivvy, even though all you girls seem to think I am. The rules of this place is that everyone has to pull their weight, an' not leave every bleedin' thing to me.'

She gave the chip-basket a good shake to remove the surface grease and then dumped the pile of roasting chips on an open copy of the *Stockport Express*. She then scooped up handfuls of damp, raw potato chips, put them in the basket, and returned it to the hot fat where the smoking and hissing started all over again.

Mona turned to Angela now. 'Don't just stand there like bleedin' Piffin – go an' give them lot a shout and tell them their tea's on the table.'

Angela headed out towards the hall, pausing at the kitchen. 'I'm really sorry, Mona,' she said. 'I did me best to get back as quick as I could . . . I didn't feel up to fightin' my way on the packed trams.'

'Go on,' Mona said with a dismissive wave of her hand, 'you'll have to toughen up a bit, or those mill girls will walk all over you. It's everyone for themselves, or you'll always get left behind.'

Tea was a bit of a sober affair, as the other girls talked and whispered amongst themselves about their plans for the weekend, largely ignoring Angela. She knew it was to do with drinking tea with Colin that morning, and that it would all sort itself out again when they saw she wasn't interested in him.

Besides, not being part of the crowd didn't bother her quite so much this evening as she had other things on her mind. She knew she definitely wasn't fit to go out tonight, because, apart from her sore throat and ears, she felt hot and sort of shaky all over. But how was she going to let Philip know that she couldn't meet him as they had planned? They had made no definite arrangements about where they were going – they were to meet outside the fire station in Mersey Square at seven o'clock and then decide on the pictures, or perhaps go dancing at one of the local Catholic clubs. She had Philip's phone number, but she was feeling so unwell that the thought of walking down to the phone-box at the corner of Cale Green did not appeal to her in the slightest. She hated phoning his house anyway, because his mother wasn't too keen on her after the trouble with Eric and the impending court case.

As she stood scrubbing at the fish-finger tray at the

sink, she decided that she would have to walk out to the phone-box whether she felt up to it or not. She had upset Nancy and her friends and Mona Kelly already today, and she didn't want to upset Philip as well by standing him up.

Half an hour later, Angela slowly walked back from the phone-box – hot and shaky, but happy and relieved that Philip had answered the phone and not his grumpy mother. He had been lovely and concerned about her, saying that if he hadn't heard from her by Sunday, he'd drop by to visit her. She stopped at the corner shop, bought herself a hot-water bottle, throat lozenges and some aspirin, then made her weary way back to the lodging-house and went straight to bed.

Chapter Fifty-Four

Elsie had been very bad with her nerves recently and, as Eric's court case grew nearer, she was getting worse. Although it meant problems with managing the work on her own, Biddy had talked her friend into going to stay with her sister for a few weeks, down in Devon.

'But how will you manage, all on your own?' Elsie had asked, with a tear in her eye. She was rarely without a tear in her eyes these days.

'I'll manage,' Biddy had assured her in a tone that brooked no argument. 'I can get somebody in to help.'

'Who?' Elsie had asked, looking alarmed. There were plenty of folks around that would love a job in the boarding-house, and maybe somebody would come in while Elsie was away, and then decide they didn't want to leave. 'What about me mate, June?' June was dependable enough to do the work, and she wasn't the type that would go trying to steal another friend's job.

Biddy had mulled it over. From what she'd heard of June, she was a bit on the rough side, but – according to Elsie – she was a great worker. Biddy had given June a ring and had asked her to call around for a chat to see if they could work something out.

Biddy had been a bit taken aback when she'd opened the door and seen the tall, thin peroxide-blonde standing there. She recognised June from out and about the shops around Shaw Heath and Davenport, and she had always considered her to be quite attractive, but in a rough, cheap-looking way.

Whilst Biddy warmed to 'salt of the earth' types like Elsie, June's type was just a bit beyond the pale. As she'd looked at the woman, she couldn't believe that Elsie had actually said that she thought June and herself were alike! For a start, June was a good ten years older.

Walking into the kitchen, Biddy had glimpsed June's dark roots peeping out through her hair, and she'd thought how right she was to have gone back to her own natural colour. Never again would she be tempted to lighten her hair – the thought of looking like June would now be the direst of warnings.

'The main thing is gettin' the breakfast in the mornin' for the lads, and then there's washing and ironing and cleaning different places on different days,' Biddy had explained, thinking she might put June off. 'And then sometimes you might have to pick the kids up from school for me, and after that we have to sort the tea for the lads coming in again in the evenin'.'

'No problem,' June had told her, taking out a packet of Embassy tipped. She had held the cigarettes out to her prospective employer, but Biddy had politely declined. 'I learned the run of the place when you were over in Ireland, and I got to know the lads as well – they're a right rum lot, aren't they?'

Biddy had nodded, trying to remember if Elsie had said anything about June and men. She knew she had been divorced twice, and was bringing up her children on her own, but she wasn't too sure what her situation was with boyfriends. The last thing Biddy needed was a problem with June and the lads or, even worse – she remembered the older nurse in the hospital – June fancying Fred.

Last week had been June's first week, and so far Biddy had not been able to find one thing to fault her with – apart from the fact that she wasn't as good with the kids as Angela had been. June was happy enough to pick the children up from school and sort meals for them and that kind of thing – but she didn't have the same way with her as Angela did. She just wasn't interested in reading to them, playing games or chatting about school with them – all the little things that Angela had been so good at. It was probably due to having four teenagers at home, and having had to manage them for years on her own – June had probably had her fill of children.

Although Michael and Helen liked June well enough, they were still complaining about Angela having gone and constantly asked when she was coming back. If the truth was told, Biddy missed her, too, and she was still upset at the way things had ended. As time went on, she began to have nagging doubts about how hard she'd been on Angela. It had been a bad time with the way things were with Fred and Gabriel and everything, and Angela telling lies had just capped it all. But there was no good in crying over spilt milk; she was gone now. In actual fact, Biddy was very surprised that Angela's parents hadn't told her to go straight back to Ireland when she'd written to explain about their falling-out. She supposed they must have thought that Angela was nearly a grown woman, and was fit enough to look after herself.

Although June wasn't quite so good with the kids as Angela had been, she had lots of good points. She had appeared on time every morning, and had got down to work straight away. She chatted to the lads when she was giving them their meals, but she hadn't been *too* forward or personal with them. She was definitely quicker around the house than Elsie, and she didn't mind what she was asked to do. Biddy also thought that June was a good laugh, although she was inclined to be a bit on the coarse side at times.

Like Biddy, June was fond of a bit of a drink, and had come over a few evenings to join her boss for a couple of glasses of sherry when Fred was out watching a wrestling match with his mates. Last Sunday night, when Fred was out for a drink with his working mates from the Grosvenor, June had brought over four little bottles of Babycham. They had made a lovely cocktail of brandy and Babycham and had sat watching a film and drinking the potent brew. Biddy had also brought out some beef and mustard sandwiches, French fancies and two chocolate éclairs.

During the boring parts of the film, June had filled Biddy in on the bits of her life that Elsie had discreetly left out. 'The biggest mistake I ever made in me life was lettin' this rich, older fella go that I used to work for.' She took a deep drag on her cigarette. 'He wanted to marry me an' everything.' She gave a deep, theatrical sigh. 'Oh, I could be in clover now, if I hadn't been so bleedin' stupid.'

'What kind of work did you do for him?' Biddy asked, intrigued.

'Housekeepin',' June replied. 'He had a big house in Bramhall. He was a widower, like.' She got herself comfortable in the chair with the ashtray balanced on one arm and her brandy and Babycham on the other. 'It were before I had the kids, like – it were before I was even married the first time.'

'So, what happened?' Biddy asked, hearing alarm-bells ringing once again. If June had taken up with one of her male employers, would Fred be safe from her clutches?

'Can I be straight with you? Elsie says you're not the kind to be easily shocked,' June said, taking a slurp of the sweet, fizzy drink. 'You see, my problem is – I've never really liked sex. An' if I'd realised that back then, I wouldn't have got into the bleedin' mess I did with men.'

Biddy's jaw nearly dropped open. 'You don't like sex?' she whispered, looking anxiously at the door in case any of the lads were going past. 'Not at all?'

June shrugged. 'Not really, I could never understand what the big deal was about. After a bit of their huffin' and puffin', I just begin to feel bloody raw downstairs, and there's nowt pleasurable about it when you start to feel like that.'

'Did you never go to a doctor about it?' Biddy asked, reaching for a chocolate éclair. 'Maybe they could have given you somethin' . . . some special cream or somethin' like that.'

'A *doctor*?' June said, her eyes rolling with amusement. 'Could you just imagine me goin' to a doctor an' sayin', "Excuse me, Doctor – but I've got a bit of trouble with me *fanny*"?'

Biddy's hand came up to her cream-filled mouth as she went into peals of laughter.

'That is the most *terrible* word!'

'Can you just imagine it?' June said in a high-pitched giggle, then took a sip of her brandy and Babycham. 'I don't think so. Besides, I don't even *want* to enjoy it – it doesn't do nothin' for me – it's a waste of bloody time.'

Biddy dabbed her creamy mouth with her hanky now, trying to stop laughing. 'Do you never think of what you might be missin' though?' she asked. 'There's times when it can be lovely.'

'What's there to miss?' June said, waving her cigarette in the air. 'I mean, it's not as if I ever had one of them organisms – or whatever the bleedin' hell they're called. Anyroads, I've heard it's just like a good sneeze – an' who wants to waste their time tryin' to make themselves sneeze? You'd need to be some kind of bleedin' lunatic.' She looked at Biddy, her eyebrows raised dramatically.

'Oh, June! You're a real scream!' Biddy started to laugh again, and this time she couldn't stop. She laughed and laughed until the tears ran down her face – and she couldn't decide whether it was the brandy and Babycham or whether it was the shock of realising that

June was nothing like she had imagined. Or maybe even relief at knowing that Fred was perfectly safe with this peroxide-blonde, tarty-looking woman. 'Oh, an' I can't believe that terrible word you used earlier!'

'What word?' June said, raising her eyebrows, deliberately trying to get Biddy to say it.

'You know perfectly well!' Biddy laughed, taking a mouthful of her drink.

'*Fanny?* What's wrong with that?' June's thin, dark eyebrows were raised high. 'There's no point in beatin' about the bleedin' bush – an' there's no other nice word for it. Anyroads, getting back to me story', June said, helping herself to a French fancy, 'about the older man from Bramhall.' She shook her head. 'As they say in all the best stories, I were too young and foolish to know what I were turnin' down. If only I knew now, I wouldn't be sittin' in a bleedin' corporation house with four kids and not two ha'pennies to rub together.'

'What happened?' Biddy said, really enjoying herself now. She hadn't had this much entertainment since Ruby Sweeney used to tell her all her lurid stories – although Biddy felt that June had definitely outdone her with this one.

'Well,' June said, 'he wanted me to move in with him, like – Geoff his name was – but me mam would have killed me, livin' over the brush with an older man. I was only twenty at the time. Anyroads, I used to stay the odd weekend at his fancy house, and I really liked it, and Geoff were dead nice to me, buyin' me nice clothes and jewellery and everythin' – but I hated havin' sex with him. The thing is, I thought it was just that I didn't fancy Geoff enough. I thought I'd be fine when I met the right man, like.'

'An' did you never meet the right man?' Biddy said sadly.

'I've met plenty of men,' June said, 'an' I've married two and gone out with more than my fair share – but

I've still never developed an interest in sex – it's just not my idea of enjoyment.' She stopped, a thoughtful look crossing her face. 'I reckon I'd have been well set up with Geoff by now – he'd have been too bleedin' old to be lookin' for anythin' off me at this stage.'

Biddy shook her head, laughter bubbling up in her again. 'So, nothin' would entice you into a man's bed now? Not even if it was Cary Grant or somebody like that?'

June shrugged. 'The only thing that would get me to do it now would be money – if I were right desperate for money, like.'

'But that's the same as *prostitution*!' Biddy said in a high voice. 'Surely you wouldn't consider *that*?'

June shrugged again. 'Probably not. As I say – only if I were right desperate. I reckon any mother would consider it – if it meant the difference between feedin' her kids or not.' She grinned. 'And anyroads – if you're not getting any pleasure out of it, a few bob might bring a smile to yer face. It's done it to mine on a few occasions.'

'Well,' Biddy said, quite overwhelmed by this take on life, 'I suppose it's a case of each to their own.' She smiled now, not wanting June to feel bad about having given her all this information. 'I have to say, I quite enjoy a kiss an' a cuddle with Fred.'

'You can tell an' all!' June said, laughing. 'He's never got his bleedin' hands off you. I often see him grabbing you around the waist when you're busy at the cooker in the middle of the mornin'.' Then, her face suddenly went serious. 'But I think that's lovely, you bein' married and havin' two kids and another on the way. There's a lot of women who would be happy to jump into your shoes.'

Biddy beamed with delight. 'Ah, well – I can't say I'm not happy with my life.'

'An' you'd be wise to keep up the kissin' and cuddlin',

for there's a lot of women who would be happy to jump into bed with Fred an' all.'

The smile slid from Biddy's face, as she wondered if June was referring to any woman in particular. June sat forward in her chair now, and started to pour them both another brandy and Babycham mixture.

'Make mine a bit lighter this time,' Biddy said, 'on account of the baby.'

'A drop of brandy will do it no harm,' June assured her, pouring a good two-inch measure of brandy into her own glass, and a smaller one into Biddy's. 'An' it'll help you to get a good night's sleep.' She topped them both up with the bubbly champagne perry and handed Biddy her drink. 'Isn't this lovely?' she suddenly said, looking around her. 'I feel all sophisticated like – sittin' here in your lovely big house, and drinkin' brandy an' Babycham, and eatin' fancy cakes.'

'I'm glad you're enjoyin' yourself,' Biddy said warmly, cheering up again at the compliments to her house, 'and, I have to say, I'm enjoyin' your company – it's a bit livelier than poor old Elsie's has been lately.'

June lifted her overfull glass very slowly to her mouth and successfully managed to take a big drink out of it without spilling a drop. She gave a little sigh of contentment, and sat back in the chair to light up another cigarette. 'That were a right to-do with her Eric, wasn't it?'

Biddy nodded, her face turning grim. 'Don't think I'm being rude, but I don't like even hearin' his name.'

'Well, it's taken it out of poor Elsie, that's all I can say. It's really done her in. She's not the same woman she was . . . her nerves are in a terrible state.'

There was a sound at the sitting-room door. Both women turned to look as the door slowly opened.

'Mum . . .' Little Helen stood in the doorway in her pink pyjamas adorned with white woolly sheep. 'I can't sleep . . . I had a bad dream.'

'Come on,' Biddy said, opening her arms. 'Come and sit on my knee for a while, then you'll be all right.'

The child came running across the room to her and stopped just in front of the coffee table. 'Can I have somefing?' she said, eyeing up the little fancy bottles and the glasses and the leftover cakes. 'Can I have a drink from that little Bambi bottle?'

Biddy winked over to June, starting to heave herself to her feet. 'I'll get you some lemonade to go with that. You couldn't drink it on its own – you're not old enough.'

'Stay where you are,' June said, jumping up. 'I'll get her some lemonade in her little plastic cup.'

Helen clambered up on her mother's knee. 'Mum,' she asked in a low whisper, 'when will Angela be coming back?'

Biddy gave a short sigh. 'Look,' she said, picking up one of the Babycham bottles, 'he is a lovely little Bambi on the front, isn't he?'

The next morning, Biddy woke early, and as she lay in bed feeling the effects of the potent brandy mixture, she vowed to herself that she'd go easy on the alcohol until after the baby was born. In fact, the way she was feeling, she might decide never to drink again even if she wasn't expecting.

'You wouldn't think there was such a kick in those little bottles,' she said, as she lay cuddled in Fred's arms.

'Just like you,' Fred said, 'small and lethal.'

Biddy pretended to punch him and snuggled in closer, delighted to hear Fred making witty remarks. She knew that the 'small and lethal' one was an old wrestling term he had often used to describe opponents, but even so, he'd used it at the right time. 'So, you enjoyed your night out at the Grosvenor?'

'Champion,' Fred said, 'I'd a crackin' good night.'

'Who was there?' Biddy asked.

Fred reeled off all the people that Biddy would know – staff they'd both worked with together and some old friends. 'Oh,' he suddenly remembered, 'and Frank. Frank Kennedy was there with his girlfriend.'

'A girlfriend? Who was that?' Biddy said, intrigued.

'A red-haired girl,' Fred said. He held his hand to measure just below his opposite shoulder. 'Smallish and quite posh.'

It came to Biddy in a flash. 'Was her name Kate?'

'Yeah,' Fred said, nodding slowly. 'Come to think of it . . . I think it was Kate.'

'I'm delighted,' Biddy said, 'it's about time he got over Tara and found himself a new girlfriend.' Although a little part of her wondered if somewhere in the future Frank and Tara could have got back together. They had so much in common – and in time maybe she could have got to forgive him for the lies he had told her the first time around.

'Did he know Tara well, like?' Fred asked.

'Yes, Fred,' Biddy said patiently. 'You're a divil for tryin' to kid me that you don't remember these things.'

Chapter Fifty-Five

On Monday morning, Angela lay on in bed for a while
longer, struggling with the burning, achy feeling all over
her body, and the terrible soreness still in her throat.
She had woken numerous times during the night – out
of the most horrible, frightening nightmares – wishing
she had someone she could ask to get her a drink of
water. Wishing she had someone who even cared that
she needed a drink of water.

But she only had Nancy and Alice in the bed
opposite, and they were barely talking to her, and
Mona, who didn't really believe she was ill, and thought
she was only dodging out of the weekend housework.

The last few nights, when she'd been on her own in
the darkened bedroom, when the other girls had been
out enjoying themselves, she had turned her face into
the pillow and wept for all the things she had thrown
away and now so desperately needed. She wept for
Biddy and the children and the boarding-house, and
then she wept for her family back in Ireland. Her lovely
mother and father who would be only too delighted to
bring her drinks of water and look after her. And her
brother and sisters who usually teased and messed with
her – but who would do anything for her if they thought
she was actually sick.

Yesterday evening, Philip had called at the house and
Mona had let him up to see her for a few minutes. Even
with her high temperature and sore throat, Angela still
had the sensitivity to be embarrassed about the general

dire conditions in the house – and her own bedroom in particular. She was acutely aware of the fact that she and Mona were both Irish, and it might look as if everyone from Ireland had awful, depressing houses like this. And she wished Philip had been brought into her nicely decorated bedroom back in Maple Terrace when she'd lived there, so's he could have seen that she was used to better things. Philip had been very concerned, saying that he thought Angela should see a doctor, and he'd brought a bottle of Lucozade and some grapes, and he'd also been polite, and hadn't mentioned anything about the house. He had offered to go up to the boarding-house and tell Biddy what had happened. 'I'm sure she'd be very worried if she knew how sick you are—'

'No!' Angela had said in a croaky voice, struggling to sit up. 'She'd think I was only puttin' it on to get sympathy.'

Philip had just sat there looking flummoxed, not knowing what to say or do to make her feel better. He indicated the glass that lay beside a small bottle of aspirin, on the floor at the side of the bed. 'Shall I take that downstairs and wash it and pour some Lucozade in it for you?' he suggested.

Angela nodded, and croaked out, 'Please.'

The only thing was, Philip had left the bottle of Lucozade downstairs last night, and she hadn't thought to ask him to bring it up when he was leaving. In fact, she barely remembered him leaving.

She stretched across the bed now, calling out Nancy's name as loudly as she could. After several minutes, the girl eventually moved and sat up. She stared over at Angela. 'What's wrong?' she said, her brows knitted together.

'My throat . . . an' I'm boiling as well,' Angela said.

Nancy hopped out of bed quickly and came over to Angela's bed. 'You look bleedin' awful,' she said in a shocked voice. 'When Mona gets up, I'll tell her you're not well.' She paused, suddenly remembering their row and feeling guilty. 'D'you want me to get you something?'

'A drink . . . please,' Angela whispered. 'I've Lucozade downstairs . . . that Philip brought me.'

Nancy bit her lip. 'Oh, Angela, I'm dead sorry . . . but we finished the whole bottle when we came in last night. I feel terrible – but honest, we didn't know it was yours . . .'

'Water', Angela struggled out, 'will be grand.' And as she heard Nancy's footsteps rushing down the stairs, Angela suddenly felt overwhelmed with relief at someone looking after her, and she turned her tear-filled eyes towards the pillow.

'I'd say you're not fit for work – I'd say you're going to need the doctor,' Mona pronounced, after feeling Angela's forehead and ordering her to open her mouth.

'D'you think you would be well enough to walk down to the surgery?'

Angela shook her head. The thought of even walking to the toilet was making her feel terrible, although she knew she would have to manage somehow. 'I'm sore everywhere,' she rasped. 'My throat and ears and my legs and everythin' . . .'

Mona lifted the bottle of aspirins from the floor, her mind racing as to the best course of action. 'Here,' she said taking two tablets out and handing them to Angela, 'take these and stay in yer bed for the rest of the morning and try to get a good sleep.' Angela took the tablets and very painfully swallowed them down with the water. 'I'll have a word with the supervisor and hopefully they'll let me come home at lunchtime.' She patted Angela's shoulder. 'If you're no better then, I'll ring the doctor to come in the afternoon, and I'll get somebody to sit downstairs so they can let him in for you.'

Angela nodded. 'I think . . .' she whispered, 'I'd better . . . go to the bathroom.'

'C'mon,' Mona said in an unusually soft voice, 'I'll give you a hand to walk out.'

Very shakily, and leaning on her landlady, the young girl made her way slowly to the bathroom.

When Mona came home in a huge fluster at lunchtime, she knew that all was definitely not well with her young Irish boarder. Her temperature was higher and she was hardly able to speak at all. She rushed into her bedroom and phoned the doctor's surgery, then made another phone call to ask her friend, Alf, to come around to wait downstairs for him coming.

'I told them it was an emergency,' she said to Angela, 'so he should be out fairly soon.' She hovered over the bed. 'I feel rotten leaving you . . . but I've got to get back to work an' I've not had anything to eat yet. There was a bad accident there this mornin' . . . a young fella lost three fingers when he was cleanin' out one of the machines.' She tutted. 'God knows what he was doin' – they're warned often enough about those machines. That's two of them that's lost their fingers since the summer.'

Angela shook her head, not attempting to speak now, as it was too painful and too much effort to get the words out.

Mona patted her over the bedclothes. 'I'd say it's your mother you'd like to be here now instead of me . . .' She sighed. 'Don't feel bad about it – we're all the same when we're in a bit of trouble – no matter how old we are. The mammies are the ones we want when we need a bit of comfort.'

Angela woke with a start some time later in a fevered

sweat, having had a series of bloody nightmares about people having fingers and arms chopped off by machines that were chasing them around the factory. She heard heavy footsteps coming up the stairs. The footsteps paused on the landing outside for a few moments, then she heard them coming towards her bedroom.

'Angela?' a voice said, then she heard a small tap on the door. 'It's Alf – Mona asked me to look in on you.' The footsteps came over now to the side of the bed.

Angela lifted her head a few inches from the pillow, and managed to make some kind of sound to indicate that she had heard. Then she felt a heavy weight on the opposite side of the bed, as though someone was sitting down on it. She turned, moaning as she did so, and opened her eyes to find she was looking up into the face of Mona's friend.

'I hear you're feelin' poorly,' he said in his broad Stockport accent, beer fumes emanating from him. 'Mona says yer not too well.' He cleared his throat. 'She said to give you a drink of water . . . or see if there was anything else I could do for you . . .'

Angela closed her eyes and swallowed, sending a dull pain coursing from her throat to both her ears – her throat had now swollen so much that she felt it was almost closing over.

She felt a hand on her forehead now and instinctively pulled away.

'That's a high temperature you have on you,' Alf said in a funny, husky kind of a whisper. 'Maybe you should throw them bedclothes back off of you . . . maybe if I gave you a cold wash . . . it would help bring that temperature down.'

Angela gripped the top of the faded old quilt and pulled it up around her neck and closed her eyes tight. *Sacred Heart of Jesus*, she prayed, *make him go away and leave me alone!*

Alf bent down to the side of the bed now, and lifted up the half-filled glass of water. 'Here,' he said, fumbling with the top of the quilt, 'take a drink . . . it'll make you feel better . . .' When he felt her resistance, he leaned away from her to put the glass back down on the floor. Then he sat up straight again, staring at the huddled shape under the bedclothes. 'I were only tryin' to be friendly,' he explained. 'I know it can't be easy . . . a young girl all this way from home . . . all on her own.'

There was a silence, then his hand came back on to the mound on the bed that was Angela. It started at her thighs and then slowly moved upwards to her hips and the curve of her back.

As she lay there, her whole body burning up and her throat swollen and tight, the young Irish girl realised that ignoring this hideous, lecherous man was not going to work. In fact she instinctively knew that lying there in a prone, unresponsive position was actually encouraging him further as she heard his breathing growing more loud and rapid and she smelt the beery breath coming closer to her again.

'I'll just loosen this around yer neck,' he said, as he reached up to touch her ear and then the back of her head.

Angela summoned up every ounce of energy she had to drag herself around to face him with both arms outstretched, to push him off balance. 'Leave me . . . *alone*!' she rasped, the effort almost hurting her lips.

'Bloody hell!' he said in a loud voice as he slid off the ancient satin quilt and on to the linoleum floor. 'There's no fuckin' need for that! You're an ungrateful little sod!'

Then, with better timing than she could have wished for, a loud rap came on the front door – heralding the arrival of the doctor.

Chapter Fifty-Six

Biddy stood in front of the mirror, twisting this way and that, trying to decide which of the outfits to buy. Which of the outfits were the most flattering over her ever-increasing baby bulge. When they had got breakfast over with that morning, she had taken the rest of the day off to go into Manchester, shopping for a new outfit for Fred's special 'do' at the Grosvenor Hotel. She had decided to start off in John Lewis's at Piccadilly, where the bus had dropped her off, because they had a good range of clothes for everyday wear and for special occasions.

Fred had insisted that she have time off, saying she had no excuses now that she had June, who had already proved herself as being perfectly capable of managing the place for a day on her own. Fred's walking had improved, and he was now able to walk down to school to pick Michael and Helen up. Up until now he had been relying on lifts from friends in cars and taxis when he went out, and so being able to walk a bit of a distance was yet another move forward in his recovery.

Biddy had spent some time looking through all the racks of proper maternity wear, and now she looked at the ordinary clothes which she might be able to get away with wearing for a while. Eventually, with the help of a young, stylish sales assistant, she'd settled on an elegant black silk suit. She knew immediately, when she looked at herself in the mirror, that it was the type of outfit that Tara would have picked for the occasion –

and she knew it would suit her dark brown hair. The silk skirt – luckily with an elasticated waistband for her increasing middle – was decorated with a subtle purple and navy beaded hem which flowed down towards her ankles. The glamorous flowing jacket had a mandarin-style collar and was more flamboyantly decorated with the same beautiful beads. It was nearly forty pounds, but Biddy felt it was well worth it, because nothing else she'd tried on looked half as good. She also bought a pair of maternity trousers, a skirt, and two flowery overblouses that were handy for working around the house and still looked nice.

As she came out of the changing room, a young girl came rushing over to her saying, 'I'll carry your purchases over to the till for you, Madam.'

Biddy felt a surge of pride at the title and, as she handed the money over at the till, she gave silent thanks to Ruby Sweeney for leaving her the boarding-house, and the wherewithal to come into Lewis's and buy all these nice clothes.

'So you had a lovely day at the shops?' June said, pouring tea into Biddy's cup and then stretching across to Fred's. Biddy had come in after six, having thankfully missed all the lads having their evening meal, and all three were now relaxing in the sitting room with the television on and eating tea and biscuits. Michael and Helen were sitting at the kitchen table with the colouring books and crayons that their mother had brought back from Manchester. The two containers of 'bubbles' she had also brought them were safely packed in their schoolbags for the playtime break in the morning.

'Grand, thanks,' Biddy told her, 'although my ankles are a bit on the swollen side from going up and down the stairs. And I treated myself to a lovely meal in John Lewis's restaurant.'

'Oh,' June said, raising her eyebrows in interest, 'what did you have to eat?'

'Steak and mushrooms in a fancy wine sauce,' Biddy told her, 'and chocolate gateau and cream to finish.'

'Ooh!' June said with a smack of her lips, clearly impressed.

Biddy lifted her carrier bags on to the coffee table now, and then dipped into them to produce each item for June's approval.

'Them's absolutely gorgeous outfits,' June said, holding the black beaded jacket up to herself, 'an' you could wear them whether you're expectin' or not – I'd definitely wear the suit and them two blouses what you got.'

'By the time the baby comes, I'll be sick of the sight of them,' Biddy said, 'so you'll be welcome to them.'

'You'll be sorry you said that,' June laughed, 'an' I'll bleedin' hold you to that promise. D'you hear that, Fred?' She dug Biddy in the ribs now, motioning over to her husband who was engrossed in the television.

'Fred!' Biddy said in a loud voice. 'June's talkin' to you, an' you're not even listening.'

'What was that, June?' Fred said, his brows coming down in concentration.

'Oh, nowt of any importance,' June said. 'I were only havin' a bit of a joke with yer wife.'

The front door bell went and June got to her feet. 'I'll get it,' she said, knowing that she was far more nimble than her pregnant employer and her slow husband.

A few moments later she appeared back in the sitting room, pulling a face and motioning out to the hall. 'A visitor for you,' she said, rolling her eyes meaningfully.

'Who is it?' Biddy mouthed, getting up to her feet.

'A young lad,' June whispered, 'and he's in a bit of a state.'

Biddy went out to the hall to find a very anxious-looking Philip standing there, still wearing the shirt and tie and corduroy jacket that he wore for work. He was hovering close to the open door, as though ready to take flight if his welcome was none too warm.

'I thought you'd like to know', he said, without any preamble, and sounding strangely formal, like an older man, 'that Angela isn't at all well.'

Biddy folded her arms high up over her bump. 'What's wrong?' she said in a low whisper.

'The doctor was out at the lodging-house this afternoon,' Philip went on, his voice slightly more confident, now that he hadn't been ejected, 'and he said she has a severe case of glandular fever . . . she's really quite ill.'

'*Glandular fever?*' Biddy repeated in an incredulous tone. 'Are you sure? That's fairly serious.'

'Definitely,' he confirmed. 'The landlady told me that the doctor left her penicillin and some other tablets – but he says it doesn't always help glandular fever – and if the medicine don't have any big effect, that she might have to go into hospital.'

'Hospital?' Biddy echoed, aghast. 'Is it that bad?'

Philip nodded gravely. 'She looks terrible.'

'And how is she . . . you know, in herself?' Biddy asked.

'Not great,' Philip stated. 'She's not able to talk or anything. And she's also very upset . . .' He looked down at his well-polished shoes now, awkward and embarrassed. 'I hope you don't mind me coming round, but I thought that somebody needed to know because she's been lying in – in *that place* all day on her own.'

A tight feeling came into Biddy's chest. 'Is there nobody to look after her?' she asked. 'Is there nobody in the lodgings during the day?'

'Nobody suitable,' Philip said, digging his hands deep into his jacket pockets and hunching his shoulders. 'In fact, I think that's one of the reasons Angela was so upset.'

'How do you mean?'

'There was a man in the house today,' he explained, 'to answer the door for the doctor.' A redness rushed over the boy's face. 'He came up into her bedroom . . . and I think the way he was behaving made her feel very uncomfortable.'

Biddy sucked in her breath. 'What', she said in a strangled voice, 'did he do to her?'

'Angela wasn't able to tell me much – because of her throat – but she was crying and she managed to say that a man had been in, and he'd been trying to pull the bedclothes back and trying to touch her.'

Biddy's hands flew to cover her mouth. 'Jesus, Mary and Joseph!' she uttered.

'I don't think he did anything *really* bad,' Philip said quickly. 'I think the doctor came in just at the right time – and then the landlady got home from work early. She said she had been worrying about Angela all day . . . that she had been fairly ill this morning.'

Biddy nodded her head, the situation slowly sinking in. 'And what did the landlady say when Angela told her about the man tryin' to interfere with her?'

'That's the difficult part,' Philip said. 'Apparently he's the landlady's brother-in-law. Her late husband's brother . . .'

'Does he live in the house?'

'No,' Philip said, 'but he comes around every night.'

'Right!' Biddy said, gripping the sleeve of Philip's corduroy jacket. 'We'll just go inside and explain all this to Fred. I'll get the address off of you, and then we'll get something done about all this business.'

In less than an hour, Angela was safely ensconced back in her old bedroom. Leaving June to keep an eye on the children, Biddy and Fred had taken a taxi down to the house in Hillgate, and told it to wait while they brought her and her few belongings back downstairs and into the taxi.

Fred stood waiting outside with the taxi while Biddy and Mona Kelly helped Angela to put a coat on over her pyjamas and get her slippers on, and then they carefully got her downstairs and out of the house.

Biddy waited until Angela was safely settled in the back seat of the taxi, and then she got in beside her to ascertain exactly what had gone on that afternoon. Biddy then told Fred she needed to speak to Mona and would be back out in a few minutes.

'Can I have a private word with you?' Biddy asked Mona in an urgent voice, her eyes darting towards the two girls gathered at the front door watching the activity centred around the taxi.

'Come into the kitchen,' Mona said, her brow furrowing. She led Biddy down the narrow, dark hallway.

Biddy followed behind, wrinkling her nose in distaste at the dank, musty smell.

'Sit down.' Mona indicated a chair with a cracked, peeling cover.

'I haven't time to sit down, I have a very sick girl outside in a taxi – so I'll come straight to the point,' Biddy said, when they closed the door behind them. 'There was a man left in this house with Angela this afternoon – isn't that right?'

'It is,' Mona confirmed. 'My brother-in-law. Alf was good enough to sit in with her until the doctor came.' She paused, her eyes suddenly narrowing. 'Why are you asking?'

'Because,' Biddy said, 'from the reports I've heard, he wasn't a suitable person for a young girl to be left with – and if it hadn't been for the doctor arrivin', God knows what might have happened.'

There was a few seconds' silence. 'Are you suggestin' that Alf did something to her?'

'I'm not *suggesting* anything,' Biddy said slowly and clearly. 'I'm *telling* you exactly what happened. It seems that he sat up on the bed beside Angela, and was touchin' her over the bedclothes and then he tried to pull them off of her.'

'Rubbish!' Mona exclaimed. 'She never said a word to me about it.'

'She was afraid to say anything to you, because she said you wouldn't believe her.'

'She's bloody right there!' Mona said, her eyes bulging with rage now. 'I certainly would not believe anything of the sort. Alf would never do a thing like that – she's got it all bloody wrong.' She prodded her finger on the table now, pressing the point home. 'Now look here – that girl wasn't a bit well this morning – she had a high temperature and was practically ravin'. I'd say she was all confused and didn't know whether she was awake or dreamin'!'

'Well,' Biddy said, 'in my opinion, she knows exactly what went on.'

Mona gave Biddy a withering glance. 'And in *my* opinion, it's a bloody terrible thing to say about a poor man that wouldn't harm a fly.'

'Well,' Biddy said in an even tone, 'Angela would have no reason to make this up. She's sitting out in the taxi, shaking like a leaf after what's happened to her.' Biddy moved towards the door. 'Why don't you come out and have a word with her? You might change your attitude when you speak to her about it yourself.'

'I've no bloody intentions of speakin' to that little lying bitch – now or ever again!' Mona spat. 'Here we were, all tryin' to help her. Me runnin' up and down from the mill like a bloody blue-arsed flea to check up on her and phone doctors for her – an' all she can do is cause bloody trouble.' She prodded the table again. 'An' I'll tell you another thing – she wasn't a bit popular with the young ones down in the mill. She caused bloody ructions the other day over a young fella—'

'You needn't worry about the mill,' Biddy told her,

'because she won't be back there. She's not going to be fit to work for a while.'

'She owes money,' Mona stated.

'She paid you a week's rent in advance,' Biddy reminded her sharply. 'That means you're paid up until next week – so she owes you nothing.'

Mona's mouth tightened, and her eyes disappeared into little slits.

'I have a *proper* lodging-house myself,' Biddy said quickly, 'so I know how it works.' She opened the door into the hallway now, having said all she'd come to say.

'I'll tell you something,' Mona said in a loud voice, coming out behind her, 'I'm well bloody rid of that one . . .' The two girls in the hall turned to hear what was going on. 'Stealing other girls' boyfriends and then makin' accusations against innocent men – God knows what she'd be up to next if she was to stay a minute longer!'

After she'd got Angela settled back into her old room and had unpacked her few belongings, Biddy bathed the children and put them to bed. On her way downstairs, she met one of the older lodgers.

'How's the young girl?' he said, nodding up to the bedroom. 'I hear she's not been well.'

Biddy nodded. 'Glandular fever,' she said, 'so it'll take a few weeks for her to come around from it.' She ran her hand through her hair, weary now with the events of the evening.

'I'm glad to see her back here safe and sound,' the man said, his face serious, 'because I've young ones back in Ireland her age, and I wouldn't like to see them lying sick in a strange country.'

'That's exactly why I brought her back here,' Biddy agreed, not wanting to go into too much detail about what had happened. 'She'll stay here now until she's better.'

'She's a grand young one,' the lodger said. 'And she's got a great way with her with the kids.' He paused, then lowered his voice so as not to be heard. 'It's just a pity she got in with that scut Eric when she first came.' He shook his head. 'I didn't want to interfere, but I heard him being abusive to her on a number of occasions. There was one occasion in particular, when you were over in Ireland.'

'What happened?' Biddy asked curiously.

'Oh, he was here very early in the morning, annoying her,' the lodger said. 'There was a bit of a carry-on going on upstairs.'

'In her room?' Biddy asked sharply.

'No, no – I was coming out to the bathroom, and I heard him at her bedroom door, rapping on it and whispering in to her – but she wasn't silly enough to open the door to him.'

Biddy felt a mixture of relief and guilt. Angela had obviously been telling her the truth after all. She went downstairs and sat watching television with Fred for a couple of hours. She scarcely spoke for most of the time, just stared at the black and white screen, going over and over the situation in her mind. A little bit of her still felt angry with Angela for the silly mess she had got herself into with Eric, but the other half of her now felt very responsible. She felt responsible for Eric being in the house in the first place, and she felt responsible for being too hard on Angela when everything erupted.

Biddy looked over at her husband now, as he sat glued to the Dick Emery comedy show on television. These days he had to give everything his whole concentration, or he lost the thread of what was going on. But all in all, he was much better than anyone thought he was going to be. He was much better than Biddy had hoped and prayed for.

And he'd been lucky again a second time around. Eric's knife could just as easily have hit the wrong place.

Fred suddenly turned to look at her now. 'Are you happy now that you've brought Angela back to stay here?'

Biddy thought for a moment. 'Yes,' she said, smiling back at him. 'Yes . . . I think we've done the right thing. And yes – I feel much happier.'

Chapter Fifty-Seven

TULLAMORE

Shay stood back to admire the clamps of turf which he had been working on all morning. He'd reared and brought home a good amount over the summer, but with the weathermen warning that it was going to be a severe winter, he'd thought better of it, and got a lad from Durrow to drop him out a couple more loads. He'd had a busy morning throwing the turf into the shed, and had spent the last hour or so putting the finishing touches to it.

He sighed with contentment now as he surveyed his morning's work. There was nothing like a bit of outdoor grafting to take a man's mind off his problems – and Shay was a man with plenty of problems at the moment. In fact, they were coming thick and fast at him, and from all angles.

'Well?' Tessie said, coming out of the back door of the house. 'What do you think?'

'I think', Shay said, taking off his cap and wiping it across his face, 'that we'll have plenty of turf now to see us through the winter. That, and a few trailers of wood, and we'll be on the pig's back. We'll be well ahead of ourselves.'

Tessie tutted loudly. 'I wonder, do you ever listen to a single word I say? All you can think about is the feckin' turf! I was talkin' about your daughter, Angela, and us going over to Stockport.' Her hands were on her hips now, a sure sign that she meant serious business. 'Wasn't that what you were supposed to be thinkin' about instead of turf?'

'You wouldn't be callin' the turf like that, when the cold nights come in,' Shay told her. 'You'd soon be givin' out if we hadn't enough turf to heat the house and cook the dinners. You wouldn't be complaining about the turf then.'

'Will ye forget the bloody turf,' Tessie said, 'and give me an answer about Angela?'

'I think', Shay said, coming over to stand by his wife, 'that we should ring Stockport and speak to her or Biddy Hart, and find out how the land lies. She could be up and running about now, and us rushing over and payin' all that money for nothing.'

'Did you think of askin' Tara about going over?' Tessie said in a low voice. 'We could all have gone over in the car.'

Shay shook his head vigorously, in the manner of a man who had made up his mind.

'Sure, you'd as well be talkin' to that turf as you would be talkin' to Tara at the minute. She wouldn't be up to driving anywhere.' They moved into the small back kitchen now. 'She's like a ghost going about Ballygrace House . . . Tara's not in the frame of mind for travelling anywhere.'

'I thought it might kill two birds with one stone,' Tessie said. 'I thought that the trip over would take Tara out of herself, and it would give us a chance to see how Angela is.' She put her hand on Shay's arm now. 'I'm fierce worried about her . . . I can't stop thinkin' about her being over there all on her own and sick.'

'She's not on her own,' Shay said. 'Sure, she's in the lap of luxury back with Biddy and Fred.' He moved now to take his wife into his arms in a consoling embrace.

'Listen,' he said in a gentle tone, 'if you can organise

394

someone to sit with Molly this evenin', we'll cycle out to Ballygrace House and make a phone call over to Stockport and speak to Angela for ourselves.'

'I don't like to be bothering Tara,' Tessie said.

'Look,' Shay said, 'Tara Flynn is me daughter – the same flesh and blood that Angela is. Now, I'm always the first one to say that she can be uppity an' full of her own importance when it suits her – but when the chips are down, there's nobody that would come to your help any quicker than Tara.'

'True, true,' Tessie said, smiling in agreement now.

'What we'll do,' Shay went on, 'is we'll speak to Angela or Biddy, or whoever is there, and if we're not satisfied with the way she sounds, then we'll make arrangements to go straight over there as soon as we can.'

Tessie buried her face in her husband's neck. 'I'm fierce worried about her,' she whispered. 'I wish we'd never let her go.'

'Well, you can quit the worryin',' Shay said, drawing her closer into his chest, 'because Shay Flynn will sort it all out.'

Molly was in one of her agitated moods. Tessie had brought her down a nice dinner of bacon and cabbage and lovely floury potatoes to have around four o'clock, which would keep her going until her supper before bed. Tessie had heated the dinner over a pan of boiling water, and made sure it was nice and hot for the old lady. But, after all her efforts, she then had to sit and watch Shay's aunt as she messed the food around the plate, having hardly eaten more than a few forkfuls.

'What did Mrs Slamman give you to eat earlier on?' Tessie checked. 'She didn't give you potatoes and meat already, did she?' Tessie was thinking now that they'd need to check on what the old woman was eating throughout the day, because she wasn't able to give any kind of report herself.

Tara and Joe had arranged for a neighbour to take turns in caring for Molly, in order to give Tessie and Shay a break from it, but it was early days, and they still hadn't got the situation completely organised. It was quite possible that Mrs Slamman – who had offered to give Molly 'a bit to ate' at lunchtimes – was giving her a hot cooked dinner instead of the sandwich that Tessie had suggested.

'Did Mrs Slamman give you potatoes?' Tessie repeated, pointing to the cold potatoes on the plate.

Molly looked blankly at her nephew's wife.

'Did you see Cecil Smith?' Molly suddenly asked. 'Did you see Cecil Smith down the town?'

'I don't know how many times I've told you,' Tessie sighed, 'I wouldn't know Cecil Smith if he walked in through the door this very minute. I don't know anybody called Cecil Smith.'

'Did they say whether he's come back from England yet?' Molly demanded, getting up from the table and going over to the window. 'It's getting dark now . . . he'll be coming home for Christmas.' She turned back to Tessie. 'Would you say Cecil will be home for Christmas this year?'

'I don't know, my darlin',' Tessie said, more to herself than out loud. 'I don't know whether Cecil will be home for Christmas or not.' Then she looked down at her own plate and thought, *I haven't the foggiest notion about Cecil Smith – all I know is that I wish our Angela was coming home for Christmas.*

Mrs Slamman appeared back at the house at five o'clock as had been arranged earlier, to let Tessie go off to Ballygrace with Shay. 'I'll be back in time to put her to bed,' Tessie promised, as she tied her headscarf under her chin.

Mrs Slamman accompanied Tessie to the door. 'Do

you think she's fit this evening to walk over to the church with me for devotions? I thought the walk out might do her good.'

Tessie bit her lip, thinking. 'It might do her no harm at all since it's a dry evening,' she said, 'but I'd sit at the back of the church just in case she finds it hard to settle.'

Ballygrace House stood in repose amongst the tall fir trees and the bare deciduous trees that had now relinquished the last of their golden and rust-coloured leaves. 'I'll have to be out here with the oul' rake at the weekend,' Shay said, as he and Tessie cycled up the leaf-strewn driveway in the fading daylight. 'Otherwise the frost will get there first, and the drive won't be fit for the car or the bike.'

'You do a grand job, keepin' this place tidy,' Tessie complimented her husband. 'When you consider the size of it, and you only having the odd evenings and weekends to spare on it.'

'It doesn't look too bad at all,' Shay said, with more than a hint of pride, 'and I'd rather do it myself than have Tara bringin' in some other lad that would only be tryin' to take over the place. There was enough of that with the oul' Scully woman, when she was the house-keeper. Sure, that oul' one thought she ruled the place.'

'I'd say it must still be stickin' in her craw,' Tessie said quietly, 'that Tara married Gabriel, and ended up the mistress of Ballygrace House.'

'Good,' Shay said bitterly. 'I never liked the oul' witch.'

They dismounted from the bikes and left them leaning against the wall of the house and, at Tessie's insistence, went to the main entrance of the house. The outside light was on, and so was the light in the hall upstairs, but the back and the downstairs part of the house was in complete darkness.

'There's only Tara in, and she's not expectin' us,'

Tessie explained. 'It's different when it's in the middle of the day and you know there will be somebody in the kitchen.' She stretched on her tiptoes now and craned her neck to see if there was any sign of a light shining into the sitting room. 'It's only manners to come to the front entrance at this time of the day.'

Shay huffed and puffed, but did as his wife asked. There was something about waiting on the doorstep of Ballygrace House that brought back all the old feelings of inadequacy, of stepping out of his class, that remained ingrained from his early days. From the days long before his daughter, Tara Flynn, became the mistress of Ballygrace House.

The kitchen was far more to Shay's liking, with the low, cottage-like back door, and the homely heat of the range and the smell of whatever delicacy was cooking or baking.

They stood anxiously now, ringing the bell several times before any sign of life came from inside the house. Eventually, the hall light came on and a few moments later Tara opened the door, a towel around her hair, and wearing a dressing-gown buttoned up to the neck.

'Come in,' she said, her brow raised in surprise. 'I hope you weren't waiting long . . .'

'Divil the bit,' Shay said, stepping into the dark-panelled hallway with the sombre pictures and the heavy chandelier, that always made him feel he was in a place he had no business to be in.

'We wanted your advice,' Tessie started straight away. 'It's about our Angela . . . I had a letter from Biddy Hart this morning, and it seems she's not been at all well. She has the glandular fever.'

'*Glandular fever?*' Tara gasped, thinking guiltily back to the series of phone calls from Biddy that she had yet to return. 'And how is she now?'

Tessie's eyes filled up with tears. 'That's the thing,' she said, fishing the folded letter out from her coat pocket. 'The letter was written last week ... so we don't know whether she has improved or disimproved in between times.'

'We'll phone over to Stockport straight away,' Tara said, moving down the hall now towards the kitchen. 'We'll phone from in here – it will be warmer than standing in the hall.'

Tessie gripped her husband's hand tightly as they followed behind.

'Didn't I tell you that we'd sort everything out?' Shay whispered, giving her hand an encouraging squeeze.

Fred answered the phone, as Biddy was out at the doctor's for a check-up, and he immediately allayed all fears by telling Tara that Angela was a lot better than she had been the previous week.

After giving Fred a message that she would be in touch with Biddy soon, Tara passed the phone over to her father, knowing that he would enjoy a few words with his old pal from Stockport.

'I'll put the kettle on,' Tara whispered to Tessie, 'and I'll leave you to have a good long chat with Angela while I go and get dressed.'

A few minutes later, as she mounted the stairs to her bedroom, Tara had an overwhelming feeling of guilt about her sick sister and her pregnant friend – who she had left to deal with the problem. She wished with all her heart that she had the physical energy and the mental capability to deal with these situations in the proper manner, but even normal things still felt like a mountain to be climbed.

As she took the towel from her head and let her damp curly red hair fall down around her shoulders, she wished she could just go straight to bed now as she had planned to do before her anxious visitors had arrived.

She looked over to the high brass bed that she and Gabriel had lain in all of their married life. Since he had left her, their bed was the only place in which she felt even slightly comforted. As though lying in it brought a small, tiny bit of Gabriel back to her.

Tara's guilt at not having kept up the correct level of correspondence with her sister and friend was slightly assuaged when she saw relieved looks on her father's and Tessie's faces when they came off the phone.

'Ah, she's the finest,' Shay stated, rather over-exaggerating the situation.

'She's over the worst,' Tessie said, her eyes moist again, but this time the tears were of sheer relief. 'She said that Biddy had been like a second mother to her – she's made her stay in her bed and has had all her meals brought up to her and everythin'. Seemingly, there's an awful nice woman in the boarding-house called June, who's been helping out while Angela's been sick, and she's been in and out, checkin' up on her, too.'

They all sat down at the kitchen table, where Tara had set out three cups and saucers for the tea that was now brewing on the range.

'She's grand now,' Shay confirmed, taking off his jacket and putting it on the back of the chair. 'Sure, there's nothing for us to be worryin' our heads about at all.'

'I wouldn't be quite so confident,' Tessie countered a little sharply. 'She says the glands under her arms and at . . .' She halted for a moment, trying to find a delicate description for the groin area. 'The glands at the top of her legs are still swollen and tender. And her throat is still a bit raw.'

'Glandular fever is a very unpleasant thing,' Tara said quietly. 'I remember one of the girls in the office in Tullamore having it. It can lay you low for quite a bit.'

Tara poured the tea, and then got out her smallest cake-stand and filled the two circles with a fancy fruit-cake and chocolate biscuits which she knew were her father's favourites. She refused all offers of help from her stepmother, feeling that entertaining them in this small way was the least she could do.

'You're surely early cutting into your Christmas cake!' Tessie exclaimed, as she took a slice of the white-iced cake. She held it up, admiring the dark texture, the thick layer of marzipan, and the generous measure of fruits and nuts. 'It looks lovely and rich.' She took a tentative bite out of it. 'Oh, it's absolutely beautiful – and you can tell it's been well-soaked in brandy. Did Kitty bake it?'

'She did,' Tara said, suddenly realising what she had done. She hadn't even noticed that it was a Christmas cake she had taken from the larder shelf. She suddenly remembered Kitty mentioning something about a cake to her yesterday – something about leaving it for a bit for the fruit to settle.

Tara silently admonished herself.

Her aunt would probably be disappointed when she next called in, and saw that the Christmas cake had been cut into prematurely.

'What's your opinion on the situation, Tara?' Shay now asked. 'Would you say there's any need for us to go rushing over to Stockport to check on Angela?'

There was a short pause.

'How did she sound?' Tara checked. 'Was her voice as cheery as usual?'

Shay and Tessie looked at each other. 'Grand,' said Tessie, nodding. 'Apart from telling us about her glands and her throat, she seemed in good enough form.'

Tara shrugged, not wanting to sway them either way. 'It depends on how you both feel . . .'

'To tell you the truth, I'd like her back home,' Tessie stated. 'We're all missing her, and from what she's told me, she's missing us.' She looked at Shay, as though hoping for some kind of back-up. 'I think the few months away has done her good . . . but maybe it's about time she came home.'

Tara bit her lip. 'I don't know if it's a good time to have her travelling – I'm not too sure if it mightn't set her back a bit, especially now she seems to be improving.'

'True enough,' Tessie agreed. 'Maybe we should see what the next few weeks bring.'

Tara took a deep breath. 'If you want to go over,' she said, trying to sound light and enthusiastic and not quite managing it, 'I could take the car, and we could all go together . . .' In her heart she knew she wasn't up to going back to Stockport just yet – that was why she'd decided to turn down Biddy's invitation to the sporting awards dinner. She just wasn't ready to meet Biddy and Kate and Mr Pickford and everybody who had known Gabriel. She wasn't ready for their kind, well-intentioned words. But she had a responsibility to Angela, having been the one who had brought her over to Stockport in the first place.

Shay looked at his wife. 'I wouldn't want to be the one makin' the decision,' he said quietly, 'but if you feel set on goin' over to visit her, then that's what we'll do.' If the truth be told, Shay felt most uncomfortable at the thought of Tessie staying in Ruby's old home, but it would have to be done.

'Maybe we should hold fire,' Tessie eventually said. 'She sounded grand enough on the phone.' She looked at Tara now. 'And there's Molly to consider . . . she's not great at the minute – it's Cecil Smith this, and Cecil Smith that, the whole time.'

'Don't be worrying about Auntie Molly if you want to go over to see Angela,' Tara said now. 'We can arrange for her to be taken care of.' She looked at her father. 'Joe and I have told you both before that we'll arrange for any help she needs around the house. You only have to say when you need a break and there will be somebody organised to come in full-time.'

'We're grand,' Tessie said decisively. She reached for another piece of Kitty's Christmas cake. 'There's no need for us to go turning everything upside down, and putting Biddy to a whole lot of trouble getting beds ready for us and everything, if Angela is getting back to her old self. Between Christmas coming up and one thing and another, we might be better to leave things as they are for the time being.'

Shay reached out for the teapot to pour himself a second cup of tea, delighted that the situation had been resolved.

'Whatever you say, Tessie. Whatever you say.'

Chapter Fifty-Eight

The bicycle journey from Ballygrace back to Tullamore was not quite as pleasant as the outward journey, due to a sudden coolness in the air and a fairly stiff breeze which whipped in their faces as they cycled along.

The house was empty when they arrived home, the two girls out at some church meeting or other, and Tessie decided to delay going down to Molly's by half an hour, so as to have some time on her own with her husband, listening to a favourite radio show. They sat together on the old wooden sofa, drinking tea and enjoying the peace and quiet.

'Do you feel happier now that we've spoken to Angela?' Shay said, running a hand over his wife's hair.

'I do,' she confessed, giving a little contented sigh. 'I feel a hundred times better.' She turned towards her husband now, kissed his cheek lightly, and then laid her head on his shoulder. 'We haven't had much time on our own lately,' she said in a regretful tone, 'what with me running up and down to Molly's, and you working during the day and going back and forth to Ballygrace House when you have any time to spare in the evenings.'

'It won't go on for ever,' Shay said. 'Something will have to be done about Molly sooner or later. We can't keep this runnin' and racin' up for ever.' He paused. 'I know that Tara pays us well to look after her, but there comes a time when you just want to be in your own corner and not in other people's all the time.' He pulled his wife closer now. 'And I don't think money compensates for an empty space in the bed. I might be getting on a bit, but I still like to have an oul' cuddle when we're in the mood.'

'And how do you think I feel, havin' to sleep in the spare room in Molly's, when I could be sleeping beside you?' Tessie asked. 'To be honest, I was even thinking that a few days over in Stockport on our own might have done us good.' Then she hastily added, 'Providing Angela was well, of course. I always had a notion to go over and see the boarding-house where you lived and to see Tara's nice house.'

'Sure, what's there to see over there?' Shay said. 'Aren't we just as well at home?'

'Well,' Tessie said, cuddling into him, 'it would have been a change – a break away from all the running around.'

'We'll get Christmas over,' Shay suggested, 'and then we'll see what can be done.'

Just after nine o'clock, Tessie packed her few belongings in her bag and Shay walked her down through the town to Molly's house. Tessie had her apologies ready for being later than usual, but Mrs Slamman waved them away and insisted on making all three of them a cup of hot cocoa.

'I have a bit of news to pass on to you,' the cheery neighbour said, when she and Tessie came to sit down with their drinks. They had left the old lady's half-cup of cocoa to cool down before letting her have it, in case she scalded herself. 'You know I said I would take Molly down to devotions with me?'

'You did,' Tessie said, glancing over to Molly, who was putting one of Joe's old jigsaw puzzles together, on a small table in front of the fire. 'And was she all right? She didn't do anything, did she?'

'Oh, she was grand,' Mrs Slamman reassured her in a

low voice. 'She sat as straight as you like and knelt and stood at all the right bits, and she was well able to join in with the prayers.'

'Thank God.' Tessie took a sip of the hot, sweet drink. 'So, what was the news?' she asked curiously.

'Well,' Mrs Slamman said, 'a woman came over to me in the church as soon as the devotions were finished, and she wanted to know if it was Miss Molly Flynn that I had beside me – the same Molly Flynn that had a sister Maggie and a great-nephew that was a priest. Of course I said it *was* Molly Flynn and all to that, and I explained that I was a neighbour who was looking after her for the evening, like.' She held her cup between both hands as though warming them. 'She had a few words with Molly, like, mentioned her mother's name and where she knew her from, and that kind of thing.'

'And did Molly understand anything of what she said?'

'Not a bit of it,' Mrs Slamman said, 'but she perked up a small bit when the name Peggy Coulter was mentioned. That was the woman's mother's name, you see.' The neighbour smiled now. 'She kept sayin' "Peggy Coulter" over and over again, real thoughtful, like.'

'And what did the woman want?' Tessie prompted, even more curious now.

'She said that her mother and Molly used to be great friends at one time. It seems they went to school together and that Molly had been godmother to the oldest boy in the family.'

'And who are they, d'you know?' Tessie asked.

'I didn't really catch the woman's own name,' Mrs Slamman explained. 'I think it might have been somethin' along the lines of May, or something like that – but the mother's name was definitely Peggy Coulter. I made sure I took a note of that in me head, so's I could pass it on to you.'

'Peggy Coulter?' Tessie repeated thoughtfully. 'I can't

say I've ever heard anyone mention the name before. Did she say where they came from?'

'I think it was out around the Kilcormick area,' Mrs Slamman recalled. 'She asked me where Molly was living now, and said she might like to go out and visit Peggy some day. Or she says if it suits, she could bring her mother out to visit Molly here.'

'Indeed,' Tessie said thoughtfully. She glanced over at Molly now, who was unusually quiet at the moment. 'Maybe it would be nice for her to have a visitor. Seeing an old friend just might lift her out of herself.'

Mrs Slamman finished the dregs of her cocoa now and got up to put her coat on. 'I gave the woman the address of the house here, and told her to call around when you were in some time.'

'Well,' Tessie said, seeing the neighbour to the door, 'it might give poor Molly something else to talk about apart from Cecil Smith.'

Chapter Fifty-Nine

As Tara walked down the stairs in Ballygrace House, she suddenly had a great urge to get away from the place. Whether she needed to go for a long time or a short time, she didn't know – and at this point it didn't matter. She just knew she had to get away from the house and the caring people around her.

She couldn't face another day of coming downstairs and trying to keep up a conversation with Ella or Kitty or her father – or whoever else came into the house that day. All these nice people who kept trying to talk about ordinary things to take her mind off the terrible thing that was now her life.

And she certainly couldn't face the thought of going into Ballygrace Village or to the shops in Tullamore. It all entailed having to talk to people who knew about Gabriel dying – and the longer it went on, the harder she found it to open her heart to anyone. To open up about the darkness that lurked just below the surface. She needed to find something different to pass the time – even if it was only travelling.

By the time she had reached the hall downstairs, she had already decided that she would go to Stockport and attend Fred's special occasion after all.

It would kill three birds with one stone: it would give her a chance to check that Angela was truly recovering from her bad bout of glandular fever, perhaps even bring her home, it would give Biddy a lovely surprise, but, most importantly, it would give Tara Fitzgerald a respite from the constant treadmill of her mind.

Tara did up the buttons of her dark brown, velvet-trimmed coat, and then she walked over to the wardrobe. She paused, regarding herself in the mirror. It was looser than she had imagined – a lot looser. It was the same coat with the matching hat which she had bought all those years ago for Joe's ordination. It was still in perfect condition and, being a classic style, still in fashion. Coat and skirt lengths were getting shorter every year, but the mid-length of the coat still looked fine on her tall figure, the chocolate-brown colour giving a fiery glow to her red curly hair. If it had fitted her properly, it would have been perfect. It would have made her look sophisticated and confident. The deep-brimmed hat would have come well down over her eyes – the vivid green eyes now darkened with a haunted look that would have given the truth away.

She shook her head at her reflection, and a few moments later the coat was hanging back up in the wardrobe, and the glorious matching hat was back on the top shelf, languishing amongst her more ordinary hats.

She would have to go with her three-quarter-length, swing-style camel coat and her short sheepskin jacket. It didn't really matter what she wore, as she wasn't planning on going anywhere special apart from the award ceremony. She had already packed an evening dress and matching stole that she'd got for a ball last New Year that would be perfectly suitable for the occasion.

She checked through the items she had carefully placed in the open suitcase, and then left it lying on the bed so that she could put the last few things, which Ella was ironing for her down in the kitchen, in later.

Tara checked her watch now. She wanted to give

herself plenty of time to catch the train up to Dublin, and then she would take a taxi out to the airport for her late evening flight. She had been very lucky to get a single available seat on the plane, and at a time when she could catch a train up. It had been a long time since she'd travelled that way, since she or Gabriel or Mick would normally drive up to the airport. But this time Tara preferred to spend most of the journey on her own, and not have to sit for several hours making small-talk to her uncle, and possibly Kitty, who often accompanied them for the change of scenery.

She needed to make this first, big foray back into her old world on her own.

Chapter Sixty

STOCKPORT

Biddy was up early the following morning, as she now found it increasingly difficult to find a comfortable position in bed with her expanding baby bulge. Besides, her bladder left her little choice. Getting up would also take her mind off all the things she had lain worrying about – the imminent worry being Fred's award 'do' that night. As she bustled about in the kitchen downstairs, she ran over the scenario in her mind again. What if he fell up the stairs of the stage when he went to get his award? What if he couldn't remember the words of the very short speech they'd worked on together? And what if everyone was looking at her, thinking that her maternity outfit was not as nice as the outfits of all the other wrestlers' wives who would be there? There were going to be some of the more famous wrestlers and sportsmen there, ones she'd never seen in real life before, and they were bound to be far posher than herself and Fred. She'd heard that Jackie Pallo, who was often on the Saturday afternoon TV wrestling, would be there, and she knew, without having met her, that he'd definitely have a very glamorous wife.

She also wished she'd had a close friend to come and sit beside her at the special table they had reserved for Fred and his guests right at the front. She'd have Fred's parents and his sisters and their husbands – but it wasn't the same as having a really good friend with her, another woman with whom she could have laughed and gossiped about who was with whom, and what they were all wearing – but there was nobody that fitted the bill for tonight. Elsie would have done perfectly well if things had been different. Dressed up and with a new hairdo and a bit of make-up, and with a few sherries inside her, she would have relaxed, and she and Biddy would have sat chatting and bolstering each other up.

Or even Angela would have been good company – a pretty-looking, cheery young girl. But she'd just gone down the other day with a second bout of glandular fever, and was only really back on her feet this morning. She wasn't as bad as the first time, but her throat was still sore and the glands in her neck and groin were very tender. By no stretch of the imagination was she in any shape to go to a Christmas party. There was June of course, but Biddy wasn't sure how her new home-help would cope with a fancy function, and she was also a bit wary of June's effect on her own drinking. No matter how much Biddy argued, June somehow managed to persuade her that a couple of drinks would actually do her and the baby good. Besides, she needed June at the house to look after the kids, since Angela wasn't up to being left with them.

So it looked as if Biddy would just have to go to the 'event' on her own.

Fred was making his careful way down the stairs when the doorbell went. When he opened the door, he found Tara standing on the doorstep. He frowned as he tried to recall the recent information he should know about her. He could remember the bit about the blond fellow she was married to dying – but any more than that at this very moment escaped him.

Tara smiled and put a finger to her lips, indicating that he shouldn't call out to Biddy that she was here. She had initially thought about turning up at the

Grosvenor, just as the function was about to start, to give Biddy a big surprise, but then decided against it. Anything could go wrong – there might not be enough tickets or a place set at the table.

She decided instead to arrive early in the day and to join Biddy in the Saturday morning endless cups of tea and breakfast atmosphere, as the builders came down in dribs and drabs. Hopefully, the activity in the house and hearing all about their plans for the night out would take her mind away from her own thoughts.

Tara now followed a very bemused-looking Fred into the warm kitchen that smelled of Saturday morning bacon and sausages. Biddy was at the cooker with her back to them, concentrating on turning over fried eggs without bursting the yolks. There were three cheery-looking builders seated at the table, whom Tara recognised from before, the two children and a blonde woman with an overall, who was obviously helping out.

'Hello, Mrs Roberts,' Tara said in a voice she hoped sounded bright and cheery.

'Tara!' Biddy shrieked. She shoved the wooden spatula back in the frying-pan and swung around, her face a picture of delight.

As the morning slid into the afternoon, Angela appeared, pale-faced and leaning against the frame of the kitchen door. 'Tara!' she said, in a husky, surprised voice. 'I didn't know you were coming – when did you arrive?'

'I'm only here a short time,' Tara said, relieved that her half-sister was at least well enough to be out of bed.

'Come in, come in,' Biddy said, pulling out a chair for Angela.

Tara went over to put her arms around the girl. 'You've not been at all well,' she said, looking very concerned.

'I'm getting better,' Angela said, as they sat down at

413

the table beside Biddy. 'If you'd seen me a few weeks back . . .' A picture of the awful, depressing bedroom in Mona Kelly's house came flooding into her mind now, and she felt like bursting out crying.

Biddy nodded sadly. 'You wouldn't have given tuppence for her, if you'd seen her at her worst.' She looked at Tara, and thought she could nearly have said the same for her – except that she wouldn't have dared say it under the circumstances – when she had turned around at the cooker to see her dear old friend looking so pinched and tired as though something had gone missing from her. And then Biddy realised what it was. The light and life had gone out of Tara's lovely green eyes.

Tara reached out her hand to cover Angela's. 'Every day you'll get a little bit better . . . until you're back to your old self.'

Angela smiled. 'I was doin' grand this last week or so, and then it just hit me all over again on Wednesday. But I'm gettin' over it quicker than I did the first time.'

'The doctor said it takes a while to go out of the system,' Biddy said gravely. 'So we just need to make sure she's well looked after.'

Two pink circles appeared on Angela's cheeks. 'Biddy's been great to me,' she said, her eyes suddenly filling up with tears. 'I don't know how I would have managed without her.' She put her elbows on the table, and let her head droop into her hands. Since she had come back to Maple Terrace, Angela had found herself consumed with floods of regret for all that had happened over the last few months. And every time she thought of the mistakes she had made over Eric, she was overcome with feelings of guilt and wretchedness. The smallest kindness from Biddy or Fred made her feel like dissolving into floods of grateful tears, realising how lucky she was to have been given a second chance.

'Are you all right, Angela?' Tara said anxiously,

putting her arm around the girl. 'Are you not feeling well again?'

Angela moved her head back and forth, tears spilling down between her fingers. 'I feel terrible about all the trouble I've caused . . . do Mammy and Daddy know about it yet? Do they know about what Eric did to Fred?'

Tara looked across to Biddy. '*What's she talking about?*' she mouthed.

Biddy looked down at the tablecloth, her brain desperately trying to think up some plausible explanation that might help her avoid telling Tara about the whole sorry saga. It wasn't just a case of not wanting her to think bad of Angela – she felt that Tara would think very bad of herself, for not handling the situation as well as she should have done. She also felt Tara had enough on her plate trying to rebuild her own life now. 'It's OK, Angela,' she said. 'I wasn't going to say anything about it . . . I didn't think it was something we should worry Tara over.'

Angela sat, shoulders slumped, a picture of dejection. 'I thought you'd told her . . .'

Biddy came around to Angela now. 'We've all made mistakes, there's nobody made more than me in my time . . . we've just got to try and learn from them. Look, you're still not at all well, and you don't need to be worrying your head about what's past.' She put a comforting hand on the young girl's shoulder. 'Why don't you head back upstairs and go to bed? If you don't feel like sleeping, you could always read or do a crossword or something.'

Angela got to her feet again, drying the last of her tears with a hanky. Just thinking about that terrible afternoon when both Fred and Philip could have been stabbed to death made her feel all trembly and weak. And the ridiculous, silly way she had carried on with Eric made her feel even worse. All the business with the fancy nightdress – it made her blood run cold just to think about it.

Everything had gone wrong since that terrible day, and nothing she could do now would change it. And Philip had been keeping his distance since she'd come back to Maple Terrace. He'd called up once or twice, but hadn't been near the place in the last week.

But, as Biddy told her, she shouldn't have been at all surprised about that. Philip's family were decent, hard-working people who had not brought their son up to get involved with the police or court cases. And anyway, she had gently told the girl, it might be no harm for her to give lads a rest for the time being, as she didn't seem to have the knack for picking the right type. 'And don't be worryin' about *that*!' Biddy had ended with. 'Because I picked a few wrong ones myself before I met Fred Roberts.'

'I'll bring you up a hot-water bottle in a few minutes,' Biddy told her gently now. 'Just go upstairs and have another little rest for yourself.' She put her arm around the girl's shoulders. 'You're still not well, and it's making you feel that things are a whole lot worse than they are.'

'I'm going to go into Stockport for a few things,' Tara said, 'and I'll bring you back a couple of magazines. What ones do you like?'

Angela shrugged. 'I don't mind . . . anything, thanks.'

'What's happened?' Tara asked, as soon as Angela was out of earshot.

There was a short but awkward pause. 'It's nothing *that* terrible . . . nothing to go getting yourself all worked up about,' Biddy said quietly. She looked up at the kitchen clock. 'I don't really want to talk about it here . . . in case anybody comes in and hears us.' Then she suddenly thought. 'I've arranged to have June here for the rest of the afternoon to sort the lads' tea, because I have the hairdresser's at four o'clock. I could ask her

416

to keep an eye on the kids and you and me could go to Stockport together. We'd get a chance to talk in peace without being interrupted.'

'Grand,' Tara said quietly, knowing instinctively that there was a lot more to the situation than her friend had originally been prepared to tell her.

They found a secluded corner in a little tea room in Princess Street, and there Biddy poured the whole story out to a shocked Tara.

'Why didn't you tell me?' she gasped. 'It's not fair that you've had to cope with all this on your own – with what all you've gone through already with Fred and you expecting another baby . . .'

'Tara,' Biddy said quietly, looking down at the fancy lacy tablecloth, 'how could I tell you? You've been going through the worst thing in your life, and you weren't even up to taking phone calls. How could I have landed all this trouble with Angela at your door?' Her voice dropped even further. 'And I'm not proud of the way I handled it all meself . . . I was a bit hard on the girl with the way things were at the time.'

Tara lowered her head. 'But it was me who landed Angela at *your* door, Biddy – and it's you who has been left with all the problems.' Tara suddenly felt a great sense of having let Biddy down – of not being there when her oldest and dearest friend needed her. Fred could have been killed or maimed for life, and God knows what that lunatic might have done to Angela if he'd got hold of her. And here was Biddy almost apologising for telling the story now – still trying to carry it all on her own. 'What's going to happen?' Tara whispered, conscious of the white-aproned waitresses bustling around. The other tables were far enough away not to overhear anything, but she knew a waitress would appear beside them to take their order soon.

'A court case,' Biddy confirmed, her face suddenly

looking pinched. 'We're all going to have to go to court over it. And it's not just ourselves I'm worried about, it's poor Elsie. She never did anybody any harm – apart from sticking up for her stupid son – and now half the neighbours won't talk to her, and she's terrified of what will happen when he gets out of prison.'

Tara gave a weary sigh. 'It seems as though Angela is far more gullible and naïve than I would ever have imagined. It seems she wasn't up to coping with life away from home after all.' She shook her head. 'If anything really terrible had happened to her – I'd never be able to forgive myself. And I can't tell you how dreadfully sorry I am that Fred got hurt, and you've had all this to deal with on your own.'

'We're grand,' Biddy reassured her. 'All's well that ends well, as they say. We're all grand now, thank God.'

'But you're *not* all grand yet, Biddy, with the court case hanging over your heads,' Tara said pointedly. 'How could you be? And I know perfectly well that it's all my fault.' She shook her head. 'If I'd been around more, or even been up to chatting on the phone to you, I wouldn't feel so bad . . . but to know that you had to manage this all on your own . . .' she repeated. She bent down to retrieve a hanky from her handbag.

The waitress came over to their table now to take their order of a tea, coffee, and two Danish pastries.

Biddy sat in silence after the waitress left, struggling with whether or not to tell Tara the rest of the story. 'I don't know if I'm right to tell you this,' she suddenly blurted out, 'but there was another little incident that happened.'

Tara looked up at her with wide eyes. 'I don't know if I can bear to hear any more bad news.'

'It's not that terrible, and anyway, you'll probably get to hear about it from Angela.' She gave a rueful smile. 'I don't think she has much cop-on about what to say or what not to say.'

The waitress returned to the table, set the cups and saucers and the tea and coffee pots down, and then went away again for the Danish pastries.

'Go on,' Tara said, pressing a finger between her eyes to ward off the headache she felt coming on.

'Before I say anything more,' Biddy said, lifting the small teapot to pour tea into her cup, 'I want you to know that it's *me* who's the guilty one here. If I hadn't let Angela go out of the house, she wouldn't have been lying sick in a terrible dump like Mona Kelly's.'

Tara stifled another huge sigh of despair. 'Get on with it, Biddy,' she urged. 'You have my nerves in shreds, waiting to hear what's happened now.' She started to pour her own drink out from the heavy silver coffee pot.

'It was about a man,' Biddy said, 'who was supposed to be keeping an eye on her, while she was waiting on the doctor. Anyway, to cut a long story short, he came up the stairs and into the bedroom, and was tryin' to interfere with her when she was too sick to defend herself.'

'Did he hurt her?' Tara asked in a shocked gasp. Then, as though her wrist had suddenly lost all its power, the silver pot came crashing down on top of the cup, sending hot coffee spilling all over the starched lace tablecloth and splashing out on to Tara's light-coloured trousers. She pushed the chair back from the table.

'Oh, shite!' Biddy said, regretting the terrible word as soon as it left her lips. She moved towards her friend with a large pink linen napkin. 'Sorry about the language! Are you all right, Tara? Have you scalded yourself?'

'No ... no,' Tara said, suddenly aware of people looking around at them. 'I'm fine ... the coffee-pot just slipped out of my hand.'

The waitress came rushing towards them with a cloth and more napkins, and in a few minutes the worst of the damage was mopped up. Another waitress came over, asking if they would like to move tables to a newly set one, but both women declined, saying they would prefer to stay where they were. A fresh tablecloth was put on, and a new pot of coffee came with the Danish pastries.

'Are you OK?' Biddy checked, when they were all settled again, tea and coffee safely poured. 'You seem to have got a real shock when I told you about that man . . .'

'I just don't believe that all this could have happened,' Tara said, 'and I knew nothing about it. I can't believe that you and Angela have had all these terrible things happening to you.'

'It's all grand now, Tara,' Biddy reassured her, taking a sip of her tea. 'And I was only telling you in case you heard it from elsewhere . . . I really didn't want to go worrying you.'

'But this thing with Angela and the man,' Tara went on, 'was it serious? Did he hurt her?'

Biddy shrugged. 'Not that I know of . . . I think he just tried to touch her . . . pull the bedclothes off her, that kind of thing. Even though she wasn't well, she fought him off.' She paused. 'I don't think it was much more than that, otherwise she would have said – wouldn't she?'

Tara sat back in her chair, her hand over her eyes now.

'Tara?' Biddy said, her voice very anxious now. 'What's wrong?'

There was a long silence – and, after a morning of awkward silences, it was the longest and most awkward of them all.

'I think', Tara said, 'that we both know that girls

420

don't always tell the whole story. That they keep a lot of things hidden.'

Biddy looked back at her friend. 'You mean *me*, don't you?' she said, her voice rising in surprise.

Tara shook her head. 'Not *just* you, Biddy . . . lots of girls have terrible things happen to them, and they don't say a thing.'

'Are you sayin' that I should tell Angela about . . . about the way I was taken advantage of when I was young?' Biddy's face had suddenly gone pale, and her eyes narrowed defensively. 'Are you sayin' that I should tell her all about the priest and . . . and the baby, and everything? That I should drag all that terrible stuff up again just to make Angela feel better?' Her voice suddenly dropped. 'Don't forget we've had to put up with a lot of trouble that Angela caused us.'

'No . . . no,' Tara said, reaching out to cover her friend's hand. 'I don't mean you should tell her *all* those things, I just feel we should—'

'But, *Tara*,' Biddy said, her tone unusually chilly, 'you're not talking about *we* – you're talking about *me* telling her everything.'

'I wasn't thinking of it like that,' Tara said apologetically. 'I'm really sorry if you felt I was being thought-less . . .'

Biddy shook her head. 'I've been happily married to Fred for a long time now, an' we've two children and another one on the way.' She fiddled with the small plate that held her untouched Danish pastry, turning it round and round. 'Maybe I don't feel like dragging all that bad stuff out again – having to tell another person that I'm not as good as they think I am.'

'Angela wouldn't think that,' Tara told her, 'she thinks the world of you. She's told me how good you've been to her – she thinks you and Fred and the children are fantastic.'

'Well, she might change her mind if she finds out all

the things that I did when I was young,' Biddy said bitterly. She lifted up her Danish pastry now and took a bite of it.

'I'm really sorry,' Tara said again, feeling awful for hurting her friend's feelings. 'I didn't mean to upset you ... you're the last person I'd want to hurt.'

Biddy took a little drink of her tea to wash down the piece of dry pastry. 'I'm sorry if I was a bit snappy with you,' she said, giving an apologetic little smile. 'I forget about all those things for weeks, and then suddenly it all comes back to me – as if it was only yesterday. Sometimes I think it'll never go away ... all about the little boy that was adopted and everything.' She looked down at her bulging stomach. 'When I think how much I love Michael and Helen ... and how much I know I'll love this next one ... I feel so guilty about the little boy I left back in Ireland ...'

'Oh, Biddy,' Tara whispered, 'I feel terrible for bringing all this up now ... I really didn't mean to.'

'I know you didn't,' Biddy sighed. 'How could somebody like *you* know about these terrible things? You're so lucky that you've only had men that were good to you. I know that losing Gabriel was the worst thing in the world that could happen ... but at least you have lovely memories of him.'

'My life's not always been as perfect as you think ...' Tara said in a low, hesitant voice.

'Oh, I know you had a hard time over Frank Kennedy,' Biddy went on, 'and I know what he did was deceitful and terrible – but in his own way he adored you. He never treated you bad ... and look at the lovely piano he bought you and everythin'.'

'Biddy,' Tara said in a very serious voice now, 'I've never told you this before ... I've never told *anyone* before ... but I had a terrible thing happen to me just before we left Ireland.' She looked around the tea room, checking that nobody could hear them.

Biddy had just started to lift her cup to her lips again. She halted with the cup in mid-air, and then brought it back down to the saucer again without drinking it. 'What are you talking about, Tara?' she asked, her brow creased in confusion.

'I was raped,' Tara said in a bare whisper, tears springing into her eyes. 'That's the real reason I left Ballygrace.'

'*Raped?*' Biddy repeated in the same low voice. '*You* were raped?' She sat back in her chair, unable to take in what her friend was saying. How could something so dreadful have happened to Tara Flynn? Biddy took a deep breath and sat forward with her hands clasped together. 'Who did it to you, Tara?'

'William Fitzgerald,' Tara said. 'Gabriel's father was the man who raped me.'

Then, over the next hour and a half and cold cups of tea and coffee, Tara poured out all the hurt and pain of what William Fitzgerald had done to her when she'd been an eighteen-year-old girl. Biddy listened and held her friend's hand – suddenly seeing this beautiful red-haired woman as an ordinary, vulnerable girl for the very first time.

Later, as they walked around the shops in the crisp December sunlight, Tara and Biddy talked about ordinary, easier things, such as the children and the expected new baby. Every now and again, they came back to the harder, darker realities. 'Everything has changed. It's all so different without Gabriel,' Tara said, as they walked towards a large newsagent's shop to get the magazines for Angela.

'Everything seems too difficult to do – and then when I try and make myself do it – it all seems completely and totally pointless.'

'They say time heals all of that,' Biddy said, squeezing

her friend's arm. 'I hope that happens. I hope it gets better for you soon.'

'I'm not sure if I want it to get better, Biddy,' Tara replied, 'because if I feel better, it means that Gabriel didn't matter enough to me.' She slowed down now as they came up towards the shop, then turned to her friend. 'What I told you about Gabriel's father – if I hadn't loved Gabriel so much, I could never, ever have married him after that happened.' Tears welled up in her eyes once again. 'I loved him so very, very much – and I know that, whatever happens, I'll never love another man ever again.'

Chapter Sixty-One

Biddy was a bundle of nerves as she helped Fred put on his fancy white dinner shirt with the ruffle up the front. What a day she'd had! She'd stayed longer than she'd meant to in Stockport with Tara, and then had had to rush straight to the hairdresser's for four o'clock to get her hair set for this evening. Then it was a quick rush home and into the bath and now she was standing with a dressing gown wrapped around her, trying to get Fred ready and out of the way so that she could get herself finished off. And in the middle of her whirlwind of getting herself and Fred ready, and listening to what the kids had done, and checking that Angela was all right – she kept going over and over all the things that Tara had told her.

And she still couldn't believe that it was true. That such a terrible thing had happened to her friend.

'Tuck your shirt in now,' she instructed Fred, and after a few moments of watching him painstakingly try to get the fiddly shirt sitting right, she ended up doing it for him. 'Now,' she said, making sure that he had done his trousers up properly, 'turn your collar up, and I'll sort your bow tie.'

A few minutes later, she told him to stand back until she got a good look at him.

'Grand!' she told him. 'You'll be the best-looking fella in the place tonight.'

'Do you think so?' Fred asked, with a beaming smile.

'I do indeed,' Biddy said, coming over to put her arms

around his neck. 'And I'll be very proud when I see you goin' up on to that stage to get your award.'

Fred tightened his grip. 'And I'll be right proud of *you*, as I always am.' He gently moved her to arm's length. 'And when they see you . . . you know, with the baby and everything, they'll know I'm back to normal.' He took a deep breath. 'This time next year I could be back in the ring . . . I could be makin' my comeback.'

Biddy's eyes suddenly grew wide with shock. 'No, Fred!' she gasped. 'Don't be thinking that . . . there's no way you're going back into the wrestling ring. You know what the doctor told you . . . you could have been killed. You could have been left like a bloody cabbage!' She stared at him now with a steely gaze. 'The only way you'll ever set foot in that wrestling ring again is over my dead body!'

Tara came down the stairs of the house in Cale Green very carefully, one hand holding up the hem of her long wine-coloured evening gown, and the other hand steadying herself on the banister.

She came to a halt at the table and mirror inside the front door. She placed her small beaded evening bag on the table, and then checked her hair and her emerald necklace and earrings in the mirror.

The sitting-room door opened. 'Oh, Tara!' Vera Marshall said in a startled tone, when she saw her. She stood in the hallway, a prim, thoughtful finger pressed in the middle of her chin. 'You look stunning . . . simply stunning! I don't think I've ever seen you in such an elegant, stylish dress.' She stared in statue-like awe – almost as a person would stare at a captivating painting.

'That's very kind of you to say so,' Tara said, giving the schoolteacher a grateful smile. She straightened the skirt of the wine-coloured taffeta dress, and adjusted the matching stole, checking that both ends were the same length. 'It's an important occasion for my friend and her husband . . . and I didn't want to miss it.'

She turned to the side now, and the teacher suddenly caught her breath when she saw how very, very thin Tara was, but she stopped herself in time and tactfully made no comment. 'I don't want to be presumptuous . . . to be too personal,' Vera said now, in her most awkward, stiff manner, 'but I know that coming over like this can't be easy for you.' She swallowed hard, unaccustomed to talking in such an intimate way. 'We were all so very sorry about Gabriel . . . he was such a gentleman . . . such a—'

'Thank you,' Tara said in an almost brusque manner. 'You're very, very kind.' She picked up her evening bag from the hall table. 'I think I'll wait in the front room for the taxi . . . just to make sure I hear him.' Then, before Vera could say another word, she went across the hall and quickly closed the door behind her. She stood with her back leaning against the door and her eyes closed. *Gabriel*, she whispered to herself, *Gabriel – how can I do this without you?*

Chapter Sixty-Two

When Fred and Biddy and Tara pulled up outside the Grosvenor Hotel in the taxi, they were amazed at the groups that were already crowded in the large entrance hall: men in black suits and bow ties, holding glasses of brandy and smoking cigars, and women in formal evening wear, milling around and admiring the beautifully dressed Christmas trees and the tasteful, festive decorations.

Tara and Biddy stood to the side of the large decorated fireplace draped with seasonal swags and tails of greenery, while Fred made his way to the bar.

'I knew it was going to be dressy,' Biddy whispered anxiously, 'but I didn't think it was going to be as posh as this.' She looked around the room, searching for Fred's parents and his two sisters and their husbands. 'I don't think I recognise anybody so far, except the girls who are working here . . . all I can say is, thank God you came along with me, Tara. I think I would have died if I had to come to a fancy thing like this on my own.'

'I'm delighted I came, too,' Tara said, squeezing her friend's arm. For even though it was difficult and a strain pretending she was relaxed and enjoying herself, Tara knew that, for Biddy's sake, she had made the right decision in coming. She leaned towards her friend now and whispered, 'I don't think we need to worry, we're as well-dressed as any of them.'

'D'you think so?' Biddy whispered back. Then she

started to laugh. 'Would you listen to me!' she giggled. 'As if *you* need to worry about not being dressed right. You're always dressed to perfection, even when you're not going anywhere special – and that dress and stole you're wearing tonight is just gorgeous.'

'That's very nice of you to say so, Mrs Roberts,' Tara said, affecting an overly formal manner. 'And, as I told you earlier, that beaded suit is particularly lovely on you, and could take you absolutely anywhere. Definitely a pregnant Jackie Kennedy with the lovely hairdo.'

'Oh, I wish I did look like her,' Biddy laughed, patting the back of her hair in an affected, preening manner, but obviously delighted at being compared to such a famous, glamorous woman.

Fred appeared now, very carefully carrying a tray with two glasses of sherry for the women, and a pint of beer for himself. Biddy sipped slowly on the sweet drink, savouring every little taste. It had been weeks since she'd had an alcoholic drink, as she had been keeping firmly to her promise about not drinking too much for the baby's sake. But tonight was a very special occasion, and in the interests of being relaxed and enjoying herself, she had decided that she would allow herself a few festive drinks.

They stood chatting for a while, admiring the other women's outfits, and then a group of men spotted Fred and coaxed him away to have photographs taken with the other sportsmen who were being given awards during the evening.

'Shall we have a wander around?' Tara suggested to Biddy. 'We can keep an eye out for Fred's family as we go along.' Then, to give her friend the impression that she was really excited and enthusiastic about the event, she added, 'I wouldn't mind a peep into the ballroom to see how they've set it up for the function. It's nice to get a proper look before it gets packed out with people.'

They started weaving their way through the crowds now, taking care not to spill their drinks.

'June was telling me that they've got all new carpets and curtains in the ballroom since we were last in it,' Biddy whispered as they went along. Then she suddenly felt Tara tug on her jacket sleeve, pulling her to a halt.

'Oh, no!' Tara hissed, her face draining of colour. 'It's Frank Kennedy – and he looks as though he's coming straight over to us. I think he has a woman with him . . .' She suddenly halted, unable to believe what she was seeing. 'Oh, my God . . . I don't believe it.'

Biddy turned to look, and there, making his way towards them, was a smiling Frank – and on his arm was Tara's friend, Kate Thornley, wearing a long, figure-hugging black velvet dress.

'Tara!' he said. 'I knew it was you – I told Kate I would recognise that hair anywhere.' He stood, not knowing how to greet her, as he knew any physical overtures such as an embrace or a kiss would be instantly rebuffed.

Kate stepped forward now, her face pink and flustered, and rushed over to hug Tara. 'You look absolutely stunning tonight in that gorgeous dress!' But as Kate's arms went around her friend, she was immediately shocked at how thin and fragile she felt. 'I'd no idea you were coming over from Ireland for this . . . I would have been in touch if I'd known.'

Tara stood looking from one to the other, knowing that there was something here that she was missing. Why on earth would Kate be here at a 'do' for Fred? She couldn't remember them ever meeting. As far as she knew, Kate and Biddy hadn't become friendly enough for Kate to be invited to this event.

'How are you?' Frank asked, his eyes searching her face.

'I'm grand, thank you,' Tara said quietly, her gaze lowered and well away from Frank's searching eyes. She

moved her drink from one hand to the other, waiting to
see how the conversation would develop.

'Wasn't she good to fly over at this time of the year,
just for Fred?' Biddy said, smiling around the group,
obviously trying to think of something conversational
to distract from the awkward atmosphere.

Kate leaned forward and tipped Tara's elbow. 'Can I
have a quick word with you?'

The two women moved across the floor to stand by
the fireplace.

'Oh, Tara,' Kate said, 'I feel absolutely dreadful
about the way this has happened . . . I never thought for
a minute you'd be here tonight.' She looked very
anxious now. 'I was planning on telling you after
Christmas if things were still going OK for us . . .'

'Telling me what?' Tara asked, although she had a
horrible feeling that she knew what was coming.

'About me and . . . Frank.' Kate's eyes were clouded
over with anxiety. 'I didn't think for a minute that it
would come to anything,' she babbled on. 'It all started
one evening when I crashed my car into his when I
dropped in to see Biddy . . .'

Tara's face suddenly stiffened. Biddy had never
mentioned anything about Kate being in her house or
anything at all about Frank Kennedy. That was very
strange and unlike Biddy. But then she remembered
Angela's trouble, and how she hadn't been told about
that, either. She wondered with alarm now if there were
other things that people hadn't bothered to tell her.
'You mean you're seeing each other?' she asked in a low
voice. 'Do you mean you're *courting* Frank Kennedy?'

Kate took a deep breath. 'Well . . . I don't know if I'd
describe it like that.' She gave a small, tense smile.
'We've been out a few times to the theatre and that kind
of thing . . . nothing serious at all. But I wasn't sure
how you'd feel about it.'

Tara glanced across the room, and caught Frank

looking directly at her. She immediately felt a stab of annoyance. He tried to hold her gaze with his usual intensity, but Tara ignored him and turned her attention back to Kate. 'It's not for me to feel anything about it, Kate,' she said quietly. 'You're a single girl and Frank's a single man now – and even if either of you weren't, it's not my business.'

'I would have rung and spoken to you about it,' Kate went on quickly, clearly embarrassed, 'but I felt it was the wrong time . . . I wasn't sure if you'd want to talk about things like that . . .'

'Kate,' Tara said gently, 'you were perfectly right . . . I'm afraid I'm not very good at social talk at the moment.' She paused, searching for the right words. 'I really, really don't have any feelings about you seeing Frank Kennedy – why should I? He's nothing to do with me . . . he's only an old boyfriend from a long time ago.'

'Oh, Tara,' Kate said, relief written all over her face, 'I was really worried in case you would think that it put you in an awkward situation – after what happened between you.'

'It doesn't put me in any kind of situation at all.' Tara halted, her eyes flickering over in Frank's direction again. 'It was a long time ago, and circumstances have changed.'

Kate nodded, smiling now. 'I'm sure it will come to nothing,' she said, 'but I'm enjoying his company while it lasts – he's a very charming, generous man.'

'Oh, he is,' Tara agreed, amazed at the starry-eyed look on her friend's face even as they spoke about him. 'He's a very charming man.'

The Grosvenor had acquitted itself admirably in all aspects of the evening. Waiters floated around in white jackets carrying trays of drinks, the tables were decorated with beautiful floral arrangements, gleaming glasses and sparkling candles, and low, flattering lights and pleasant background music set an easy, relaxed atmosphere.

Tara concealed a small sigh of relief when Frank and Kate were seated a few places along to her right, which meant she didn't have to either sit talking to them or gaze across the table at them. She was placed in between Biddy and one of Fred's sisters, and opposite Fred's parents, and she was overwhelmingly grateful that they were cheery, chatty types, who were happy with a nod here and an odd word there as they related various stories about Fred when he was growing up.

Even though she had given Frank Kennedy no thought over the past few months, she knew instinctively by the way he had looked at her when they had met earlier on that his feelings for her had not in any way diminished. But it posed a big question as to what exactly he was doing seeing her close friend, Kate Thornley.

'Tara,' Biddy whispered as the waiters gave out the dinner menus, 'I had no idea they were coming . . . honestly. If I'd thought for a minute they were going to appear together, I would have warned you. I didn't know myself until the other night, when Fred mentioned that he'd seen Frank out with a woman whose description sounded very like Kate.' She paused, clearly upset about it. 'Honest to God – I had no idea they were actually a couple.'

'Don't worry about it,' Tara said in a low voice. 'I'm delighted to see him with someone else – although I have to admit to being shocked that it's Kate. I thought she would have known better.' She gave a little shrug. 'For all I know, he might have changed – he might have learned a lesson after what happened between us.' She gave a small, careless laugh, which Biddy could see was not genuine. 'At least it means that he won't be bothering me again.'

433

'That's true,' Biddy said, laughing along with her now.

But, as both women laughed on the surface, deep down Biddy knew that Tara was suffering quite enough in her life now, without having to endure a trusted friend's betrayal.

The Christmas dinner was as perfect as the traditional dish cooked for over a hundred would allow, and for those not so partial to turkey and ham, there was a choice of steak or poached salmon. Large tureens of steaming potatoes and seasonal vegetables were placed in the centre of the tables, and, beside them, porcelain dishes of the accompanying sauces.

Tara was still struggling with her appetite, and felt ambivalent towards all of the dishes, but she made enough of an effort to allow her unfinished plates to pass without comment.

Her weight loss, however, had been commented on by both Kate and Biddy at different times – although they had both been careful to couch the comments in a complimentary way, saying how well her evening dress looked on her even slimmer figure.

But in the privacy of the ladies' toilets, and well out of Tara's hearing, Kate turned to Biddy. 'I'm really worried about Tara,' she gasped. 'I can't believe how much weight she's lost. I hope she didn't see the shock on my face when I first saw her.'

Biddy nodded her head very slowly. 'She has lost a lot of weight . . .'

'Is she eating?' Kate asked anxiously.

Biddy shrugged. 'She picks at things . . . but I don't actually think she eats very much.' There was a little pause. 'You know what Tara's like . . . she's not the kind of person you can give advice to easily. And it's very difficult to say anything just now – I don't think she's even started to get over what happened to Gabriel.'

'She still looks beautiful,' Kate said in a low voice, 'and that claret-coloured dress and stole looks stunning on her . . . but she looks so very, very thin and fragile. And she's so pale – she looks almost transparent.'

'She's just reached the wrong side of being slim,' Biddy agreed. 'When she was wearing a jumper and trousers she looked a bit thinner than usual, but the tight dress really shows just how much weight she's actually lost.'

Kate turned to the mirror to reapply her lipstick. 'I hope she starts to feel a little better soon, because she really cannot afford to lose another ounce in weight.'

Tara held Biddy's hand tightly as they both watched Fred mount the stairs at the side of the stage when his name was called to come and receive his honorary award from the Wrestling Association. There was a hushed silence in the audience as he took his time, slowly and carefully negotiating each step upwards until he reached the safety of the stage where the MC waited alongside Jackie Pallo, who was going to present the award.

'Now, didn't he manage that perfectly?' Tara whispered encouragingly. 'And doesn't he look lovely, standing up there in his dinner suit and bow tie?'

Biddy nodded, unable to speak because of the large lump in her throat. A mixture of pride and fear raced through her at the same time, as she watched Fred standing calmly to the side of the podium, while the evening's host gave an introduction outlining Fred's great achievements over the years in the wrestling ring. Biddy didn't catch a single word of what was actually said, as she sat scrutinising every little move that her husband made.

She watched as he slid the piece of paper from his

jacket pocket, then held it behind his back so that it wouldn't look too obvious. Then she watched the confident, almost serene look on Fred's face as he listened intently. He looked better now than he ever did. The bit of weight he'd kept off since the accident suited him – giving him a trim but well-built look as opposed to looking too heavy or too thin. And the easygoing, bemused manner he had been left with since coming out of hospital had somehow left him looking more relaxed and younger than previously.

This night, Biddy thought with great emotion, *is the best night of my life*. And as she watched her husband, an overwhelming feeling of love and gratitude enveloped her. She was so very, very lucky! After the terrible life she'd had growing up in Ireland, and after the terrible mistakes she'd made, she was so lucky to have found a good, decent man like Fred Roberts.

She thought back to the day she had agreed to marry him, and although she hadn't known it at the time, she now realised that it had been the best decision she'd ever made in her life. She cringed now, thinking back to how she had kept him waiting in the wings, wondering if she just might find somebody better or more exciting.

And of course there hadn't been anybody better. The lads in the boarding-house had only wanted her for one thing: for a laugh and a bit of slap and tickle – but definitely not as a proper girlfriend or as serious marriage material. And it had taken her a long time to realise just exactly what she had nearly thrown away, in her silly quest for what she thought were the more exciting aspects of life.

She realised with a start now that she hadn't fully appreciated what she had until very recently. As she sat wearing her expensive, elegant suit from John Lewis, she suddenly thought back to that night with Lloyd. The night when she put all those precious things at risk once again. How stupid she had been – and how very, very dangerous.

As Biddy watched her husband step forward to receive the award shield from Jackie Pallo and then shake the famous TV wrestler's hand, she made a silent vow to herself that nothing would ever come between herself and Fred. She would never look at another man again, and she would do her utmost to ensure that Fred never felt the need to look at another woman. Thankfully, he had calmed down in his enthusiasm for the physical since he had come out of hospital. But if there were any needs to be met, Biddy Roberts would make sure that she was the woman to meet them.

She observed him now as he stood, taking a few moments to slowly organise himself. Calm and unflustered. Eventually, when he had his speech safely placed on the lectern, he lifted his head and gave the audience a big, beaming smile. Then, just as he prepared to get his first word out, the Wrestling Association – and then the whole audience – rose to its feet and gave Fred Roberts a rousing, thunderous round of applause.

Throughout the rest of the evening, whenever she felt any doubts about her trip over, Tara remembered that overwhelming applause for Fred, and was truly grateful that she had been there to share that moment with her old friend. Any feelings of anxiety that Biddy had had regarding her outfit or Fred falling up the stage steps had completely evaporated, and were now replaced with euphoria and emotion as Fred came back to the table with his silver award.

When the awards to the other sportsmen and all the speeches and formalities were over, Frank Kennedy and Kate moved up the table to sit beside the Roberts group. Kate came over to sit with the women, and Frank sat beside Fred and his father and his brothers-in-law. A few minutes later, two waiters appeared carrying ice-buckets with bottles of champagne, and trays carrying a dozen fluted glasses.

'We couldn't have an occasion as important as this without champagne,' Frank announced, as the waiters popped the corks on the expensive bottles.

'This', Fred's father said, holding out his glass, 'is a night in a million. This is a night we'll never forget.'

Tara smiled at everyone and joined in with the toast to Fred. One half of her felt very emotional and delighted for Fred and Biddy, but the other half of her couldn't help thinking just how very typical of Frank Kennedy the champagne part of the evening was.

Expensive, bubbly and exciting – just like Frank.

Later, as she watched him topping up Kate's glass, Tara saw the sparkly look in her friend's eyes, and she realised that it was this side of Frank that Kate liked. The showmanship, the confidence and the generosity – and the not knowing what lay around the corner with him.

All the things that Tara herself had liked about him at one time – until she had found out exactly what had lain around the biggest corner of them all.

Later, when Fred and his award were whisked off again for more photographs, and the others, including Frank and Kate, had wandered off to watch, Biddy turned to her friend. 'You know the bit that Fred added to his speech – the bit about him making a comeback in the wrestling ring – d'you think I'm being silly for worrying that it could happen? You don't think that he would ever be able to go back into the ring, do you?'

Tara took her friend's hand in both of hers. 'I think Fred has made a wonderful recovery,' she said quietly, 'but I don't think the promoters would ever take the risk again – not after what happened. I don't think you need worry about him going back into the wrestling ring.'

'Ever?' Biddy checked anxiously.

Tara nodded her head in a slow but definite gesture. '*Ever.*'

She would never say it in so many words to her friend, but she couldn't imagine Fred's co-ordination or speed of thought ever coming back to the way they were. Whatever improvements Fred had made up until now were likely to be the greatest he would ever make.

After the tables were cleared, the lights were dimmed further and a band struck up, and soon couples were taking to the floor. Tara had immediately felt uncomfortable, realising that she would be in the awkward position of not having a partner. Biddy was also anxious, aware that Fred no longer had the co-ordination necessary for dancing – not, as she wryly thought, that he had ever been the slickest of dancers before.

As it turned out, in the security of the dim lighting, Fred made a passable attempt at the basic waltzes, and took both Tara and his wife around the floor several times – constantly repeating that he couldn't believe that the Wrestling Association had honoured him the way they had tonight. And imagine them having someone as famous as Jack Pallo to present the award to him.

Tara found fairly quickly that she needn't have worried about being a wallflower, as Fred's very pleasant family and friends came to ask her to dance any time she was left on her own.

In fact, one or two of the friends went a little further, emboldened by alcohol and the general festive atmosphere of the evening, asking if she was single and intimating that they would be delighted to spend the rest of the evening dancing with her. Tara was pleasant and polite, but very quickly dispelled any notions of that sort that they might harbour.

At one point, just as she was returning from the dance

floor to her table, Frank Kennedy appeared beside her and very quietly and politely asked her to dance. His manner was respectful and suitably distant and, given the occasion that it was, it would have seemed very churlish to refuse him. Tara was aware that Kate had sat down at the table beside Biddy and Fred, and although she was chatting in a lively manner to them, Tara knew that she was carefully watching herself and Frank.

Frank guided Tara on to the dimly lit floor, and in a few moments they were moving around in the same easy manner as they had years before.

'How are you, Tara?' he suddenly asked, lowering his head to look her in the eye.

Tara moved her head to keep her gaze fixed firmly over his shoulder.

'Are you feeling anything like your old self?' Frank asked.

'I'm grand,' she replied in a stiff, cold manner which she hoped would discourage any personal talk.

'It's bound to have been hard on you,' he continued on the same track.

'I don't want to talk about it,' Tara said in a low hiss, 'and I'd be very grateful if you didn't say any more.'

They danced around in silence for a while, then he attempted conversation once again.

'I saw Mr Pickford the other day,' he said. 'We were talking about the Cale Green Hotel, and he told me that you had viewed it a few months back. Would you be interested in buying more property over here?'

'I've no plans to buy more property either here or in Ireland,' she said quietly. 'I have very little interest in anything at the moment.'

'Fair enough,' he said, 'fair enough.'

The dance eventually finished, and Tara thanked him and walked back to her table without having once looked him in the eye.

Although she had drunk much less than she would have normally done, the few glasses of champagne and sherry and the whole success of the evening had suddenly made Biddy brave enough to tackle a little issue that had been niggling away in her mind.

'Can I ask you something, Tara?' she said, her face going red with embarrassment. She checked now that the others at the table were too engrossed in their own conversations to be listening. 'It's going to sound fierce silly . . . but you're the only person I'd trust to give me an honest answer.'

'What is it?' Tara said, feeling slightly alarmed.

'It's about my *name*,' Biddy said, giggling self-consciously.

'What about it?'

'I hate it,' Biddy confessed. 'I've hated it since ever since I came here to England.'

Her face was now serious, upset almost. 'It never bothered me when I was growing up . . . I didn't know any different. But I've always felt self-conscious about it here, and for some reason it's really, really bothering me. I'd far rather be called by my proper name – Bridget.'

'What does Fred think?' Tara asked, amazed that her friend had been feeling like this all these years and she didn't know.

Biddy shrugged. 'He doesn't care what name I want to use – and anyway, some of the staff in the hotel used to call me Bridget.' She paused, thinking. 'Frank Kennedy often calls me Bridget, too. It just sounds more sensible and more respectful.' Her eyes suddenly filled up with tears. 'I was the only one at school with that name, and I don't know one other person over here who's called "*Biddy*". It was that oul' witch Lizzie Lawless that stuck the name on me for badness.' She looked up at her friend now. 'D'you think I'm being stupid? Do you think people would think I'm trying to be uppity if I change my name?'

'No, I don't think you're being one bit stupid,' Tara said in a definite tone. 'If you want to be called Bridget – which is, after all, your correct name – then you're perfectly entitled to ask people to call you that.'

Biddy sat back in her seat as though a great weight had been lifted off her.

'There's only one problem,' Tara suddenly said. 'What will happen to people who are so used to your old name that they forget to call you Bridget?'

'I'll be writin' it down,' Biddy said, laughing. 'I'll be writing their name down in a black book every time they say the wrong name.'

Tara looked at her friend, and then she started to laugh too. It was almost a real laugh, like the kind of laughs they used to have long ago. The kind of laugh she'd had before Gabriel died.

As the night was drawing to a close, it suddenly dawned on Biddy that Tara was planning to go back to Ireland the day after next. With all the worries and anxieties leading up to tonight, she hadn't really taken in the fact that Tara was staying for such a short time. 'Wouldn't you think of staying on for Christmas?' Biddy asked in a pleading tone. 'You wouldn't need to do a single thing; you could come and go from Cale Green down to Maple Terrace as it suited you. You could have all your meals with us . . . it would do you good to have a nice rest.'

'I have to go back,' Tara said quietly. 'I really only planned to come for Fred's special night – I never intended to stay for long.'

'If you wanted to go out anywhere in the evenings I'd organise a babysitter,' Biddy rushed on, trying to think of things that would make staying on more appealing. 'I'd even go into Manchester to the theatre – or one of those musical evenings that you like. There're lots of things like that advertised at the minute.'

'I'm sorry, Bridget,' Tara said, giving a little smile of acknowledgement as she tried out her friend's new name, 'but I really feel I need to be back in Ballygrace House this Christmas. To be honest, it's taken every little bit of energy and courage that I possessed to come here – and it's starting to run out on me.'

'I wish with all my heart that you could stay longer,' Biddy said, 'but I accept your decision.' She touched her friend's arm. 'I can't even begin to imagine what you're feeling . . . but I know it's terrible for you, and you have to do what you think is the best thing for yourself.'

'There's another thing . . .' Tara said, slightly hesitant this time. 'I think it might be a good idea if I take Angela home with me.'

Biddy looked up at her now in surprise. 'Why?'

'For a few reasons,' Tara explained. She took a sip of the glass of sherry that Fred's father had placed in front of her ten minutes ago. 'Firstly, I think she's missing home, and secondly, I know for a fact that Tessie is definitely missing Angela. When she called at Ballygrace House last week, she was very worked up about her.' She put the drink back down on the table. 'I also think that you need a break from her. Apart from all the running around you've been doing since she's been ill, you've been through a lot with that Eric fellow.'

Biddy's face fell at the mention of it.

'It might be the best thing all round if I bring her home with me,' Tara explained. 'She's not in the same position as you and I were when we were young, with nobody to look out for us. Angela has a family who care about her, and I think she'll recover a lot more quickly if she's back home.'

'But what about the court case?' Biddy suddenly remembered. 'It's only a few months away.'

'She can come back for it,' Tara said. 'In fact, I'll

bring her back myself. It's the least I can do after all you've been through.' She paused for a moment, her eyes darkening. 'And if I get the chance when we're on our own, I'll mention to her about that man that interfered with her . . . and I'll try to find out if there was any more to the story.'

Biddy nodded her head. 'Maybe you're right,' she sighed resignedly. 'Maybe it would be best if she went back home to her mother and father.'

'Thanks for being so understanding, Biddy,' Tara whispered. Then she gave a little laugh – a laugh which did not quite reach her eyes. 'I hope you're not going to write my name down in your book, since I've already forgotten to call you Bridget!'

Chapter Sixty-Three

CORK, DECEMBER 1962

Father Joseph Flynn sat at his desk, staring down at the open ledger. It had fallen to him this year to organise the collection of the Christmas dues. There, in front of him, were piles of unopened envelopes containing offerings from families he knew could not afford the money. Offerings that would have been better spent on winter fuel and warming food for their needy families at this cold, harsh time of the year.

This was another of the Church's traditions that he did not agree with, for he knew that most of the money went into Father O'Leary's bank account, simply to gain more interest on the large sum already deposited there. In one way, he knew he shouldn't complain, because Father O'Leary was a fair enough man by the standards of some parish priests, and he made sure that his curate was well-fed and clothed, unlike some less fortunate priests. Joe was lucky that he also had his own little private income from the money Auntie Maggie had left him, which helped with his car, and luxuries such as his books – so he took no more from the parish funds than was absolutely necessary.

But there were certain things that Father O'Leary did without question, simply because it was the way things had always been done in the parish, that truly irked Joe. And the collection of the Christmas dues was one of them. At least, Joe thought, they had moved away from reading out from the altar the names of the donors and the amounts the families did or didn't give.

He shut the ledger and leaned his elbows on the closed book. He had agreed this afternoon that he would remain in the parish over the Christmas period to allow Father O'Leary to spend Christmas Day afternoon and St Stephen's Day with his brother's family down in Kerry. The parish priest would be there for the morning Masses on Christmas Day and would then head off in time to arrive at his brother's for dinner later in the afternoon.

This would leave Father Joe Flynn spending Christmas on his own in the presbytery – which did not dismay him quite as much as it might have done in previous years, for the alternatives were equally as bleak. In fact, the more he thought about it, the more appealing the idea of having the presbytery to himself came to be. The picture of himself sitting and reading a new novel, or perhaps listening to a festive radio programme in front of a roaring fire, presented itself very nicely.

In the normal course of events, the parish priest encouraged the curate to be fairly frugal with the turf or coal, but the festive season allowed for a few extravagances, and there would be no need for him to count the sods over those special few days. The housekeeper had given in her Christmas lists at the local shops, which meant that there would be delicacies in the presbytery larder and fridge that Joe could help himself to without waiting for Father O'Leary to suggest it first. Several of the better-off families had also issued invitations to him to drop into their homes for a drink on Christmas night or St Stephen's Day, or any time over the Christmas period.

All in all, the prospect of staying down in Cork alone was actually more appealing than a visit up to Offaly this year. Tara was in no frame of mind for hosting celebrations this Christmas, and had in fact told him when she'd been down that she would probably spend a few token hours up at Kitty and Mick's and then spend the rest of the time on her own at Ballygrace House.

And then there was Auntie Molly. Though he felt riddled with guilt over it, he just couldn't face the thought of spending a Christmas night lying awake listening to every unfamiliar sound in the house that just might herald a disaster, even though he knew that Tessie and his father and the family would do their best to see that he wasn't burdened with his aunt over the whole holiday, and even though he felt that his aunt deserved some time and attention from the nephew she had lavished so much love and attention on.

But, guilty as he felt, there was nothing he could do about it. With the parish priest gone, the ministering of the flock on Christmas Day had to fall to the curate. Joe got up from the desk now, the decision about Christmas already made.

Chapter Sixty-Four

Angela had received a rapturous welcome from the whole family, and a week after her surprise return home it had not lost any of its warmth. On arrival, after a lengthy chat over numerous cups of tea and several comforting slices of her mother's home-made brown bread, Angela had been made to go straight to bed. She had been well-cosseted and minded by everyone for several days until she felt strong enough to be up and about again.

'I think half of her troubles were caused by being homesick in the end,' Tara explained, when she had dropped the girl off at the house. 'She settled in great and got on grand with everyone, but it's a very different story when you're away from home and feeling ill.'

'She's already talking about going back over to help Biddy when the baby's born,' Tessie said, shaking her head. 'Young ones – you never know whether you're coming or going with them.'

A few days before Christmas, there was a knock on Molly Flynn's door. The old lady was sleeping in the chair, and Tessie, who was in the middle of baking an apple-tart for her, dusted the flour from her hands and bustled out into the hallway to answer it.

'Mrs Flynn?' A small, bright-eyed woman of around forty stood on the doorstep. 'My name's May Coulter ... I met your Auntie Molly in the church the other week.'

'Peggy Coulter's daughter?' Tessie remembered.

'That's right,' the woman said. She motioned to a small black car parked across the street. 'I had to bring my mother in to the doctor's, and I just thought I'd look in as we were passing . . .'

'Well, I'm delighted you did,' Tessie said, opening the door wide. 'I was just putting an apple-tart into the oven, and then we were going to have a cup of tea.' She gestured towards the car. 'Bring your mother in and she and Molly can sit and have a bit of a chat. Won't it be lovely for them?'

'Are you sure now?' the woman checked. 'I wouldn't like to be imposing on you . . . just turning up like this.'

'Not at all,' Tessie reassured her. 'Sure, aren't we only too pleased to have the company? Especially an old friend of Molly's, for she doesn't get too many visitors of her own age these days.'

'Well,' May Coulter whispered, stepping closer so as not to be heard by anyone. 'I suppose there aren't too many of their own age left.'

Although Peggy Coulter was sounder in mind than her old schoolfriend, she was a lot frailer in her body. It took a good five minutes for her daughter to help her across the street, and that was with the aid of two stout walking sticks. Tessie came out to help her up the final steps of her journey and into the house.

'I remember it well,' Peggy Coulter said, walking along the dark little hallway. 'I remember being in this very house when I was a young bit of a girl.'

Molly was sitting up straight in her chair in the little room off the kitchen, having been gently wakened by Tessie. She peered closely at the mother and daughter as they entered, and then she turned to look at Tessie. Her face was blank and devoid of any recognition.

'This is Peggy Coulter,' Tessie announced, guiding the old friend into the chair at the opposite side of the fire.

Peggy looked hard at Molly, her bird-like little head

cocked to the side. 'Don't tell me you don't remember your old schoolmate?' She took her woollen hat off to reveal a head of nice, wavy silver hair, then she took her outdoor coat off.

Tessie motioned to May, Peggy's daughter, to come into the kitchen with her. 'If we leave them on their own for a few minutes, maybe it'll jog her memory a bit.'

A short while later they went back to join the two old ladies, Tessie carrying a tray with the teapot and cups and saucers, and May with a plate of sandwiches and some slices of coconut cake.

As soon as the things were set down on the coffee-table in the middle of the room, Molly reached out for a piece of the coconut cake.

'I hope you're not going to find any fault with it now,' Tessie said in a mildly teasing manner. 'This is one of Molly's favourite recipes,' she told the guests, 'and she's very particular about how it's baked. She showed me how to do it a few years back when she used to do all the baking and cooking herself.'

They watched now as Molly scrutinised the top and bottom and side of the cake, and then proceeded to take a good-sized bite out of it. She sat chewing and waiting patiently while Tessie poured out her half-cup of tea and then added a good drop of milk to cool it down.

'I think she's beginning to remember me all right,' Peggy informed them, with a conspiratorial wink. 'I think it's all coming back to her now ... isn't it, Molly?' She shook her head. 'You wouldn't think it was over sixty years ago that we used to go to the dancing together in Tullamore and Daingean.'

Molly suddenly stopped – the remainder of the cake held in mid-air. 'Dancing?' she said, turning around to look at Peggy Coulter now. 'Did you used to go to the dancing?'

'Of course I did!' Peggy said gleefully. 'Sure, didn't

yourself and myself go together? Weren't we two of the best dancers in Tullamore?'

'And did you see Cecil Smith?' Molly demanded, with a hint of aggression in her tone. 'Did you see Cecil Smith at the dancing?'

Peggy turned to look at Tessie and May with wide, shocked eyes. 'What did she say?'

'Don't pay any attention,' Tessie whispered, 'she's always going on about Cecil Smith, whoever he is.'

'Well, she's not as far back as you all think she is,' Peggy said. 'Not by a long chalk.'

'What d'you mean?' May asked.

'Have you seen Cecil Smith?' Molly repeated, getting up to her feet.

'No, my darling,' Peggy Coulter said, reaching out to take her old friend's hands in hers. 'I haven't seen Cecil Smith this long time.'

Molly looked straight into the old lady's eyes. 'When is he coming back? When is Cecil Smith coming home?'

'Do you know whom she's talking about?' Tessie asked urgently.

'I do indeed,' Peggy said, tears coming into her eyes. She smiled, jogging Molly's hands up and down with her own. 'Cecil Smith is an old boyfriend of Molly's . . . a young lad she was engaged to, many, many years ago.'

'Engaged?' Tessie said in a shocked voice. 'You say Molly was *engaged*?'

'That's correct,' Peggy said, still smiling into her old friend's eyes. 'They were engaged all right, and planning to get married – although they only told a few people at the time.'

'And what happened to him?' Tessie gasped, hardly able to take it all in.

'He was a Protestant lad,' Peggy sighed, 'and when both families found out, they weren't having it. He wanted Molly to go away with him to England, but she never had the nerve for that kind of thing. In the end, he went off heartbroken to England and he never came back.'

Molly suddenly pulled her hands out of Peggy's and went back to finishing off her cake, as though the conversation about Cecil Smith had never taken place.

'She took an awful long time to get over it,' Peggy said in a low whisper, 'and once she did, she never mentioned his name again.' She nodded her head slowly. 'And to my knowledge, she never looked at another lad for the rest of her life.'

Chapter Sixty-Five

BALLYGRACE, CHRISTMAS 1962

Tara went to first Mass in Ballygrace church on Christmas morning with Kitty and Mick. She had purposely suggested the early Mass, knowing there would be fewer people there and that she could go in and out barely noticed. Kitty had agreed without comment, knowing that Tara was finding it increasingly difficult to mix with people and that she visibly winced when anyone mentioned Gabriel's name.

In previous years, if they were not spending Christmas with Gabriel's family in London, Tara would have invited her own family members for a cold buffet on Christmas night or for their dinner on St Stephen's Day.

But any kind of celebration was out of the question this year. And no one would have expected any different, as it was the custom in Ballygrace and the surrounding districts for families in mourning to dispense with the usual Christmas rituals of sending cards or giving gifts – although Tara had given monetary gifts to her own family, to William, and to Biddy and Fred and the children, knowing that things must be a little bit tighter now that Fred was unable to work.

No one had expected Tara to join in wholeheartedly with any kind of frivolous celebrations – but they had hoped that she might be making some move to pick up the strands of her old life again.

The whole family had been delighted when she'd

made her recent trip over to Stockport – but so far the signs showed that since then she had gone even further into herself. Even a trip over to London to spend Christmas with Elisha and young William would have been better than staying cooped up in Ballygrace House each and every day.

But that was what Tara chose to do. To all who cared about her, it looked as though she had gone backwards instead of forwards.

The Flynn family in Tullamore were set to enjoy one of the best Christmases they'd ever had. The whole crowd, including Auntie Molly, were together for a splendid Christmas dinner of goose and ham and all the accompaniments, and presents this year were more generous than ever. For having the wherewithal to afford this Christmas, Tessie and Shay gave a silent thanks to Tara. She had given them both envelopes with large amounts of money which she explained was a bonus for all their work looking after Molly and helping around Ballygrace House.

'But it's far too much!' Tessie had exclaimed when herself and Shay had opened the envelopes in the privacy of their own kitchen. She rifled through the ten-pound notes in her envelope and then watched as her husband did the same. 'We can't take all this . . .'

'Indeed and we can,' Shay said in the manner of one who had never looked a gift horse in the mouth. 'And who else has she to spend her money on?'

Tessie shook her head. 'That's not the point – it's still far too much . . .'

'Look,' Shay said, holding out the envelope, 'Tara has never been short of a bob or two – and now that Gabriel's gone – God rest his soul – she has everything that he owned on top of it. Houses, auctioneer's businesses and all the rest. In fact,' he contemplated for a moment, 'it could be said that my daughter, Tara Flynn, is a woman of very substantial means.'

Chapter Sixty-Six

Kitty tapped on Tara's bedroom door. 'It's only me,' she called in a soft voice. 'I have a cup of tea and some toast for you . . . can I come in?'

There was a few moments' pause, then the thin voice told her the door was open.

'It's a lovely morning,' Kitty said, striding over to the bedside cabinet and putting the tea and toast down on it. 'Your father let me in, he's working outside on one of the fences.'

Tara pulled herself into a sitting position. 'Thanks for the tea,' she said, reaching for the cup and saucer.

Kitty sat down on the side of the bed. 'I have a cousin down in County Clare who has a beautiful house,' she suddenly said without any preamble, 'and she's gone off to America for six months. She says if I want to have a holiday in the house at any time, she's left the key with a neighbour.'

There was a silence, and then Tara lifted her eyes to look at her aunt, wondering what the point of the conversation was.

'I think it would do you good to get away for a few days, Tara,' Kitty told her. 'I think this particular place would do you the world of good. I've seen photographs of it, and it's right by the sea.'

'You're very good for thinking of me,' Tara said, 'but I don't really feel like a holiday just now . . . I wouldn't have the energy for travelling, and I don't feel like meeting people.'

Kitty leaned forward. 'I know you don't,' she said in a kind but firm voice, 'but you've got to *make* yourself feel like it.'

Tears flooded into Tara's eyes. 'I'm sorry, Kitty, I know you mean well . . . but I'm just not in the right frame of mind. I couldn't face it.'

'It's nearly seven *months* since Gabriel died,' Kitty said gently, 'and you've got to start living your own life again . . . you're only a young woman, Tara.'

Tara put the cup and saucer back down on the table. 'What life do I have now?'

'It's time you stopped talking like that,' Kitty said, 'and if you don't stop soon, we'll have to think of calling the doctor in to you.' She went on quickly before Tara could protest, because it had taken her a few weeks to build up the courage to tackle this. 'You've got to do *something*, Tara – if Gabriel were here, that's exactly what he would be telling you.'

'But he's not here, Kitty,' Tara whispered, 'and he never will be again, and I just don't feel I have anything to live for . . . every day feels as though there's less and less reason to get out of bed. It's not as if I've got children or anything . . .'

'You're depressed, Tara,' Kitty said, taking her niece's hand, 'and you need to do something about it before it really gets in on you. While it's only natural that you should be grieving for Gabriel and still missing him – you're getting worse instead of better, and that's not good.' She paused for a moment. 'I lost my own husband, and I know what it's like . . . but life must go on. Gabriel would want you to go on, wouldn't he?'

'I don't know anything any more, Kitty,' Tara said, 'and I just feel that all I want to do is sleep. I don't have the energy for anything else.'

'But how could you have energy? You're not eating

properly, Tara,' Kitty said. 'And you've lost far too much weight . . .' She passed the small plate of toast to Tara now. 'Would you not think of going over to Stockport for a few weeks? You used to love going there. Or even London,' Kitty suggested. 'You've said you'll go over and pick up Gabriel's nice car some time . . . and the young lad has written to you a few times recently, asking you to go over. Why don't you go over and collect the car and bring the boy back with you? Having a youngster about the place would liven things up – you could take him down to Clare for a few days over the half-term break, and then he could go back on the plane.'

Tara took a small bite from one of the slices of toast, and as she chewed it, tears started sliding down her face.

'Oh, Tara!' Kitty said, hugging her. 'We've got to do something, for watching you going downhill like this is killing all of us. Your father is worried sick, and then Biddy's ringing up all the time to see how you are . . . and it's not good for her to be worried and her expecting a baby now.'

Tara leaned against her aunt, her shoulders heaving as she sobbed. 'I'm sorry,' she cried, 'I'm so, so sorry . . . I wish I was dead and gone with Gabriel.'

Kitty held her like a child in her arms, letting her cry until she was no longer able to. Then she gave Tara the lukewarm tea and told her to take a few mouthfuls from it.

'While you're finishing that drink,' she told her now, 'I'm going to run you a nice hot bath, and while you're in it, I'm going downstairs to make you a decent breakfast.' She looked at her watch. 'You've a quarter of an hour, and then I want to see you downstairs bathed and dressed.' She held up a warning finger to Tara, but her eyes were kind. 'And I'm not taking "no" for an answer. I'm not leaving this house today until you're up and about on your feet.'

Kitty had poured some scented bath oil in the water, and had left a clean flannel and shampoo and two big bath towels on a chair by the side of the bath for her. Tara tested the water with her fingers and it was a perfect temperature. Recently, she'd found even the thought of running a bath a huge effort, and it had taken her half the day to get up the energy to sort out all the things she needed. It was such a struggle that on a couple of occasions, she realised it was dinner time and she hadn't even got out of her dressing gown yet.

She lay in the water for a while, then she soaped herself all over, feeling the bones on her shoulders and neck more obvious than usual, and aware of Kitty's comment about her having lost weight. Then she got the jug that she kept in the corner of the bath, and started to wash her hair.

Around twenty minutes later, having taken some time deciding what to wear, she was downstairs, dressed in brown corduroy slacks and a thick Aran-style sweater. She came in to find the kitchen cosy and warm in spite of the freezing February morning outside. Shay had obviously cycled in from Tullamore and raked and reset the range for her as he did most mornings since the funeral. The radio was on in the background – Kitty's attempt at giving a feeling of normality and joviality to the morning.

'Good girl,' Kitty said, pouring her a mug of hot tea. She went over to the oven and took out two hot plates of bacon, sausage, black and white pudding and fried eggs. 'Just eat as much as you are able, but try to get what you can of it inside.'

Tara's stomach clenched at the sight of the food, but she thanked her aunt politely and prepared to make the best attempt she could.

Kitty went out to the front door and called Shay for his breakfast, and a few minutes later he was round at the kitchen door, kicking the wet grass off his boots. His face lit up when he saw Tara at the table. 'Grand morning,' he told her, taking his cap off and hanging it on the back of his wooden chair. Then he sat down at the place Kitty had set for him.

'Thanks for working on that fence,' Tara said quietly. 'It's a cold morning to be doing anything outside.'

'Ah,' Shay said, with a toss of his head, 'it keeps me out of harm's way, and out from under Tessie's feet.' He winked at Kitty. 'And I get a better breakfast here without any of the scaldin' I get at home.'

They both laughed and Tara even managed a bit of a smile.

'What's Mick at this morning?'

'Oh, when I left him he was sorting out some chicken wire to fix up at the back of the garden. We've had a fox on the prowl recently, and lost a couple of the hens.'

'Shockin'!' Shay said, spearing a circle of black pudding and a circle of white on top of it, then proceeding to put the lot in his mouth.

After a few minutes, and when he could take no more of the silence, he put his knife and fork down. 'Well,' he said, 'any news?' He looked from one woman to the other, as if he didn't know that Tara hadn't left the house for weeks.

'Not a ha'p'orth,' Kitty reported. 'All very quiet in Ballygrace this last while.'

'Ah, well,' Shay said, 'I suppose they had a busy enough summer with all that went on out here ... I suppose they had their fill of news watching all the comings and goings at the funeral.'

Kitty shot her brother-in-law a withering look, thinking that thoughtlessness must run in the Flynn men, as even the mild-mannered Mick could come out with the most inappropriate things at times. She glanced at Tara, and wondered if she even heard what her father had said.

Whether she had or not, she did not react.

There was a silence now as Kitty and Shay pondered over how much news the Fitzgeralds had indeed given the village over the last few months. Not just news, but entertainment as well, with neighbour reporting to neighbour and gossiping in shops any time they caught a glimpse of Biddy Hart or the grieving Tara Fitzgerald, whom they would always refer to as Tara Flynn.

Gradually, when the funeral was all over, and Biddy Hart had returned home to her invalid husband and children, and Elisha and the London crowd had left – the concentrated interest in Ballygrace House started to die down. Then when they saw neither sight nor sound of Tara Flynn, the village gossips moved their attention on to more lively cases, such as the local guard who had been caught in bed with another man's wife.

And as the weeks passed from summer into late autumn and now into winter, people passed by Ballygrace House oblivious to the light and life that had vanished from the house.

Oblivious to the light and life that had vanished from Tara Flynn.

Chapter Sixty-Seven

CLARE

As they slowly rounded the bend on the narrow, wet road, Tara looked through the rain-splattered glass and thought that the house – from the outside, anyway – was exactly as Kitty had described it. It was just that bit too big to be called a farmhouse, but slightly smaller and somehow more untamed-looking than Ballygrace House. The red-painted door and window frames shouted loudly against the white-washed walls. 'A bit gaudy-looking' as Kitty had described it, but Tara's first impression was that the house was big enough to take the colour, and it looked welcoming and friendly, and perfectly suited to the sea location.

She brought the car to a halt, window-wipers swishing noisily against the glass, and turned up a rough track running along the side of the house and the field in front. As she drove carefully along, she could see the stable buildings at the back in the same whitewash and red paint. And then, when she turned her head to glance towards the greenish-blue sea, she noticed the white Victorian-style conservatory tagged on to the side of the house.

Kitty hadn't mentioned the conservatory, but then she'd said it was a good five years since she'd visited Sheila Barry. It was the sort of detail that Kitty would have mentioned had it been there, because at one point Gabriel and Tara had been considering adding a conservatory to Ballygrace House. They had never actually got round to doing anything about it, because the idea of knocking down the solid old walls, and then digging up the paths and gardens at the side or back, had always frightened them. Even Gabriel, who had a good eye for extensions and would point out all sorts of possibilities to purchasers of new properties, had always hesitated when it came to disturbing the perfect lines of the old house.

But as Tara looked at this white and red house, she could see that it was a place that looked happy with change and adaptation. Whoever had designed the conservatory had given careful thought to adding decoration and capturing the perfect sea view from the house.

She glanced at her sleeping companion in the passenger seat and gave a terse little smile. Something about the young boy's trustful, innocent face made her feel lighter in herself, and yet she had the nagging feeling that bringing him over here was total madness. She could hardly cope with herself, far less be responsible for a ten-year-old boy.

Tara got out of the car and, picking her steps quickly but carefully over the muddy wet ridges, she slid back the bolt on the heavy black-painted farm gate and swung it back and bolted it down into the ground to let the vehicle through. When she got back into the car, she wiped her wet hands on the small towel she kept on the dashboard. Then she inched the car forward until she was as close to the back door of the house as she felt was practical and safe.

She turned the engine off and sat for a few moments, staring at the old stone wall in front of her. Waiting to see if the dreaded empty darkness would take her over. The awful feeling that made a mockery of exercises deliberately designed to occupy her mind, like driving or cooking or shopping, or visiting. The feeling that whispered that every single thing was pointless and only a way of filling in time until the total darkness eventually found and completely consumed her.

Then, as the blackness started to rise up in her, she leaned forward until her head was resting on her arms on the driving wheel.

'Have we arrived yet?' a small voice beside her asked. William pulled himself up into a sitting position, rubbing his eyes and looking around. 'Have we got to the sea yet, Tara?'

The key for the back door was awkward. After a few moments' wrestling with it in the rain, Tara fastened the toggles of her black duffel-coat and then pulled the hood up to keep her hair and Aran sweater dry. 'We'll run for it to the front door!' she said, taking William's hand.

They made a dash around the side of the house, past the white conservatory and around to the front.

'Look!' William exclaimed. 'There's the sea, right in front of us! We'll be able to swim in it when the rain stops.'

'I think it's much too cold for swimming,' she told him. 'Have you forgotten what time of the year it is?' She inserted the key into the lock. Thankfully the Yale key opened the heavy red door at the first try, which let them into a stained-glass porch with stone benches at either side, under which were neatly placed several pairs of wellingtons. On one side, there was a row of outdoor coats and on the other, white and pink busy Lizzies and vivid red hanging geraniums tumbled out of two hand-crafted plant stands. And three lilac-painted shelves held displays of driftwood, marbled-pebbles and shells, and a rough blue and yellow Spanish-style bowl filled with dried lavender. In the corner there was an old brass stand filled with an assortment of umbrellas and fishing nets and rods.

William opened the half-glass-panelled door and they went into a large, white, airy hallway with old brown and blue and white mosaic-patterned tiles. 'This is brilliant!' he said, going over to examine the curving staircase and the paintings and photographs that hung on the walls. 'Is this *Irish*?' he asked, pointing to a poem in an old, ornate gilt frame.

Tara came to stand beside him. 'Yes,' she told him patiently, 'that's written in Gaelic, in the Irish language.'

'Will you read it to me?' he asked eagerly. 'Read it in Irish first, and then tell me what it means.'

Tara stifled a tired little sigh. This was so, *so* difficult. It was much easier back in Ballygrace House on her own, where she could just close the curtains and pull the bed-covers up over her eyes. Where she could shut out the whole difficult, demanding world.

She took a deep breath and read in the native language she had not used for a long, long time:

Scoil fé'n spear

Is deas liom scoil
Amuigh fé'n spear
Fé scáth na gcrann
Leis an rang go léir
Crónán na mbeach
Agus ceol ná n-éan
Bo binn im' chluais
I rith an lae

'What does it mean?' William urged enthusiastically. 'What is it about?'

'It's about children at school,' Tara told him. 'It's about the teacher bringing the whole class outside on a sunny summer's day to do their lessons in the open air, under the shade of the tree.'

'It sounds lovely,' William said wistfully, fingering

the old picture frame. 'I wish our school would bring us outside on hot sunny days.'

'It *is* lovely,' Tara agreed, wishing she could feel more enthusiasm herself. 'It reminds me of summer days when I was back at school in Ballygrace.'

'The people in this house have very interesting things,' he remarked now, looking around the walls. 'It's a bit like being in an art gallery or a museum.'

As she stood beside him, Tara's thoughts flickered to what Kitty had told her about the owner of the house. A cousin – a widow who was an eccentric type, who dabbled in writing poetry and was involved in a kind of arty-style life. A lively woman, by all accounts, who spent a lot of time travelling between Ireland and America where both her son and daughter now lived.

William moved on down to the bottom of the hallway, then stood in front of an array of framed posters, reading all the printed information. Some were old ones from theatres in Galway and Dublin, advertising plays and concerts, and there were some brightly coloured vintage posters from Paris.

As she looked at them, Tara suddenly felt the familiar claustrophobic feeling tightening in her chest. *Paris* – where she and Gabriel should have gone just after he died. *Paris* – the beautiful, romantic city she would never see with her beautiful, blond-haired husband.

The city where she had hoped at long last to conceive their baby. The baby that would never be.

Just thinking about it gave Tara a tight pain across her chest.

'It's really different from our house in London and Ballygrace House, isn't it, Tara?' William said, his arms moving dramatically. 'This house feels much more exciting ... probably because it's by the sea.' Then, humming the tune of 'I Do Like to Be Beside the Seaside', he wandered back up the hallway and looked again at the fishing nets in the porch, completely oblivious to the devastating blackness that had just enveloped his sister-in-law. He picked one up and then held it out as though trying to catch a fish. 'If it's too cold to swim in the sea, we can at least have good fun fishing with these nets! Maybe I'll catch some crabs.'

Tara took a deep breath, suddenly feeling this was all a very big mistake. She would never keep up with his enthusiasm and energy – even at her best it would have taken everything she had. Already she wanted to drive back to the safety of her bedroom in Ballygrace House.

'Can we look around?' the young boy said excitedly, pointing to another shelf overflowing with bits of bleached driftwood and assorted pebbles painted dramatically in black with gold and silver Celtic symbols. He lifted the largest pebble and traced the gold-painted circular pattern with his finger. 'And after we've looked downstairs, can we go upstairs to see what my bedroom is like?'

Tara took a deep breath and followed him on a tour of the old, bohemian-style house that smelt of beeswax polish, dried lavender and things that had come from the sea.

Half an hour later, Tara was standing with her back to the range, looking around the warm, yellow-painted kitchen and vaguely wondering who had been good enough to light the fires for them, and generally make the house so welcoming. The bedrooms upstairs had shining old pine furniture with American patchwork quilts on the beds, and Tara was surprised to see vases of early spring flowers there as well as in the rooms downstairs. Any spaces in the rooms were filled with overflowing bookcases. In the brightly coloured sitting room there was a fire – kept alive from earlier on with dampened coal – and two comfy Indian-patterned sofas filled with lots of cushions.

The house was brighter and not as formal as

Ballygrace House, but it had a comforting warmth and lots of charm. Most importantly, it didn't hold any memories of anyone who knew her. And it didn't hold any memories of her and Gabriel.

Although she didn't feel in the slightest bit hungry, she knew she would have to make William something to eat, and she had faithfully promised Kitty she would eat three regular meals a day herself. But nothing she had brought in the large cardboard box now sitting on the marble worktop appealed to her in the slightest.

'Shall we have an Irish breakfast?' William suggested, on his tiptoes and peering into the high box.

Tara looked at her watch. 'But it's after one o'clock,' she told him, her eyebrows raised in surprise. 'Isn't it a bit late for a fry-up?'

'Well,' he said, tilting the box on its side to get a better look, 'we didn't have a very big breakfast this morning . . . I only had cereal and a piece of brown bread and marmalade.' He grinned, holding out a packet of sausages. 'We can have a *brunch* – just like the Yanks. They always have a mixture of breakfast and lunch.'

Tara fought back feelings of reluctance and resentment at having to cook, and having to cook something she positively did not want to *eat*. But then, that was one of the reasons she had brought William – to *make* herself do things. She turned toward the cooker to check on equipment for cooking the meal. Yes, there was a heavy black frying-pan hanging on a hook on the wall, and when she checked in the fridge, there was a large block of lard. No excuses.

'Shall we empty the box?' William suggested, going over to lift the egg container that Kitty had filled with fresh hen and duck eggs that morning.

'That', Tara said, 'might be a good idea. We'll know exactly what we have, then.'

Ten minutes later the big round kitchen table had two

places set with cutlery and napkins and a cup and saucer. The plates were warming in the oven while sausages and bacon and black and white puddings crackled on top.

'I didn't realise you were so well trained,' Tara said, as William busied himself buttering a quarter of a fresh brown loaf.

'I help Mrs Saunders at home,' he explained, putting the slices of bread neatly on a plate. 'You know, our housekeeper. When Mummy's having a lie-down, or when she's out, then I do things with Mrs Saunders.' He gave a big smile. 'She's even taught me how to bake.'

'And what sorts of things can you do?' Tara put on an oven glove, and opened the door of the oven. She lifted out the hot plates, then filled both up with the food from the frying-pan and put them back into the oven while she fried two eggs.

'Oh . . .' he said, clapping his hands together, 'my favourite thing of all is meringues. I love making meringues with fresh cream and fruit.'

'Very impressive!' Tara said, cracking the eggs into the hot, spitting fat. 'And what else?' She felt she had to keep the conversation going, because if she ran out of things to say, she was afraid of the silence which would echo through the old house.

'Lots of things,' he said, smiling and licking his lips theatrically, 'especially desserts. I can make a lovely toffee and banana cake with a biscuit base, and, ooh . . . let me think . . . chocolate pudding, bananas and custard. Things like that.' He came over to stand at the cooker beside her. 'Would you like me to make something for dinner tonight?'

Tara turned one of the eggs over with a flat wooden slice. 'Let's get this meal over first,' she said, turning around to him and wagging the slice, 'before we start planning the next.'

William started laughing. 'Did you used to say that to

Gabriel when he asked about meals? You knew Gabriel when he was my age, Tara,' he said, his voice suddenly quiet. 'Didn't you?'

There was a silence, then eventually Tara said, 'William, I don't mean to be awkward with you . . . but I'm really not up to talking about Gabriel. Not yet.'

'I'm sorry, Tara,' the boy said quickly. 'I'm really sorry . . . I didn't mean anything.'

She came over and tousled his hair. 'You've nothing to be sorry about, William . . . none of us have anything to be sorry about. It's just the way things are.'

Tara was surprised to look at the kitchen clock some time later, and discover that two whole hours had passed. Recently, she only allowed herself to check the time every half-hour or so, finding it excruciatingly painful in its slowness – but this afternoon had been the opposite.

After their 'brunch', they both washed up and then, since the rain had eased, they went out to the car and lifted in their cases. William was very excited and Tara was doing her utmost to keep up with him, but trying at the same time to bring his energy down to a level she could handle.

'Now look,' she told him when they had brought the stuff inside, 'you're going to have to find things to entertain yourself with while we're here.' She raised her eyebrows. 'I did warn you when you said you wanted to come back to Ireland with me . . . it's not the same as London, and we don't have all the city things here.'

'But I *love* it,' he told her earnestly. 'You don't know how boring it is for me back home . . . mother's always tired or upset, and Harry spends all his time doing things to cheer her up.'

They went upstairs with the cases. Tara put hers in one double bedroom at the front of the house and then she guided William into the identical room at the other side.

'Now, take your time,' she told him, opening the large empty pine wardrobe, 'and unpack your things and then put them in here on the shelves.' She pointed to the top shelf. 'You could put your pyjamas and socks and smaller things here, and your sweaters and jeans on the one below.'

William nodded his dark head. 'No sooner said than done, Ma'am!' he said, giving her a salute. 'And then can I go down to have a look at the sea?'

'One thing at a—' A noise halted Tara mid-sentence, and when she paused, she realised it was the brass knocker on the front door. Feeling slightly alarmed, she went downstairs quickly, wondering who would know that she was staying in the house. She opened the door.

'Beggin' your pardon, Ma'am.' A solid-figured elderly man took off his cap respectfully. He steadied his old black bicycle against the wall, then quickly untied a small, bulky sack from the pannier on the back. Then he held out his work-weathered hand. 'Michaeleen Fahy,' he announced, 'and you must be the lady from Offaly who's come down for the few days?'

Tara smiled and shook his hand. 'I am indeed,' she said, holding the door open for him. 'Come in, out of the cold.'

'Bad old weather we're getting over here, but sure it's the same everywhere. What else can we expect, this time of year and everything?' He stepped into the small entrance hall, then put the sack down on the floor.

'Herself baked ye a nice fresh brown loaf,' he said, reaching into the sack for it. 'She wouldn't let me come down earlier on, until she had left it out to cool for a while.'

'Oh, that was very kind of your wife,' Tara said and, as she took the wrapped loaf, she could still feel the warmth of the oven coming through it.

Michaeleen lifted the sack up now. 'There's some spuds and carrots, and a few Brussels sprouts to keep you going,' he said. 'We drop them down regularly for the lady of the house when she's at home.'

'That's so very good of you,' Tara told him. 'I was going to go out looking for a shop later.' Vegetables were one of the foodstuffs she had decided not to carry with her, due to the dirt and the weight – and the bread she had brought was white, so the brown would give them the choice.

'My wife Mary was down at the house yesterday, and she said to tell you that if there was anything else you needed, just to let us know.' He pointed over her head. 'We're in the cottage above, just beyond the Post Office, the one with the black door. Mary has the key for the house here, and she slips in and out and keeps it aired, and that kind of thing, when the lady herself is gone.'

'Well, it was more than grand when we arrived,' Tara said. 'And it must have been one of you who lit the fires in the house?'

'Sure 'tis only a five-minute job,' he said. 'We set fires every few days when the house is empty, otherwise you could be attractin' damp and oul' mildew and the divil-knows-what.' His face grew dismal at the thought. 'You wouldn't last too long in here without a fire at this time of the year, I can tell you. We're bad enough ourselves up above, but below here you're so close to the water and the wind.' He waved his hand towards the door and the wintry-grey sea beyond. 'Sure, there's nothing here between the house and the sea. There's nothing here at all to protect you . . . nothing to protect you at all.'

Tara was exhausted by ten o'clock that night. Physically, she had done more today than she had done in the last few months. And it was all down to guilt – guilt at bringing the young boy with her in this terrible weather with little or nothing for him to do.

After they had sorted out all the stuff from the suitcases, she had suggested that he sat quietly and listened to the radio or read his books, while she had a half-hour lying on top of her bed. He had quickly run upstairs to get a Billy Bunter book he was reading, and had settled down in front of the fire to read as she had asked.

Tara reluctantly left him to his own devices and went upstairs, knowing that she needed this little space to herself if she was to cope for the rest of the evening. Within five minutes of lying on the big, comfortable pine bed, she ended up fully clothed under the bed-clothes, because she was both tired and cold. She knew she should have lit the fire that Mrs Fahy had set for her, but once she had lain down, it was easier just to crawl under the covers and warm herself up that way.

As she lay, half drifting off to sleep, she was conscious of William downstairs, trying not to make her feel that she had deserted him.

Chapter Sixty-Eight

BALLYGRACE

Shay wheeled the bike around the side of Ballygrace House, and then stood in the shelter of the doorway as he took off the wet black plastic cape. He gave it a good shake to get rid of the worst of the water and then he took off his cap and tapped on the door. 'Bad oul' day,' he said, coming into the kitchen.

'God, I wasn't expecting you to cycle out here on a day like this,' Kitty said, pulling the plug of the iron out of the socket and putting the hot iron end-up on the worktop. She left the half-ironed white linen pillowcase on the ironing-board until later. 'Give me that,' she said, taking the cape from him. 'I'll leave it to dry out in the big sink in the laundry-room.' She went through a small door at the back of the kitchen. Shay went over to the hot range and balanced his cap on the bar at the front. It would be dried out by the time he left – and, hopefully, so would the weather.

Kitty came bustling back into the kitchen now. 'I have the kettle boiled,' she told him, 'and I'll make us a nice cup of tea.'

'Grand,' Shay said, taking off his jacket and putting it on the back of one of the chairs around the big pine table. 'Any news?' he asked. 'Any word from Tara and the lad?'

'None,' Kitty said quietly. 'I hope to God they're all right . . . I hope she got down there safely in all that

474

rain. I heard on the news earlier that there was some flooding down in the west.'

'Ah, she'll be grand,' Shay said, crossing his legs. 'Sure, the engine on that car is shining – you could fry an egg on the top of it an' you wouldn't find a speck of dirt on it. The car isn't a year old, hardly been used – grand tyres – everything. A bit of oul' rain wouldn't do it the slightest harm – not a bit of it.'

'That's something, anyway,' Kitty said, putting the teapot down on a wooden mat on the table beside the milk jug and the sugar. 'What'll you have to eat?' she asked him. 'I could do you some bacon and sausage . . .'

Shay held his hand up. 'A bit of bread and butter will do me grand.'

'Did you have a fry already this morning?'

He inclined his head. 'Ah, sure, I threw a few sausages and eggs in the pan for myself, and a bit of pudding.'

'Was Tessie up at Molly's last night?'

Shay nodded. 'She's up and down there the whole time – you can't leave Molly alone for five minutes. Sure, you'd come back and she'd have the whole house burned down on top of you.'

'Has Joe said any more about her going into the hospital?'

Shay shrugged. 'Ah, he can't make up his mind; one minute he says we have no alternative, and the next he's saying maybe we should give it a while longer.'

'He did his best the few days over the funeral,' Kitty said, bringing a loaf of soda bread over to the wooden cutting block. 'There're not many priests that I know who would have stayed on their own in the house with Molly – Joe's to be admired for that. There are plenty of priests who like to be waited on hand and foot, but he's definitely not one of them. He's grateful for anything anybody does for him.'

'True for you,' Shay said, 'and I think he has enough

on his plate with the crowd down in his parish. It can't be easy working in a big city like Cork. Sure, they have problems down there we'd never even dream of.'

Chapter Sixty-Nine

CLARE

Tara lay awake in the dark, listening to the far-off sound of the sea and the low whistle of the wind through the trees. She wondered if it would have been any better if she had come here at a different time of the year. If the weather had been warmer and kinder, would she have felt any different in herself – would it have made a difference? As she turned her face into the pillow and closed her eyes, she knew the answer. But she had actually slept better here the last two nights than she had slept for months. She had turned the lamp on that morning when she first woke to discover it was twenty past five, which meant she had slept for over *six* hours.

Over the last few months, she'd not managed to sleep for more than two hours at a time. Not since she had slept on her own. She would waken in the dark and lie there, thinking the same dark thoughts – night after night. Then eventually she would go back to sleep for another two hours at most, and repeat the same thing until morning came. And often, when she had energy for nothing else, she would repeat the same pattern again during the day – always hoping for that relief from her inconsolable tiredness.

However difficult it was to achieve, sleep was the only real escape. She lay awake now, until eventually the early morning light started to filter through the slit in the curtains, then she suddenly decided to move out of bed and go downstairs. She slipped her feet into her sheepskin moccasins and put on her thick dressing gown, then she padded quietly out of her room and down the stairs into the warm, homely kitchen. She raked through the hot ashes in the range, and then put some small pieces of wood on it to get it going again. A few minutes later, she added some small pieces of turf to the flames to get a decent, long-lasting heat to boil the kettle. When she went to the tap, she only filled it halfway up so that it would boil quickly.

Then she moved around, opening cupboards to look for a plate for her bread and taking a nice-sized flowery mug from a row of hooks on the old painted dresser. She looked at the large electric toaster, thinking it would be nice to have a hot, even piece of toast: they had never got around to buying an electric one in Ballygrace House, and the toast that was made on the range was often white in the middle and burned around the edges.

She studied the toaster carefully, wary of using it, because it was completely different from the kind she had back in Stockport – and it seemed to have collapsible sides. After a few moments, she took a chance and plugged the toaster in, then she placed a slice of bread in one side and closed it up.

At one point, as she poured the boiling water into her coffee, she heard a noise upstairs. She paused, listening – and was grateful when there was no further sound. She really needed a little while to herself before William was up and about, talking and expecting some kind of normal conversation back from her.

William paused – his spoonful of cornflakes held in mid-air. 'What do you think we should do today?' he asked. He was dressed in stripy pyjamas and a navy woollen dressing gown with a red trim.

Tara looked at him, grateful that he had slept until half past nine. 'What would you like to do?'

'It's dry,' he said, pointing to the window with the spoon. 'So we could really do anything, couldn't we?' He guided the spoon back to his mouth.

Tara fought back her overwhelming reluctance to do *anything*. 'What would you *really* like to do?' she said, forcing herself to sound interested.

He crunched on his cornflakes, thinking. 'How about a walk out on the beach first?' he suggested. 'And then after we've had something else to eat, we could maybe go for a drive out someplace.'

'OK,' Tara said, going to make herself another coffee to gear herself up. 'After we've finished breakfast, we can go and get dressed in warm clothes and heavy boots.'

'Would they have any bookshops around here?' William asked, his face serious.

Tara raised her eyebrows. 'Around *here*?' she said, smiling. 'You can tell that you were obviously sleeping when we came off the main roads.'

'So . . .' he said, taking another spoonful of cereal, 'there *aren't* any bookshops around?'

'There aren't any *shops* around here at all, as far as I could see when I was driving in yesterday,' Tara told him, 'far less bookshops.'

'So what is there?' he asked. 'And where are all the shops?'

'I think', Tara said, realising that going out might be preferable to sitting here answering a never-ending stream of questions, 'we should have a walk out, and then you can see for yourself.'

'This is the strangest beach I've ever seen!' William stated, as they stood on the grass verge looking across at the wide expanse of rock and shale. But it was not the usual beach landscape of white sands or coral or even

479

giant flat pebbles. This was acre upon acre of large, flat slabs of solid limestone – the origins of the Burren gradually laid bare by constant scouring from the sea over thousands of years.

'Do you think people carried these big stones here?' William asked, stepping on to a big whale-shaped stone.

Tara shook her head. 'I wouldn't think so, I would imagine that it's just the natural terrain . . . you know, the way the land is around here.' She paused, the dark weariness creeping up again inside her, making her want to head back to the comfort of the house and the bed upstairs.

She stood now, staring over the white rocks and the blue-grey sea to the hills and the small cottages dotted around at the other side of the bay. Staring but not seeing. Both she and William were very well wrapped-up against the winter chill; Tara with a soft tweed scarf over her hair and tied loosely at the back, her duffel coat buttoned up to the neck and black slacks tucked into socks and boots, and William in jeans with socks and boots and a thick navy hooded jacket.

The tide was out, the sea having left behind a trail of blackish-green seaweed strewn over the more distant rocks. William moved off the whale stone now, and very cautiously started to move from rock to rock until he was some distance away from her.

Tara turned her gaze towards him, wondering if she should call him to come back, because she knew he wasn't a rough-and-tumble type of boy. Any physical activities he engaged in were along the lines of the safer sports, like swimming and tennis, as he was over-protected by the anxious Elisha. She waved now, and shouted, 'Don't go too far!'

He came to a halt on a particularly large flat rock. 'Come on, Tara!' he called back to her excitedly, the wind lifting his normally tidy hair into little black

peaks. 'Come on, it's easy . . . you can just walk across.'
He started to come back towards her now, jumping
over the cracks in the rocks. 'Here,' he said, holding his
hand out, 'I'll help you.'

Tara tightened the knot at the back of her scarf as
best she could in her leather gloves, then she moved off
the grass and on to the rocks. She stepped from rock to
rock until she reached him, then took the boy's
outstretched hand and allowed him to guide her down
to a low, flat rock.

'It's brilliant!' he told her, pulling her down on to the
shale. He waved his hands around. 'It's like something
from outer space . . . it's so weird.' He jumped up again
on to a higher platform of rock. 'It goes on for miles,' he
said, holding his hands to his eyes like binoculars. 'How
far do you think it is to the end? D'you think we could
walk it?'

Tara smiled at his enthusiasm. 'If you want to run on
ahead, then on you go. But keep near enough for me to
see you, and be careful you don't slip on the rocks or try
jumping too far.'

'What about you?' he said, a little frown of concern
on his forehead, his upbringing with the tense Elisha
making him used to considering the feelings of adults.
'What will you do? Will you be bored?'

'Don't mind about me,' Tara said, ruffling his hair.
'I'll be grand following behind you . . . I'll just take my
time.'

Tara heaved a sigh of relief as William moved on a
few yards ahead of her, leaving her to the sound of the
sea and her own thoughts. Within a few minutes he was
a good distance away, stopping every so often to look
back and wave.

Tara moved along the beach, feeling herself warm up
a little with the exercise.

Although it wasn't a quick, strenuous walk, she
found herself having to climb up and down in bits

481

where there wasn't a straight path of smaller stones. After a while, when she looked back, she realised that the house was quite far in the distance, and that they had covered a reasonable bit of ground.

After another ten minutes, they reached a bend in the road, and Tara noticed that the tide was starting to come in. William kept up the distance between them, as though sensing that Tara needed the time to herself, but continued to wave and shout every so often to remind her he was still there.

But even as she plodded along the stony beach, Tara was struggling. Struggling to force back the heavy weight inside her that threatened to rise up and completely swamp her. Struggling to feel there was anything in the world that would ever matter to her again.

But she had William to consider and, whatever happened, she had to get through the next three or four days with him. She forced herself on, climbing up and down the flat white rocks. After jumping over several gaps in the rocks, Tara stopped to catch her breath, and turned to look backwards – estimating how far they had come – and she realised that the house was long lost in the distance. It was the furthest she had walked in months.

She looked up at the sky, and noticed the dark grey clouds coming in from the sea. She checked her watch. They had been out of the house for over an hour. Most of the time had been spent going backwards and forwards between the rocks, and she knew they would walk it much more quickly back on the path. She checked the sky again. She really didn't fancy them both getting soaked and having all the fuss of trying to dry out coats and scarves and everything.

Just as she decided to call to William, she heard his voice first.

'Tara!' the boy shouted, his hands cupped around his

mouth to help his voice carry. 'Come and see!' He had climbed up from the rocks and on to the grassy hill, and was now back on the path. He pointed across to an area that was out of Tara's vision, and then he suddenly started to run and within a few seconds she could no longer see him.

Tara negotiated her way up over the rocks, and followed the direction that William had taken. Then, as she rounded the bend, with the sea on her right-hand side, she could see a little sheltered cove on the left, which she presumed was where the boy had gone. She walked quickly now that she was on the flatter, even surface, scanning the reedy edge of the water to see where on earth he had gone. Then, suddenly she heard a muffled sound coming from a few yards below her, down near some small straggly bushes – the only tree-like plants that grew in the Burren. She looked and suddenly saw him standing quite still, his finger pressed firmly against his lips to warn her to keep quiet.

Very quietly, she made her way down the bank towards him, and when she looked to where he now pointed, she could see the reason for the silence. There, gently moving along the banks of the water, was a pair of adult swans and three little brown cygnets. When she came to stand beside him, she could see his hazel eyes sparkling with delight.

'They're beautiful,' he whispered, 'aren't they?'

Tara nodded slowly, her gaze following the family of elegant birds and the little trail they left behind them in the water. They watched them in silence for five or six minutes, then Tara touched William's elbow.

'I think it's going to start raining soon,' she said quietly, 'and we'll get soaked if we don't head back to the house now.'

The boy took a deep breath as though disappointed. 'Can we stay for one more minute, please?' he asked and then turned his serious little face back to the swans.

Half an hour later, they turned the corner and walked back up the path at the side of the white house with the red door and windows.

'Soup?' Tara suggested as they hung their coats in the porch beside the purple shelves and the fishing nets. 'I think it would be the quickest and the warmest thing to make just now.'

'What kind of soup?' William checked, his face serious.

'Tomato or chicken,' Tara said, wondering if she was going to get the first signs of childish fussiness from him now. 'And the soup's out of a tin before you ask – it's Heinz soup.'

'Great,' he said, gleefully. 'I'll have tomato, please – it's my favourite . . . Mrs Saunders often makes soup for me at home.'

'Mrs Saunders has been with your family quite a long time, hasn't she?' Tara said, as they went into the kitchen now. She took a medium-sized pan from one of the cupboards and a tin-opener which she had seen peeping out from a flowery yellow jug. She put the soup to heat on the range, then put out two bowls and started to slice up a quarter of the bread that Mrs Fahy had baked for them.

'Sometimes Mrs Saunders bakes bread at home,' William said, as they sat at the kitchen table having the soup and bread, 'but sometimes we just buy bread from the baker's. There's a van that comes around every day. We buy all different kinds, and buns and cakes at the weekend.'

'Are you missing home?' Tara suddenly asked. It was something that hadn't struck her until now, but with him constantly mentioning the housekeeper and all the things he had at home, she wondered now if he might well be missing it.

'No!' William said, looking startled. 'No, I'm really enjoying being here. I love the house and that it's so near the sea and everything . . .' He fumblingly put his spoon back into his soup bowl and the piece of bread back on his side plate. 'It's much better than being with my mother, because she's so cross and unhappy all the time . . . and it's got much, much worse since . . .' His face suddenly crumpled, and his shoulders slowly drooped until his head was almost touching the table. His shoulders started to heave, and tears trickled down his face. 'I miss him, Tara – I miss him – I miss Gabriel so much! He was the only one who knew what to say to me.'

And all Tara could do was fight back her own tears, and come round the table and take the boy in her arms.

Tara knew that she would have to find the energy to take William out that afternoon. After she had comforted him and he had stopped crying, she had put his soup back in the pan and heated it up for him again. Then, when he was back settled and eating his lunch, she did the same with her own, going to and fro to check on it. Small things to keep herself busy, and to keep them from talking about the big, black, terrible things.

As she stood at the sink washing up the crockery, Tara stared up at the sky. It was quite clear; the dark grey clouds had passed, and so far the threatened rain had come to nothing.

'Shall I dry the dishes for you?' William asked, holding out a stripy tea towel. 'Sometimes I help Mrs—' And then he caught himself and stopped.

'OK,' Tara said quickly, 'that would be great.' She tried to push out of her mind the picture of a ten-year-old boy who was so bored at home that he had nothing more exciting to do than to help the elderly housekeeper dry and put away the dishes. How had she and Gabriel not known how desperate things were for him? He had always seemed so happy and excited when they arrived, and had kept that demeanour up all through their visits.

But then, Tara wondered, that must have been precisely why Gabriel had decided to stay on while she came up to Stockport last summer. But if it was the case, why hadn't he said something to her? Why hadn't he said he was worried about his younger brother? She could only presume that he must have sensed something from the boy. Something that made him want to stay and give him a bit of time. He had given the boy the last days of his life, taking him swimming and playing tennis. William had got the last few days of Gabriel's life.

The last days that Tara had missed.

William looked at her now. 'What should we do this afternoon?'

'I think', she said, looking out of the window above the sink, 'that it might be a good afternoon to go to Galway . . . I think we might find a decent bookshop there for you.'

'Brilliant!' he said, his whole face lighting up.

'Can I buy this, Tara?' William asked, holding out a boy's adventure comic. 'I have all my own money.'

'Yes,' she said patiently, 'you can spend your own money on anything you like.'

He went off to the till, the comic under his arm. Tara turned back towards the shelves of children's books, waiting for him to come back. On the drive into Galway, he'd gone on about all the books he was looking for, and they'd only been in the shop a couple of minutes when he came across the American comic that he'd gone hot-foot to the till with.

She scanned the shelves of children's books, looking for the familiar books she had read as a child. There were a few, but most were written by modern authors that she had never heard of. Then she suddenly recognised a title. A book she had loved as a young girl: *Heidi*. Her throat suddenly went tight as she picked the book out of the shelf, but as she did so, she realised that the storyline echoed bits of her own life. Her life growing up with her granda.

It was just like the way Heidi's gruff old grandfather was landed with the young girl in the story. Just her granda and herself ... and sometimes her father and her Uncle Mick. How had she never realised it before? On at least one occasion it had been read aloud to her class in school. She couldn't place the time, or who the teacher was – but she knew she had definitely heard it read aloud in school, before she reached the age of being able to read it for herself.

And as she turned the book around in her hands, it dawned on her that the storyline very effectively echoed the situation that she herself was in – this very moment – with William. The only difference was that William didn't know it. He had no idea that she was looking after him with great difficulty.

They spent a while in the bookshop, and William came out with three books, his comic and a large jigsaw of Robin Hood. Afterwards, they went for a late afternoon tea to the Great Southern Hotel in Eyre's Square. They shared a pot of tea and sandwiches and cakes, and as Tara forced down the last of a piece of cherry cake, she thought how she'd be able to truthfully tell Kitty that she'd eaten well while they'd been away. Not that she had really felt like it, but at least she'd stopped feeling sick every time she ate.

On the way back out from Galway, Tara heard the church bell in Kinvara ringing for the Angelus, and she realised with some surprise that it was six o'clock. William brought in several baskets of turf while Tara got the range burning brightly again. When she checked the time again, it was well after seven. It was the quickest-passing day since Gabriel had gone.

The books and jigsaw puzzle kept William busy for the rest of the evening, then he helped Tara make them a supper of scrambled eggs on toast.

At round ten o'clock, Tara told him it was time for bed, but that he could bring his books upstairs with him to read.

When he reached the top of the stairs, William suddenly turned back. 'It's been a lovely day, Tara – hasn't it? Seeing the swans and then going into Galway.'

'I'm glad you enjoyed it,' she said, giving him a smile.

'But I think *you've* enjoyed today, too – haven't you, Tara?' He stood looking at her, almost holding his breath as he waited for the answer he wanted.

'Yes,' Tara said, knowing it was what the boy needed to hear. 'I've enjoyed myself very much, William.'

Chapter Seventy

There was a strange silence when Tara woke on the Wednesday morning. There was also light. When she looked at the clock, it told her that she had slept for eight hours. For the first time in many months, she had not wakened in the blackness of the night.

She climbed out of bed and went over to look out through the curtains. A fine white veil of snow covered the garden and the rocky beach beyond, stretching out so far it seemed to merge into the white foamy sea. Looking at the beautiful natural scene gave her a lightness inside she had not felt for months.

She padded across the bedroom floor and put on her dressing gown and slippers and went downstairs very quietly. A few minutes later, after restacking the range with turf and wood and putting a full kettle on top, she went back upstairs.

A short while later she was fully dressed in a thick sweater and matching woolly pull-down hat, and heading out of the bright red front door into the crunchy white, cold morning. She had left a note on the kitchen table telling William that she had just gone for a short walk and wouldn't be long, and had moved the kettle off the range so that it wouldn't boil dry while she was gone.

She had also taken a few slices of the loaf that was now going a bit stale. The weather was a combination of sun and snow, and within minutes of walking along the sea path, Tara loosened the scarf around her neck and stuffed her gloves in her coat pocket. She began at a fast pace, and then slowed down to a comfortable walk. For some reason, she had it in her mind that she wanted to see the white of the swans against the brilliant white of the snow. Also, she was a little worried about them finding food with the water having iced over.

She made it to the bend in the road in under the half-hour it had taken them on their way back the previous day, and as soon as she followed the turn, she could see the white shapes moving around in the reeds. The closer she got, the clearer she could see the three little cygnets hiding in the denser reeds.

Tara moved slowly and quietly until she came to a large stone at the edge of the water, then she sat down to watch the birds for a bit and to rest her legs.

After a while, she got up and started to throw small bits of the bread in the direction of the reeds. At first, the swans moved further away, then suddenly – as though having given it considerable thought – one of the parents glided out into the open water and took up the bread.

By the time she had finished off the end of the loaf, both adult swans were clearly in view and one of the cygnets had ventured out, too. She stood for a while longer and then she decided it was time to head back to the house. As she turned to go, the bright morning sunlight suddenly caught the surface of the water, turning it into a sheet of dazzling, dancing diamonds.

The sight of it made her hold her breath – and then the tiny feeling that had been there this morning suddenly rose up inside her into a glorious warmth. And she continued to stand, taking in every bit of the white wintry scene, as though photographing every little detail in her mind.

A word suddenly came into her mind. *Lucky*. In a strange, weird way – that's exactly how she felt this morning. Lucky to be alive and experiencing this wonderful sight. Experiencing the piercing white cold of the snow. Seeing and feeling the real, natural things of life. Seeing and feeling things that Gabriel would never see and feel again.

As always, when she thought of him, she felt hugely sad. But this sparkling, glorious morning had told her that she was alive and part of the living world around her. A world with places she'd never seen, like this strange flat-stoned shore on the west coast of Ireland, and a much bigger world that lay beyond.

A world Tara Fitzgerald could hide away from no longer.

As she walked back to the house, Tara realised that Kitty had been right all along. She had been right to nag her to get up and out of her bed and start moving again. Right to insist that she ate when she wasn't hungry. Wise Kitty. She had done all these things in the last few days just to make things seem normal with William – and things had become normal now.

She speeded up a little as she neared the house, feeling guilty for taking longer than she had meant to. And then she saw the figure coming out from the side of the house, running towards her.

'Tara!' William called, waving his arms to catch her attention. He was still in his pyjamas and dressing gown.

Tara broke into a run now, too. 'What is it?' she called, alarmed that something had gone amiss in the house in her absence.

'Are you all right?' he said, coming to a breathless halt beside her. 'Are you feeling all right?'

'Yes,' she said, nodding, 'I'm fine . . . I just went for a walk.'

'I thought . . .' he said, 'I thought you might have been upset and gone away and left me.'

Tara moved forward and pulled him close to her,

then she tousled his hair. 'I'm absolutely grand. It was just the weather – it was so beautiful that I decided to have a bit of a walk.' She took his hand in hers, and they started walking back to the house. 'I'd never have gone and left you, William – and anyway, I left you a note. Didn't you read it?'

'Yes,' he said quietly, 'but I was still a little bit worried in case . . .'

'Well, don't be worried,' she told him, swinging his hand. 'We came here to have a nice time, and that's what we're going to do. And I'll tell you what – when we've had breakfast, I'll come outside into the garden with you, and we'll build a snowman together.'

'Can I have sausages, Tara?' he asked, his voice much chirpier now.

'You can have sausages and anything else you want,' she told him, and then smiled as he ran on ahead to get dressed.

A short while later, they sat down to eat the sausages along with bacon and mushrooms and fried bread, and Tara felt a small sense of satisfaction as she looked at her own empty plate.

Her appetite – like her zest for life – was slowly starting to return.

The snow went as quickly as it came, and the following days slid away with walks in the winter sunshine and visits to the surrounding villages in County Clare. They found a small pub down by the harbour that served them hot soup and sandwiches, and they took to visiting it in the afternoons. William was delighted to be allowed to sit up at the bar on a high wooden stool, and then later they sat by the roaring fire, watching the sea crash on to the rocks just a short distance from the bar window. Tara watched the boy's enjoyment, oblivious to the admiring glances she drew from any males who came into the bar.

On their second last morning, Michaeleen Fahy appeared up at the house again to check that they had enough wood and turf inside the house to keep them going. He also brought another loaf of fresh bread, then asked William if he'd like to come up to their house for a few hours as they had a grandson around the same age visiting from Galway.

'Ye can kick a ball around for yerselves for a while,' he suggested, 'or take a spin out on the bikes.' He motioned to the shed outside. 'You'll find one out there that'll fit ye, and ye can ride back with me now if ye like.'

'I'd love to come up,' he said, looking at Tara with hopeful eyes, 'if I'm allowed . . .'

Tara felt a great sense of satisfaction as she watched the boy and the old man wheeling the bicycles down the sea path until they reached the flatter road. This was exactly what he needed – fresh sea air, and children of his own age.

She pottered about in the house for the rest of the morning, tidying and then listening to the radio or reading. Then, when she started to feel hungry at around mid-afternoon, she put on her thick sweater and jeans and duffel coat, put a book in her pocket, and set off to walk down to the pub.

As the pub building came into view, Tara suddenly thought that she must phone Biddy as soon as she got back, because the baby was due in the next few weeks. She would let her know that she was coming over to London with William at the weekend, and that she would stop off in Stockport for a couple of nights on the way back.

It seemed an awful long time since she had seen her friends and her house in Stockport. And there were an awful lot of things that she needed to catch up on.

She turned in the pub doorway now, the smell of the hot soup bringing a smile to her face. She was almost sorry to leave this lovely seaside place, but her real life was waiting for her back in Ballygrace and beyond.

The life she was now ready to return to.

Chapter Seventy-One
STOCKPORT, APRIL 1963

They hadn't been long in bed when Biddy felt the need to get up to go to the toilet again. She leaned over the sleeping Fred to check the time on the alarm clock that he kept on the table at his side of the bed. It was nearly one o'clock. She sat up, swinging her legs out on to the floor, then, taking a moment to catch her breath, she heaved herself up on to her feet. She moved across the floor to get her dressing gown from the back of the door, not wanting to chance running into any of the lodgers coming in from their boozy Saturday night out with only her nightdress on.

She had just locked the bathroom door behind her, when suddenly she felt a gush of warm water running down her legs and on to the linoleum floor. Startled, she rushed to the toilet just before a second avalanche came on her. She sat there pondering for a few moments, and when a sharp pain suddenly hit her low down in the back, she decided that it was time to phone for the ambulance.

On the way back up from the phone, another pain hit her and she had to sit down on the stairs until it passed. By the time she had wakened Fred and had located her packed weekend case, she knew that her labour was well and truly underway. She was both scared and excited at the same time, although the baby was a few weeks earlier than the date the hospital had given her. But it didn't matter, a few weeks early was nothing, and, hopefully, if the baby was smaller because of that, it would make the birth all the easier.

'What can I do, love?' Fred asked anxiously. He had got himself dressed more quickly than usual, with the new short-sleeved shirt that he just pulled over his head. It was much easier to manipulate than the ordinary Bri-nylon shirts that buttoned all the way up. Biddy had tried to think of anything that would make life easier for him when she was in hospital, and had bought him three of the casual shirts to keep him going.

'Just carry my case, and hold my hand,' Biddy said, attempting a brave smile as another pain came on.

When they arrived at the hospital, Biddy was whisked away on a trolley and Fred was shown to a waiting room where he joined two other men waiting for their wives to give birth – a small thin man in his early twenties, and a big, pleasant-looking man in his mid-thirties.

'It's Fred Roberts, in't it?' the older man suddenly said, looking up from his paper.

Fred smiled vaguely, trying to work out who the man was, and where he knew him from.

'The wrestler!' the man said, grinning broadly. He folded his paper up now. 'You're Fred Roberts, the wrestler. I've seen you loads of times in Belle Vue and in the town hall.'

Fred nodded and gave a beaming smile. 'You're spot on, mate,' he told him, going red with delight.

The man stretched out his hand towards Fred. 'I'm proud to shake hands with you. Neil Singleton's the name.' Then he turned to the younger man. 'This lad's one of the top fighters in Manchester,' he said, 'a bit of a legend.' He caught Fred's hand again, his face serious now. 'I heard you had a bit of a fall in the ring a few months back . . . are you OK now?'

'Top notch,' Fred said, holding his thumb up. 'I'm brand new, Neil.'

'Are you back fighting again?' the younger man asked, looking at Fred curiously.

'In training,' Fred told him. 'The hospital won't let me back in the ring . . . till I get the all-clear.' He held his hands up in a boxing gesture now, as though hitting a punch-bag. 'A few more months and I'll be back in there again.'

'So what happened, mate?' Neil asked. 'What was the story about the accident?'

Fred shrugged. 'Just – just an unlucky landing.' He tapped his forehead. 'Went straight down on the head.'

The door suddenly opened and a nurse came through. 'Would any of you boys like a cup of tea?' she checked. All three signalled yes.

'How is the wife?' Fred asked. 'Is there any news yet?'

'I'll sort the teas out,' the nurse told him, 'and then I'll look in. What's the name again?'

'Fred . . .'

The nurse's face broke into a big grin. '*Second* name!' she told him.

'Roberts,' Neil Singleton said quickly. 'His name is Fred Roberts.'

'Have you been waiting long?' Fred asked the two men when the nurse went off to get the cups of tea.

'I've been here since ten o'clock,' Neil said, then he pointed towards the younger man, 'and Tom's been here since the late afternoon.'

'Is it your first?' Fred asked.

'Yeah . . .' Tom said, biting the side of his finger. 'They said it could be a while.'

Biddy lay in the high iron bed, her pains coming and going, complying with everything that the nurses and doctors asked of her. She breathed in and out at the right times, pushed when she was told to, and held back when she was instructed to.

In between times, she replayed in her mind the other three births she had had. The first one had been by far the worst – but she'd only been a young girl at the time, terrified and all tensed up. She wondered now, as she had when she had given birth to Michael and Helen, what her first-born son looked like. He would be . . . ten? Ten years old by now. She wondered if he bore any resemblance to herself . . . and once again hoped with all her heart that he didn't look anything like his monster of a father, the man who had abused her rather than helping her. At one stage when the pains got really bad, she was given an injection that made her feel a bit more relaxed and her thoughts drifted off again.

This time she thought of her own mother. The mother she never knew. And her father. Both complete mysteries to her. They could have been anybody from anywhere. As a young girl growing up, she had often wondered about them, but when she asked Lizzie Lawless one day if she knew who her parents were, she immediately wished she had never brought the subject up.

'Tinkers,' Lizzie had told her, 'pure dirty tinkers, from what I heard. Nothing to be proud of in the breeding there.' Then she had said very darkly, 'Let's just pray to God that the breeding doesn't break out in you or any of your offspring – for there's definitely bad blood there.'

Biddy wished with all her heart that Lizzie Lawless could have seen her two lovely children, in their lovely spotlessly clean clothes. Unlike their mother, Michael and Helen had never known a day's hunger in their lives and they'd never had to sleep in a dirty bed. If Lizzie Lawless could only have seen the lovely big boarding-house that they lived in – sure, in its own way it was nearly as grand as Ballygrace House. Well, maybe not just as grand – but bigger and better than anything anybody else had in Ballygrace besides the Fitzgeralds.

Another sharp pain hit Biddy and this time the midwife gave her the mask with gas and air. She had been well used to the mask when she'd been in hospital with the other two children, and she took it in both hands with gratitude. And then the pains started to come overwhelmingly close together, and things escalated in the room as the child started pushing its way into the world with all its might.

'A girl!' the midwife called out delightedly, as she wrapped the newborn child in a white towel. Immediately the child gave a healthy, squawking cry. Then, as she studied the baby closer, a frown crossed the midwife's face and she looked at the nurse across the bed from her, then nodded to the bundle in her arms. 'I'm not too sure whether she might have a touch of jaundice . . .'

'Is she all right?' Biddy asked anxiously, trying to move higher up in the bed so she could see what was going on. 'There isn't anything wrong with her?'

'I think she just needs a little cleaning up, love,' the midwife said. 'I'll bring her back to you in two minutes.'

The younger nurse came round now to pat Biddy's hand encouragingly. 'Having a baby's never easy, but you've got off fairly lightly,' she told her. 'It was a fairly quick and straightforward labour – not even a stitch. I'll bet you're ready for a nice cup of tea?' She helped Biddy to move into a sitting position now.

The nurses seemed to be gone quite a long time, and as she waited for them to bring the baby back, Biddy found herself beginning to worry more and more. This had never happened with her other babies – they'd always been given to her as soon as they were born.

Eventually, the younger nurse came back with the promised tea and a slice of toast.

'Is the baby coming back up soon?' Biddy asked, taking a sip of the sweet tea to calm her mounting anxiety. 'They haven't found anything wrong with her, have they?'

'Not a thing,' the nurse said.

'Can my husband come in now? He'll be anxious to know what's going on – he's a real worrier, especially when it comes to me. And he'll be real worried about the baby.'

'Is he in the fathers' room?' the nurse asked. 'What's his name?'

'Fred Roberts . . . he's a big-made fellow with dark hair. You can't miss him.'

The nurse nodded. 'Don't worry, we'll have him and the baby up to you very soon.'

More time elapsed, the tea and toast were long finished, and there was still no sign of the baby, the nurses or Fred. And then Biddy heard footsteps approaching the room.

'Mrs Roberts . . .' The midwife came into the room with an older nurse alongside her. 'Sister and I just wanted to check a few personal details with you . . . if you don't mind.'

Biddy sat up straight, her hands clasped on the bed sheets in front of her. Her mouth had suddenly gone very dry and her breathing tight.

'Your husband, Mr Roberts, is he English?'

'Yes,' Biddy said, her brow becoming furrowed. 'He's in the waiting room, like I said.'

'He's the tall, well-made man?' the nurse checked.

Biddy nodded, swallowing hard on the lump that had formed in her throat.

'And is he the baby's father?' The ward sister spoke up now. Her voice was very officious and her face severe.

'Yes,' Biddy repeated. 'Like I said, he's my husband.' She looked from one serious face to the other. 'It's the baby, isn't it? There's something wrong . . . is she sick?'

'Your little girl is perfect in every way – perfectly healthy.'

'Thank God!' Biddy breathed, blessing herself now.

'But there is a little problem . . . we thought at first it was caused by jaundice, but when we gave her a little wash over . . .'

'What is it?' Biddy demanded.

'She seems to be . . . well, she has the appearance of a half-caste baby,' the sister said in a low voice. 'We checked her out with another darkish baby in the nursery and their colouring is almost identical.'

Biddy's hands flew to her mouth, her eyes wide in shock. 'Holy Mary, Mother of God!' she uttered, almost choking on the words.

'I'm sure when you've had time . . . you will be able to work it all out for yourself,' the midwife said kindly. She went over now, and put her arm around Biddy. 'We just thought it would be better if we came and told *you* first, before we bring your husband in to see the baby.'

'Can I see her?' Biddy whispered. 'Can I see my baby now?'

And as the nurses' footsteps echoed down the corridor as they went to fetch her newborn child, Biddy knew that it wasn't her husband's baby they were bringing back. They were bringing back Lloyd's baby daughter.

Biddy looked down at the newborn child in her arms, and was filled with the most enormous rush of maternal love. She was beautiful! Quite the most beautiful baby Biddy had ever seen in her life. She had the softest coffee-and-cream-coloured skin, and the most perfectly formed face and little rosebud mouth.

She stirred slightly now, her face turning towards her

mother's breast, and the movement caused an almost violent feeling of protectiveness to rise up in Biddy.

Whatever happened, this child was *her* daughter – and she would have everything that Michael and Helen, her other children, had. And like them, she would protect this new baby with her life if necessary – she would protect her from anyone who tried to cause her any kind of harm.

But first, there was Fred to deal with.

Biddy knew that how Fred reacted to the baby was going to make all the difference to how other people reacted. So Biddy was going to have to ensure that Fred was on her side from the start.

'Fred,' Biddy said, after he sat down in a chair beside her bed, 'I have something to tell you . . .' She took a deep breath, trying to keep her voice steady.

'Is the baby all right?' Fred asked, squeezing her hand tightly. 'I was right worried about the pair of you . . .'

'Well,' Biddy said slowly, 'there's a tiny little problem.' Her voice was calm, but inside her heart was beating like mad. *Please, please, God*, she thought, *let me get this story right, for the sake of my little daughter. Make Fred believe me.*

'What's that?' he said, his eyes wide and fearful.

'Well, you know I was brought up an orphan in Ireland? That I never saw my mother or father or . . .'

'I know all that, Biddy,' he said, reaching to clasp her other hand now.

'Well . . . I never knew anything about my background . . . I never knew a single thing about my family or my grandparents.'

Fred listened carefully, slowly nodding his head all the time to show he understood what his wife was saying.

'Something's happened to the baby, Fred,' Biddy said

now, 'that must have come from somewhere back in the family . . .'

'Is our little girl . . . is our little girl handicapped?' Fred suddenly blurted out.

'No, love, no,' Biddy reassured him, 'she's not handicapped . . . but her skin is darker than ours. Her skin has got a touch of brown in it.'

Fred's forehead wrinkled in confusion. 'Brown skin?' he repeated. 'She's got *brown* skin?'

Biddy's head bobbed up and down in confirmation, while her heart continued to thud inside. 'I think my mother and father must have had some foreign blood in them . . . somewhere. You see in Ireland, there are a lot of people with dark skin – they call them the Spanish Irish . . . I think it's something to do with the Spanish sailors back in history somewhere.'

'You think your family might have been Spanish, then?' Fred asked now.

Biddy shrugged. 'I don't know . . . and I'll never know now. There's no way I could ever find anything out about my mother and father now. Lizzie Lawless said they might even have been gypsies . . . and a lot of them have dark skin, too.' She squeezed Fred's hands really tight.

'But what about you?' he asked, still clearly confused. 'How come *your* skin is an ordinary colour, if your family were foreigners?'

Biddy shrugged again, an overwhelming tiredness coming over both her body and her brain now. A tiredness reminding her that she had just given birth only a short while ago, and that she should be resting. 'The nurses have said it's quite common . . . things often skip a generation.' Her eyes widened now. 'Or even *two* generations. It could have been my grandfather or my grandmother who was from . . .' Her brain raced now, trying to remember if Lloyd had ever said anything about his real origins. He had a strong London accent, and she was sure he'd said he was born in London, but his family must have come from somewhere like Africa or India or Nigeria or somewhere like that. 'One of my grandparents . . . or my parents must have come from a country with people with dark skin.' She halted, sheer tiredness completely taking over now. 'I just don't know any more, Fred,' she said, fighting back the tears that had suddenly sprung into her eyes. 'But I'm not sure she looks like either of us . . .'

'It's OK, love,' Fred said, standing up and coming over to put his arms around her. 'It'll all be OK.'

A nurse appeared at the door. 'Everything all right?' she asked, her gaze directed at the exhausted-looking mother.

'Can you bring the baby?' Biddy asked in a frail voice. 'I think it's about time that Fred saw his new little baby daughter.'

Biddy watched anxiously as the wrapped child was placed in her husband's arms. Apart from her overwhelming worry about his reaction to the child's appearance, his movements were still a bit unsteady, and she was terrified that he might not be able to hold her properly.

Fred stared down at the little bundle, his face a picture of concentration. Then, like the sun finally breaking through the clouds, a huge, delighted smile spread all over his face. 'She's gorgeous!' he said, nodding his head. 'She's bloody well gorgeous!'

'Do you really think so?' Biddy breathed, feeling light-headed now.

'I don't know what you were goin' on about,' he said, moving the baby's blanket back off her head to get a better look. 'Her skin's just a lovely tanned colour – the way some people get when they get a bit of the sun.' His brow furrowed again. 'I think she's the spittin' image of you . . . and look!' he exclaimed now. 'She's even got

the Roberts jet-black hair – the very same hairline an'
all!'

Biddy leaned over the bed and peered closely at the
child now. Apart from the dark hair, as far as she could
see there was nothing – absolutely *nothing* – about the
baby that resembled Fred. But whatever happened, Fred
was going to be this baby's father, and if he thought she
looked like him – then God must have listened to her
prayers.

Half an hour later – after four in the morning – a weary
Fred called in at the fathers' room downstairs, while
waiting for his taxi back home.

'Another daughter!' he told the wrestling fan, with a
wink and a big grin.

'Congratulations,' the man said. 'I'm still waiting;
they're not sure if it was a false alarm or not . . . they
might even send her back home. We had the same
damned thing happen a fortnight ago.' He pointed up to
the ceiling. 'The young lad, Tom, has just gone upstairs
ten minutes ago. He has to sign a form for his wife to
have an operation . . . I think there's been some
complications there . . .'

'The nurses are very good in this hospital,' Fred said.
'They've looked after my wife well – her and the baby
are champion now. A bit tired, like – but champion.'

'And who does she take after, then?' the man asked,
smiling. 'Is she a big bruiser like yourself?'

Fred beamed. 'No . . . she's small and dainty like her
mother . . . I'm pleased to say. But,' he said, his eyes
dancing with delight, 'she definitely has *my* black hair.'

Chapter Seventy-Two

Tara walked around the shelves filled with blue and pink and yellow baby clothes, occasionally lifting the tiny, soft things to examine them. Now she was actually in the shop, it wasn't quite so bad. Standing outside the recently opened, very modern Mothercare chainstore, looking at the cots and prams and baby clothes, had made her feel as though she had a heavy weight crushing her chest.

It wasn't as though she grudged Biddy – or Bridget, she now reminded herself – her new baby. She was delighted for her old friend, but there were times when she found it very difficult mourning both Gabriel *and* the much-wanted baby they never had.

She moved along the shelves, picking up a little gown here and some baby vests there, until she had a collection of all the things she would have bought if she were shopping for her own baby.

After seeing William off at the airport, she had travelled with the car on the boat overnight, and had stopped on her way through Manchester to have breakfast in the Midland Hotel and then call at the shops before heading on to Stockport. She had slept surprisingly well in the little cabin, going to bed fairly soon after the boat set off, and had woken just as it was drifting into the dock in Liverpool.

She would have loved a bath in the morning, but knew that would have to wait until she got to the house in Cale Green later. Instead, she made do with a strip wash, using the tiny cabin sink, then pulled on a fresh cream sweater and beige trousers. She had put on just a touch of make-up and lipstick and then packed up and headed off to collect the car.

It had been a lovely, clear morning and as she drove along, admiring the fresh green countryside, Tara once again was grateful that she could enjoy the beautiful natural things in life that she had lost in the blackness of Gabriel's death. She would always wish he was there to enjoy them with her, but she knew it would make things much more awful to deny the good things she still had.

She left Mothercare now, laden down with two big bags filled with the baby stuff she had gone in for, and also a new outfit each for Michael and Helen. Passing through Levenshulme, she pulled up outside a bakery and went in and bought fresh rolls, two gingerbread men for the children, and some fresh cream cakes that she knew were Bridget's favourite.

A short while later, as she pulled up outside Maple Terrace, Tara felt a surge of excitement at the thought of seeing this latest new addition to the Roberts family.

Although in a very different way from herself, Bridget had had a terrible year. Starting off with Fred's accident, and then having to live with the worry of him never making a full recovery – and now all this terrible court-case business that hung over their heads.

A new baby to brighten up everyone's life was definitely the best thing they could have wished for to balance up the rest.

Angela opened the door, and Tara knew straight away that her young sister was well on the road to being back to her old self. Her blonde hair was in a new, shorter style, but was glossy and shining with health again. And the colour was back in her cheeks. She wore a pair of nicely fitted jeans and a casual blue gingham blouse that picked up the bright blue of her eyes.

After a few months of being looked after back at home in Tullamore, the sunny spring mornings and the thought of the children's excitement over the expected new baby had lured Angela back to Maple Terrace.

'I'm grand now,' she had pleaded with her mother, as they sat over the breakfast table the previous month, 'and there's no decent work around here for me.'

'But Tara has told you that she can get you work in Fitzgerald's Auctioneer's office, and there's always work for you out in Ballygrace House,' Tessie pointed out.

'I don't want office work,' Angela told her gently, 'and Ella can manage anything that has to be done in Ballygrace House by herself, now there's only Tara there.'

'But look what happened to you the last time you were over,' Tessie had said in a worried, exasperated tone.

'I'm older, Mammy,' Angela had said, 'and a whole lot wiser than when I first went over.' She moved to the other side of the table to put her arms around her mother's neck. 'I love working in the boarding-house, and I'm dyin' to look after the brand new baby. Oh, please say you'll let me go back? Just until the end of the summer?'

Her mother's face had softened. 'I suppose we can't hold on to you for ever – you can go for a while and see how you get on.' She kissed her daughter lightly on the cheek and squeezed her hand. 'Look after yourself, and make sure that you don't come back with a brand new baby of your own.'

'Come in, come in,' Angela said now, excitedly ushering Tara into the hallway. She automatically reached out to take one of the bulging bags from her. 'Bridget is upstairs,' she said in a low voice. 'She's having a bit of a rest, as she was up a good part of the night with the little one.'

508

'How is she?' Tara said, her green eyes sparkling with excitement at the thought of seeing the new baby.

'Grand,' Angela said. 'Both of them are. The baby's absolutely beautiful . . . gorgeous.'

Hearing voices in the hall, Fred came out from the kitchen to see who had arrived.

Tara gave him a wave, then pointed upwards. 'I'm just going upstairs to see the new arrival.'

Fred nodded, beaming. 'They're champion!' he told her, giving her a 'thumbs-up' sign. 'She'll be so pleased to see you.'

When they reached the top of the stairs, Angela suddenly stopped and turned back to Tara. 'In case you get a surprise,' she said in a low voice, 'in case Bridget forgot to tell you . . . the baby takes after some of her family that she didn't know.'

Tara frowned, completely confused. 'Her *family*?' As far as she had ever been aware, her friend had never known anything about her family.

Angela nodded. 'I don't think she likes to talk about it . . . well, not to me, anyway.'

Tara took a deep breath. 'Is the baby OK?' she whispered. 'There's nothing wrong with it or anything . . . is there?' Surely not, she thought. Surely not after everything that's happened to poor Fred.

'She's perfect!' Angela said, smiling. 'It's just that she looks a bit—' And then she suddenly cut off, seeing Fred coming up the stairs behind them with a pile of fresh towels for the lodgers' bedrooms.

'No rest for the wicked,' he said, giving them a wink as he passed them by.

Angela knocked on the bedroom door and when Bridget called out, she motioned Tara to follow her. 'You've an old friend here to see you!' she said. 'One that can't keep away!'

The two old friends hugged, and as they did so, Tara felt Bridget clinging to her more tightly than she would normally do. 'You're looking great,' Tara said, 'lying there in your fancy frills and flounces.'

Bridget rolled her eyes, but there was a wary, slightly anxious look about her. 'I bought them before I went into the hospital,' she said, fiddling with a ribbon on her pink satin bed-jacket. 'I remembered when I'd had the other two how I felt like a beached whale, and I decided that I'd make sure I had a couple of nicer items to brighten me up.'

Tara moved off the bed now, and moved around to the other side, towards the wooden crib. She bent her head down towards the sleeping child and stood looking in for a few moments, trying to make sense of what Angela had told her out in the hallway. Then she straightened up and turned towards her friend, a curious look on her face.

'She's absolutely beautiful,' she said quietly.

'Isn't she a little dote?' Angela put in enthusiastically.

There was a pause. 'Have you decided on a name for her yet?' Tara asked.

'Lucinda,' Bridget said, her voice flatter now. 'I always liked the name after I came across it in a book years ago.'

'That's a lovely name,' Tara replied, glancing over to the cradle, 'and I think it really suits her.'

'Would you check the kettle is on downstairs, Angela?' Bridget said now, in a low, strained voice.

When the girl had left the bedroom, Bridget lifted her eyes to meet Tara's, and their gaze held. 'She's beautiful,' Tara repeated and stood waiting. When nothing was said, she sat down on the side of the bed again and took her friend's hand in both of hers. 'Do you remember what we said back in December? Do you remember what we said about not keeping any more secrets?'

Bridget's head suddenly drooped down on to her

chest. 'What d'you mean?' she said in a slightly aggressive tone. 'What are you suggesting?'

Tara sat in silence for a few moments, just stroking her friend's hand.

Eventually, Bridget lifted her head very slightly, still not quite able to meet her friend's gaze. 'I didn't even know . . .' she whispered. 'I'm still not sure . . .'

'Bridget,' Tara said in a patient, quiet voice, 'I know this is obviously very difficult for you . . . but you must know if something has happened that has caused the child to have dark skin.' She sucked in her breath, wondering if it would have been better to have said nothing. Wondering if it would have been better to pretend.

'I know what you're thinking,' Bridget said, her voice unsteady now, 'but I don't remember anythin' happening.' There was a silence. 'And anyway . . . I never knew my family. Maybe my granny or even my father . . . or somebody . . . had dark skin.'

Tara squeezed Bridget's hand tightly now – gearing herself up to ask the unaskable question. 'When . . . when did you last see Lloyd?' she whispered.

Bridget's whole body suddenly shuddered. 'I don't know . . . I don't know,' she said, shaking her head.

'You told me you saw him back last summer . . . around the time we got the dog. If you count nine months back, you'll know if it could have been then.'

Bridget covered her face with her hands. 'I can't remember anythin' about it . . . I honestly can't remember a thing.'

'You must know if you . . . you must know if you did something with him?'

Bridget shook her head. 'Honest to God . . .' she uttered in a small, strangled voice. 'Honest to God and his blessed mother – I have no memory at all of anythin' that happened when he was here.'

Tara took her friend by the shoulders now. 'You

must know if there's even a chance ... surely you remember *something* about when he was here?'

There was a painful silence, then Bridget finally lifted up her head high enough to look Tara in the eye properly. 'I'm really, really telling the truth when I say I can't remember,' she said with a sob in her voice, 'because I was *drunk* ... I was drinking more than I usually do because I was all upset with Fred bein' in the hospital and I was dead lonely ...'

Tara looked shocked and shaken at what she was hearing. 'So are you saying that Lloyd might have taken advantage of you when you were in no fit state to know what he was doing?'

Bridget shook her head violently. 'No ... no,' she whispered, 'it was nothing like that. He didn't do a thing wrong – he's not like that.' She looked at Tara with sad, haunted eyes. 'You know Lloyd – he's not got a bad bone in his body.'

'But you don't have to be bad to make a mistake, we both know that.' Tara gave a deep sigh. 'Can you really not remember a thing?'

Bridget shrugged helplessly. 'I know we came back to the house after being in the pub ... and I remember us cuddling and kissin' a bit ... but that's all.' She hung her head. 'It would be easier for me if I did remember ... at least I could be sure.'

There was a deathly silence as Tara tried to take in the ramifications of what Bridget had just told her. 'I'm going to say this because you're my oldest and dearest friend, and because I'm desperately worried about you. I hope,' Tara said, her face white and tense now, 'that you will never, *ever* allow yourself to get into such a terrible situation due to drink again.'

'I know,' Bridget said in a hushed, contrite tone. 'I decided that myself ... because I'm shocked and let down with myself.'

'Well,' Tara said, 'if you've made that decision

yourself . . . then there's no point in me saying any more . . .'

The baby suddenly let out a little cry, and Tara turned around again to the crib.

'Can I lift her?' she said to her friend. When Bridget nodded, Tara went over and very carefully lifted the little bundle wrapped in a fine, hand-made lace shawl. She moved her gently to lie in the crook of her arm, then she came back to sit on the bed. She looked again at the baby's face – back again in perfect repose – and the smooth softness of the coffee-coloured skin quite took her breath away. 'Oh, Bridget . . . she's the most beautiful, the most perfect little thing I've ever seen.'

And as Tara felt the warmth of the child close to her, and then as the little face suddenly turned towards her as though seeking her breast, a strange ache ran through her whole being. An ache that had echoed a long way back in time.

An ache that told Tara that her own body was still yearning for a child.

The child she would never have – her beloved Gabriel's child.

Bridget's hand came across to gently stroke the side of her daughter's face. 'She *is* beautiful, isn't she, Tara? Her dark skin doesn't take that away from her.'

'Her skin only adds to her beauty if that's possible,' Tara said.

There was a little silence. 'As God's my judge, Tara,' Bridget whispered, 'I cannot remember a single thing about that night.' She halted. 'I'll never know the real truth about it, because of that.'

'Have you asked Lloyd?' Tara said. 'Have you checked with him what he remembers?'

'No . . .' Bridget said. Then her hands came to her face again.

'Does he know about the baby?'

'Well . . . he knew there was another baby on the way.'

'But does he know she's been born?'

Bridget shook her head and shrugged. 'No . . . sure, he'd have no reason to know. It's not as if he called here that often. It's only when he was working up around here, or up on business to do with work.' She looked at the baby again. 'For all I know, I might never see Lloyd ever again.'

'Would you not get in touch with him . . . phone him or something?' Tara said. 'Just so you know one way or the other.'

Bridget's face suddenly crumpled. 'What would be the point in that?'

'But you'd know the truth . . .'

'But maybe I don't want to know the truth, Tara. If the truth is going to cause a whole lot of problems for me and Fred, then I'd rather not know it.'

Tara thought for a moment. 'How is Fred reacting to the baby?'

'The same as he did with Michael and Helen – he loves her the very same.'

'So he didn't remark on the baby's dark colouring?' Tara asked. 'Wasn't he shocked when he first saw her?'

Bridget fiddled with the bedspread. 'I warned him before he saw her . . . I explained that there might have been dark skin in my family that I never knew about.' She halted. 'He never asked anything else – nobody really has. I've told them all the very same thing . . . and you're the only one that ever questioned it.'

'And would you have told me about Lloyd, if I hadn't asked?' Tara said quietly.

Bridget nodded. 'You know I would have . . . eventually. But I was still pretending to myself that nothing must have happened.' She bit her lip, deeply embarrassed now. 'I had got it into my head that my granny or somebody must have been foreign . . . or one of those

Spanish Irish. I'd really begun to believe that's what happened.'

The baby gave another little cry, and this time Bridget instinctively reached for her and, when she held her in her arms, lifted the tiny little face close to her own cheek. 'I don't care who she belongs to, Tara – whether it's Fred or Lloyd. All I know is that I love her with all my heart.'

Tara looked at her friend now – and saw only a beautiful new baby held in the arms of a loving, besotted mother. 'I suppose at the end of the day,' she said quietly, 'that's the only thing that really matters.'

Chapter Seventy-Three

Tara closed the car door, then held her umbrella aloft and ran across the street to Thornley's Estate Agents in Bramhall. Joan, the plumpish girl who lived in the house in Cale Green, gave her a welcoming smile and then ushered her into Mr Pickford's office, saying she would bring them both tea in a few minutes.

'Tara, my dear!' Mr Pickford stood up, smiling, then shook her hand in the fashion of an old friend as opposed to an old boss. He indicated a comfortable chair at the opposite side of his desk. 'And may I say how particularly well you're looking.'

'Thank you,' Tara said, sitting down and opening the buttons on her rust suede jacket that toned with the brown and rust geometric-patterned skirt. 'I feel much better, and I think that the time has come to seriously consider my future.' She paused, then gave him a big smile. 'You'll be pleased to know I've finally succumbed . . . I've decided to have another look at this decrepit old building you've been driving me mad about.'

Mr Pickford joined the tips of his fingers together, a tiny, satisfied smile on his lips. 'I have a good feeling about this, Tara. I think you're the perfect person for the project . . . and I think perhaps the project is perfect for you.' He opened a folder containing all the information pertaining to the sale of the Cale Green Hotel. 'There have been a handful of viewers, but no real offers in the last nine months, and they are desperate to sell up now. In my opinion, you have a chance of getting it at a rock-bottom price.'

Tara nodded thoughtfully, then she leaned forward, her elbows on the desk and her hands joined together. 'I need to do something,' she told him honestly. 'I need to put my energies into something new.' She lifted her eyes to meet his now. 'I'll go mad if I stay cooped up in Ballygrace House – and the businesses back in Ireland don't have the same interest for me. Besides, the managers now run them very well without any help from me.' She took a deep breath. 'I started off here in Stockport, and it's where I feel I have the most confidence and knowledge about the property market.'

Mr Pickford nodded understandingly, then he handed her the folder across the desk.

'This would be a *real* challenge ... as you know, there's a lot of work to be done.'

'Hard work has never worried me,' she said, 'and I definitely need to be occupied.'

The secretary came in with the teapot and milk and sugar, and then returned a few moments later with cups and saucers, two scones, and some butter and jam. She poured the cups of tea and gave them one each. 'If there's anything else you need,' she said, smiling in Tara's direction, 'just give me a call.'

There was a companionable, thoughtful silence now as they cut the scones in half and buttered and spread jam on them.

'Would it take you long to raise the mortgage?' Mr Pickford enquired.

Tara shook her head, and took a sip of the hot tea. 'No,' she said simply, 'I have the money ready and waiting.'

Mr Pickford lowered his gaze, knowing the heart-breaking source the money had come from. 'In that case,' he said, smiling broadly now, 'there's no point in us wasting time. When we've finished our tea, we'll drive over and have another look at it.'

As she stood outside the sad-looking, neglected building, Tara couldn't decide whether the Cale Green Hotel was better or worse than she had remembered. But it didn't matter. She was looking at it now through very different eyes – critical but confident eyes. And as she scrutinised the shambles of a red-brick building – she knew she could do this. She could resurrect this very faded Edwardian beauty – and bring it back to the former dignified hotel that it once had been.

With a reasonable amount of money and dedication – and a good team of builders and the relevant tradesmen – Tara Fitzgerald knew that anything was possible.

As though reading her thoughts, Mr Pickford suddenly turned to her. 'I could put you in touch with a good contracting team – in fact, Kennedy Contractors have been out several times looking at this place already.'

'No,' Tara said quickly, 'I'd rather sort the workmen out myself.' She looked at her old boss now, and decided that it was time to put him in the picture – to save any future misunderstandings. 'Much as I respect him as an excellent businessman and a thorough worker, I have no desires whatsoever to work alongside Frank Kennedy. In fact, I'd drop the whole idea if I have to have any contact with the man.'

Mr Pickford's eyebrows shot up, surprised at her words.

'He has already been in contact with me about the hotel, and I've told him in no uncertain terms that I do not need any help or advice from him.'

'I see,' the estate agent said, as Tara's words now left him without any doubts as to their relationship. 'I think we're quite clear on that now – and I shall make sure that I don't encourage him in any way, should he suggest that he gets involved in your work.' Amazingly, it had never dawned on him that there was any kind of conflict or antagonism between them. He had always found the Irishman to be courteous and honest in any business dealings – and there were no shortcuts or half measures when it came to any work his contractors took on, which was very unusual in this day and age.

But, business was business, and Mr Pickford valued Tara's friendship much more than any feelings of admiration he had for the Irish contractor's business skills. Satisfied that the point had been made and taken on board, Tara looked at Mr Pickford now and smiled. 'Put my offer in, when you get back to the office this afternoon,' she told him.

'At what figure?' he asked briskly, not at all surprised at her decision.

'Whatever figure is necessary to buy it,' she told him.

And so it began, the next phase in Tara Fitzgerald's life.

'My God!' Bridget exclaimed, her mouth agape. 'A hotel? You've really bought a *hotel*?'

'I've really bought a hotel,' Tara confirmed, grinning broadly now at her friend. 'Well, I've put in an offer, and I'm pretty sure it will be accepted.' She shook her head now, her red curls tumbling around her shoulders. 'I can't actually believe I've bought it myself!'

'Oh, Lucinda,' Bridget said teasingly, bringing her nose close to the baby's, 'your Auntie Tara has gone really posh this time – and now she's going to be the owner of a fancy hotel as well as hundreds and hundreds of big houses.'

'Oh, don't say that!' Tara scolded. 'You make me sound like some big billionaire business tycoon . . .'

'I wouldn't put it past you,' Biddy laughed. 'No better woman to do it.'

'What's all the laughing about?' Fred said, sticking

his head around the kitchen door. He had been outside oiling the wheels on Lucinda's pram, in preparation for the christening the following Sunday.

'Tara's bought a hotel!' Bridget told him.

'The Grosvenor?' he said, in a shocked tone.

'No, not the Grosvenor,' Bridget said, rolling her eyes to the ceiling. 'The Cale Green Hotel – it's the smallish one down Cale Green Road. It's on one of the roads near the cricket club.'

'Ah,' Fred said, nodding his head slowly. 'Down near the cricket club.' He thought for a moment. 'I could be ready for work by the end of the summer,' he told Tara now. 'So, if you're looking for a good barman – you don't need to look any further. It would be very handy, only a five-minute walk away. Oh, and I know a brilliant chef . . .'

Tara stared at him for a few moments. 'Good Lord!' Her hands suddenly flew to her mouth. 'What on earth have I let myself in for?' she breathed. 'I'd only thought as far as getting the building renovated, and very vaguely considered the kind of furnishings I might have . . . but I hadn't given any thoughts at all to what I would do when it was all finished . . . I'd never really thought what would be involved in the actual running and the organising of a hotel. What experience have I got of hotels?'

'You'll cope,' Bridget told her. 'I have every confidence in you.' She waved her hand around the kitchen. 'If I can own and run a boarding-house like this, Tara Fitzgerald can easily own and run a hotel. Besides, you already have hotel experience – didn't you run the reception in the Grosvenor Hotel when you were only a young girl?'

Tara nodded her head. 'You're right,' she agreed. 'I did learn how to work a reception.'

'And you'll have me and Fred to advise you on the bar and the kitchen,' Bridget went on, growing more and more excited at the prospect. 'It'll be brilliant, you'll be able to have weddings and christenings and every kind of occasion in the hotel – and we'll walk down and have a meal in your restaurant every Saturday night.' Then she giggled. 'And I might even go mad and allow myself a weak lemonade shandy in your bar.' Then, ignoring her friend's exaggerated disapproving look, she clapped her hands together. 'Oh, I can't believe it – you owning a hotel! It's brilliant! Really brilliant!'

'Do you think so?' Tara said, clasping her friend's hand. 'Do you really think I can do it?'

The following afternoon, Tara got a call from Mr Pickford to say that her first offer for the Cale Green Hotel had indeed been accepted, and it was now simply a case of running through the necessary paperwork.

'How long?' she asked, holding her breath. 'How long until it's officially mine?'

There was a silence on the other end of the line as Mr Pickford calculated. 'There's no property chain or anything like that,' he said carefully, 'so I think we could have everything over and done with by June.'

'Wonderful,' Tara said, smiling. 'That gives me a couple of months to tie everything up back in Ireland.'

'You're not thinking of selling up there, are you?' he said in a surprised tone.

'No,' Tara said quickly. And then without knowing why, she suddenly added: 'Not for the time being, anyway.'

'Tara,' Bridget said solemnly, as they sat in the front room that night after Angela had gone upstairs to put Michael and Helen to bed, and after Fred had gone to watch a wrestling match. 'I have something to ask you.' She bit her lip. 'It's a really big favour ... and I'm almost frightened to mention it.'

Tara shifted the sleeping baby into a more comfortable position. 'Is it money?' she asked in a gentle voice. 'Is it with Fred being out of work?'

'No,' Bridget said, smiling and shaking her head. 'We're grand for money . . .'

'Are you sure?' Tara checked. 'Because you only have to ask – I've told you that before.'

'Honestly,' Bridget reassured her. 'We're absolutely fine where money is concerned. The money we make from boarding more than covers the bills and that kind of thing – and besides, we're not big spenders. I'm not one for wanting the latest furniture and things like that, or the kind that has to have the latest fashions.' She halted. 'We're very, very lucky to be in the position we are in, and I never let meself forget it . . .'

'You would come to me if you ever needed money,' Tara checked, 'wouldn't you?'

Bridget nodded her head. 'I certainly would,' she smiled. 'Yours would be the first door I would knock on.'

'So,' Tara said, stroking the side of Lucinda's face, 'if it's not money – what is the problem?'

Bridget took a deep, deep breath. 'Frank Kennedy . . .' Then, the minute she saw the set of Tara's jaw, she rushed on before she could be interrupted. 'Hear me out, Tara – for once – hear me out about Frank Kennedy!'

There was a painful, protracted silence. Then, after a big, weary sigh, Tara said, 'Go on . . . get it over with.'

'The christening,' Bridget said, feeling that now she'd started, she might as well be totally direct. 'Fred wants to ask him to Lucinda's christening on Sunday . . .'

Tara stared down at the sleeping baby.

'And,' Bridget went on, 'if I'm really honest, I want him to come, too.' She held her hands up, expecting an onslaught now. 'He's been really good to us both over the years – and especially good since Fred had his accident.'

'You know how I feel,' Tara started, her voice low so as not to disturb the baby. 'And you know what happened. You know what that man did to me.'

'I do,' Bridget agreed, 'but that was a long time ago . . .' She paused. 'He learned his lesson from what happened with you – and he's really, really changed. He's come back and forth to us all these years without ever seeing much of you. In fact, he went *years* at the beginning where he never saw you at all, and he *still* called out here to visit us. And all the times he drove into the hospital to visit Fred or came to collect me to drive me to the hospital to see him.' She held her hands out again now. 'Everybody is entitled to a mistake, but they're also entitled to make up for it, and Frank Kennedy is a decent enough man – better than most.'

'I'm not saying he doesn't have any good points,' Tara said in a heated whisper now. 'Everybody has some good points – but I'm afraid there's nothing that you or anybody else can do or say that will make me feel any different about him.'

'I think you're being really unfair now,' Bridget said heatedly. 'And it's not just him. He's still seeing Kate Thornley – and she's been a good friend of yours for a long time. You've hardly seen or spoken to her since she started going out with him.'

'Well,' Tara said, her voice rising in spite of herself, 'maybe Kate should have thought of that – maybe Kate should have realised that true friendship matters more than nights out at expensive restaurants and bottles of champagne. Frank Kennedy knows exactly how to buy people – he just finds out their price. He's found out your price and he's found out Kate's.'

'That's a terrible, hurtful thing to say,' Bridget whispered. 'I'm shocked at you, Tara, and I can't believe you're taking this so badly.'

523

There was a tension now between the friends – a very serious tension.

'Maybe', Tara said, getting up to put Lucinda into her cradle, 'it would solve things if I didn't come to the christening . . . maybe it would make it easier on everyone else.'

Tears sprang into Bridget's eyes now. 'Do you really hate him so much,' she said in a strained, shocked voice, 'that you would be prepared to miss that innocent child's christening?'

'It's the last thing I want to do,' Tara said sadly, lifting her coat and bag now. 'But it's quite obvious that I'm the odd one out – that everyone else would be much happier and have a better time if I wasn't there.'

'Don't be so silly, Tara!' Bridget called, but it was too late.

Without a backward glance, Tara Fitzgerald strode out of the room and out of her friend's house.

Chapter Seventy-Four

The women had all left for work and Mrs Winterbottom had banged the door and gone off to do the weekly shopping before Tara ventured out of her bedroom. She had gone into the bathroom, run a bath, and lay soaking in it for ages, then she had dressed in casual khaki trousers and a brown linen blouse, and towel-dried her long red hair before going downstairs.

She had had the most awful night – sleeping for only an hour or two before waking again for the same length of time – and just could not face the thought of meeting up with anyone in the house this morning. As she lit the gas under the kettle and then found a mug for her coffee, she went over the conversation with Bridget again for the umpteenth time – and still could not come up with any answers that might rectify the dreadful situation that had suddenly erupted between them.

This was not the first disagreement the friends had ever had – in fact they had had numerous disagreements over the years. But nothing like this. Nothing that had ever threatened to smash their friendship wide open.

Tara took her coffee into the sitting room and sat drinking it, staring out of the large bay windows, the weak April sun struggling through cloud to glint through the smaller stained-glass windows at the top.

The last thing she truly wanted to do was miss this baby's christening. It was vitally important to Bridget that she had Tara, the one and only person who knew Lucinda's true parentage, with her just in case anybody raised the delicate question of her skin colour again. She needed Tara to divert the conversation and discreetly inform any inquisitive, insensitive individuals about all the dark-skinned Spanish Irish that still roamed the length and breadth of Ireland.

Tara wanted to be at the christening for that reason, and also because she wanted to be part of a joyous celebration of a new life. She had spent too many days in the last year mourning the loss of life, and this beautiful new baby had somehow given her a sense of belief and hope in the future.

She walked, coffee mug in hand, from the sitting room into the hallway and then into the front drawing room. She paused at the doorway, looking at the black, well-polished piano. So many times in the last week she had come into this room . . . and had almost lifted the lid on the beautiful instrument that had once given her so much pleasure – had given her pleasure right up until the time of Gabriel's death.

She ran a hand over the top of the shiny ebony wood, and if she had been looking for dust, she would not have found a single speck, for Vera Marshall had fallen in love with the handsome instrument and cared for it with the same loving attention that Tara had once given it.

Tara was on her way back out to the kitchen when she heard the distinct ring of the front doorbell. She took a deep breath; her first instinct was to ignore it, but then, with a sudden lift of her heart, she thought it might just possibly be Bridget coming to sort out this dreadful mess.

She moved quickly towards the door, but as she got nearer she realised that the figure outlined in the glass panels to the right of the door was much too tall for Bridget and was most likely a man. Swallowing her disappointment, she opened the door wide and there, standing on the doorstep, was Frank Kennedy – dressed not in his usual distinctive business suit, but in a casual sweater and jeans.

'No!' Tara said, shaking her red hair furiously. 'I have nothing to say to *you*! I'm not interested in getting involved in business deals with you, and I don't want you doing any work for me – and that's the last time I'm going to tell you!'

'I'm not here for any of those reasons this morning,' Frank said in a steady tone, although his face was taut and white. 'I've come to try and help sort this situation out between you and Bridget—'

'That', Tara said in a bitter, angry voice, 'has got nothing whatsoever to do with you. And I'm very upset that Bridget has involved me with you – of all people.' She turned away from him, and went to close the door.

Frank stepped forward and put a strong hand on the heavy Edwardian door. 'Tara,' he said in a firm voice, pushing the door open again, 'we need to talk. Please hear me out.'

'Why should I?' she said, blinking away hot, angry tears.

'Because', he said, his foot on the threshold, holding the door open, 'I might be able to make things better ... and because I feel I've caused a lot of this.' He halted – desperate to choose the right words for this very fragile situation. 'I know I deserve the worst word out of your mouth for what I did all those years ago – but you're punishing not only me, but also innocent people who really love you ... and really, really need you.'

Tara was leaning against the banister now, trembling – but she was listening.

'Bridget and the child need you at that christening on Sunday,' Frank said in a low voice. 'She needs you there because of the child's situation ...'

'What do you mean?' Tara asked slowly.

'The child's appearance – her colour,' he said baldly.

'It's perfectly obvious that there's a big question over who the father is.'

Tara was shocked into complete silence for several moments. 'Has she talked to you about it?'

'Of course she hasn't,' he said, 'but a blind man on a galloping horse couldn't help but notice it.'

There was no point in denying that she knew the truth about Lucinda, and anyway, she knew he would only see through it. 'Does everyone think that?'

Frank shrugged. 'I think the story about her background has satisfied most people . . . what can they say? And poor old Fred isn't going to push it too hard, whether he has any doubts or not.'

There was a silence, then Tara moved into the hallway. All she wanted was for things to go back to the old way with her dearest, oldest friend – and Frank Kennedy was obviously the key to that outcome. She suddenly realised that to fight it would only make the situation worse – maybe irrevocably worse. 'Come in,' she said in a quiet, calm voice. 'We might as well finish talking inside.'

He followed her down the hallway now, down past the front room where the black piano he had bought her stood, and down past the sitting room where the chairs and sofa were much too cosy – and into the safety and practicality of the kitchen.

He didn't expect tea or coffee and the offer was not forthcoming – but he was being listened to, which was much more important. Tara pulled a chair out for herself, and indicated that he do the same.

'Bridget rang me last night in a terrible state,' he started, 'and I dropped everything and drove over to talk to her and Fred.' He paused. 'Not that Fred said much about it, but he was obviously worried about the trouble between you and her.'

'The trouble between Bridget and me', Tara said, 'is *you*.'

Frank lowered his eyes. 'She told me . . . she told me the whole story.'

Tara took a deep breath. 'Look, Frank, I've just had the most terrible year in my whole life . . .' her voice started to crack now, 'and I'm desperately . . . desperately trying to make a new start. Trying to build a new life for myself.'

Frank nodded his head. 'Of course, I understand that . . . I really do.'

'As you probably know,' she went on, 'I've actually bought the Cale Green Hotel, and as soon as all the paperwork is complete, I'm planning to start a full renovation job on it.'

'Yes,' he said. There was no point in pretending that he didn't know.

'Well,' Tara said, 'I just don't think I can give it everything I have – I don't think I can go about my work relaxed and confident – if I know you're lurking in the background, always trying to be involved in my life in some way.'

There was a long silence. 'Is that how it feels?'

'Yes,' she said truthfully, looking him straight in the eye now, 'that's how it has always felt since you and I split up – and it has got to stop.'

Frank turned his head to the side, staring out of the window and into the back garden.

'I'm sorry,' he whispered. 'I'm truly sorry I've made you feel like that.'

And as she looked at him now, something started to thaw inside. Not something big – just a tiny piece of what seemed like a huge block of ice that she had carried around inside her for so many years. The block that she had kept firmly between herself and Frank Kennedy.

'I've no feelings left for you, Frank,' she told him honestly now, 'and I never will have again.'

Frank nodded, but there was a great sadness in his

eyes. 'I know that,' he said in a low voice. 'I think I've always known it on and off over the years since we parted. But over the last few months, I think I've eventually come to realise and accept it.'

'Really?' she whispered. 'Do you mean that?'

He gave a great, shuddering sigh. 'I'm not a stupid man,' he said, 'although I know I've behaved like one at times.' He turned his head to look at her, painful for him though it was. 'And I know that I have a life to live, too. That I have to find an alternative life to the one I've made a complete mess of . . .' His voice cracked a little now. 'I suppose I just got used to hoping . . . I convinced myself that once you got rid of your anger at me for lying . . . that you might come to love me again.'

'No,' Tara said, shaking her head vigorously, her Titian-coloured curls flying around. 'That was never, ever going to happen.' Her green eyes gave him an intense stare. 'If you want to know the truth, the way you carried on at times almost frightened me . . .'

'I'm sorry,' he said again, 'I am truly sorry for any upset I've ever caused you, I'm ashamed that I made you feel like that. I promise you that you can go about your life now . . . without worrying about me bothering you ever again.'

'Truly?' she asked him, feeling that a huge weight was finally being lifted from her.

'Truly,' he confirmed, and she knew he was speaking the truth.

'What about Kate?' Tara suddenly said. 'What's going on there?'

'I like her,' he said simply. 'She's good company and she's good fun.'

'I was worried that you were using her . . . to somehow get to me.'

'In the beginning,' he admitted, 'I suppose, if I'm honest, that's exactly what I was doing.' He shrugged. 'Stupidly trying to make you jealous or something of that nature. But then it changed – I got to know her properly and I really got to like her.'

'And has she feelings for you?'

'Yes,' he said, 'I think she has quite strong feelings for me.'

'Well,' Tara said hesitantly, 'if that's the case, I hope that things work out for you both . . .'

Frank looked at her now. 'We'll see what happens . . . I won't rush into anything. Now,' he suddenly said, 'what about this christening? What are we going to tell Bridget and Fred?'

Tara considered his question. 'If everything that you've said is true,' she said, 'then there shouldn't be any problem. You can tell her that I'll be there at the christening, and I'll be civil and friendly to all the other guests – including yourself and Kate.'

'Grand,' he said, getting to his feet now. He gave her one last look. 'I'm delighted that we've sorted all this out. I would have felt very, very bad if I'd come between you and Bridget . . . as well as having caused all these problems between yourself and me.'

She showed him to the door. 'I think', she said, looking at the blue sky breaking through the clouds, 'that things will start to look up now.'

Chapter Seventy-Five

LONDON

'A hotel?' echoed Elisha Mortimer, a fluttering hand coming to her throat. 'My dear . . . have you any idea of the work involved?' She gave a brief, almost panic-stricken smile now to Mrs Saunders as she cleared the dinner plates from the table.

'Fantastic!' William said, punching the air gleefully. 'We can come and visit you and stay in your new hotel. Can I help to serve behind the bar?'

'William,' Elisha said in a stern voice, 'would you please go and tidy your bedroom, and stop listening into adult conversation that doesn't concern you.'

'Oh, please, Mother,' William said, smiling appealingly across the room to Tara, 'let me stay and hear all about Tara's hotel . . . I'll be really, really quiet.' He went and sat in one of the low floral antique chairs by the fire. 'You won't even know I'm here.'

'Let the boy stay,' Harry said, reaching across to pat William's knee in a companionable manner. 'He's old enough now to hear good, honest business talk, and that's how boys learn these things.' He took a mouthful of his brandy, then leaned this head back against his high-backed leather chair and closed his eyes.

Elisha paused, clearly flustered by the news. She turned away from the two males, concentrating on the problem in hand. 'Please don't take this the wrong way, Tara, because I would truly hate you to think that I was interfering in your business – but do you *really* think that it's a suitable thing for a young woman in your position to be doing? Do you really think that you can cope with all the work involved – dealing with building people and tradesmen . . . and all those kinds of things?'

'I need to do *something*,' Tara said simply, taking a sip of her red wine. She hadn't really expected Elisha to fall behind her idea immediately, and had only come to discuss it with her out of a sense of duty – to give her the respect due to Gabriel's mother. Whether Elisha agreed or not, it was much too late, as Tara had already set the wheels in swift, irreversible motion. 'This project is one I feel that I can get completely absorbed in . . . I feel it's something I can put *myself* into.'

'Well, indeed,' Elisha said, brushing a stray hair back into her loose, elegant chignon, 'if you really feel that this is something you have to do . . . I suppose all we can do is support you, and hope and pray that it works out.'

'Tara?' William ventured from the corner. 'Do you think it might be OK if I came up to Stockport during my summer holidays to help you out? I would really love to watch the men doing the building work . . .'

'That would be lovely, William,' Tara said, a smile spreading on her beautiful face, 'if your mother doesn't mind . . . It's really up to her.'

'Fan-tas-tic!' William said, getting to his feet again, his eyes dancing with sheer excitement.

'We shall have to give it some thought,' Elisha said carefully, glancing anxiously over at her husband.

'Not very much thought,' Harry put in, suddenly wide awake and very alert. 'If William were to be safely occupied over the summer, it would give us the chance to go on that nice, hot Mediterranean cruise that we're always promising ourselves.'

Chapter Seventy-Six

BALLYGRACE, JULY 1963

As soon as Tara got the go-ahead from Mr Pickford, the first thing she had to do was to close up Ballygrace House. She had considered it from every angle, and there was no other sensible way around it.

She was going to have to move to Stockport for a good, solid six months to oversee the major work on the hotel, and there was absolutely no point in having Ella come in on a daily or every-second-day basis just to keep the house going. She decided she would pay the housekeeper a nominal wage that would give her a basic income, and allow her to pick up work in one of the local hotels or restaurants.

Shay, they had decided between themselves, would continue working in the grounds at the weekend, keeping the lawns and the bushes cut over the summer, and generally keeping an eye on the place.

'There's no doubt about it,' Kitty said sadly, looking around the kitchen in Ballygrace House, 'you'll be sorely missed.'

'I'll only be over in Stockport,' Tara reminded her, 'and I've already been going backwards and forwards these last few months. In any case, yourself and Mick can come and visit me at any time. Bridget would be delighted to see you, too.' She smiled broadly now. 'And by next summer, please God,' she held her crossed fingers up, 'you could be coming to stay in my new hotel.'

Kitty clapped her hands together in delight. 'Oh, we will,' she assured her. 'Have no fear about it – we'll definitely be there.'

'Funnily enough,' Tessie mused, as she and Tara sat in Molly's small sitting room, 'I'm not so worried about Angela being over in England this time as I was the last. I feel she's changed . . . she's matured.'

'She definitely has,' Tara agreed, 'and I can guarantee you that she'll be watched very closely. I'll only be five minutes away from her, and I'll be calling around to Maple Terrace very regularly – so you won't need to worry about a thing.' She paused. 'If the hotel works out, I might be interested in her doing reception work for me or something like that – what do you think?'

'It would be a great opportunity, and we won't stand in her way,' Tessie said, 'and I know that you'll look after her and make sure that she behaves herself.'

'Good,' Tara said, 'and I'll make sure that she gets back home often.' She picked her car keys up from the coffee table. 'Are we all ready?'

Molly looked up at her grand-niece expectantly. 'Where are we going?'

'We're going to visit your friend, Peggy Coulter.'

'Where is she?' Molly demanded, her brows down, as though ready for conflict.

'Her daughter told you all about it when she called last week,' Tessie reminded her gently. 'She's in the nursing home in Mullingar.' Tessie helped her out of her chair now, and into her lightweight summer coat. 'We're going to visit her in the lovely nursing home with all the lovely nuns.'

Molly put one arm in the coat, then turned a half-circle to put the other one in. 'Will Cecil Smith be there?' she asked.

They drove up the flower-lined avenue and then circled around the fountain in the middle of the courtyard, and came to a halt at the front door of the nursing home. Between them, Tara and Tessie helped the old woman out of the car and then very slowly – an arm at either side – helped her walk into the building.

'It's lovely here,' Peggy Coulter said, handing a box of Cadbury's Roses around the group. 'We get nice dinners and we have cards and dominoes, and a sing-song on a Friday and a Sunday night. There's a fella that comes with a fiddle, and he's a fierce lovely singer.'

Molly took a sweet wrapped in purple cellophane paper without a word of thanks, and proceeded to untwist it very slowly and deliberately.

'This is a lovely place, isn't it?' Tara said to her grand-aunt, her eyes darting across to Tessie. 'And there's plenty to do.'

'Would you like to come here, Molly?' Peggy Coulter asked, her bright little eyes scanning Molly's face. 'Would you like to come and stay here, too? We could keep each other company.'

Molly looked up at her with a blank face.

'Would you like to come and live here with your old friend – and have the lovely nuns look after you?' Peggy repeated. 'They look after me grand – for my poor oul' legs have given out on me, and my heart's not great . . .'

Molly looked at her for a long time. 'I don't know,' she whispered. 'I'd have to talk to Maggie . . . I'd have to see what she thinks.'

'Well,' Peggy said, winking at Tara and Tessie, 'you go home and have a chat with Maggie, and see what she has to say.'

Molly nodded her head thoughtfully.

'But if you do decide to come and live here,' Peggy told her, 'we could look after each other.' There was a little silence. 'What I'm saying', the small, bird-like woman explained, 'is that if you look after me, Molly Flynn, then I'll look after you.'

Molly turned to look at her old schoolfriend. 'And if you look after me, Peggy Coulter,' she said, 'then I'll look after you.'

'I think it's nearly settled,' Tara told Joe on the phone. 'The nuns have said they'll ring as soon as they have a room for her.'

'How long do you think it will be?' Joe checked. 'Weeks or months?'

'I've no idea,' Tara said, 'but Tessie will ring you as soon as they get word about it.'

'I've arranged with Father O'Leary to get a few days off when she has to move in,' he said quietly. 'I want to be there with her . . . and I suppose I'll have to meet up with the auctioneer about selling the house, and then make arrangements to dispose of her furniture and that sort of thing.'

'It's not easy, is it?' Tara said quietly. 'Closing the door of a house you've lived in – akin to closing the door on a part of your life.'

'That's exactly what it is, but there's no avoiding it.' He halted for a moment. 'How do you feel about leaving Ballygrace House?'

'Grand,' Tara said, her voice full of optimism. 'I know it's the right thing to do – but I'm not going to make any drastic decisions. I'm just going to go over to Stockport and throw myself into overseeing all the work that needs doing in the hotel.'

'And when the work is finished,' he said, his voice full of curiosity, 'what will you do then? Will you sell it or will you try to run it as a going concern?'

'I haven't decided yet,' Tara said honestly. 'It's something I have no experience in. I'm just going to take it a step at a time. If it works out, it works out – and if it doesn't, it doesn't.'

'Tara,' he said, 'although you are my sister, I have to tell you – I admire you very, very much.'

Coming up to the final weekend before she departed Offaly, Tara suddenly decided that she wanted to give Ballygrace House a fond and fitting, albeit temporary, farewell.

She was acutely aware that the last gathering of people in the house had been for Gabriel's funeral – and she did not want that to be the lasting, abiding memory when she returned. She checked that the dependable Ella would be there to organise the catering, and then she invited all her family to an informal, buffet-style hot Sunday lunch to say goodbye and to thank them for the understanding, caring and support she had received during the worst year of her life.

Kitty and Mick came early for Mick to check all the fires and for Kitty to give Tara and Ella a hand with organising the food, and then the crowd from Tullamore arrived after the midday Mass, all resplendent in their Sunday clothes.

The big table in the dining room had been spread with a white lace tablecloth and two big vases of flowers that Tara and Kitty had picked from the garden that morning. Rather than face everyone with formal settings at the table, Tara had organised that the plates were stacked in a pile, and the cutlery settings were wrapped up in napkins and laid in a small basket, to allow everyone to choose where they sat.

Ella put out dishes of hot chicken and sliced beef, with tureens of mashed and roast potatoes and the traditional Sunday vegetables. A big dish of trifle and apple-tarts with jugs of cream sat on a small wooden trolley, and there was beer for the men and sherry and wine for the women.

The lunch went off perfectly and ended up with Mick and Shay having their usual constitutional walk around the grounds, putting the world to rights, while the younger generation of Flynns and their respective spouses sat listening to long-playing records of Bill Haley and Connie Stevens on the radiogram.

Tara joined her stepmother and her aunt in the kitchen as they discussed Molly's forthcoming move to the convent nursing home, and the weekend visiting rota they would draw up to make sure she was not neglected. Hopefully, they said, the chattering company of Peggy Coulter would see her happily through the rest of the week.

As things were winding to a close, Kitty took Tara gently by the arm and drew her aside. 'I want to ask you a favour,' she said. 'I want you to do something for me . . . for us all.'

'What?' Tara said, her brows lifting in surprise.

'I'd like you to play some music for us . . .'

'What would you like to hear?' Tara said. 'Shall I bring you through some of the records?'

'No,' Kitty said, shaking her head. 'Not that kind of music.'

'Well,' Tara said, 'what kind do you want to hear?'

Kitty hesitated for just a moment, then decided there was nothing to lose. 'The piano,' she said, 'we'd all like to hear you playing the piano again.'

Tara looked at her aunt, clearly taken aback. 'I couldn't . . .' she said in a low voice. 'I'm just not ready . . . I haven't played for ages.'

'Please, Tara,' Kitty said, squeezing her hand.

'Maybe next time,' Tara hedged, moving over to the worktop to make a fresh pot of coffee. 'When I've got back into practising.'

At around five o'clock, as they were all finishing off their final round of drinks, accompanied by a large box of chocolates which Kitty had brought, the phone rang and Tara went out to the hall to answer it.

It was Bridget, checking what time Tara was expected

later in the week. They chatted briefly, Bridget bringing Tara up to date on Lucinda's latest developments, and on the continuing progress that Fred was making.

'Elsie is selling the house,' Bridget also told her, 'and is goin' to live with her sister full-time. The trouble with Eric has really taken it out of her, and she says she couldn't come back to face all the neighbours after what's happened. It's a pity, because she was a good friend and a good worker . . . but I suppose she has to do what's best for herself and for her nerves.'

Bridget rattled on a bit longer, omitting to tell Tara that Elsie had also called over to see the new baby. The horrified look on the older woman's face when she saw Lucinda had told the landlady all she needed to know, and confirmed Bridget's worst fears about the reception the child might get in certain ignorant quarters.

From that time on, the child would be the yardstick that Bridget would use to measure her friendships. The loud-mouthed, peroxide-blonde June – who had never offered a word of comment or criticism – would now fill the gap that Elsie had left.

Tara hung up the phone and turned to join the others in the dining room. Then suddenly something stopped her in her tracks. She looked across the hallway to the drawing room and to the grand piano that she had first played when she was a young teenager.

A few minutes later, a sound echoed through Ballygrace House that had not been heard for too long a time – a beautiful, familiar sound – as Tara Fitzgerald's slim, elegant fingers played her old favourite, *Moonlight Sonata*.

Chapter Seventy-Seven

Tara's days were now filled with visits to the Cale Green Hotel, to consult with builders and plumbers and electricians – often under the guidance of Mr Pickford – and to watch as windows and doors were ripped out and chimney stacks were dismantled, brick by dusty brick. The roof was scrutinised by the builders for missing or broken slates, damaged and missing guttering was replaced, and the pointing was carefully restored between the red and orange and sand-coloured bricks. The original conservatory, with its decorative glass and wood mouldings, was carefully taken apart, and then carefully rebuilt to the original specifications.

The work on the outside gave Tara a feeling of immediate gratification, as any changes or replacements could only be improvements.

But the interior of the hotel had been a different matter.

As she had gone through the downstairs reception and function rooms and then upstairs into the guest bedrooms, she had experienced an overwhelming sense of guilt – a guilt at ripping out what she felt was the heart and soul of the old hotel. In a ridiculous way, she almost began to feel that the furnishings and draperies were the clothes of an elegant but flamboyant old lady who had died. As though she were rummaging through the grand old lady's wardrobes and closets, and deciding what would or wouldn't stay.

She felt almost heartless as she discarded the embroidered antique chairs and sofas that were now damaged beyond repair, the fringed and tasselled velvet curtains that had once matched boudoir-style chairs and the trimming on four-poster beds. Most of the soft furnishings were now frayed and torn, fit only for the filthy skips in the back garden.

The Oriental-style rugs that had welcomed thousands of gracious guests into the reception hall and the large but cosy sitting room at the front of the house had been ruined by countless cigarette burns and cruel stiletto heels. And then there were the old wardrobes and matching dressing-tables in the bedrooms that were too far gone with woodworm, and the coffee-tables and plant stands that would never stand repair.

Tara Fitzgerald had gritted her teeth, and, with her small but dedicated army of workers, had swept like a tornado through the rooms of the Cale Green Hotel, demolishing everything and anything that got in the way of her vision. The vision that would eventually lead to the grand old Edwardian lady rising elegantly again, from the dust and the ashes and the years of neglect.

July, August and September had arrived and flown away, as did the visitors who came to view the work and the restoration that was being undertaken, and to join in Tara's excitement and enthusiasm as the old building started to take on a more encouraging shape.

In late July, young William Fitzgerald was put in the care of a guard at London's Euston station, and he made the journey up to the North-West for the first time, to stay with his sister-in-law for the greater part of the school summer holidays. He settled into the small spare boxroom in Tara's house, and spent every day following her around and charting the progress that was being made by the builders and the carpenters. At first he was shy of approaching the workmen and self-conscious of his public-school accent compared to theirs, but gradually he gained in confidence. By the end of his holiday, they were all on first-name terms, and it had become a Friday afternoon ritual that he ran down to the local fish and chip shop for the workmen's order, then joined them eating out of newspapers in the summer sunshine.

Tara watched with quiet pleasure as he quickly adapted to a freer life without the anxieties of his mother and the constant attention of the servants with which he had grown up. He bathed and dressed himself every day, and was delighted to be able to wear the t-shirts and jeans that became his daily working apparel.

Over the weeks, Tara watched him gradually develop into a more relaxed, carefree boy, running up and down to visit Bridget and Angela in the boarding-house and playing with the Roberts children. She had even come into the boarding-house one Saturday afternoon to find William and Fred glued to the wrestling bouts on the television, both yelling encouragement at the small square box.

Tara smiled to herself, thinking how strange it was that she should feel happy to see William casting off all the stiff formalities of his gentrified upbringing – all the trappings that she herself had aspired to as a young, ambitious girl.

Eventually, as the new school term beckoned, and Elisha and Harry returned from their cruise, William said tearful goodbyes to all his new friends, and headed for the train back to London.

'I hope you don't mind, Tara,' he told her as he hung out of the window of the guard's van, 'but I've told all the men I'll be back for the half-term holidays in October, because I want to check up on all the work they've done.'

Tara stretched up on her tiptoes and leaned against the train door to give him a kiss on the forehead. 'Don't worry,' she told him, 'I'll keep you up to date with a weekly written report.'

'You promise?' he asked, his face deadly serious.

'I promise!' Tara called, as the train chugged away.

Chapter Seventy-Eight

NEW YEAR, 1964

The main topic of conversation on New Year's Eve was the same as it had been all month – the assassination of America's President Kennedy. Television, radio and newspapers had carried references to the tragedy on a daily basis, and everyone waited breathlessly for more news to come through regarding the apprehension of the assassin or assassins.

But the newly refurbished Cale Green Hotel gave all the local business people an entirely new subject to discuss, and excitement grew as the invitations were issued to the party on New Year's Eve that would relaunch the hotel.

At one stage, around late autumn, there had been discussions about opening the hotel in time for the Christmas trade of office parties and business lunches – but Tara had decided against it. She had taken too many weeks and months overseeing the rebuilding of the hotel, and had poured too much of her energy and her heart into choosing the subtly classic furniture, carpets and curtains for reception rooms and bedrooms, to rush things at the last minute.

She decided that she would take the whole month of December to calmly review all the work inside and outside that had been done – and then decide on any additional features that might be needed to add the finishing touches.

A company in Macclesfield supplied thick, fluffy white towels and bathrobes for the guests, with the hotel's initials embroidered on them in dark green, and Tara had two solid weeks of scouring auction rooms, department stores in Manchester and local florists for small occasional tables, footstools and an abundance of plants for both the hotel and the beautifully restored Edwardian conservatory.

She stopped on Christmas Day and Boxing Day to spend that special time with Bridget and Fred and Angela, who was spending her first Christmas in Stockport – and as soon as the shops and businesses were reopened, she was on the go again, phoning and organising, so that the bar was well-stocked and everything was in order for the buffet party on New Year's Eve.

The manager of the Grosvenor Hotel had been more than helpful, and had spent a whole afternoon with his old receptionist, advising her on the business guests she should invite to the relaunch of the hotel.

'You must ask people who have been helpful to you, Tara,' he said, 'and especially ask those who *will* be helpful in the future.' Then, he gave her a long list which included local councillors, the brewery suppliers, the architects and planners who had been involved in all the work, and the local newspapers which would help with publicity.

Mr Pickford had been on hand throughout the renovations, and had added his own list of people whom he thought she should invite. 'Tara,' he told her, 'this will be a showcase for your ability to regenerate – literally bring back to life – an intrinsically beautiful but dilapidated and neglected Edwardian building. And not only to accomplish everything that you set out to achieve – but also to accomplish it with your own inimitable talent and style.' He had paused. 'There may well be influential people who would be interested in sharing some of that talent or perhaps interested in putting more of these buildings or businesses in your hands.'

'Thank you,' Tara said, truly touched by her old employer's words, 'but I think I have probably achieved all I've set out to achieve. I'm delighted with the result and very proud of it – but I can't imagine myself going through this process again.' Her voice had dropped a little. 'Besides, I haven't started running the hotel yet ... it may not work out. I don't know if I have the experience and knowledge necessary to carry off a successful business venture. The rebuilding was one thing – running a hotel is another.'

'I have a feeling, Mrs Fitzgerald,' the estate agent said, his eyes glistening, 'that anything you set your mind to cannot help but be a success.'

Tara had dressed with great care for the evening, having bought a low-necked, old-gold evening dress that flattered her slim but voluptuous figure. The shimmering dark gold brought out the rich tones in her hair and the piercing emerald glints in her eyes.

Seeing how sophisticated the dress made her look, Tara had decided, on a whim, to have her hair piled up with a few soft, curling tendrils escaping at the nape of her neck.

After dressing and applying her make-up and perfume, Tara had sat at her dressing-table going through her jewellery – looking for the perfect pieces to complement the dress. And then her hand, with its dark-red varnished nails, came to rest on the small tissue-wrapped cameo brooch and earrings that she and Gabriel had bought for Madeleine's eighteenth birthday. The sight and touch of them brought a rush of tears to her eyes and a lump to her throat.

She gave herself a few minutes to compose herself, and to think lovingly of the young, caring man who, in life, had given her every single thing that he had been capable of giving, and had continued to give to her even after death.

She lifted the brooch and the earrings to her lips, and then carefully rewrapped them in the tissue paper and returned them safely to the jewellery box, to be brought out on another, more suitable occasion. Tonight was the beginning of a whole new year – it was not a time to look backwards with sadness. It was time to look forward with hope.

Tara reached for a sparkling gold and diamond necklace and a matching pair of earrings, and then, satisfied with her appearance, headed down to greet her guests.

Bridget and Fred and Angela were amongst the first guests to arrive, all suitably dressed for the occasion. The three women stood admiring each other's glamorous evening dresses and new hairdos, while Fred went off to test the beer, and to check out how the bar was being run.

'I can't believe the difference in the place,' Bridget said, looking around her. 'Apart from not being as big, it's better in every way than the Grosvenor.'

'Tons better!' Angela stated. 'And the smaller the place, the more attention you can give the guests. Places like the Grosvenor are fine and grand – but you can't beat the personal touch in the smaller hotels.' Angela was now becoming an authority on hotels since Tara had suggested that she might like to come and work for her. She had already checked with Bridget, and she would continue to stay on in Maple Terrace and help with the babysitting and housekeeping when she wasn't working in the Cale Green Hotel. It would be a long time before Angela was ready to spread her wings and try anything new after her disastrous experience of working in the mill and her ordeal at Mona Kelly's.

'I wouldn't go that far,' Tara had laughed. 'But I'm just delighted you think that it's in the same class as a hotel like the Grosvenor.'

More guests started to arrive, including Frank and Kate. Tara greeted them both warmly, and graciously accepted Frank's good wishes and his bottle of champagne, realising with some surprise that she no longer had the old overwhelming feeling of animosity towards him. And when Kate kissed and hugged her, Tara suddenly felt that it was quite possible that some day they might return to their old, comfortable, close friendship.

Within half an hour, the reception room in the hotel was packed and Tara was swept off in a sea of kissing cheeks, shaking hands and introductions – and, as always, her striking looks and confident bearing turned the heads of men of all backgrounds and ages.

But there was more about her now than there had ever been – looks were all well and good, but Tara Fitzgerald had now proved herself in a world that many women would not dare venture into. And it was only the start.

Almost against her will – and encouraged by her success so far with the Cale Green Hotel, and the belief that people like Mr Pickford had in her – little seeds were already forming in her mind. Seeds generated by the property and businesses, both in London and Ireland, that Gabriel had left to her.

But she would do nothing about them at present. It was much too early. It was too early for a lot of things. She would take one step at a time. She would just wait and see what happened.

The evening of good food and drink, music and then dancing flowed steadily towards the end of the night and the end of another year. The end of a better year for Tara Fitzgerald.

She had just finished a lovely, rather sedate waltz with Mr Pickford, when her attention was drawn to the time by one of the staff. There were only three minutes to go before the New Year. 'Don't move,' she told her old boss. 'I'll be straight back.' She set off towards the edge of the dance floor, and found herself being stopped every few yards to be congratulated on the wonderful night and the fine job she'd made of the Cale Green Hotel. And then, just as she craned her neck once again to scan the crowds, she felt a hand suddenly gripping hers.

'I've been looking for you for *ages*!' Bridget exclaimed. 'And now I've finally found *you*, I've managed to lose Fred!'

Tara gave her a big smile and pointed across to the bar, where Fred was gesturing to them and holding up a bottle of champagne in one hand and glasses in another. The women waved him over, and then, hand in hand, the two friends made their way back to Mr Pickford with Fred following behind.

The crowd suddenly hushed as the bar manager started the countdown to midnight and the start of the New Year.

There was a split second's silence as the first bell rang out, and then the revelling crowd erupted noisily.

'Cheers!' Fred Roberts called, expertly popping the cork on the champagne bottle.

'Happy New Year, Tara!' Bridget said, kissing her dear friend's cheek.

Then Mr Pickford took Tara's hand. 'And every success for the Cale Green Hotel.'

Tara looked around her now – at all her friends, old and new – and felt a surge of something that was very nearly happiness.

It was as close to happiness as she could get without her beloved Gabriel – but she would keep trying.